The Crawshaw Inheritance

The Crawshaw Inheritance

John M Dore

© Wendy Dore, 2011

Published by Spinney Corner Publishing

A CIP catalogue record for this book is available from the British Library.

ISBN 978-0-9570764-0-2

Book and cover design by Clare Brayshaw

Prepared and printed by:

York Publishing Services Ltd
64 Hallfield Road
Layerthorpe
York YO31 7ZQ

Tel: 01904 431213

Website: www.yps-publishing.co.uk

About the Author – John M Dore

John was born and brought up in Bradford and spent most of his working life in West Yorkshire. He spent many weeks researching the historical background to his story and began writing in January 2007. He completed the story in April that same year and sadly passed away in May.

John wrote the story in long hand and asked me if I would type the manuscript on the computer as he carried on writing. It was quite fun but also frustrating as John would often forget the names he had given to some of the minor characters and I was left with many blank spaces and lots of dot dot dots. I would ask him 'what is this?' He would say 'I thought you would remember, as you are good at remembering names.' We decided that I should carry on typing until I had finished and then we would print off two copies of the manuscript and go through it page by page and correct the errors and maybe he would change a few things that he thought necessary. Alas this did not happen.

When John died I had still to type part four. I found this very difficult to restart as it was the last thing we did together and it was heartbreaking to try to carry on the whole project now that he was no longer here. It has taken me a long time but with the help of John's daughter Helen, and some good friends one of whom has read it four times not always looking for errors!, and still thinks it is a good read. We have done our best to bring it all together, we have spent many months and indeed years going over it page by page making sure it makes sense and is ready to be published. It is exactly as John has written it, we haven't changed the storyline and we think that this is exactly how he would have presented it himself.

We hope that John would approve of our efforts in bringing his novel to the reading public. Although difficult at times, above all it has been a labour of love.

Wendy Dore and Helen Jackson 2011

Acknowledgements

With grateful thanks to Ann who has been a great help. To Glenys, Will, Vincent, Margaret and Mike.

A special thanks to Ted Childs, for his help and good advice in the earlier stages of our endeavours and for his continuing words of encouragement.

To Duncan, Paula and to Clare especially for all her hard work and patience in bringing it all together.

Thank you

Spinney Corner Publishing

Part 1

Chapter 1 – April 1856

Albert-Edward Crawshaw was a big man with a small-holding; his ability to value a flock a field away and to gauge the quality of a fleece from a run of one finger from a tail to a skull was admired throughout the Heights between Bradford and Halifax.

Lacking a head for business, expanding his fields and his flocks did not interest him. He had a comfortable home, a good wife and a son of fifteen. Helped ably by two local hands and less so by two brothers who shared a cottage on his land, he worked hard in that harsh climate and was content with what living it provided.

The brothers, now in their early twenties, had been employed and given housing by Albert-Edward five years before. Locally, they were referred to as 'backwards.' Less kindly, Joe, the elder, was regarded as 'Tenpunce tu't shilling.' This elevated him above his brother Luke, who was even less bright, and was known in The Plough and Pair as Ninepunce.

Local talk had it that Tenpunce and Ninepunce were at Crawshaw's Dyke Hole Farm because of some arrangement between a charity in Halifax and a schoolmaster in Illingworth where young Henry Crawshaw was getting part-time schooling. Nobody knew the facts and there were far more interesting things to discuss in The Plough and Pair.

That was certainly the case following the discovery of Albert-Edward's body.

Snowfall in April was not unusual on those hills but the weight of the fall and the depths on the fields had not been predicted – even by those respected weather predictors who had spent their lives on those hills.

Lambing had not finished and Albert-Edward had gone out with a shovel in the night to a flock that had, too early, been placed in the upper fields. He did not return. Large numbers joined his wife and son in the search, trudging through the waist-deep fall all through the following day, but the snow had continued after Albert-Edward had set out and his trail was totally covered.

The numbers returned with the next day's light and worked without rest. The body was found late that afternoon. He was face down in a ditch alongside a dry-stone wall, frozen. There was blood in the snow about his head and there was a hole in the back of his skull.

The body was carried to the farmhouse and laid in front of the kitchen fire. No one knew how long it would take but all were agreed that the physician and the Coroner's Officer would be unable to do their work until the body was thawed out.

Henry and his mother, despite their own need for sleep, spent the night stoking and re-stoking the kitchen fire, watching over the body, watching the steam rise from the huge overcoat, and turning and turning the body.

The Coroner's Officer arrived first and stood there saying little, trying to appear knowledgeable while awaiting the arrival of the physician. The thaw was as sudden as the fall and the lanes were no obstacle to travel so the doctor should not be delayed, he told them.

The physician had come from Horton. He did not consider the body to be sufficiently thawed for a proper examination so he asked the Coroner's Officer to arrange for the body to be removed in order that the thawing should occur naturally, not by way of roasting. This was addressed to Mrs Crawshaw. Henry and his mother could take some rest but there was a funeral to arrange; though she didn't know when that would be permitted.

The Plough and Pair was unusually busy that week. There was no shortage of theories or people who supposedly knew someone who knew something. The wound to the back of Albert-Edward's head was variously described (by those who claimed to have seen it and those who claimed to know someone who had) as a hole, a gap you could put a fist in and a crushing that had pushed his brains out of his nose.

Tenpunce and Ninepunce, the Ogden brothers, had not been in The Plough and Pair since the night of the death. This fuelled several theories and, as the ale flowed each night, a consensus was eventually reached among the amateur detectives of the Heights.

It was agreed that the brothers had been in the inn that night and that they were undoubtedly drunk. They would have gone back to the hovel they call a home and been unfit for anything. Albert-Edward would not have been able to dig the lambing-ewes out of the top field alone. He would have gone to the Ogdens' cottage, found them incapable of work, or refusing, and had to do it all himself.

'That doesn't explain what happened to him though.' One voice.

Another voice, 'Crawshaw wouldn't leave them two idle buggers in bed when he were digging out 'issen. I know what he would have done. If they couldn't or, worse to my mind, wouldn't do what they were getting their keep for he'd have telled 'em, they was sacked. And so would any man here.'

That brought full agreement and mugs were refilled as he continued. 'So I'll tell you what I think happened.' This was said with a glance around to make sure the Ogdens hadn't come in.

He waited, wanting full attention. Rarely did Nathan Dodd have an audience and he was going to wring everything from his tale that could be wrung. Hunched over the bar, his flat cap touching the tops of his ears and his coat collar the bottoms, all that was on view was a pink face, two peephole eyes and a turned up nose. If ever a man more resembled a piglet he had not been seen in those parts.

His account was torturously drawn out and punctuated by exaggerated turns to the door and sips from his mug, which the landlord was happy to keep topping up without charge. A full bar, all buying ale and showing no inclination to leave was well worth keeping Dodd's mug well filled.

The meat of the be-capped piglet's conclusions, each morsel prompting vigorous nods and encouraging mutterings, was that Albert-Edward had been murdered by one or both of the Ogden brothers, and there was good reason for believing that.

He asks his audience whether anybody else would have been on Crawshaw's fields on that night other than those two, the wife and the boy. For being unable or unwilling to dig out, the brothers would surely have been sacked. By morning they would be out of house and home and who else would have them.

He continued, slowly, 'All right, they are barmy but not so barmy not to know what everybody here knows. They are neither use nor bloody ornament.'

This drew no disagreement so he continued, still pausing to sup, still pausing to check the door. He tells them that it might be that Ninepunce wouldn't have the gumption to work out what should be done, but Tenpunce would. If Albert-Edward never came back from the top field then nobody would ever know they had been sacked.

'So one of them', said Dodd, this time in a dramatic whisper, 'and I think both of them, followed his boot-holes and made sure he didn't come back.'

Still there was no objection, not even to the length of time he was taking over getting to the point. Dodd wanted to know if any man there thought Crawshaw didn't know every inch of every ditch and every wall on his fields. None did. Or if any one thought that he would fall into a ditch he didn't know was there and bang his head on a wall, none thought that either. Wasn't it more than likely that someone had broken his skull with a rock or a stone from the wall and rolled him into the ditch?

Dodd pushed the peak of his cap up an inch or two, revealing a little more of his pink porker features and said, 'Oh aye, they was lucky they was. The snow kept on coming and there were no holes in it to follow when they went searching. To my mind it was them two. Never been more certain.'

More ale was drunk and more pipes were lit. The case had been investigated; the Ogdens had been charged, tried and convicted. Since there was no tradition of lynching on the Heights, there was no more to be done that night. The inn emptied eventually and the jurors made their ways home with heavy bellies, light purses and the satisfaction that comes of a night's work done well.

It was to be four days between Doctor Phillips receiving the body and completing his examination. His conclusions were passed to the Coroner's Officer, from him to the Coroner and from him to the constable to undertake enquiries and arrange an inquest.

The Coroner would not be presiding. He was to marry that weekend and was then to go travelling. A bachelor for fifty years, he had succumbed to the charms of a widowed lady whose husband's inquest he had conducted. There were those who were happy that he should find, and that she should regain, happiness at their time of life. Less charitable souls wondered if the wealth of the deceased, revealed in the course of the inquest, might have made her more attractive than the lady's outward appearance. Either way, the Crawshaw Inquest would have to make do with a deputy coroner.

Carlton Devereux was a recently qualified solicitor who had secured a position with Messrs. Spencer & Hartley of Bradford just one month before. His initial enthusiasm for his position, given the nature of the town in which he was to practise, was fading. His appointment as a deputy coroner, though, lifted him a little. Such rapid advancement. A doubt lurked that others may have declined the appointment, and a curiosity as to why that should be.

Raised in comfortable circumstances in Staffordshire, educated at Oxford, Devereux had all the social skills necessary for a young lawyer to gain good standing, and commensurate earnings, from his chosen profession. The choice of Bradford was, he thought, a mistake. It was a filthy town comprised of soot-covered buildings, when they could be seen through the smoke. The people, drawn in by the growing industry, were, to his mind, as foul as the putrid canal in the town centre, the stench from which had caused him to retch.

Having been unsuccessful in two applications for a position he ought to have been more circumspect, he thought. Instead, like a desperate spinster, he had too quickly accepted the first offer to come his way. Still, here he was and, for now, would stay – but only until such time as a more suitable position could be secured. Stay, that is, unless the air should ruin his health or his inability to understand the languages, accents and colloquialisms of this stew-pot of nationalities made it impossible to do his work.

Tomorrow, however, he would be able to travel out of this stinking bowl. He was to conduct an inquest into the death of a hill-farmer who had been found dead in his fields ten days before. Reading the papers in the case, he was looking forward to dealing with a local community rather than those who inhabited the town centre slums. The Italian, German, Irish and Scottish accents defeated him – almost as much as the grunts and verbal and vowel shorthand that passed for language among the local people.

The inquest was held at noon in the bar of the Plough and Pair, on the Heights. Devereux saw a long rectangular room with a bar running almost the full length on the right hand side when viewed from the door. At the far end, in front of the fireplace, was a table, facing the door at which would be seated the Deputy Coroner flanked to his right would be the Coroner's Officer and to his left be the Coroner's Clerk. The constable stood to the left of the table and the witnesses were seated in a row across the width of the centre of the room.

Behind the witnesses stood the spectators; a large and noisy gathering, some of whom had come quite a distance. There was little entertainment on the hills and such that there was ought not to be missed.

Deputy Coroner Devereux was determined that the dignity of the Coroner's Court and the respect to be afforded the bereaved were not to be compromised. He had not been to the Heights before, though, nor to any place like it.

'Landlord, proceedings are about to begin. Stop serving ale please.'

'Cannot Sir. 'Tis a coaching inn and it's a requirement that food and ale be always available.'

'And do you have residents at present?'

'Nowt to do with it, Sir. Applies just the same. A rule you see.'

The landlord didn't know whether there was or was not any such rule, but there was a lot of ale to be sold, if he could. Devereux's studies had not included obscure licensing laws so did not know whether they took precedence over a coroner's proceedings. He felt it should suffice to say, 'Well be quiet about it.' Then to the rest, 'Every one present should be aware that unless they observe absolute silence throughout these proceedings the constable will eject you. In the case of a serious failure to comply with my instructions, the constable will arrest you and the case against you will be presented to the magistrates by me, in person.'

His words had their effect. Not so much their meaning as the educated tones in which they were spoken. There was a certain deference paid to class and education no matter how the reaction might be resented. It was a conditioned reflex.

With a nod to his right he signalled the Clerk to commence. The Clerk bellowed, 'Come forward the Widow Crawshaw.' And Devereux winced at the insensitivity of this crude, fat man of ill-kempt appearance with whom he had to work.

Margaret Crawshaw stood before the table and to show respect to her husband and to the Court she wore her

Sunday clothes. This was a misnomer since she wore those clothes only three times a year. These were for church on Christmas Day, for church on the Sunday nearest to the anniversary of her mother's death and on the one Saturday each year when she attended Sir Isaac Ambrose's garden party.

Margaret, then known as Meg, had been in service at Thornton Old Hall, the Ambrose home, from the age of twelve until she married Albert-Edward Crawshaw when she was twenty. Her husband was a gruff bear of a man but never anything but tender in his love for his wife and, later, for their only child Henry. She was proud of her family and proud too that Sir Isaac should invite her and her family to the annual party he held for his staff, his employees, the locals of Thornton and his friends. Margaret was counted among the latter.

Albert-Edward was invited but never accompanied her saying that he never felt comfortable in the company of such folk: didn't have the manners. She often told him, and others if the opportunity arose, that when she was a skivvy she was treated as a person and when she became a person she was treated as a friend. As the wife of Albert-Edward Crawshaw and a friend of Sir Isaac Ambrose she felt doubly honoured.

'Constable, bring a seat forward for Mrs Crawshaw.' It was placed behind her but she continued to stand. She gave her account without self-pity and with a dignity that prompted many behind her to remove their caps. She had gone out with her son at first light but the snow was waist deep and she needed help, She would, she said half turning, always be grateful to those who gave up two days to help her search.

No, she had not gone to The Ogden brothers' cottage that first morning as she expected that they would have been out with her husband through the night and when one was found the three would be found. Yes, she had seen them among the searchers later that morning and Joe Ogden told her that he had not been home that night. She had tried to speak to Luke but could not make any sense of what he said.

She confirmed that she had identified her husband's body to the Coroner's Officer in the field and to Doctor Phillips in the kitchen at the farm.

Young Henry was called. He shuffled forward and it was a pathetic figure he presented to the Deputy Coroner. His hair, washed and well brushed, was still a tousled dark mess. His boots that were well cleaned and while his clothes were most presentable they could not rescue his defeated appearance. The little natural confidence he possessed had been destroyed by his grief. Although not yet fully grown it was apparent that his eventual height would still fall well short of that of a mature man.

Having mumbled his way through the oath with head bowed, he could add nothing to his mother's account. He had not spoken to the Ogden brothers on the first morning of the search. It was not usual for him to speak to them or them to him.

This was not true. Ever since arriving at the farm, but never in Albert-Edward's hearing, Joe Ogden had bullied, insulted and taunted him. His vulgar comments about animal functions and about women had disgusted Henry and had been a constant source of fun to the leering Tenpunce. This wasn't the place to talk of such things though, and he decided to say nothing.

The clerk called Luke Ogden and a voice at the rear shouted, 'Come on Ninepunce, your turn'. This caused raucous laughter but the Deputy Coroner had spotted the voice.

Devereux, concerned for the dignity of his court and for the feelings of the widow and her son who had just given evidence, was angered. He spoke. 'Constable, the rude bearded fellow, still wearing his cap. See him out and you may cuff his ears as an example to those who find his conduct amusing', Then to the others, 'Those still wearing caps, remove them now'. All did. 'And landlord, stop serving until these proceedings are concluded. If not, the licence of which you affect such knowledge and to which you are, no doubt, attached may well be forfeited. I would, without fee, prosecute the matter myself.'

There was not a murmur in the room. There would be no more ale and should be no more interruptions. Devereux was fully in command.

The oath that Mrs Crawshaw and Henry had sworn and repeated solemnly defeated Luke Ogden. Even when asked to repeat the words singly he was incapable. The previously raucous few at the bar would have been incapable of containing their hilarity had they not been in fear of the Deputy Coroner and of the constable who had returned and nodded to the Bench to signify that instructions had been fully complied with.

Devereux began, 'Where were you on the night of Mr Crawshaw's death?'

Ninepunce replied. To Devereux it sounded like 'Want Eye'. Same question, same reply. A question to his clerk 'What is the fellow saying' The clerk answered, 'he's saying it wasn't him' Further questions to the witness. Every reply 'Want Eye'.

Devereux studied the unwashed brute before him. Tongue lolling out and eyes darting about, sometimes together, and sometimes independently. It was apparent that the witness was a moron and Devereux told him to go back to his seat.

Joe Ogden was called. Quite as wild in appearance as his brother but with a marginally more acceptable countenance, he was able to repeat back the words of the oath.

'Did Mr Crawshaw visit your home on the night of his death?'

'Wunt no. Weren't 'ome'. After a whispered translation from the clerk he continued,

'Where did you spend that night?'

'Under that table of yours' This proved too much for one at the rear and the constable was dispatched to dispense summary justice on another pair of ears.

Tenpence's tale was that he was too drunk to make his way home and he had slept under the table until first light. When he got back to Black Dyke Hole he found the search in progress and he joined in. He was questioned at length but could not be budged.

The constable was called. He had made enquires when he was informed that an inquest was to be held. The facts that the Deputy Coroner had elicited did not differ from the accounts that had been given to him. There had been no-one in the Inn that night that could say with any certainty that they saw Joe Ogden leave and the landlord could not be certain that Joe Ogden or anyone else for that matter had slept under a table. It wasn't unusual for it to happen.

The constable concluded that there was one person who claims to have seen both Ogden brothers walking home that night but he considered her to be an attention seeker. He wouldn't lay much store by anything she saw, he added.

'Her name constable?'

'Maisie Buckley Sir.'

'I'll hear from her.'

'She's not been called, Sir.'

'Well fetch her man. Now!'

Having reminded all present that the hearing was still in session, Devereux occupied himself with re-reading the very detailed and lengthy report of Doctor Phillips. It wasn't to be a long wait before the constable returned with a well built girl in her late teens.

'Miss Buckley, you have just taken an oath. Do you understand what it means?'

'Yes Sir'

'Well tell me then'

'Sir it means if I tell a lie I will burn in hell when I die'

'A good answer. Now tell me what you know about the night Mr Crawshaw died'

'I know he (she pointed at Joe Ogden) didn't stay in the Plough. I passed 'em both on Back lane on t'way to Crawshaw's'

'And why do you remember that?' asked Devereux

'Cos they were both drunk, saying very rude things to me and waggling their thingies at me. Their thingies, you know, their pissers. Do it all the time, they do, ask any of the girls round here'

The Ogdens muffled their giggles but couldn't hide the jiggling of their shoulders.

'So what time was this?'

'Well past eleven Sir'

'And what were you doing up Back lane at that hour?'

'Coming home from visiting my young man, Sir. It's all right me mam knows.'

'Tell me, Miss Buckley, how can you be sure it was the night of Mr Crawshaw's death?'

'It were the night of the big snow. I was on and out of bed all night. The ale we'd had, me and me young man, it was well sour and it give me the runs. I saw the snows and wished it would bury them two mucky buggers before they got 'ome.' She turned to the Ogdens and her last words were directed at them. Devereux thanked her and released her.

He asked the Coroner's Officer why Doctor Phillips was not there and was informed that the doctor was not normally inconvenienced from his many duties. His reports usually sufficed.

'Well then just read the first two paragraphs for the record.'

The Coroner's Officer cleared his throat, and with as much importance as he could muster read. 'The cause of death was a breaking of the skull and bleeding into the brain. The cause of wound was most likely to have been a blow with a heavy object of irregular surface – perhaps a rock or a stone.'

At the rear a hatless piglet faced man nodded vigorously so vigorously in fact that his colour changed from pink to puce.

'However, having regard to the deceased's height and weight and the reported conditions underfoot, I am unable to discover the possibility of a slip of the feet causing a falling back on to some such object as previously described'.

Devereux thought for a moment, his hands together, as if in prayer, pressed to his lips. Then he spoke. 'Mr Clerk, I wish you to record fully and accurately my findings in this case and then to make two copies. One of those should be delivered to the Coroner on his return from his er, travels. I would wish it to be impressed upon him that there are matters here that are unresolved.' He paused to allow the Clerk to record these words.

'One course open to me is to adjourn this inquest until a more diligent investigation is undertaken. This I would do if I felt there was any likelihood that further enquires would resolve matters. My experience here of the investigative abilities of those concerned' and he deliberately looked first to the Coroner's Officer then to the constable, 'provides one with no such confidence.'

The constable at least had the grace to flush.

'I am minded that there is a woman and a son who have yet to bury a well-loved husband and father, a man who was highly respected. I therefore intend to order the release of the body for burial. My verdict in this case is to be recorded as an Open Verdict. For the record this is because the evidence in the case is insufficient to rule out criminal activity by a person or persons unknown. I was impressed by the evidence of Miss Buckley. Much less impressed by that of Joseph Ogden'. With this he stared at Tenpunce, who returned his stare unblinking. 'It is word against word yet I feel I am entitled to have a preference for one version rather than the other.'The clerk completed his writing and asked.

'To where should I send the second copy?'

Devereux rose and collected his cloak, hat, gloves and papers before responding.

'To the Head Constable, with a suggestion, that if he has officers capable of conducting a diligent investigation they would be well employed on this matter.'

With that he left the table. He stopped in front of Margaret Crawshaw, 'My condolences Mrs Crawshaw', a brief bow, 'Master Crawshaw,' with a nod.

Carlton Devereux directed the driver of the trap to deliver him to his lodgings with a stop at a wine merchants in Westgate to buy a bottle of claret. The letter he had dreaded to write that evening would be difficult for him.

Messrs Spencer & Hartley

'My Dear Sirs,'

I shall be forever grateful for the opportunity you have given me to practice. Moreover having had the privilege of witnessing at such close proximity the diligence and professionalism you apply to services you provide, I shall always hold you and your firm in the highest esteem.

When I came to Bradford from rural Staffordshire and from the surreal environment that is Oxford University it was in the full understanding that I would be required to make adjustments. I knew the town to be growing at a rapid rate and to becoming renowned, even abroad, for the wealth its quarries, coalmines and textile industries was producing.

In the month I have lived and worked here I have seen how that wealth is being built on the broken bodies of infants, less than half of whom survive until the age of four, and on its illiterate population that has twice been decimated by cholera. Indeed, on more than one occasion I have vomited in market street from the stench from the open sewer that masquerades under the name of canal. The poisonous smoke that stings my eyes and burns my throat can do no less to those who live their lives in the squalor of the town. Those who cannot, as I, escape to lodgings in the streets above the centre.

The town cannot accommodate its present swell, when it is added to, it seems, daily. It is a magnet for the worst examples of the many nationalities that comprise this stew. I find I cannot understand the language or accent of people with whom my work brings me in contact. It is sadness to me that intelligent conversation, a well-loved pleasure of mine, is denied me in any company other than yourselves, your members and your staff.

As you are aware, Sirs, my duties took me to the Heights above Clayton today. While the air was cleaner than in the town my understanding of the people and their language was no clearer to me at all. With few exceptions the people I encountered were inbred, ill bred, ill mannered, or illiterate. Some fell into all four categories. A sensitive, intelligent person having the misfortune to be born into that community would have all spirit and ambition crushed from them.

It is in this low mood that I pen this letter, determined upon my course to tender my resignation from my position. I do it in full realisation that I am blighting my future prospects but as dear as they are to me they are no less dear than my health and my sanity.

I wish you both, Sirs, every good wish for the continuing reputation and prosperity of Messrs Spencer & Hartley. I wish I could offer the same for Bradford but I fear that this town will never amount to more than the midden it is.

My affection for your selves will never diminish.

Yours

Carlton Devereux.

Devereux was at his Principal's offices early next morning and when those gentlemen had arrived he requested a meeting with both. He gave them his letter of resignation and was asked to sit while they digested the contents. Joshua Spencer the senior of the two, made no attempt at discussion. 'Carlton, dear boy, may we ask that you return at noon to say your goodbyes to your colleagues and staff and to take a glass of sherry with us. We would wish to part with a handshake and in friendship'.

This was a far more pleasant reaction than the young lawyer had anticipated and that he too would wish to part on such terms.

With trunk and case packed by noon, he was back at the offices of Spencer & Hartley where he took his leave of his former colleagues. They were perplexed, puzzled and disappointed to lose the company of a popular young man who had quickly demonstrated his promise. Any speculation that misconduct personal or professional might be involved was quashed by the knowledge that the Principals were providing a sherry reception. A ritual reserved only for the most highly prized clients.

Sherry served, the three of them sat in armchairs around the fire in Sheldon Hartley's office. It was Joshua Spencer though who led the conversation. With a mane of white hair worn over the collar and balanced by bushes of side-whiskers, his appearance approached the theatrical a fondness for colourful waistcoats, and spats. When walking out in a crimson lined cape, carrying a silver capped cane the illusion was complete. He would engage in flowering language but this was a device to wrong foot those who failed to recognise soon enough the precision of thought he brought to his detailed knowledge of the law.

'Carlton,' and Spencer patted Devereux's knee in reassurance, 'Mr Hartley and I, on the basis of so short a relationship with you are convinced that the law will be a good mistress for you and you a fine lover for her. This town may not be the place where you can display your affection to its greatest effect but in another place you should find yourself more able to embrace her in the manner in which she deserves.'

Devereux sipped his sherry, listening respectfully.

'Yet, before you depart, I need to offer another view of this town, which, with good reason I concede, disgusts you so. You see an ugly malformed child, mewling and puking. Yes? I too saw only that, when I arrived here over thirty years ago. Since then I have seen the child growing and not only in the monuments to power and wealth that its many and increasing fine buildings represent. A town is not its buildings, noisy mills, its choking dirty quarries or its dusty mines. A town is its people.'

(But what people they are, thought Devereux.)

'No, dear boy, in its people, Bradford to me is no longer the ugly child: it is the ungainly, unconfident girl and only taking the trouble to know of her foibles, uncertainties and growing pains we come to have affection for her – and more –to see the attractive young woman that she is destined to become.' He paused, looked to the ceiling and continued with emotion. 'Yes it's poor who live in squalor. How can they live like that you ask? I'll tell you. By a dependence upon each other for there are no others to whom they can turn. They have little yet they share; they clothe their naked neighbour; they visit the sick neighbour; they act as midwife, doctor, and nurse. Do you consider that losing a fourth or fifth infant to illness is less or more grieving than losing a first? Think on it'.

This pause was longer and Carlton Devereux felt embarrassed to have insulted a town for which Joshua

Spencer had such obvious concern; but Spencer had not finished; his theatrical flow was now given full rein.

'These people, those worst examples of the nationalities that comprise its stew as you would have it, how can they live in this cesspit? They do so by compulsion. They do so by supporting each other in a myriad of daily kindness that could never be numbered. In supporting one and being supported by another, they strive to keep each bottom lip above the level of the effluence floating on top of the mire into which they have been pitched one and all.'

If it had been Joshua Spencer's intention to make Devereux feel like a public school snob, an over-privileged ingrate who felt qualified to sit in judgement on the less fortunate he had achieved his aim, but that was not, Spencer said, his intention.

'Carlton, I spoke as I did in order that, as the accomplished advocate you will surely become, you will be able to identify, and hereby to argue, the opposing case. It is an ability that must be practised. It is fundamental to your profession; we leave on the happiest of terms and with every wish that you will prove to be a success we believe you will become. We should be pleased to be kept informed of your progresses.'

The three rose, then shook hands as Sheldon Hartley handed him three sealed envelopes.

Devereux took the railway to Halifax, then from there to Manchester, where he intended to stay overnight before continuing on his journey to his family home in Staffordshire.

During his journey he opened the three sealed envelopes. The first contained his earnings. A generous fourteen pounds. The second, his fee for the Crawshaw inquest two guineas and two crowns for the hire of the trap. The third was a testimonial.

'To Whom It may concern'.

Throughout his employment with this company Mr Carlton Devereux has applied himself assiduously to his duties and his clients. He came to us with a highly creditable grade from his studies of law undertaken at one of the more esteemed universities for a qualification of that discipline.

In his brief time here he displayed the pragmatism necessary to apply his academic knowledge to the practicalities of everyday practice.

His reasons for terminating his position are personal to him, explained to his principals and fully understood and supported.

We wish him success in his career and should be pleased to provide references if requested to do so.

Rather than be signed formally, *Messrs Spencer & Hartley*, as was custom, it was personally signed by Joshua Spencer and Sheldon Hartley. Devereux was both relieved and humbled.

As the train passed through the Lancashire countryside he thought of those he had met. He dismissed from those thoughts the Ogdens as well as the incompetent constable and the crude clerk. He thought better of Maisie Buckley but thought her situation would never permit her to amount to anything. Mrs Crawshaw had his sympathy but young Henry, what of him?

He could foresee that it would not be many years before a flat capped Henry Crawshaw would be at the bar of the Plough and Pair most nights, laughing at crudities. The horizons would be no further than he could walk with a full bladder.

No. For Henry Crawshaw he saw no hope.

Chapter 2

The early May weather, blue skies and warm breezes, mocked the widow at the graveside of a fine husband, found dead and frozen in an April blizzard. The lane to Queensbury churchyard was lined with friends, neighbours and the merely idle and curious. Margaret Crawshaw was determined to maintain her dignity and to give strength to her son Henry who was inconsolable at the finality that the hole in the ground before him represented. Firm of purpose and of step she had followed Arthur Edward's coffin the full two miles from the Catholic Church in Horton. It had been carried on Selwyn Jenkins's cart, pulled by his pony. Her husband's chestnut mare was not trained to the harness.

Father O'Donnell was visiting his dying mother in Cork. This was his third such pilgrimage in eighteen months, each financed by 'special collections.' Rumours that on the last occasion he had been seen in Scarborough gained little currency, even in the Plough and Pair since they could not be traced to anyone who had ever travelled further than Bradford. A curate from Bradford deputised. He could not have spoken more movingly of Albert-Edward's qualities as a husband, father, shepherd, friend and neighbour, had they had a life long acquaintance. His words were as reassuring as the resurrection and he had such a presence that the memory of the service would long be spoken of. Also to be long remembered was the sight of the cortege, being led by the handsome young curate on the white stallion.

Margaret and Henry would not have to walk back to Black Dyke Hole. In the lane outside the churchyard a fine carriage pulled by a matched pair of grey horses. The gentleman who greeted them introduced himself as the representative of Sir Isaac Ambrose and he handed Margaret Crawshaw a letter. It was late evening before the last of the mourners had left and she and Henry read the letter together.

'My dearest Mrs Crawshaw,

Had I been able I would surely have paid my respects in person today. It is with profound regret that I am reduced to conveying my condolences in this way.

Since my election, my constituency duties detain me in Huntingdon and though I miss my Thornton home it is infinitely more convenient here for my frequent journeys to London.

I would wish you to know that the Old Hall estate is now being managed by my son Charles who you will remember from his childhood and who remembers you with affection. He shares my concerns for you and for your son. He awaits a request from you for any assistance you may require of him and will respond as readily and as happily as I would.

I am, dear Margaret,

Isaac Ambrose.'

Henry rose next morning with a new resolve. He would be the man of the house, the manager of the farm, and the provider for his mother. His mother however, was determined that Henry should complete the education to which his father had attached such importance. The resolve of a schoolboy against the determination of a Yorkshire woman was not an even contest and the following Monday found Henry back at Simon Pepper's School in Illingworth.

Margaret was pleased and relieved to accept the offer of a neighbouring sheep-farmer, Ernest Hargreaves, to oversee the management of the Crawshaw flocks. The time he could devote to this was limited but the two long term hands who had worked under Albert Edward responded well to their new responsibilities. He considered the Ogden brothers worse than useless. Margaret, though, while unaware of the details, knew that Henry's education and the Ogdens' 'employment' were dependent on each other. They would have to stay.

Henry, now out of the shadow of a father to whom he had been devoted, grew greatly in confidence, though only a little in stature. This would be his final year in school and he saw his future in the running of Black Dyke Hole. The knowledge of rearing a flock, gained from his father, was supplemented by the knowledge of managing hands he was gaining from Ernest Hargreaves. Astride Albert-Edward's chestnut mare he would ride with Mr Ernest Hargreaves, as he addressed him, over his neighbour's fields at Upper Denholme. Hargreaves had far larger flocks, over a dozen full time hands and several tenants on his land. Henry watched and learned while this farmer, employer, landlord complimented, encouraged and occasionally criticised his staff and tenants. This was Henry's first experience of practical management. His father had been a gruff, uncommunicative man who set an example to those who worked with or for him. Ernest Hargreaves was a manager whose skill was to fetch the best from others.

Margaret had no immediate money worries. Her husband had been a prudent man who, while by no means wealthy, did have a good sum in savings. Income had reduced significantly following his death and she, still had running costs, feed for stock and wages for hands, including the Ogdens who were now thoroughly idle and frequently drunk. Still, Henry had convinced her that with his schooling finished next year and with the guidance he was receiving from Mr Hargreaves he would have Black Dyke Hole back in profit before his father's savings became too depleted. Watching him astride his mare and seeing him instructing the hands, she was proud of the fine young man who had changed so much in the course of the summer. He had no contact however, with the Ogdens and Margaret felt that was sensible. What was she to do about those two once the arrangement with Mr Pepper's school was concluded next summer?

At the beginning of the autumn school term in late August, Henry met and made a friend of Desmond Hardcastle, who told him of an afternoon function he had attended in Halifax while at school in that town the previous term. This was Miss Petunia Peel's Social Afternoons for Young Gentle People. They were held on Fridays from four o'clock, Desmond told him, and one could hear music, learn to dance and, most exciting of all, meet well brought up young women. Henry told his mother, who was enthusiastic and ensured he had suitable clothes and shoes for such an occasion. Unsure that he would wish to attend for more than the one occasion he had agreed with Desmond, he worried about this extravagance.

Desmond's description of this function was proved accurate. It was well attended, the music lively and there were at least as many young women as young men. The majority were a year or two older than Henry and Desmond but caught up in the atmosphere, Desmond was soon off from the boys' side of the dance floor to the girls' side. Henry admired his friend's confidence. Desmond's dancing style was no more than an awkward shuffle but he smiled at and laughed with each partner and he actually had girls in his arms. What girls they were too. Not the farm girls of the Heights but pretty, well spoken, young women in colourful dresses. Did he have the nerve to cross the floor? If the girl he approached rejected him, what then? He was still in this quandary when the decision was taken from him. She crossed the floor a vision to Henry in a white dress with a pink sash and pink silk dancing slippers, her dark curls framing laughing eyes. She took his hand and asked him for the honour of a dance.

Henry was smitten. He had a girl in his arms and her hair stroked his cheeks as she swayed in time to the jig he was attempting. The touch of her hand, the scent of her perfume, the giggle in her voice, each alone had him in her power. The combination won him completely.

The music stopped, she bowed and said 'Miss Alice Miles Sir'.

Henry returned her bow, 'Master Henry Crawshaw' wishing, as he said it, that his accent was less guttural and that he could have more closely matched her pleasing tone.

Returning to his side of the room he had an interest in no other than Miss Alice Miles. He would not be asking another to dance but worried about the protocol of returning too soon to ask Miss Miles. She stood with a group of young woman, laughing and enjoying each other's company. He watched as other young men requested dances, he agonised to see her in their arms. The pain he felt in his stomach was as real as if he had taken a blow.

It seemed that Desmond missed not one dance, while Henry had had but one. Lacking in confidence to return to Alice, and unwilling to be unfaithful to her by dancing with another, he stood, stared and longed. Before the function ended he braved his nerves, set out on the long, lonely walk across the floor and asked Miss Miles for the honour. She smiled, curtsied and once more she was in his arms. Henry felt he would never wish to be anywhere else, never wish to be doing anything else. Any time not spent with Alice, his Alice, would be a wasted time, a wasted life. Henry was in love.

How could he live without her until next Friday? What if Alice should not be there? Worse still, what if something was to prevent him from being there and she was to dance with others? She should only dance with him.

Friday did come again, eventually. The function room began with Miss Petunia Peel announcing that the purpose of her Social Afternoons for Young Gentlepeople was not only an opportunity for music and dancing. She insisted that there be no girls on the boys' side of the room, but there should be conversation between the two. She instructed that half the girls should take themselves across the floor and half the boys should do the same. Henry set off at once, leaving a couple of dozen stragglers, but was dismayed to see Miss Alice Miles crossing in the opposite direction. The music didn't start for sometime and Henry watched as Alice and her friends were grouped with a number of young men, including Desmond.

On the first note from Miss Peel's piano, Henry was across the floor, almost elbowing his way through the group to reach Alice and request the honour. The dance, done too soon to Henry's mind, accompanied Alice back to her group and joined them. He resented her dancing with others, begrudgingly admired the easy conversation of the other young men who told entertaining tales and he asked for, almost demanded every third dance with the radiant Miss Miles.

A person who had the appearance and mannerisms of a gentleman but whom Desmond knew as a braggart and bully dominated the conversation in the group. He was Julian Dexter. When Henry asked Alice for yet another dance, Dexter embarrassed him, by saying to her 'I once had a pup that was similarly devoted but shot it when it pissed on my boots,' his friends laughed. Alice did not and she danced with Henry once again. Henry was convinced she loved him too.

In school, Desmond attempted as politely and sensitively as he was able to suggest to Henry that paying attention to and dancing with other girls would make him appear more attractive to Alice. As sound as this advice was, the enraptured Henry was deaf to it and for the next two weeks his dances with Alice were ample compensation for Dexter's insults. These were repetitive and usually involved pups and Henry's height. Typical of these would be the greeting, 'Hello little fellow, not on my boot if you please'.

For two Fridays in December Alice was not at the function. These were miserable afternoons for Henry who had decided that he too would no longer go if she didn't soon reappear. The next function was to be the last before Christmas and it would be three weeks before the next one. Happily Alice was there and even as happily Dexter was not. Without their leader, his friends were quite affable and Henry shamelessly monopolised his Alice's company and her dances.

She told him that she had visited with her cousin in Shropshire and that Carmel would be staying with her over Christmas. She described in detail the wonderful Christmas Eve parties held at her parents' home in Wilsden. The games they played, the feast of food, the unending fun, the music and the dancing 'til dawn. He was mesmerised, hardly hearing her words but lost in her eyes and gazing at the moving lips that he dared hope that one-day he would kiss.

Holding both his hands in hers, she said, 'Henry you would find it a wonderful occasion if you were able to come'. Returning home in a state of high excitement he told his mother of the invitation, so lost in love that his mother's Christmas the first without her husband to be spent alone, never even registered in his thoughts. Happy for him to be happy, his mother shared his excitement.

When he rode out that Christmas Eve afternoon, he had gifts for Alice's parents in his saddlebags. For her mother a fine wool shawl and for her father a fleece of the finest quality fashioned as a saddle blanket. It was a four-mile ride down narrow tracks and darkness fell by three o'clock. Snowflakes were settling on the tracks but the mare was sure footed and with his riding coat wrapped tightly around him, Henry's anticipation grew with every step.

There would have been no light to be had on the final climb once past the Dye Houses and Tan Houses, had Edmund Miles not arranged for braziers to lead his guests over the final quarter mile to the drive of the family home. Henry rode to the stable adjoining the right side of the house, tethered the mare temporarily while he announced his arrival, and climbed the stone stairs to a grand front entrance. The house was lit at every window through which he could see many guests already gathered drinking, talking and laughing together. Well dressed and in all appearances, people of some standing. He had with him a change of clothing and hoped it would be appropriate.

The door was opened by a manservant who requested Henry's name and that he present his invitation. Having explained that he was there at the personal invitation of Miss Miles, he was asked to wait in the entrance. The servant soon returned and asked him to attend at the kitchen door, which could be reached through the stable. Perplexed, he made his way as instructed and was met by Edmund Miles, ruddy of face and most unwelcoming.

'What is the purpose of this visit young man?'

Standing two steps below the door and looking up at the tall, fat man above him, Henry felt small, insignificant even. 'I am here, Sir, at the invitation of Miss Miles.'

'Are you indeed, an invitation which I as the head of this household have no knowledge.'

Henry hesitated. 'Perhaps, Sir, if you were to speak to Miss Miles.'... He was interrupted. There appeared from behind Alice's father a figure Henry knew and disliked, Julian Dexter and two others who he did not know but in appearance fops, all three of them. Dexter spoke to Edmund Miles,

'I know this lowborn fellow. Progeny of a hill farmer I understand. Hardly fit company for your guests I should think.'

Henry protested. 'I wish to speak to Miss Miles.'

The father was angry. 'I would not wish that. You came to my home on the Eve of Christmas and insult me by your implication that my ambitions extend no higher than one such as yourself.'

Incensed and insulted Henry responded, 'Sir, I would have you know that my father...'

Dexter interrupted, mimicking and exaggerating his accent 'Ah wud av thee no that mi fether...' 'I doubt that you knew who your father was or that with any certainty your mother.'

Henry attempted to strike the smirking Dexter but could reach no higher than his waist. Edmund Miles turned to the three with him and told them to get this unwelcome visitor off the grounds.

Dexter and his friends bundled him back to the stable. There was a muttered conversation then the two pinned Henry to a stall, lowered his breeches and Dexter struck at his buttocks twice with a coachman's whip. The consequences nauseated Dexter as much as it traumatised Henry. An intention to only humiliate resulted in two deep and free bleeding wounds. The three hurried back to the kitchen, ashamed of themselves. Henry collapsed in pain.

Staggering, he led his mare back into the lane. Each step was agony, riding was impossible and, the braziers passed, there was no light from the Tan Houses, the Dye Works or from the sky from which a steady but heavy snow was falling. The blood from his wounds was running down the legs of his breeches and gathering in his riding boots. It had to be staunched and he tore a length from his best linen shirt from his saddlebag. His boots were unsuitable for walking. His dancing shoes would have been no better and after less than a mile he was spent. If he was not to freeze in the snow as his father had done just eight months before, he would have to find shelter but where?

At the edge of Ridge Wood he came across an open sided but roofed structure that was used by sawyers. Having led his horse in, he took the fleece that would have been Edmund Miles's gift, and rolled in the sawdust. The blood was still flowing and he was resigned to die there. What hope could there be of any assistance in Ridge Wood on Christmas morning?

At eight o'clock Margaret Crawshaw left her home to meet up with neighbours for their walk to the service at the church at Horton. She would, as she did every year, celebrate the birth of Jesus, give thanks for his blessings and this year pray for the soul of her husband and to express her gratitude to God for the changes in the introverted son that she was witnessing.

The living of a sawyer depended on his productivity and his sales. Christmas was not a day to be idle, especially not a cold and snow covered Christmas day when Yule logs could be sold and would be burnt as fast as they could be sawed. A day without work and pay was a day for high summer not for a day such as this.

Henry was found, roused and, with his mare tethered to the rear of the wood cart, he was carried to the Heights. The two sawyers considered it an act of charity on this holiday but they were rewarded nevertheless with a shawl, a quality fleece and two half crowns. Before stabling his horse he hoped to be able to clean himself rather than have his mother return and find him in that state. Too weak to do either he was kneeling and shivering close to the kitchen fire when his mother returned. Had he had the strength to object to her stripping him and discovering his wounds he would have done so, but he had not.

By evening, in his bed, the fever set in. At first drenching sweats then shivers and convulsions, delirium set in and he was incoherent, drifting in and out of consciousness. For three days there was no improvement and his mother spent every minute of those days and nights bathing and cooling his burning body. Every attempt at feeding him broth resulted in vomiting and retching. The bleeding had stopped but his mother's poultices appeared to be having no effect on the angry weals on his buttocks. That evening Ernest Hargreaves called. Exhausted and terrified by her son's deteriorating condition she asked that a request be passed to Doctor Phillips to call.

It was mid-morning when Henry awoke. His mother was not at his bedside and the fire in his room had burnt out. He shuffled down the stairs on his bottom, each step sending searing pain through his body. The house was cold and the kitchen, when he finally reached it, was colder still. Here too the fire was out. On the flagstones, as cold and as blue as the flagstones themselves, lay the body of his mother in the place where his father's body had been laid before her. Henry sank to his knees, placed his perspiring forehead against her cheek and sobbed until he had nothing left.

Doctor Phillips arrived at noon, at the same time as a neighbour, Kate Mellor. The doctor pronounced Margaret Crawshaw dead and he found Henry to be seriously ill. He despatched Mrs Mellor to arrange care for the young man. The hill farmers' wives were nothing if good organisers and within the hour fires were lit, Henry was in bed. the ointments left by Doctor Phillips were applied and tinctures administered. The local wives had arranged round the clock care. There was a huge lamb casserole on the kitchen range and Black Dyke Hole was not unattended at any hour of any day for a week. Ernest Hargreaves undertook to make arrangements for the service and the funeral but when he visited Father O'Donnell he was informed that the arrangements had already been made for the following Monday.

The first carriage of the matching pair that had brought home Margaret and Henry Crawshaw from Albert-Edward's funeral was at the door of Black Dyke Hole that Monday morning. Neither of the gentlemen who alighted was the same as before. They escorted Henry, still weak but improving, and as he stood once more before that hole in the ground of Queensbury churchyard, he collapsed. Awaking in bed, in a room that he did not recognise, he attempted to sit up. The room swayed, his stomach lurched and he vomited.

Sometimes aware that his wounds were being tendered, sometimes not, not knowing where he was nor how long he had been there, his days passed in dreams and hallucinations, the faces of dead parents, a girl in his arms, being the object of humiliation, laughter and cruelty, music and pain. He was attended daily by a physician and constantly by a young woman who sponged his body, applied balm to his wounds and stroked his wet hair until he slept again. As his strength returned and his periods of consciousness increased he recognised Marianne and grew close to her.

With the physicians approval he was wrapped in a blanket and led to an armchair by a fire in a drawing room where he was joined by a man he did not recognise. The man offered his hand. 'You are most welcome young cousin.' This was a courtesy term amongst children of parents who were not necessarily related but were well acquainted.

Henry's thoughts were now clearer and full of questions, he listened as Charles Ambrose told him that he was at Thornton Old Hall. He had been there for three weeks; that his body was now recovering from its infection and that he was a welcomed guest for as long as he wished. When

Marianne joined them Henry attempted to rise to thank his nurse when Charles introduced him to his wife.

Within a few days, apart from soreness in his buttocks Henry improved immeasurably. Charles spent time with him each evening over a glass or two of wine and he raised the young man's spirits. One evening at the end of that miserable January they had a third glass and Charles turned to practical matters.

'Cousin Henry, during your illness I have taken certain liberties as regard to your affairs. None of these arrangements are irreversible and if you were to disagree with any of it, indeed, all of them, then I shall of course cancel them forthwith. I have with the complete agreement of Mr Ernest Hargreaves, appointed a temporary manager to conduct your affairs at Black Dyke Hole.' (Charles had in fact offered a generous sum to compensate Hargreaves for the work he had done on Margaret Crawshaw's behalf following her husband's death. This had been declined.)

'This manager, Mr. Nathan Stein is an accountant by qualification and a man of some talent, employed by my father before me, to our complete satisfaction. He has produced detailed accounts on your behalf which he will be pleased to present to you at your convenience.'

Mr Stein had in fact, done more than that. He had spent his first nights at the Plough and Pair where he had gleaned information that Charles was not yet ready to share with Henry. Also Stein had enquired into the history of the Ogden brothers' employment. Now living in the Crawshaw farmhouse Stein was examining every penny earned and spent and was preparing further reports and recommendations for Charles Ambrose.

'Tomorrow, cousin, I must travel to Huntingdon to visit my father to settle some business matters. Since his election to Parliament I am entrusted with his estate and business interests here and he has resumed his interest in the Huntingdon estate that I was managing previously. I expect to return in no more than ten days and in the meantime I would wish you to rest, enjoy everything my home has to offer you. I look forward to returning to find you restored to full health.'

Henry missed his evening conversations with Charles but Marianne, to whom he had become so attached during his illness, spent time with him. Her gentleness and concern for him contrasted with the business like conversations he had enjoyed with Charles. With Charles there were some barriers, which excluded personal feelings. With Marianne there were none.

When on the second evening she suspected a tear in Henry's eye, she sat on the arm of the chair and held his head to her breast. The awareness was more than he could bear and the dam of his emotions burst and everything poured out. His childhood, emotions, his insecurities, the feelings of inferiority when watching his tall powerful father working, his dependence on his mother, the death of his confidence, the taunting by the Ogden brothers, his suspicion that they murdered his father, the devotion to Alice Miles, the insults of her father, the thrashing by Julian Dexter. None of which he could have admitted to a man. He had not told his mother, nor the doctors or Charles, the cause of the still raised welts on his buttocks. As Marianne consoled and reassured him, he felt love again. Not the love he had felt for Alice Miles, but the love he would have had for a sister.

Nathan Stein had been opening and responding to mail on Henry's behalf. Some mail was clearly of a personal nature and the next day he gave Henry those letters, unopened. Some were messages of condolence from neighbours, some from school friends including Desmond. One was from Miss Alice Miles.

Dear Master Crawshaw,

I am given to understand from my father that there was unforgivable unpleasantness at our home on Christmas Eve. He was displeased that I should issue an invitation to his festive celebrations without his agreement. It was only with a deal of persuasion that I convinced him of no such thing.

The wish I expressed that you were able to see the wonderful way in which we celebrate Christmas was no more than that, a wish. I would not, nor could I issue an invitation without my father's approval which, given the disparity in our families' standings, would not have been forthcoming.

Moreover, I was distressed to learn of your assault on my friend Julian Dexter. I shall not be attending the social afternoons again and I intend this letter to conclude any correspondence between us.

Alice Miles.

If Alice Miles letter was intended to wound, it had the opposite effect. Cured of his infatuation he was filled with a resolve to place pragmatism over romantic notions, to rise above the station that others looked down upon and to be the man of whom Albert-Edward or Margaret Crawshaw would have been proud. He could not aspire to be a Charles Ambrose. His privileged upbringing, his education, his wealth and his place in society were beyond Henry but, with Charles's help, he could learn to be the most of which he was capable of being.

The business of the two estates was complicated and his father's attendance at Parliament extended Charles's stay in Huntingdon but the time was found to discuss Henry Crawshaw. Sir Isaac recalled the boy who accompanied Margaret to the annual garden party although he barely knew him even less than the boy's father but he had affection for Meg, as he knew her. Charles outlined his intentions and sought his father's agreement, which was readily given.

Henry's afternoons were spent riding with Marianne over Thornton on his mare, now stabled at Old Hall. Other than some discomfort from the saddle, he was fit and in good spirits when Charles returned after three weeks. On the terrace that first evening Marianne told Charles of all she had learned from Henry. It was no breach of confidence, she felt, (she knew there were matters where she could not reassure,) but believed that Charles could. He told her of his conversation with his father concerning Henry and of his intentions. She was pleased. The agreement of his father, the additional information from Marianne and the further reports he received from Nathan Stein the next day convinced the young master of Old Hall that the course upon which he was to embark was right and just.

On the afternoon following Margaret Crawshaw's funeral a slim bald, dome headed man had taken a room at the Plough and Pair. If the professional police force had been better established at that time, Nathan Stein would have been a detective, the attention he paid to the detail of columns of figures he paid to other accounts – accounts of events and inconsistencies. That first evening he invested three mugs of ale in a piglet faced man and heard the theory of Albert-Edward Crawshaw's demise. This explained the dissatisfaction evident in the conclusion of the Deputy Coroner whose report of the inquest he had examined in Bradford that morning. Stein was also alerted to an arrangement under which Henry was being educated and the Ogden brothers were being kept.

The following evening Tenpunce and Ninepunce were in the bar. The accountant stood behind them, ordered a large pot of rum and offered them the same. Round after round they drank it like ale, while Nathan Stein, whenever they were distracted, tipped his in to the spittoon. Affecting surprise that the brothers were employed at Black Dyke Hole, in fact they actually managed the farm, he told them in strict confidence, they should understand, that he was looking to buy the farm.

Tenpunce did. Ninepunce understood nothing.

Tenpunce disclosed no details about the death of Albert-Edward but he did reveal his attitude towards Henry whom he referred to as 'the whelp' and who would do as he, Joe, would tell him. 'I say boo. He cries. Always did. Always will, on his own now he is. He'll be happy to sell if I speak to 'im, you see.'

Stein's third day was spent in Halifax where he examined registers of the charities that supported the Subnormal and the fourth, fifth and sixth day at the farmhouse, fathoming and calculating the Crawshaw accounts. After this, purporting to have been sent by the commissioners of the Halifax charities for the in educable, he visited Simon Pepper's school in Illingworth. Pepper was not anxious to co-operate in any way with Stein's enquiries or readily offer his accounts for auditing.

Chapter 3

Sir Isaac Ambrose's business interests in Yorkshire were complex and demanded close attention. His son Charles attended them as assiduously as he would have done had they been his own, which one day they would be. The time he could allocate to Henry was limited but he would set aside at least an hour each day, normally after dinner, to spend with his young houseguest. Charles was pleased that Henry was well but concerned that after two months he was not now raising the question of his future. There was a danger that once he was well settled, with having no responsibilities and content to do nothing but ride each day, Henry would become dependent and devoid of motivation.

Their wine glasses filled, a good fire in the grate, Charles broached the subject of Henry's plans for the future. Henry felt that while he would never have his father's ability with a flock, nor would he for some time be able to emulate Ernest Hargreaves's Management skills, he had learned something from both. His seventeenth birthday was approaching and he would honour his father's wishes that he should complete his education with Mr Pepper this summer then assume Management of Black Dyke Hole.

'Tell me Henry, what are your intentions regarding the Ogden Brothers?' His face darkened, 'They are a problem to me.'

Charles continued, 'and what more will you learn from Mr Pepper that you have not yet gained in your years attending his school?'

Henry didn't know.

The gentle probing continued, 'How well are you acquainted with the value of Black Dyke Hole and its flocks and of the costs associated with its running as opposed to its income?'

Henry felt increasingly awkward. 'These are matters I'll need to be looking into.'

It was obvious that this young man was directionless and it would be no kindness to let him drift in that state. 'It is some weeks now since I told you of certain liberties I had taken with your affairs. One of these was the appointment of Nathan Stein who has produced detailed accounts that he will present to you when you are feeling ready. It is a source of much disappointment to me that you have shown no interest in these.'

Henry was chastened but attempted a defence. 'It's no lack of interest. I was worried you might think me rude to be wanting to know how much I am worth because.' He became flushed. 'I'd rather not have a penny and have back my father and my mother'.

Had he been too harsh with Henry? He must rebuild him. 'You have learned more from your father about rearing a flock than I shall ever know. You have learned about management, not a skill I have ever been able to practice since I have been raised and educated to instruct rather than to manage. I employ others to do that. My skill is in business, not in trade, not in employment. It concerns an understanding of values that appreciate rather than costs that escalate. With your agreement I'll demonstrate that business is a skill that can be acquired. If you wish we will speak more of this on the morrow, but for now, think on this. Why does every employer pay his employee less than his worth?'

Without a pause Henry replied 'Workers are exploited. Mr Pepper regularly said this'.

'A worker can never be paid his worth. It is the difference between the cost of the labourer and the worth of his labour that provides the profit. Without profit there could be no employment. If you were to manage Black Dyke Hole, even though you would be the proprietor, you would be its employee. As an employee you could never be paid the value of your work. We'll finish for tonight while you decide if you wish to be wealthy. Should you desire that, put all thoughts of employment out of your mind, for it is not in that direction that wealth lies.'

Henry retired enthused, excited even. Wealth. He had never aspired to wealth but he was fired by Charles's apparent confidence that principles of business could be taught and that wealth was attainable. Of course, Charles had had the benefit of a privileged upbringing, an expensive education and might not have his wealth without those. But he did have wealth, understood its creation and he, Henry, could learn from him.

Dinner came and went the next evening without Charles having returned. Henry had dinner with Marianne and was about to retire when Charles returned. Henry informed him that he would place himself entirely in his hands. Charles replied that he would not. Henry would trust the first steps that Charles planned then his future would be in his own hands. They would be riding in the morning to put Henry on the road to his future.

They rode out early on a bright, still morning across the lanes of Denholme and Queensbury, passing close by Black Dyke Hole, and arrived at the school at Illingworth. Charles's stature in riding coat, spurred boots and sword at his belt lent him an air of authority. His personal confidence completed that authority as he strode along the school corridor and summoned Simon Pepper from a classroom to his office. Henry stood behind, unaware of what to expect. He was in awe of his headmaster but filled with admiration for Charles who was a powerful presence.

'Mr Pepper, Sir, I am Charles Ambrose and I am conducting affairs on behalf of Mr Crawshaw who you will know is recently bereaved.'

The headmaster, surprisingly Henry thought, addressed Charles with no more deference than he would show to a new boy on the first day of term.

'And most sorry we were to hear of it, Sir. As sorry as I am that you did not show me the courtesy of making an appointment to see me before arriving here uninvited. If you intend to return to your studies, Crawshaw, go to your desk. If that is not your intention, collect your books. You know where they are.'

Henry found himself turning, not knowing what he should be doing when Charles continued, 'I have come here today concerning matters of actionable fraud and the falsification of accounts. I did not expect to find you adding arrogance and ill-manners to your other sins.'

Pepper was outraged, 'You will leave now, and you, Crawshaw, collect your books, failing which you will find them in the road.'

Charles took a step towards Pepper, looked down at him and said, 'I shall leave if you wish and return with an officer of the constabulary and a collector of Her Majesty's Taxation office.'

'Explain yourself,' demanded Pepper.

'No, Sir, you explain yourself. Explain the two shillings a week you have been receiving from the Charity Commission for fourteen years for a registered retard and the three shillings you have been receiving for his brother a certified imbecile. It can be established that you have had the care of neither for ten of those years A fraud for which a lengthy term of imprisonment must surely follow.'

Pepper blanched but Charles was not done. 'And during those same ten years Mr Crawshaw's father has been paying what he thought was a discount rate for his son's education but was in fact for the full rate of half a crown a week. No record of those fees appear in your accounts but Mr Crawshaw's accounts contain each of your receipts, signed, dated and stamped. I am sure you would agree that the tax collector who will return with me will show interest, not only in your transactions with Mr Crawshaw, but with all your receipts and expenses.'

Sinking into his chair, head bowed, Pepper appeared defeated. He recovered a little and offered, 'I believe this matter might best be dealt with by a full refund of Mr Crawshaw's fees.'

'But no dear fellow,' Charles patronised him, 'There is more to this matter. Master Crawshaw has had his education, such as it has been. It would be unfair to ask you to re-pay his fees for which you have provided your service.'

'What then?' Pepper, could not see where this was leading. Nor could Henry who had calculated that Charles was rejecting an offer of over one hundred pounds. A huge sum.

'You see Mr Pepper, for ten years you have had payments for the care of the two brothers who would, at greater expense to the Borough, have been kept in an asylum. During these years that care was provided by Mr Crawshaw. As it would be unfair to deprive you of the fees for Master Crawshaw's education, would it not be similarly unfair to deprive Mr Crawshaw's estate of the fees for the services he has provided?'

Pepper had no answer. Henry calculated that this was a sum of over two hundred pound.

'Is that it?' demanded Pepper striking the desk with the heel of his fist.

'Almost, dear fellow. Almost. Throughout those ten years at Mr Crawshaw's farm the brothers have been paid a half crown a week each, all of which in recent years has found its way across the bar of the local ale house. Had they been worth their labour then their wages would not be an issue between us. The fact is they have been worse than useless. A handicap to Mr and Mrs Crawshaw that they bore, believing their son to be receiving a discounted education; those wages represent a loss to the Crawshaw estate and must be reimbursed.'

Pepper was ashen. All arrogance departed, he was reduced to pleading. He could not pay the sums involved, which amounted to two hundred and fifty pounds. How, he asked Charles, was he to settle the matter without the involvement of the authorities?

Charles told him that there should, by then, be a carriage outside the school. In it would be a Mr Alistair Wild, Master Crawshaw's solicitor and a member of the highly respected Bradford practice of Messrs Spencer and Hartley. 'The sum you owe the Crawshaw's estate equates to twenty two percent of the value of your school business and assets. The documents Mr Wild brings will allocate a twenty two percent interest in this school and its future earnings to Master Crawshaw. You may wish to have your own legal representative present but, then again, you may not wish to explain why you are signing over this interest without a concomitant consideration. Good day, Sir.' Pepper was angry. 'You are uncommonly well acquainted with my accounts and my business. There has been a recent audit. Your man, I take it?'

Charles did not reply and Henry followed him out, not fully understanding the transaction that had just taken place. With a nod to the gentleman in the waiting carriage, Charles mounted his horse and with Henry alongside, set out for Black Dyke Hole. The horses were set at a slow walk. The business with the headmaster had been concluded sooner than Charles had allowed for and he did not want to arrive at Crawshaw's farm before the arranged time of one o'clock. Even at that pace they would have arrived too early had they not watered at the top of Back Lane on the Heights where Henry enquired of Charles, 'Is that the end of my education?'

'On the contrary, young cousin, today it begins.'

They rode, still a slow walk, into the yard of the farm that Henry had not seen since the day of his mother's funeral. Stopping at the door, but not dismounting, Charles saw Nathan Stein at the window and received a signal. The two continued their slow ride the few dozen yards to the doors of the Ogden's cottage on which Charles, remaining mounted, beat with the hilt of his sword.

Both brothers appeared, apparently roused from their beds. 'Gentlemen', said Charles, 'Master Crawshaw has arranged a sale of this farm.'

Tenpunce interrupted, 'Nowt we didn't know but nice to be tolled, all the same.' With that the brothers made to return inside.

Charles shouted angrily, 'Impertinent rogue, stand still,' and enforced his command by prodding the back of Tenpunce's neck with the point of his blade. The elder Ogden, marginally more intelligent and swifter to anger and violence, wheeled menacingly but held his tongue.

Charles continued in a calmer tone. 'The new owner wishes this cottage to be kept in better order than you have kept it so he intends to house his pigs here. For that reason the two of you are to leave. Now.'

Joe Ogden, raised the sleeves of his filthy shirt, made fists and stood defiantly, 'and if we was to say no, who's to say different. Eh?'

Henry heard boot steps behind him and turned to see three of the roughest fellows imaginable. Each carried a club and had the look of a man who would alone be more than a match for the two Ogdens. The choice was clear, even to a retard and an imbecile. Leave now or be thrown out after a beating. They put on their boots and coats and set off for the gate.

Charles instructed the three men who had been hired by Nathan Stein, to see them off the farm and explained to them in words that they would understand the consequences should they ever return. 'Mark this though, I wish this to be done without violence.'

The brothers and their three escorts, followed by Charles, still mounted but with sword now sheathed, reached the gate.

Ninepunce turned. 'Where we to go? Where we to go?'

Reluctantly sympathetic to the pathetic child in this huge man's body Charles said, 'Go to Pepper's School in Illingworth and tell him that his partner, Master Crawshaw, wishes him to find you accommodation. Now be gone.'

Turning to Henry, 'We'll go to your farmhouse. I have matters to discuss with Mr Stein. You might wish to take the opportunity to gather those belongings of your own and parents that are precious to you. Mr Stein will arrange their delivery to you at Old Hall. We will have two visitors tomorrow. Before their arrival you will have some difficult decisions about your future and that of your farm.'

The light was failing when they arrived back at Thornton. Washed and having changed their clothes they dined with Marianne without the business of the day being discussed. Afterwards, in Charles's office, rather than the drawing room, Henry listened intently to his mentor's advice.

'The value of Black Dyke Hole, Henry, diminished significantly on the death of your father whose ability at breeding and rearing established the farm's reputation. The lands are themselves of little value, as are the buildings. The flock however, if well managed and quality maintained, is of value. Mr Stein has agreed a valuation of four hundred and eighty pounds, and I'll wager that no man could calculate a value to within a shilling. He has located more than one buyer prepared to meet the price.'

'And do you believe I should sell?' asked Henry.

'I believe that you ought not be employed by the farm, even as it's owner. Should the quality of the flock deteriorate, should you be unfortunate in the hands you employ or should ill-health prevent you from working the farm from dawn 'til lost light, it may not even provide a living for you.'

'If it is your advice I should sell, then I should take that.'

'Wait on. Although you ought not to be employed by the farm, you ought to have an interest in it, an interest from which you will derive an income. One interested buyer is Westhead Mills of Shelf, a customer of your father's wool and an admirer of its quality. They are an established firm who would put experienced management into the farm. They would be agreeable to you retaining a twenty percent interest if you were to accept their seventy five percent of the value. This is the course I recommend to you. Sleep on it. Our visitors are to be Mr Stein who will discuss an option for an educational opportunity and your solicitor, Mr Wild, who will explain certain legal provisions designed to protect your position and investments until you come into your majority. I now have business to attend to that needs my attention.'

Henry went to his room and stood for a time by the lamp in his window. Looking along the drive to the Hall, he wondered how the wealth that built such a great estate was amassed by the kind of transactions that Charles had conducted with Simon Pepper and was now advocating for Black Dyke Hole. He could, he calculated, have had two hundred and fifty pounds from his schoolmaster, almost four hundred had Charles not declined the offer of a refund of the school fees. He could have four hundred and eight pounds for the sale of the farm but was being advised to accept three hundred and sixty pounds. These decisions, some he was being asked to make and some being made for him, were of no little consequence to his future. With no home, no qualifications and no means of earning a living, three hundred and sixty pounds, the significant sum that it was, would not last forever and he would be ruined. He began to doubt that Charles Ambrose, who had been born into wealth, was qualified in any way to advise another on how to acquire it. In that mood he attempted to find sleep. The sums in his head and the pain in his buttocks from a full day's riding meant that sleep would be a long time coming.

Marianne was at breakfast but Charles had gone early to Bradford and would not be back before noon. Nathan Stein would be arriving soon, however to see Henry, who was disappointed not to have the opportunity to tell Charles of his decision. He would have to tell Nathan Stein.

The slight, dome headed accountant sat across the width of the long table in the library of the Old Hall. Henry sat opposite, his mind made up. 'Mr Stein, I believe I would be best served with the full sum Mr Pepper owes my father. I accept that managing the farm might not be a success. Others with more experience than me have failed. So again I would prefer its full value rather than a reduced sum.'

Stein, a shrewd man, seemed at first, encouraging. 'Well certainly, Master Crawshaw. Although my purpose in coming here today was to propose some options for your immediate future, I shall of course discuss these matters that are causing you some obvious concern. Yes, if you were able to have the sums owed by Mr Pepper, about two hundred and fifty pounds, the value of the farm, four hundred and eighty pounds, taken together with the residue of your father's savings of sixty two pound, you would indeed have an admirable total of about eight hundred pound.'

Henry nodded in agreement:

'And you would have the enviable problem of deciding what to do with such a sum. You might purchase a desirable property but its upkeep would, week by week deplete the balance of your fortune until it was gone and the property would have to be sold. Or, you might securely invest the full amount and earn an interest from the income of, say, two and a half percent per annum. The twenty pounds a year would be a useful sum for a gentleman who did not require a home, food, clothing, and all other expenses of day to day living, but insufficient for one who did.'

Less sure than he had been only a few minutes before, Henry pressed on. 'If I were to retain the farm, Mr Pepper's refund would sustain me through any difficulties I might encounter until I was better established in farm management.'

Stein, still, ostensibly helpful told him, 'It is a good sum and might be worth considering, had Mr Pepper the means of paying it. However, having examined his accounts, I can say with confidence that he has not. His wealth, like that of most, is in his business income and not in his bank account. How many businessmen could realise twenty two percent of their assets and continue to trade? Could you Mr Henry, raise twenty two percent of the value of your farm? Of course not and nor could Mr Pepper. What could he do? Sell a class room, a half-dozen pupils?'

Henry was frustrated by, but saw no flaws in the accountant's logic. 'Are you aware, Mr Stein, of the course my cousin advises?'

'Mr Ambrose and I have discussed how your future interests might best be advanced and we are agreed on the course on which you have been advised.'

Receptive now to the counsel of the older and more experienced men in whose hands he was, he asked Stein to explain how the interests to which he referred might be advanced. Over the next hour Nathan Stein presented a lesson in financial management, the difference in the value of a pound spent, a pound saved and a pound invested in an appreciating asset on the multi-plying factors that govern compound interest. It was a lesson that an open mind, eager for knowledge was ready to fully absorb; and being received from a man who knew and could teach his subject so well, could be readily understood and remembered.

And remember Henry did. It was an hour that removed his doubts about Charles and which would influence the rest of his life, not least Stein's recommendation on the completion of his education.

When Alistair Wild, his solicitor arrived at noon he spoke to Henry alone, explaining that the principles of lawyer and client confidentiality applied to their meeting and Charles Ambrose would be excluded. The legal business was quickly concluded. Charles would assume the role of guardian, his representative until he reached the age of twenty-one. Documents were completed to arrange the sale of Black Dyke Hole for seventy five percent of its value, other documents for the opening of accounts at the Bradford Bank into which quarterly payments would be received from Westhead Mills and Pepper's school and finally authority for regular transfers from the account to pay his fees and accommodation costs at the Clarendon Commercial Academy in Bradford.

Chapter 4

The Academy off Eldon Place was a short walk from the town centre but sufficiently elevated to be spared the worst of the smoke that hung in the bowl and the stench from the canal. Not long established, the building on four storeys provided classrooms, a reading room, a lecture hall and a library on the ground and first floors. The upper floors housed the residents' rooms, which were adequately equipped. Henry had a wardrobe, tallboy, a desk, a chair, an armchair and a bed.

Joining in April he was more than part way through the annual programme and he had notes to study and projects to complete before he could join the programme on which his year was engaged. The majority of his contemporaries were the sons of managers of mills, mines and quarries. Some were sons of senior foremen; owners' sons were either still in senior education or at University. Those owners sons who did not have the intellect for university would not have had the mental rigour for the Academy. Since many of those in his year lived not too far a distance it was usual for the Academy to be quiet from Friday afternoon until late Sunday evening. At first Henry spent his weekends at Thornton Old Hall but as he became to appreciate, that he would need to spend long hours in study if he was to reach the level of those in his group, he tended to weekend at the Academy more often than not.

The two-week recess in July known in the college as the summer breather to distinguish it from the Christmas breather, was spent at Thornton but Henry, even then was not idle. He was a young man with an urgent desire for progress and Charles agreed that Nathan Stein could spend some hours with him during that breather to answer some of his many questions and to give him some guidance on how he ought to approach the coming term and how to pace himself. The curriculum consisted of a rolling programme of modules, each of increasing difficulty, and which included accounting, company law, taxation, directors liabilities, stock holding, share trading, banking practices and a host of sub-group under each subject. Henry had a system, which involved exercise books for each major topic and cross-referencing from one to the other.

The Ambrose accountant expected some detailed sessions explaining the rules concerning ledger entries and then amortisation of debts and assets. He was gladdened to find how well Henry had applied himself to his studies and was not expecting Stein to teach and re-teach what could, with diligence, be found in text books. Instead Henry's interest lay in a more strategic approach and the philosophy and morality of business.

This engaged Nathan Stein to such an extent that he enjoyed and looked forward to his sessions with his student, so much so that he devoted more hours and more days to him than Charles had anticipated. Ambrose accepted that the breather would soon be over, however, and he was pleased with Henry's progress.

The shares Henry owned in Westhead Mill's, Black Dyke Hole and the Illingworth school skewed his interest towards the advantages and disadvantages of employing others as opposed to earning an income from shares in enterprises that employed others. He wrestled with issues such as rewarding employee loyalty, in the way that he had benefitted from the service his mother had given to the family in whose house he was now seated then veered to discussing the damage that could be done to an enterprise by a few Ogdens. Stein's views were balanced and explained the wider issues of who is the ultimate employer of those who are employed by the state or by the local corporation. Henry valued Nathan Stein's opinions, they broadened his own perspective and he would return to the Academy determined to master the fine detail that would put the muscle and the flesh on the bones of his vision.

As she and her husband bade Henry farewell, Marianne was uneasy. Six months ago she had met and nursed a very ill, grieving and disturbed young man. Just six months later he was focused, driven, almost obsessive and in all those months she had seen him neither laugh nor even smile.

His days spent in class rooms and the lecture hall, his evenings engaged in writing notes and committing them to memory and late evenings, into the night, deriving business scenarios and comparing the long term performance of those that involved providing employment and those that did not. September found him the equal of everyone in his year group but he continued relentlessly. Every third week he would have a weekend day with Nathan Stein who now asked him to give him written notice of the topic he wished to discuss in order that he could give thought to the issues involved and be better prepared to make good use of their time together.

Marianne confided her worry to Charles about Henry. He appeared tired, lacked any facility in conversation and skills and seemed to be ignited by talk of business and the accruing of wealth. It was agreed that on his next weekend visit Stein should not be there, Charles would take him riding and try to get him engaged in some healthy pursuit or activity. When Henry arrived on the appointed Saturday he expressed annoyance at Stein's absence, declined Charles's invitation to ride and hunt and stayed only for lunch before returning to his college.

The young men of his year were sociable and would often spend evenings out in groups. So often had he declined to join them that he was no longer invited. His sole pleasure was gained from reading, over and again, the quarterly reports he had received from Stein at the end of June and September, detailing his bank account and the sums paid into it by Westhead Mills and by Simon Pepper. He was not universally unpopular. He was most popular with those young men whose allowances didn't keep them until month end. Henry would provide loans, repayable with interest, and he was soon able to provide loans from the interest he received while causing no dent to his capital.

Stein's advice concerning the difference on a pound spent and a pound invested in a profitable venture and would have continued to do so had one of his customers, Percy Braithwaite, not found himself in such difficulties that he had no other recourse than to confess his situation to his father. His father complained to the Academy Principal, Bullivant Theakstone who wrote to Charles Ambrose. In his absence Nathan Stein received the letter.

Henry was summonsed to the office of the Principal at nine o'clock on the morning of the Thursday of the second week of December, two weeks before the Christmas breather. 'Tell me Mr Crawshaw, do you understand the term Usury?' Henry believing this to be some test of his studies replied, 'yes, Mr Theakstone, would you prefer the Oxford English Dictionary's or Flaubert's definition?' Theakstone was furious; 'I would prefer no insolence from you'. It was his Principal's reaction than the sight he caught of Nathan Stein seated to his rear that caused Henry to realise that his situation was serious.

'I intend no insolence, Sir'

'Did you not indeed. So tell me now, do you know Theakstone's definition of Usury?'

'I confess, Sir, I do not.'

'Usury, Crawshaw, is not merely the applying of extortionate rates of interest to loans, it is not even the aggravation of the practice by laying increasing rates of interest on outstanding interest, it is a practise that is injurious to the spirit of the victim, destruction of the soul of the perpetrator and is an anathema in the world of commerce. The moneylender who preys on poverty is lower than a whore. She will provide value for a man's shilling and the business is transacted. For people like you Crawshaw, like Shylock, like others of your ilk the transaction is not completed until the victim is bled dry.'

Henry was stunned and glanced briefly at Stein whose expression offered no encouragement.

Theakstone was not done. 'I abhor usury and will not brook it in my academy. There can be only one consequence and that is expulsion. The ignominy you bring on yourself is your doing alone.'

Henry's mind raced. Were all those months of study, single-minded application, and the plans he had made come to nought? He must attempt a defence.

'Mr Theakstone, Sir, kindly permit me a hearing. I came to my group a year late. The hours I had to devote to catching up meant that I was unable to socialise with colleagues, as I would have wished. Some socialise too well and, knowing I was spending little, sought loans. These were unsecured. I would have preferred not to give them and realise now I should not have done so.'

'You seek to minimise your offence, Crawshaw. Since you have applied yourself so diligently to your studies you should have little difficulty in giving me the answer to my question. What is the annual rate of interest on a sum loaned at one percent per week, per week, per week, compounded.'

Henry answered him directly, 'I can certainly answer that given a moment to make the calculation.'

Theakstone stood, beat his fist on the desk and, through heavy breath, told him, 'I do not need a moment to do the calculation, I know the answer Crawshaw. The answer is usury. Usury! Now wait outside.'

Composing himself and re-seated Theakstone turned to Stein. 'There is nothing else for it I fear. The reputation of the Academy is based on the integrity of its graduates.'

If Henry's future was to be salvaged Stein would need to call upon all the clarity of thinking he could muster and all the powers of persuasion he possessed. He began, 'Principal Theakstone, I too am a qualified accountant but with none of the eminence you have in that field. As both an accountant and a human being I detest usury and would confront it wherever I encountered it. Having made plain my position on that point I would ask you, in coming to your decision regarding Master Crawshaw, that you give weight to some failures, not offered in justification but in mitigation.'

Theakstone waited politely but showed no inclination to be receptive to as Stein continued, 'Last year he was bereaved of both parents in tragic circumstances and saw in this year in serious health occasioned by an injury. The demeanour of a young man you see today is a transformation from what he was just twelve months ago but what you will still detect in him gives an indication of his former, poorer state. He lacks conversation; he is bereft of social skills, incapable of forming friendships within his age group, conscious of his lack of height and embarrassed about by his accent. From somewhere within himself he has found the confidence to enrol in this esteemed institution and pit his intellect against his contemporaries where level of education far exceeds his own. Your staff, and you too Sir because I am confident that nothing in this college escapes your attention, will concede that his application to his studies and his progress have been faultless. I would ask therefore that you consider some punishment, for punished he must be, but some penalty that falls short of expulsion.'

It was the only mitigation Stein felt he could offer but knew he was only able to seek sympathy for the perpetrator not minimise his offence. He scrutinised Theakstone's expression, seeking signs of a softening of stance, but there were none.

'Mr Stein. You have spoken eloquently on young Crawshaw's behalf and I am not unmoved by his personal difficulties, not un-appreciating of his efforts to overcome them. However, I have two considerations that must be paramount in my decision and these are the reputation of this academy and my assurance that I would apply a most severe sanction.'

Stein had his clues. Theakstone had revealed his soft underbelly and that would be the target of his final assault.

'Mr Theakstone. On leaving may I thank you sincerely for allowing me, albeit unsuccessfully, to plead Master Crawshaw's case. I shall be certain to convey to his family the deep consideration you applied in coming to your decision. I trust it will be some consolation to his uncle (he exaggerated the family connection) Sir Isaac Ambrose

M.P. who will I know share the shame his nephew has brought on the family. I believe though that he will harbour some disappointment that your academy felt unable to give a second chance to a young man who when first away from the guidance of his family fell into foolishness. You may well know Sir Isaac as not only an employer of large numbers in this city, including some of the managers whose sons, attend here, but also as a renowned raconteur. He has regaled dinner parties with his stories of undergraduate indiscretions at the Cambridge College were he holds high office, but he prides himself that he has not yet had the need to send any down. I fear that this may not be a matter for humour around his table any longer'.

Stein noted a slight shift in Theakstone's resolve but not yet a sufficient one.

'May I ask you Mr Stein to convey to Sir Isaac my deepest regret at the decision which Master Crawshaw has forced upon me.'

A final thrust Nathan and you're there thought Stein, 'I shall certainly do that Mr Theakstone. I anticipate he may ask me, or, indeed, enquire of you, what opportunity his nephew was afforded to show penitence and make reparation; a practice employed at his Cambridge College for serious breaches.'

It was now apparent to Stein that Theakstone seeking a solution that would keep a nephew of Sir Isaac Ambrose in his college keep faith with Mr Braithwaite senior and keep face for himself.

'That was not a tradition at Oxford, Mr Stein, where sendings down were not common but not unknown. Give me an example of how it works at Cambridge, do.'

Stein had never been a guest at Sir Isaac's dinner parties but that was a detail and need not spoil a good story. 'There was an occasion, Mr Theakstone, when an undergraduate, a son of a Lord whose name you would not expect me to disclose, took a party of his colleagues to dine at one of the better hotels in the city. They arrived intoxicated and in high spirits. The young gentleman in question considered it good sport to flick food at his colleagues. When some splattered the uniform of a waitress at his table he upbraided her for what he considered to be a disapproving look. Her supervisor, a lady, attended to intervene and he thought it amusing to spray her clothing with soup spitting it at her. Encouraged by the laughter of his friends he pelted both women with bread rolls, subjected them to a foul mouthed tirade and led his party out refusing to pay the bill. He was arraigned before a disciplinary board of his masters who took the view that his insufferable behaviour had distressed two ladies, harmed the good name of the hotel and damaged the reputation of his college. His masters concluded that he was a boorish young fellow who had not a vestige of humility about him and their decision was that he should be sent down.'

'Quite right too' said Theakstone.

'Unless...'

'Unless, there could be no unless' was Theakstone's view.

'Unless he might have the penalty suspended subject to no recurrence of ill conduct, a proposal of a display of penitence and the making of appropriate reparation. These two to be agreed upon by his masters, the members of his college and the proprietors and the staff of the hotel'.

His Lordship's son made his proposal and it was accepted.

Accordingly he appeared before the whole college in sackcloth and made a long and profuse apology for his conduct for which he expressed deep shame. The college signalled its approval in the time honoured way by a stamping of feet. At that month's college dining in night, at the miscreant's expense, the two ladies of the hotel dining staff were conveyed by carriage to the college where they were honoured guests at the top table. There they were served by the penitent, wearing a waiter's uniform. He was attentive and deferential to his victims all night, presented them with bouquets and acted as outsider on the carriage that returned them to their lodgings at the hotel.'

Theakstone pondered this and asked Stein, 'And you believe that Master Crawshaw should be permitted to propose penitence and reparation before his penalty is confirmed?'

'Mr Theakstone, I would not presume to suggest how you might conduct your disciplinary proceedings. I only offer it as practice that Sir Isaac finds useful in providing young men with lessons in life that they will not gain from their formal studies.'

'I see some merit Mr Stein, in the practice that Sir Isaac employs and I would wish to hear Crawshaw's proposals for a display of penitence and an act of reparation.'

Stein had him, he hoped. 'May I suggest Mr Theakstone that you exclude Master Crawshaw for one day, on the understanding that he will return and make a proposal to you that you consider appropriate for him to make to his course year'

That was agreed and Stein was relieved but no more than Theakstone who had found himself on a hook on learning of Sir Isaac's interest in the matter and now saw a compromise that might release him.

Henry waiting dutifully in the corridor outside the Principal's office and was resigned to his expulsion when

Stein eventually appeared. 'Henry, pack a bag for one night. You may yet be returning tomorrow for your other belongings.' As Henry climbed the stairs Stein called after him, 'And bring your tally-book.'

Henry returned to find Stein waiting in a carriage. He didn't question it when the driver took the road to the Heights rather than the Thornton Road. He was too shamed. Once beyond the town Stein asked him, 'How many of your fellow students owe money to you?' 'Eight' 'And what is the total sum still owed to you?' Henry consulted his tally book, made a quick calculation and told Stein. 'One pound, twelve shillings and four pence halfpenny' 'and the largest sum owed and by whom?' Again a glance at his record, 'Percy Braithwaite, twelve shillings and eight pence.'

They travelled in a difficult silence for a while until Stein, a little angrily, said, 'the total sum owed to you amounts to less than your earnings from Westhead in the past four weeks. The sum owed by Braithwaite exceeds the sum his father has earned in that time. He has mortgaged his future allowances for months to come. He is a fool and you have taken advantage of a fool. Your father did not take advantage of fools. He suffered them taking advantage of him because he felt that served your interests and they were more important to him than his own.'

Henry's self esteem, never better than low, was now destroyed, but Nathan Stein could not relent if he was to save this young man's future.

The carriage halted at the Plough and Pair and the two went in. Stein ordered two mugs of ale, not a drink that Henry was accustomed to and Henry stared at the bar. Some heads turned, one voice to the side of Henry said, 'your family are missed up here Henry. Your father was a fine man' He turned and thanked the voice. Another then, 'Westhead's man'll never match your dad, but I have to say the flocks looking good.' One more, 'Aye, I'll not begrudge him that.'

This done Nathan Stein told Henry, 'look around, take in what you see. Some honest hard-working men and some idle. All will leave here with a shilling spent and not a penny earned. Look hard and think whether this is what you want. Drink up.'

They took the carriage to the entrance of Black Dyke Hole where they got out and leant on the gate. Henry had only been back once since his mother's funeral and that was a brief visit when Charles evicted the Ogdens.

'Your share in this farm does not entitle you to managing it but it would permit you employment. Would you wish to be back here?'

He had pushed Henry too far and he turned on Stein, 'Yes I would. I surely would. But not like it is now. Not as a hand, I want to have my father and my mother back. I want things as before. I'll tell you what I want Mr Stein, I want what I cannot have. What I can never again have.' And the tears began to flow.

Stein hugged Henry who was now inconsolable. His sobbing wracked him with pain. The stinging in his buttocks had returned, his legs were too weak to hold him and he would have slumped to the ground had Stein's embrace not still been supporting him. Henry, back in the carriage on his way to Old Hall sank into a despair from which he could never recover. The man alongside him, a man who he had respected and on whom he had relied had become his tormentor.

On the road to Thornton, Stein lectured Henry. If he was to keep at the Academy he would have to return tomorrow, propose to Mr Theakstone how he would express his regret to his class year and how he intended to make appropriate and proportionate reparation for his conduct. Stein would collect him at eleven o'clock next morning and Henry ought to spend his evening planning how he was to satisfy the conditions explained to him. Mr and Mrs Ambrose were away from home and he would not be disturbed. Henry was not receptive. He felt the detour to the Inn and the farm had been needlessly cruel, Bullivant Theakstone had been bullying and insulting and if some of his fellow students chose to incur debts to fund drinking and female company then the fault lied with them, not with him.

Stepping down from the carriage, Henry was defiant. 'It was you Mr Stein who explained the difference between value of a pound spent and a pound invested.' Stein was unabashed. 'I assumed that Common sense would inform you of the pleasure to be had from a pound well spent and a pound donated to a needy person or cause. I hope you are able to devise means to continue your studies. You have much to learn. Goodnight, Sir.' As the carriage was driven off Henry called after it, 'I've not seen much evidence of pounds donated to needy causes.'

Henry climbed the stairs and crossed the terrace to the main entrance to Old Hall. Unusually, the east wing where he, Charles and Marianne live, slept, and ate was in darkness. The west wing unopened in his year there was ablaze with light but Henry was too tired, emotional, frustrated and angry to be curious. A visit to Mrs Leek in the kitchens procured some cold beef sandwiches and a bottle of wine, which he took to his room. Would he grovel tomorrow for the entertainment of Theakstone and the young men of his year, not one whom he regarded as a friend? No he would not. He had been bullied enough and would grovel no more. As he drank, too much and too quickly, he considered Joe Ogden, Julian Dexter, Bullivant Theakstone and Nathan Stein. Nothing to choose between them. No doubt when Charles heard of his expulsion he would be expected to abase himself in front of him too. Well damn them all. He had had enough.

The men and women of the Heights he thought were for the most part honest toilers like his father and mother. Their banter and their insults were good humoured and even their arguments and disagreements were soon forgotten. When a neighbour needed help they were there in numbers. Those were not false friends like Nathan Stein. Why hadn't Stein defended him against Theakstone's insults? Why was his only advice that he, Henry, should crawl on his belly and beg forgiveness? Yes, he would be home back on the Heights and Theakstone could go to hell.

There was a tap on his door and he opened it to Mrs Leek who suggested that he might like to see the way the west wing was being prepared for the Christmas festivities. Henry had no interest in doing so but felt it would be impolite to refuse. Hilda Leek had been in service at Old Hall from the age of eleven. She had been a friend and work-mate of his mother and each year at the garden party the two would meet and spend most of the afternoon in each other's company. He had gathered from overheard conversations between his parents that she had married a groom at the Old Hall but, within a year, he had run off with a launderess from Allerton. Old Hall had been her life.

She showed him the great hall, the dining hall and the guest rooms. Staff, most hired for the purpose, were cleaning, polishing, airing rooms and hanging festoons. Mrs Leek could not have been prouder of the rooms she guided round had they been her own. 'Sir Isaac kept

Christmas well and Mr Charles does it no less, Master Henry,' she told him, 'You'll never see more jolliness,' No thought Henry, and I'll not be here to see this, no more than last Christmas when I got no further than the kitchen doorstep of Alice Miles's house.

For all her pride in conducting the tour, Hilda Leek, had employed it as a ruse. It was obvious to her that the young man who had arrived that night, Meg's lad, was weighed down by unhappiness and she needed some reason to speak with him. Meg would have done as much for her. The circuit of the west wing ended in the kitchen, the stores of which were already hung with game and carcases, ready to be skinned, boned and prepared for the spit.

With mugs of malted milk they sat and Hilda told him that she had attended his mother's funeral but had been unable to speak to him because of his illness, as she put it. She had been delighted that Mr Charles had taken him in and she had asked if she might nurse him. 'But Mrs Marianne had insisted on bearing the workload herself. Mrs Marianne thought that so many nights without sleep would be too much for a woman of my years, you see. How she managed it without making herself ill, I'll never know.' A pound donated to a needy cause thought Henry and he flinched.

'And look at you now Henry Crawshaw. A real gentleman. A student of business no less. Oh how I wish your parents could see you. They wanted you to have the education they had not had and would have seen themselves poor if they'd had to. Meg was not much of a reader and a writer and she told me that by the time you were eleven you had passed your father and could almost match him in adding up sums.'

'Could I ask you, Mrs Leek, if my mother spoke to you of their plan for the farm, for me to work with him, rear larger flocks?'

'Dear me no. The chill winds on the tops had given your father the aches in the knees. He knew they'd not improve and provided they did not give out sooner they wanted to see you educated, in well-paid employment. Then they would sell up and buy a cottage in Clayton. They worked on the Heights for a purpose and once that was done they wanted to be off from there, them and you all. No cottage in Clayton now but seeing what you are growing into, well, I know they'd trade the cottage for that.'

Henry's half hour with Mrs Leek had left him in confusion. If his parents were looking down upon him his return to the Heights would destroy their hopes for him. But what if Hilda had been put up to this by Nathan Stein to fill him with guilt. How could that be? There had been no opportunity. He had been in his bed, still distressed, not sleeping but watching figures in his mind and listening to voices; his parents, Bullivant Theakstone, Nathan Stein, even Percy Braithwaite. The ache in his father's knees could have been no more painful than the ache in his head, not occasioned by chill winds but by his being manipulated by others. He would be manipulated no longer.

Nathan Stein arrived at the Old Hall shortly after ten o'clock to find Henry had gone. Away early and without breakfast according to Mrs Leek. Stein arrived at the academy at eleven o'clock and went straight to the Principal's office. 'Mr Theakstone, Master Crawshaw is not with me...'

Theakstone interrupted, 'No Mr Stein, he is at his class, his exclusion lifted temporary until his penitence and his proposal for reparation are accepted by his fellows and brought to fruition.'

Stein concealed his surprise, and his pleasure. 'And his proposals are acceptable to you? I ask, not knowing what they are, because they are his alone. Anything other would be apparent to you as contrived.'

Theakstone nodded 'they are somewhat unconventional but, knowing him as I do I am in no doubt that they are his own. Should they meet with approval of his year and should I have no objection from Braithwaite's father, then, upon their reaction I should be prepared to re-consider Crawshaw's expulsion. Indeed, if this disciplinary procedure should prove a success I too might one day have a store of tales with which to regale at dinner parties.'

Theakstone appeared pleased and Stein was relieved that he might yet avoid disappointing Charles Ambrose and darkening his mood in advance of his grand plans to celebrate Christmas.

That afternoon, it was Friday and the students, mostly, would be dispersing for the weekend at three o'clock. Henry's year, a class numbering thirty two, were assembled in the lecture room. The Principal and the year head, Egbert Jennings stood at the rear. At the lectern was Henry. Addressing an audience amounted to torture. Any utterance he made always betrayed his hill farm origins. He had broadened his vocabulary but had made no progress with softening his vowels. Standing nervously before this gathering, all silent, none appearing sympathetic, he doubted his ability to express his regret at his conduct in a way that would meet with approval. To assist him he pictured a parent at each side, and a hand on each of his shoulders and he grew in stature, if not in height.

'My fellow students, since arriving at this academy nine months ago I have rejected every offer of friendship I have had from you. Your invitations to socialise, I have rejected. Opportunities you have given me to engage in pastimes more engaging than some of our studies, I have spurned. I have as you know, been immersing myself in these studies and in doing so I have treated you as competitors rather than colleagues. Finally and to my shame when some of you have had financial worries I regarded you, not as fellows but as a business opportunity. In taking advantage of your difficulties I have behaved shamefully and I am contrite.'

Henry paused, attempting to control his breathlessness he looked for any reaction from his audience but, as a man, they were expressionless. He would plough on. 'Being contrite is insufficient. I must show that contrition' with that he produced his tally-book which was familiar to over a third of his audience. With a flourish that some thought over theatrical he tore pages from it and ripped them into small pieces. Still there was no reaction and Henry was having difficulty maintaining his composure.

'I have calculated every farthing of interest owed and every farthing of interest paid. All sums owed are cancelled. Every farthing of interest paid will be refunded in full.' This time there was a brief but quickly aborted attempt by three or four to instigate clapping.

'I was late to my classes this morning because I needed to await the opening of the bank from where I withdrew the funds to make the refunds. I withdrew further funds to refund the initial sums I had loaned since a loan to which interest is attached is not the action of a friend, a loan to which an exploitive rate of interest is attached is the act of a shylock,' he glanced at an approving Theakstone, 'so they were not loans at all, so all these will be returned and should be regarded I hope as gifts.'

This time there was spontaneous applause from a good half of those present. Now encouraged, Henry grew in confidence and said, 'I trust my penitence will be regarded as genuine in that it has been demonstrated. However, I have done nothing more than attempt to put right my own wrong. It is appropriate that I should make reparation, not just to those whom I have wronged financially but also to all of you whose offer of friendship I have so arrogantly rejected. The reparation I am anxious to offer is dependent on your acceptance. I have no right to seek it but with sincere regret and in all humility I do.'

The year awaited his proposal. The anticipation was tangible and Henry, knowing that without the approval of his peers his contrition would count for nothing and it was likely he would be expelled in ignominy. He detailed his intentions which, as he elaborated on them, caused murmurs around the lecture hall. When he finished the year stood as one and Henry received the applause and approval of his year. Theakstone beamed.

In the crush to leave for the weekend, the students milled in the hallway. As confidentially as he was able, Henry passed envelopes containing cash to eleven of them. Some shook his hand. Percy Braithwaite pressed a trembling bottom lip against Henry's cheek.

Chapter 5

Henry remained at the Academy that weekend. With a list of arrangements to make he did not have time to spend at Old Hall. The Academy operated two class years, both actually fifteen months long. Henry had joined the first year three months late and it would be his, and his first years Christmas at the Academy. Although not long established, the custom was that senior's year dispersed for the Christmas breather on the twenty second of December, depending upon the day of the week on which Christmas day fell. The first year dispersed the following day. The evening before dispersal the year attended a festive dinner for which they paid a half crown each. This provided a sizeable feast and wine, which would be enjoyed by the Principal, the year head and their wives in the dining hall and by the kitchen and domestic staff below stairs.

Arrangements for the festive dinner for Henry's year were to be rather different. Each student would invite a guest and the total cost would be borne by Henry alone. Charles Ambrose was disquieted by Henry's request that Marianne should be his guest as a token of his gratitude for the nursing she had given him. Charles was concerned about the propriety of a married lady attending a function without her husband but she was insistent that she should be permitted. When Henry arranged for a member of the family staff to accompany her, although the lady in question, Mrs Leek, would eat in the kitchen, and when he employed two outriders from Donald Dawson's detective agency to afford protection to the two ladies, Charles relented.

The guests began to arrive, some escorted by their student host, some met at the door, and what a mix they were. Some had invited a mother or father, a few a younger brother anxious to see the college they would be attending, more invited their young ladies and one brought his grandmother who was funding his studies. The cooks and kitchen staff had been given a generous budget, latitude and bonuses and they responded with a banquet that drew gossip and applause. The three fiddlers employed to play from the gallery through the meal had the diners tapping feet and even singing along. Mrs Theakstone entered fully into the spirit of the occasion while the Principal was harbouring some reservations about whether some parents might consider the event somewhat indecorous.

The meal done, the tables and chairs moved, the fiddlers now on the floor, the dancing began. Marianne, enjoying herself thoroughly danced with Henry, then with Theakstone whom she charmed then with a queue of fathers. The jigs proved particularly popular and they filled the floor. When twelve-year-old Hanson junior danced a jig with Mellor's grandmother the floor parted to watch. When the lady danced the boy to a standstill the circling dancers collapsed in laughter.

Henry was a dutiful host and danced with Mrs Prudence Theakstone and Mrs Amy Jennings, the wife of his year head. Theakstone himself was more relaxed and re-assured when he saw Percy Braithwaite's father clap Henry on the back and shake his hand, He felt vindicated when the same man raised a glass to him from across the room and, to cap his evening, he had the memory of having danced with the daughter-in-law of Sir Isaac Ambrose no less. No animosity from that distinguished quarter, he thought.

The evening finished with the cooks and staff gathering around the walls of the rooms to lead to a long lasting round of applause. A voice at the rear, Hilda Leek's Henry could have sworn, offered Hip Hip Hooray, which was quickly taken up and echoed throughout the college.

Arriving back at Old Hall at noon the following day, Christmas Eve, he was met by Charles Ambrose. He appeared stern and said, 'I have an issue with you Master Crawshaw' Not Henry, or cousin, thought Henry. This was worrying had Marianne been waylaid on the road home? 'Marianne informs me that she has not enjoyed an evening so much as last evening in a long time. This is a source of no little disappointment to me, given the grand affairs we have attended.' Charles laughed, put his arm round Henry's shoulder and led him in. Still in high spirits from the unqualified success of the dinner he had organised, his expulsion suspended subject to continued good conduct, he was even more uplifted by the sight that greeted him in the entrance hall. The festive decorations were exquisite, the atmosphere throughout the hall reeked of celebration. He wanted to share in this. His cases were packed with his books but it would be a dull two weeks indeed if he ever felt any inclination to open them. The previous Christmas Eve had been an awful and painful experience. In the year ahead of him he was determined to put thoughts about things behind him.

He washed and dressed and had high anticipation of the days ahead. A tap on his door and it was Hilda Leek again to thank him for the evening at the Academy. The music from above had been heard below where they had been feasting, drinking and dancing and she had been made fully welcome. She then told him of how the next days at Old Hall were expected to be filled. Guests would be arriving from four o'clock; there would be dinner at eight and dancing until the guests could dance no more. Some would be staying for two days, some for three and some for four. Tonight he would have no host duties to perform. A guest like any other there was nothing for him to do but join in and enjoy the occasion.

As good a host as Henry felt he had been the previous evening he had to concede that Charles and Marianne were better. Practised, tireless, attentive, they didn't fail to introduce the guest to another; they were faultless in making every person present feeling that each was an honoured and valued guest. At Henry's estimate that there were in excess of forty persons in the great hall, a figure he confirmed when they were seated in the dining hall. Introduced as Charles's cousin he felt the equal of them all.

Henry was going to enjoy the meal but he was also going to try to unravel the mysteries of dinner table conversation. Charles headed at the end of the table, Marianne the other. Along each side were twenty guests with Henry close to the centre. Through the first two courses he was attentive to the conversations about him. Third course, roast geese, legs and shoulders of lamb and a beef haunch with a centre piece of a spit roast porker was expertly carried by staff hired for the purpose. This party, more sophisticated than his of last evening, did not applaud the comments of admiration passed amongst it.

It was Henry's intention to identify the more accomplished conversationalists and to learn the secrets of the skill. What he discovered was a revelation to him. Those he most admired were, in fact saying little. Some hardly spoke. What they did was ask questions, brief and succinct prompts on the subject on which the person to whom they were speaking were interested, invariably themselves.

On the arrival of the fifth course, compote, with or without a cognac moat, according to taste, Henry decided to experiment with his discoveries concerning the art of dinner table discourse. To his left was Hubert Holmes, a ruddy balding man with a pleasing smile. Henry had gathered from his listening-in that Hubert had abattoirs, supplied meat wholesale and sold it retail in shops, on market stalls and by deliveries to doors. Unsure whether the slaughtering or butchering of beasts was a suitable for dining in polite conversation he chanced a short prompt to Hubert on the subject. Immediately Holmes was chatty, soon he was in full flow. This was his topic and each additional query from Henry spurred him on. When dinner was done Hubert Holmes considered Henry to be a most agreeable dinner companion and a fine conversationalist.

Henry had not been fully occupied by Hubert's accounts of slaughtering, hanging, jointing and boning. Seated next to Hubert was his daughter Adeline and Henry took several opportunities as presented themselves to look beyond the father to the daughter. When the sign was given for the ladies to retire to the drawing room, while the men were served brandy and cigars, Hubert held Henry captive still with tales of escaping bulls rampaging through the town and the problems of trampling and goring with which he had had to deal.

Eventually, and none too soon for Henry, the gentlemen entered the great hall where they were joined by the ladies. A pianist accompanied the assembly; first in Christmas hymns then in a rollicking sing song. This was followed by dancing. Risking another story of a headless chicken being pursued along the length of Canal Road, Henry approached

Hubert and sought permission to ask Adeline to dance. Hubert, not a man to affect graces said, 'Most polite of you to ask young man but no need. If she doesn't want to she'll tell you and if not her mother will. No doubt about it. I've, had more no's than yes's of her mother over the years.' He said it with a laugh and with obvious affection but there was more brandy than Hubert in what he said.

Adeline didn't refuse him and he gazed at this young woman, so graceful and so demure. Many young women were taller than him but not Adeline. He didn't know many too well but he knew enough who had a confidence and self regard that he found unattractive. Her golden hair, her skin fine as porcelain, her hand tiny, and soft and in his. He would have danced every dance with her had she permitted but he felt an obligation to dance with his hostess Marianne and considered it good manners to dance with Adeline's mother, Jane Holmes, a most likeable woman whose company he enjoyed greatly. Through these duty dances he hoped that Adeline might still be free to dance with him. She was and the smile she gave him when he returned won him over. Henry was taken with her.

When her parents were ready to retire to their rooms she joined them to retire to hers. Henry, as a resident of the hall, thought it polite to continue to remain with the guests until the last eventually found their beds. He hoped to be able to get to know Adeline better but reminded himself firmly that he should not make groundless assumptions as he had done with the worthless Alice Miles one year ago this very night.

Breakfast next morning was a light affair, served early for those attending the Christmas morning service. Oats and milk, tiny pastries topped with butter and morsels of fruit. Carriages were at the door. Henry accompanied

Charles. Marianne would remain to host those guests who would lie longer abed. Her absence would be accepted since the whole parish knew of the celebrations at the hall. It would, however be regarded as most irregular should the front right pew of the parish church not be occupied by an Ambrose.

Adeline and her parents had not attended church and Henry's hopes for her company that afternoon were not to be realised. Charles was to visit some widows and widowers, valued former employees who occupied cottages on the Ambrose lands. Henry was asked to accompany him and thought it impolite to decline when he could think of no reason to do so. They rode mounted and were followed by a trap carrying boxed gifts. Each contained a game pie, a roast foul, a wedge of cheese and a spiced pudding. Six calls this year for Charles, who spent time at each home enquiring as to health and making notes of problems with which he could assist. Henry was fascinated by this aspect of operating a business, thinking at first that this attention to retired staff was entirely altruistic then coming to realise that valuing long term loyalty in retired staff bred loyalty in those still in employment or service. A shilling purchases labour but small acts of appreciation purchased commitment-something money could never buy.

The two arrived back too late for the afternoon tea but joined their guests for dinner, a less formal affair than before but the cold pork and pickled vegetables followed by a selection of pastries and goblets of mulled wine was heartily enjoyed. Henry was not seated near Adeline and, at the same side of the table but some places distant, she was not even in view. He occupied himself by practising the art of conversation that consisted of saying very little but showing interest in the responses of those about him who he prompted with short enquiries. It worked again because as the ladies retired and the men stood for brandy and cigars more than one thanked him for his company over dinner.

Dancing now, he thought, but again he was to be disappointed. When all gathered in the great hall, Christmas hymns once more sung, a group sing song done, a Mr Jeremy Irwell, an outgoing character with large round eyes that were framed by bushy side-whiskers grown wild and a waxed moustache, announced the evening's entertainment that he would lead. Guests would be called upon to sing to the accompaniment of the pianist, recite a piece of poetry or narrate an amusing or entertaining tale. Henry, certain that he was incapable of doing any of those decided that he would not be putting himself forward before learning, to his horror, that it would not be a question of volunteering, all guests would participate as called upon by the irrepressible Mr Irwell.

This caused consternation among the guests and there was much chatter as to how they might satisfy requirements when their turn was called. Henry took this opportunity to give Marianne her Christmas gift. A half-day spent speaking in Bradford had left him no clearer as to what might be suitable as a gift to a married lady. It would need to be acceptable to her and not considered too personal by her husband. Eventually he made his choice and now to hand it to her. It was a small bound volume of poetry, each poem on the theme of the changing nature of the land through the seasons. Marianne expressed delight and also said she was relieved. Henry did not understand the last comment but soon would.

Before the guests, the performers indeed, took their seats Henry insured a place next to Adeline. Her warm smile thrilled him as much as the prospect of giving a performance before this audience terrified him. Pray God that he would not be called before he had thought of something-anything.

The first to be called was Hubert Holmes. Irwell considered him to be a gregarious fellow who would get the proceedings off to a good start. Hubert announced that he would sing a duet with his wife Jane and they would be accompanied on the piano by their daughter Adeline. The song was unfamiliar to Henry but it was evident that baritone Hubert and contralto Jane were well practised in its delivery. It was Henry's opinion that the song was an over-long dirge salvaged only by the playing of the delightful little figure at the piano. Others clearly disagreed since the performance was rewarded with enthusiastic applause. When Adeline returned she took her seat next to Henry. He was pleased to be with her and would be even more pleased once his own ordeal was over.

There were more songs, some recitations, a tale of adventure in Egypt and amusing anecdotes, one of which Charles told when his turn was called. It concerned a quarry-man, up before Sir Isaac when he was a magistrate in Bradford. The man claimed not to have been drunk as charged. When questioned as to what he had drunk the previous night he had said 'Sixteen Pints of Wilson's Strong Ale, Sir.' 'Sixteen pints you say?' 'Sixteen pints before I stopped counting' 'And you were not drunk?' 'I was not Sir' 'So tell me, my man, what is your capacity for Wilson's Strong Ale.' 'Cannot say, Sir. Never reached it.' Sir Isaac had laughed so well that he did not have the heart to convict or fine the man. Instead he told him that such a defence would not wash again. The cheeky chap had replied, 'Thank you Sir, I'll be sure to have a different one next time.'

Marianne was next, stood and produced a small bound volume that Henry recognised. She read from it beautifully a poem concerning appearances of wild meadow from autumn to winter. 'Damn' thought Henry. He could have done that. But what was he to do. Still undecided he was alarmed to be called forward and quite unprepared chose to tell an amusing story he had heard from Desmond in school. It concerned a young lady in a department store who mistook the drapers counter for the furniture counter. The assistant was elderly and hard of hearing. Part way through his story he remembered that the comedy in the story was in the misunderstanding of the assistant and the different meaning in the word drawers. His story would need an immediate re-crafting and it lost all sense when she enquired about a sideboard and the assistant produced some dress material. He returned to his seat to polite but muted clapping. At least it was done and with no damage other than to any reputation he might have hoped for as a raconteur.

The very next performance though was to convince him that had been right to sabotage his own story. Brendan Lowe had obviously over indulged and on unsteady legs burped and perspired through a risqué tale concerning a visiting tradesman and a busty kitchen maid. When he had finished the ladies did not clap, and the few gentlemen who did were quickly silenced by reproaching digs to the ribs by wives' elbows.

The last performance of the evening was to be given by Jeremy Irwell himself. In his directing of proceedings that evening he had a story himself of those who had not known him previously to have a personality too big for this great room to contain. Now he called for all lamps to be extinguished other than the one which he turned down to just a flickering glow. He pulled forward the piano stool, set the lamp on a low table below his chair and his face was transformed into an eerie mask. The only other light in the room was the log fire that cast dancing shadows on the drapes and on the ceiling.

His stage set, Irwell started his ghost story, displaying an extraordinary talent. His voice, soft then harsh, the pace of his tale, rapid then laboured, his ability to mimic the voices of his characters, built the atmosphere in the room and instilled fear in his audience. They were transported to the ancient mansion where the spirit child floated and passed through walls and ceilings and when Irwell asked if they could feel the child's icy fingers touching their necks, some could. When he repeated the question in the voice of the ghost child, most could. His description of the crone who he introduced to his story was frightening and when he employed her voice Henry felt a tiny hand pressed into his. Was it Adeline's or the child ghost's? He dare not look.

The revelation that the child and the crone were the same spirit whose appearance was altered by the purity of heart of those who witnessed the apparition explained the appearance of both in the crumbly mansion and the audience were relieved to learn that the spirit had been exorcised by the fearless priest. Their relief was dashed when Irwell told them in a booming voice that the spirit now roamed Thornton Old Hall and asked his audience how it would appear to them when they were visited that night.

Lamps were lit and Henry saw that Adeline, her hand in his, had swooned. Her mother assisted Adeline to her room where she would spend the night with her. The reaction of the guests to Irwell's performance was mixed. Now embolden to be in a well-lit room some felt that he was a powerful and accomplished actor.

The events of the day had prevented Henry from spending time with Adeline that he would have wished and he was to fare no better the next day. Charles had invited those who rode to Hounds to joining him with the Thornton Hunt. Henry pleaded ignorance but Charles would have none of it and was insistent. It was not only that Henry wanted time with Adeline, and that night was to be the last night of the Holmes's stay, but the ride on Christmas day had inflamed the weals on his buttocks and any riding today would be painful.

Riding was riding, but riding in pursuit of a pack over ditches and hedges was all together different and Henry was not unhappy soon to be left behind and to return to the Hall early. Had he not done so he would not have seen the Holmes family boarding their carriage to return home and his future might have been so different to what it was to be. He was later to ponder how lives are changed by events that seem to have no relevance to any perceivable pattern at the time but may, in retrospect, give rise to a belief in fate. Is there for each of us, he was to wonder, a destiny that does in fact shape our ends?

Henry said his good-byes on horseback at the carriage window and received a smile from a wan Adeline enveloped in a coachman's blanket. They had felt it best, Hubert had explained, to return early due to Adeline being unwell. Wondering how he might employ his newly acquired power of conversation to delay the party until he could consider how he might meet Adeline again all he could offer was, 'I have enjoyed your company, and that of your family, immensely, Sir.'

Hubert replied, 'and we yours equally young man. In fact, we are to have a small number at our home over the Eve of New Year; a small number but an uneven one for our table. Thinking I would not see you I would have left an invitation for you with Mrs Ambrose but didn't know how you might receive it. But anyway it would be a pleasure to us if you would join us.' Adeline nodded her encouragement and Henry said that he would be honoured. With details of directions passed, Hubert instructed his driver and Henry watched the carriage until it left the drive and was lost in the lane.

Chapter 6

Bolton Villas was a crescent of double fronted white painted houses with three storeys above ground and one below. The ground floor provided four spacious high ceilinged rooms, the first four bedrooms and the third three more. At five o'clock on that last day of the year Henry presented himself at the door of number three with a gift for his hostess, a box of candied fruits. Anxious not to arrive too early he was in fact the last of the guests and he was introduced to three couples, none of whom he knew from Christmas at Old Hall. They were of an age similar to Hubert and Jane and Henry considered that he had been invited to provide company for Adeline, which was what he wanted anyway.

Happy to be seated next to Adeline he planned to continue his dinner table conversational skills but would be unable to do so. The nine people around the table knew each other well. Henry was the novelty and the centre of attention. He didn't have to prompt any conversation as he spent the whole meal answering questions from every direction. Mostly they concerned his studies and there was a lot of interest in every subject on the curriculum. All the men were businessmen and they were genuinely curious about the theory of commerce and how it was currently being taught. It was difficult to find opportunity to put fork to mouth, so much was he asked to explain. He did feel that Adeline appeared proud of him and he also noticed that her portions of each course were small and all left unfinished.

There was no after dinner entertainment just a sitting in the drawing room where the questioning of Henry had turned to his own business intentions and his ultimate ambitions. Loathed, as he was to leave Adeline it was nonetheless a relief to him when it was time to go to his bed. There had been a short ceremony involving a sherry toast and exchanged good wishes to greet the New Year. The men had shaken hands and the ladies had given brief kisses to cheeks. Adeline's to his had been particularly welcomed.

Breakfast was a huge meal of hot rashers of steamed ham and duck eggs, served by the housekeeper, a Mrs Mollie Tutt. At dinner the previous evening Henry had not been able to take notice of her, being engaged as he was in a detailed and lengthy interview. Over breakfast though he did look at her and what an unprepossessing sight she presented. Old before her time, her hair scraped back and neglected, she was the least attractive example of her sex he had ever seen with jowls of which a bloodhound would have been proud. Her cooking though could not be faulted. His dinner, interrupted as it was, had been delicious. This breakfast, in taste, and portion could not have been bettered. Still Adeline ate very little.

There were no plans for the day. The other guests had departed before noon and Henry, un-used to the conventions that applied, thought he too should take his leave and he returned to the upper floor to pack. The view across Manningham Lane, across the valley beyond extended all the way to Bolton Woods. This was a gentleman's residence of a kind he would be proud to own. It housed a young woman of whom he was fond and whom he hoped to get to know better and she lived here, less than a mile from his college. If he was successful he might have a house such as this and a wife such as Adeline. He would, be successful. He would.

That Monday was the first day of the final three months of his first year at the Academy. The workload increased, as did the frequency and difficulties of the examinations. Henry did not neglect his fellow students who received him well after the Christmas breather and he ensured that at least one evening a week was spent with them socialising at the restaurant, hotel or public house in the town. These evenings provided him with a store of amusing stories, but still none that could have been told to the guests at old Hall.

Adeline was often in his thoughts and when his final first year examinations were completed, and when an early spring day brought warmth to late March, Henry decided that it called for bold action if he was either to get Adeline into his life and that of his heart. He was resolved to take that action and to take it that evening. Striding up to her door, appearing more confident than he felt, he was admitted by Mrs Tutt and received by Mrs Holmes. Hubert was not yet home and Adeline was at her piano lesson.

Henry cleared his throat, took a breath and began, 'Mrs Holmes I have called un-invited for which I seek your understanding.' It was a speech he had prepared for Hubert but it would have to be made to Adeline's mother. 'I came to ask permission to call upon Adeline and, if she is agreeable, to ask permission to walk out with her.'

Jane had found him likeable at Old Hall, even more likeable at her home on the New Year and was charmed by his manners. 'Please take a seat, Henry. Neither my husband nor I would have any objection to your calling upon Adeline. It is a matter we have discussed. I have no reason to believe that Adeline would have any objection to you calling upon her. This is not a matter we have discussed but relies on a mother's instinct. Shall we agree this coming Sunday at two o'clock.'

Within minutes he was back at Manningham Lane. Had he been agonising for so long, rehearsing his speech so many times, unnecessarily. No matter. Sunday it would be. Happy Sunday. The first of those happy Sundays was the day before the first day of the final fifteen month of the Academy year. The curriculum would be more wide ranging, more searching of the Students' ability and the final examinations would be more testing than any they had ever experienced. But the first Sunday was to be followed by Sunday after Sunday. Each Tuesday evening found Henry with his fellows out for their entertainment. For some this meant seeking female company but not Henry. One Saturday in three would be spent at Old Hall but the rest of Henry's time was devoted to his lectures and his books.

On Sunday afternoons, from the first, Henry and Adeline were left together in the parlour, where they would talk, become familiar with each other's opinions, likes and dislikes and where they would develop a closeness that both found precious. This became Henry's pattern, when invited to attend the Ambrose garden party in June he would have dearly desired to invite Adeline but felt that her parents might have regarded an invitation away from home for Adeline that excluded them as improper.

By July, with Adeline's agreement, he spoke to her parents and asked if they might consent to him walking out with their daughter. Jane appeared doubtful and turned to Hubert who said, 'You'll know Henry, that Adeline is frail' his wife corrected him, 'delicate Hubert.' And he continued, 'delicate and I'm happy for you to walk out but not strive out, she is not to be exerted and on that understanding, and you're on trust mind you, I'll agree once. Now see you don't bring her back over-tired.' Henry promised and that next Sunday the two young people visited the nearby public park.

The southern boundary of the park, a good quarter mile or more in length, consisted of a straight, flat avenue benefited by benches below the trees from end to end. Sunday afternoons would see the avenue filled with an assortment of people. Nursemaids pushing perambulators meeting other nursemaids and exchanging gossip of nursemaid land. Young people would walk in small groups – groups of young men hoping to make acquaintanceships with groups of young women. Young couples would walk together, often supervised by a mother or maiden aunt occupying a bench. The larger numbers were whole families dressed in their finest Sunday wear promenading to and fro and engaging in the favourite pastime of the managerial classes – seeing and being seen.

Henry was proud to be seen with Adeline. Conscious of her father's instructions he matched his stride to her short, slow steps. Adeline, noting the behaviour of other young couples, was emboldened to link her arm to her young man's and, walking in this manner they covered the full length of the avenue, there and back again. They were agreed that neither would rather be anywhere else with any other person and in that contentment they passed the afternoon, oblivious to any other world than the exclusive one that they inhabited.

Each Sunday of that July, each blessed by dry warm weather, was spent in the same way but on this last Sunday of the month Adeline asked if she could take a seat. Concerned that she might be feeling over-exerted they did at once but Adeline's purpose in sitting was to inform

Henry that she was to travel with her mother to stay for some weeks with her Aunt Doreen in Dorset. They had done this for the past two years since her mother's sister had been widowed and Adeline's mother considered that the company benefitted her sister and the Dorset air was more salubrious for her daughter than the fog of Bradford. Taking both of his hands in hers she said, 'I would that we should not have to be parted and I shall miss you desperately.' Adeline wept and caught the tears in her lace edged handkerchief. Henry, deeply saddened but not wishing to add to her distress, spoke of the affection he had for her, told her that they should exchange letters no less frequently than weekly and that he would count the days until her return.

Adeline pressed her hands into his and whispered, 'Do not think me forward Henry but my feelings for you are feelings of love and they will make our separation a torture for me.' Henry inclined his head to peer below her bonnet, to see her beautiful soft features and tear filled blue eyes. He assured her, 'my feelings for you, dear Adeline are no less and I shall think of you every hour of every day and never think of another.'

Throughout a lonely August the lovelorn young man was in a state of agitation, pacing, unable to concentrate, he neglected his studies. The only peace he could find was in penning the long and detailed letters he sent to his sweetheart and his only happiness was in repeatedly those he received from her. He excused himself from the students Tuesday social evenings believing that laughter, indeed any form of enjoyment would amount to disloyalty to Adeline-unfaithfulness even. Henry needed a jolt to introduce some balance into his life and it came in the form of an admonishment from his year head. Some of his work had been admitted late and was not of a standard to achieve his qualification. Some assignments had not been completed. Should there not be a dramatic and immediate improvement in his performance, then the suspended expulsion might be activated.

Henry's response was decisive. What kind of a husband would he be to Adeline as a failed student whose only prospect was a share that entitled him to employment as a hand to a sheep farmer on the Heights. He must succeed for Adeline and he would now dedicate every study session, every lecture note and every assignment to his love for his future wife and he would tell her that in his next letter during the time he would set aside to letter writing-each Sunday afternoon.

October came and Adeline's letters still made no mention of a date on which she and her mother intended to return. He had made good use of September, all sub standard work re-done, all outstanding assignments completed and each to an impressive standard. Further assignments would be sat and were to be submitted one a week until Christmas. Also the final year students, assembled in the lecture hall, were informed of their final assignment. Each student was to find for himself an attachment to a commercial enterprise where he would attend on the Tuesday and the Wednesday of each week in January and February. The first two weeks of March would be reserved for the preparation of a report that would compare the theory of their studies to the practicalities of the application of those theories in day to day business. The final two weeks in March would be spent sitting final examinations.

Students were advised to make an early start on finding suitable attachments. Henry thought immediately of Hubert Holmes and his range of business interests

– slaughtering, butchering and the selling of meats both wholesale and retail. He wrote to Hubert and received a prompt reply inviting him to visit the Sticker Lane abattoir that coming Monday.

Hubert received him warmly but Henry thought his future father-in-law appeared comical in white gum boots, a full length white cotton frock and a white collar cap all liberally sprayed with blood. The first experience of the Holmes's business was a tour of the abattoir, with Henry similarly dressed to Hubert. Henry had seen his father slaughter the occasional sheep, lamb and chicken but these had been killed singly and in the open air. He was not prepared for the sights and sounds or scale of killings he was witnessing. The cries of the beasts or animals, bellowing and bleating, the fear in them as if aware of their fate, and the violence with which the slaughter men dispatched the animals was repulsive to the once farmer's son but now an aspiring young gentleman. The smell of the blood and gore that ran in rivers over his gumboots was nauseating and the coarse language and cruel humours of the slaughter men was offensive to him. This was not a business which he could ever have any interest and, before January, he would have to find a way of telling Hubert.

Henry was well ahead of his assignment programme when Adeline returned in November. The weather being unsuitable for walking, they met each Sunday afternoon in the parlour of her parents' home. With no news to catch up on, it all having been told in the letters, the conversations were mainly about their feelings for each other. Adeline told him of her desolation at being so long away from him and Henry answered that he could not face the prospect of such a long separation next year. He proposed marriage which would take place in the Spring when he had graduated and he sought her permission to seek the consent of her parents. Adeline had no hesitation. She was delighted and excited.

Applying all the knowledge he had gained at the academy he set about calculating the expense of setting up a marital home and making assumptions about income and expenditure in the early years of marriage. He rehearsed an objection Hubert might raise and how he might counter them. There was one aim and that was that he or Adeline should not suffer a lengthy separation again that coming year. This meant marriage even though it would have been better to wait until he had an established position and income.

It was two weeks before Christmas and Henry was prepared. Leaving Adeline in the parlour he joined Hubert and Jane in the drawing room. He hoped that all his preparation would not be required and that he would have consent as quickly as he had consent to call upon their daughter. It would be an ideal time since he could picture himself making an announcement with Adeline at his side at Charles's Christmas table. He was prepared for Hubert's refusal on the grounds of Adeline's age but he had what he considered to be persuasive arguments. What he was not prepared for was the response he received. His request had been respectful, polite and well presented and he watched as the parents exchanged pained looks.

Hubert spoke, 'If Adeline were to marry I could wish for no better son-in-law than you. More than that, I would be proud if you were my own son. However, there are matters on which I need to take advice and I can say no more than that today. If you'll return tomorrow at seven I'll have my answer.' After a hurried few words to Adeline, Henry left.

Next evening he was back to find Adeline's parents with a visitor, a Doctor Schroeder. At Hubert's invitation the doctor addressed Henry. 'Miss Holmes was born with a defect of the heart, a serious condition that usually results in death in infancy, if not in childhood. Very few people survive beyond that age and almost none to the age Miss Holmes has attained. I have been asked to advise on the question of her marriage.'

Silent for a moment, the doctor fixed Henry with a stare and continued. 'It is my opinion that the exertions of the marital bed would prove too much for her. If not, I am convinced that child birth would prove the end of her. She will not in any event live long into adulthood but however near or distant her loss of it will, no doubt, be hastened by a marriage. I must be elsewhere now but please allow me to offer some advice to you. Find a strong young woman who will bear your children and who will be a comfort and support to you through life.'

With that the doctor was gone and Henry was distraught. Hubert and Jane's attempt to comfort him had no effect. He wanted to see Adeline but she was not there.

Hubert spoke. 'Henry, you now know more of Adeline's condition than she herself has ever been aware. She suffers the symptoms without knowing the serious nature of their cause and it is vital that she should not know how little life she has left to her. You will understand that I cannot consent to your marriage and so that Adeline will not be alerted to the critical nature of her condition, since the alarm would be detrimental to her, I have to request, reluctant as I am, that all contact between you now cease.'

'What of Adeline' asked Henry, 'what is she to be told?'

'I shall say nothing against you and will explain my objection on the grounds of your respected ages, the short period of your acquaintanceship, the fact that you are as yet unqualified and have yet to demonstrate your ability to obtain and hold a position that would support a home and a wife. I shall tell her that you have my permission to return when you are established.'

Henry, angry and disappointed, asked Hubert, 'And when I do return, qualified and well established, that I surely will however long it takes, what then? Is it your hope that I fail and, that by the time I succeed, Adeline will be dead.'

Hubert, wounded by this last comment, demanded that Henry leave, forbade him to return or to attempt any contact with Adeline.

In the days that followed only once did Henry consider the doctors advice to find another wife. Did he really want a childless marriage to a woman who would be an invalid and would leave him a widower while still a young man? Immediately ashamed of his thoughts he determined to qualify, to establish himself, to prove Hubert wrong to having met all the conditions that Hubert had laid down to Adeline, to return and claim the hand of the young woman he loved. He would not hasten her death. Children were less important to him than her health and he was in no doubt that he would rather have a platonic marriage with Adeline than a physical relationship with any other woman in the world.

The Holmes family had, with regret, they said, declined Ambrose Christmas invitation, citing Adeline's ill health and between the formal celebrations at Old Hall Henry spent long hours at his books. As the last guests were leaving on the fourth day, Henry saw Nathan Stein arriving and greeted him. It had been a year since they had last met and had not parted on good terms.

'Mr Stein, I wish to offer a belated but still sincere apology. Your intercession with Mr Theakstone, about which I did not learn for sometime afterwards, saved my position at the Academy.'

Stein accepted the apology graciously and enquired of Henry how his studies were progressing. Henry explained that he would have to find a two day a week attachment for two months to complete his final assignment and he would have his final examinations at the end of March. Stein proposed that, with Mr Ambrose's agreement, the attachment could be to the Ambrose industries estate. Explaining that the purpose of the attachment was to compare theory and practice and to propose how the business to which the student had been attached might be improved, Henry declined. His reason was that he did not feel that a business managed by Nathan Stein would provide any material for proposing improvements.

Stein chuckled in appreciation and asked Henry if there was any other assistance he could offer. Seizing the opportunity Henry said, 'Mr Stein' 'Nathan please,' 'Nathan. One module with which I am having difficulty, and it is one in which I have more than a little interest, concerns the appraisal and valuation of enterprises and acquisitions. It is a subject that others of my year are having difficulty with too. The theory, I understand, the practice, however, remains, to me, a black art. It is two years ago now that you valued Mr Pepper's school and Black Dyke Hole. Your appraisal of both businesses and your advice on the transactions I entered into continue to earn me more than the theory of my studies suggest they should. What I am asking, Nathan, is how it is done in practice.'

Over that Christmas period Stein spent three full days with Henry. Charles was happy for Henry to have this assistance so close to his final examinations and Henry was a grateful and attentive disciple to the wizard Stein. He jotted as quickly as he could, posing questions, clarifying points and testing at every juncture. For his part, Stein had to call upon theory learned twenty years before, practice gained in the interim and experience. The ingredient he couldn't teach but could only encourage was the cultivation of instinct and the courage to apply it. By the time they had finished their three long and exhausting days, Nathan Stein was impressed by the enthusiasm of his pupil. He could not know why Henry had such an enthusiasm for such a difficult and obscure aspect of a business course. Only Henry knew that this was to be his route to establishing himself and returning to satisfy Hubert's every objection to his marrying Adeline.

Chapter 7

Returning to Bradford three days early, Henry set about finding an attachment that would accept him to start the following Tuesday. For different reasons the Holmes meat business and the Ambrose industries were not options. His favoured attachment would be one that helped him to prepare for the business he wanted to conduct, valuing and acquiring business interests for clients and for himself. At first disappointed, but, on reflection encouraged, to find no business specialising in that work he turned his attention to accounting firms. Businesses in the town were being formed and growing at an unprecedented rate and a number of companies were providing accountancy services. By the afternoon of the second day of his walk around the offices of the dirty smoke choked town, Henry felt he must have called on them all. None was prepared to offer an attachment. Some cited client confidentiality others, stated that they were not prepared to have their business practices dissected at the Clarendon Commercial Academy.

A different approach was called for, but where. Extending his search beyond the business area of the town to its fringes he came across Turners Yard and the modest office of Scowan Perkins, Accountants. His confidence undiminished by two days of rejection, and with his new tack mentally rehearsed Henry entered.

'Mr Perkins, Sir, I am Henry Crawshaw. In the hope of one day achieving the position of a qualified accountant I am presently undertaking studies which might provide a foundation to such a qualification course. My studies, at present are part time and I am available for two days unpaid experience per week for two months. I have a facility for calculation, bookkeeping and work to a high degree of accuracy. If I could assist you, unpaid, in undertaking some laborious calculations on your behalf I would gain the experience to know whether I have the talent for this work.'

Scowan Perkins was a young man, barely ten years older than Henry and, although only recently in business, was attracting more work than he could manage. His premises were modest and he employed one clerk whose job was to book the work in and out so, with low overheads and seeking to attract clients, he was charging lower fees. 'So Mr Henry Crawshaw, let us see whether you do or do not have a talent for this work. Please sit beside me.'

He had a ledger before him and placed another in front of Henry. 'We have here two columns of figures. Mine longer than yours. You can calculate the sum of your page, I'll calculate mine. Let us see who is the quicker and let us see whether you have the high degree of accuracy you claim.'

Henry accepted the challenge and Perkins said, 'let us start.' Within what seemed like seconds he spoke again. 'I'm done. How about you Mr Crawshaw.' Henry had completed the columns of part pennies and pennies but was only part way down the column of shillings and had not arrived at the column of pounds. Perkins smiled and said, 'continue and give me your total.' That done, the accountant said he would check Henry's calculation. Henry, disbelieving that Perkins could have reached his own total so quickly, asked if he could check the accountants total.

Both columns had been totalled accurately to the farthing. Henry amazed and impressed, asked Perkins how a ledger page could be calculated so quickly. Perkins explained that he did not add the figures one column at a time but added each row of four figures to the next. Henry was prepared to admit defeat but Scowan Perkins had been equally impressed with Henry's accuracy and pointed to piles of accounts filling the floor around the feet of the clerk at his desk.

'Let us be clear on this Mr Crawshaw. You are offering me two days a week unpaid work to provide totals for me, from the heaps of documents you see there?'

'I am Mr Perkins. Tuesdays and Wednesdays. Starting next week' It was agreed.

Arriving early and remaining late, Henry, determined to succeed, inspired by the ambitions to marry Adeline, worked tirelessly for Scowan Perkins and by the last day of his attachment, the last Wednesday in February, he remained later than usual. He had a question for Scowan Perkins that he had been anxious to ask since his first days of examining the accounts he had been calculating.

'Mr Perkins, some of the accounts here I have worked on are the accounts of similar business- haberdashery, bakers, and the like. Their income and expenditures varies wildly. Some of this is explicable by the scale of their operation but one aspect makes no sense to me. The profit element of their enterprise bares no comparison, one similar business to the other. That is the profit element as a percentage of their turnover. Do you see a business opportunity in advising your clients on how they might reduce expenditure, increase income and maximise profits, with advice on investment to achieve that where required.'

Perkins replied, 'Henry, the floor that was once littered with mountains of accounts is now clear but it will fill again.

Even had I had the time, energy and the ability to do what you suggest, how do you feel such advice would be received. The operators of modest business concerns come to me to have their accounts put in to an order that will satisfy taxation purposes. To offer unsolicited advice on how the proprietors might better conduct their business affairs would be no better received than if he were to suggest how they might treat their wives and raise there children. Not only do I see no opportunity in it, I see the ruination of the ambitions for this business.'

Henry thanked him for the opportunity he had been given. Scowen Perkins complimented him on the standard of his work then added, 'Please don't be too unkind about my business when writing up your assignment for the academy' Henry was abashed, 'You know?'

'Henry, I knew when you first walked through my door. I had been informed the previous evening that a student was seeking an attachment and he would act as a spy on the business practices of any firm fool enough to take him on.' 'Yet you did.'

'Without similar kindness and assistance I could not have qualified. When you form your own business you might look back on the road you travelled and not put obstructions in the path of those who would follow. In saying good-bye and in offering my good wishes, I would wish you to know that I have enjoyed your company and, should you consider a position here you would be welcome.'

Henry's assignment concluded, written up and submitted by the end of the second week of March. He had invested his report with every detail of his theory and practical experience and was well satisfied that it met every requirement. Two weeks of examinations and he ought to graduate.

The Sunday before, a full day of papers on business law was spent in his room, checking and revising every aspect he could anticipate being tested upon. In the early evening he was interrupted by a call at his door to inform him that he had a visitor. In the entrance hall was a messenger with a note asking that he attended at once at the home of Hubert Holmes. Books abandoned, he was there at once.

Met at the door by Hubert, a finger to his lips to signal silence, he was led to the drawing room where Jane sat in obvious distress. It was Hubert who spoke in a lowered tone. 'We fear Adeline is failing and I may be the cause. She has been the centre of my life for nineteen years and Jane will not object to my saying it. She has known it and understands it, I have protected her, provided all the care I could and I now fear that I have damaged the one I hold so dear. The fault is Henry, my objection to your marriage until conditions were met were not accepted by her. She has pined and the pining has damaged her. She is now so weak and wishes nothing better than to see you, do you wish to see her?' 'I wish nothing other'.

'Then I must caution you against the sight that she is reduced to. She is bedridden in the parlour. The stairs have been beyond her ability for two months now.'

Henry went in alone and was shocked. The girl he loved was shrunken. Her face once translucent was now drawn and transparent, the skull showed through. Her once beautiful blue eyes were dark circles and her lips, dry, cracked and black and were drawn back revealing discoloured gums and teeth. Aware of his presence she attempted to speak but he could not hear her and leaned forward to listen. Her breath was rank. This was not the Adeline he had last seen three months before but she was still the girl he loved and for whom he would do anything.

Henry, returned to the drawing room, sickened.

'Doctor Schroeder tells us to expect the end soon,' said Hubert, and our heartache will be increased by her final days being spent in unhappiness caused by us. I have no right to ask this, Henry, but I must. I wish to tell her that I no longer have any objection to your marriage and this would involve you making visits to her perhaps a couple of times a week. It will not come to marriage of course, indeed it could not, but it would deal with the lack of will she has to live and give her hope and happiness in her final days.'

Henry, still reeling from Adeline's appearance and enraged at Hubert's plan to deceive his daughter through her final days could only offer. 'I cannot agree to that.'

Hubert's, insensitivity continued. 'I appreciate that these visits would prove an inconvenience to you but do not anticipate them going on for a long time and you would be rewarded for your time.'

Henry bristled. He struggled to contain his rage, paced the room until he had done so and replied, 'If you loved your daughter as I do you could not want such days as remain to her to be spent in deception and manipulation. And if you had half the respect for me you previously professed you wouldn't insult me by offering payment to join you in your deceit. I shall leave now and want to hear from you that you have told Adeline that you have no objection to our marriage. I would also wish to hear from you that you mean that then I shall return, spend all the hours I am able with her and if she cannot recover I would wish to marry her on her death bed. Good night, Sir.'

As he left Jane followed him. She did not speak but kissed his cheek.

Henry was back at his desk by eight o'clock, needing to revise his notes, worried about what the examination paper might contain and, with his mind in turmoil, unable to take any of it in. Within the hour there was another message at the academy bringing a note. 'It is agreed. A visit as often as you wish. Remain for as long as you wish.' He returned at once, sat beside Adeline's bed and held her hand, dry, bony and cold, until the early hours.

The first of his two weeks of examinations were spent in this way. Long evenings spent with Adeline followed a revising of his studies and, after little sleep, a full day of examination papers.

By the second week his lack of sleep was telling on him. Exhausted, yet buoyant by the improvement that was visible in Adeline, now eating, now able to speak coherently and, once more smiling, he was determined to complete his examinations and continue his vigil. Some evenings he would fall asleep in the chair beside Adeline's bed. This did not help his revising but made him more alert for his next day's papers.

Thursday evening of the second week brought a relapse in Adeline's condition. It was Doctor Schroeder's opinion that the long hours spent with Henry were taxing for her but she demanded he be allowed to stay. Feeling it may be her last night, Henry remained beside her until morning and rushed to the Academy hoping to arrive in time to sit the most difficult paper – the appraisal and evaluation of enterprises and acquisitions. Arriving at his desk as the papers were distributed he had difficulty focusing on them. Deprived of sleep for so long he began to hallucinate but then he had an experience that he would never forget. In the dreams that came were the pages of his books, as clear as if they were before him and the face and voice of Nathan Stein, explaining patiently and in detail the answer to every question in his paper. The hand guiding his pen hand was huge and rough – the hand of a huge sheep farmer.

As the students filed out of the classroom at four o'clock they saw Henry slumped over his desk. Roused, he was assisted to his room where he lay on his bed and was soon asleep again. He had meant to return to Adeline as soon as his examination was finalised and he rushed there when he awoke at ten o'clock. At the gate of the Holmes's house he met Doctor Schroeder who was leaving. Henry asked the doctor how he had found Miss Holmes and the physician said. 'Your presence over the last two weeks has been highly beneficial in motivating her but that benefit has been diminished by you exhausting her for long hours each day beside the bed upon which she ought have been resting. Your absence over the past two days has aided her immeasurably. Nature performs its wondrous work during sleep and you will see a remarkable improvement in both her spirit and her appearance but not this night. She is sleeping. I suggest you return tomorrow, but not early and that you do not remain long. Goodnight.'

Returning to college, happy at the news of Adeline's improvement but puzzled at the doctors reference to two days absence, Henry visited the kitchen where other students were having supper. He was the subject of some ribbing – the student so relaxed that he could sleep during the hardest paper by far. Indeed some had felt that yesterday's paper had been impossibly difficult. As the banter and complaints continued Henry realised that he had slept twice around the clock and beyond.

Mindful of the doctor's advice he waited until noon on Sunday to visit Adeline and the transformation in her was incredible. He found her seated in the armchair that he had been occupying for hours and days. She was spooning a fair portion of the soup made for her by Mrs Tutt and greeted Henry with a smile. Her cheeks, for so long pallid now showed traces of colour but, and this was unmistakable, she was animated and enthusiastic.

Henry explained that it was her doctor's opinion that it would speed up her recovery if she was permitted long periods of rest and as much as he wished to spend his every waking moment with her, he would sacrifice that to hasten the day they would marry. He could visit daily but for no longer than two hours until such time as she regained her strength.

The Tuesday of the following week was the day on which the final year results were to be announced and the final year was to disperse. At nine o'clock the twenty nine students who had completed the thirty month course and the final examinations assembled in the lecture hall. Bullivant Theakstone gave a long opening address then announced that twenty two students had received the required standard in all papers and would graduate, five had failed to reach the standard in one paper and two in two papers. Those seven students would have the option of enrolling for a further quarter and could re-sit the failed papers in June. Henry hoped, fleetingly, that he might be one of the seven as this would take care of his accommodation needs for three months while Adeline grew in strength. He then withdrew that wish. As a young man intending to marry that year he should be qualified, independent and in suitable employment.

Envelopes were handed to the students and eagerly opened. Theakstone might just as well have named those who had passed and those who had not. Expressions on faces around the room, congratulations and commiserations betrayed the confidentiality the Principal had attempted to protect. Henry had passed in every subject. He would graduate today and need accommodation tomorrow.

Thornton Old Hall would have him but it was less convenient for the daily visits he would be making to Adeline's home.

Theakstone announced a prize for the best assignment report following the student's attachments. He gave a précis of four, one of which was Henry's and he praised it highly. It concerned he said, the commercial opportunity of an accountant to advise clients on the information gained from their competitors accounts. Mr Crawshaw, he went on, had accurately identified the ethical dilemma and had provided a succinct argument balancing the client's right to confidentiality and the accountant's duty to provide the best advice he could on the basis of his knowledge and experience, irrespective of how and where those were gained.

The prize did not go to Henry though but to Norbert Harrison who had spent his attachment at a stone quarry at Bolton Woods. It was established and accepted practice that the quarrymen, parched by the stone dust they created, would stake their thirst with a flagon of Wilson's Strong Ale at the adjoining Masons Arms. Harrison had calculated the cost in lost productivity occasioned by absence of the workforce for, on average, six minutes per hour ten times a day. He proposed the employment by the quarry owners of a pot boy to fetch ale by the pitcher to the workers on site. His wages would be covered by increased productivity within the first hour of every day and each subsequent hour would represent profit.

Finally, Theakstone called Henry to the platform, where he stood while the principal concluded his presentations. 'The choice of student of the year has been a difficult one with a number of worthy considerations and little to differentiate them. Together with my staff I have debated the matter to exhaustion but we agreed that if deserved weight was given to a particular piece of work then a clear distinction between the candidates could be made. We have been made aware of the student body concerning the exceptional difficulty posed by the paper on valuations and acquisitions. This was taken into account and the pass mark was adjusted accordingly. One paper though would have surpassed the standard no matter how high it had been set. Mr Crawshaw's paper is regarded by me, and acclaimed by my staff, as the most comprehensive and detailed exploration of this complex subject and his introduction of instinct that comes with experience and a buccaneering spirit as a factor added an esoteric dimension to an otherwise mundane subject. His paper is well worthy of publication as a treatise. For that, for his application to his studies and for the continuing high standard of his work the prize for student of the year is awarded to Mr Henry Crawshaw.'

With no dissent nor any feelings of jealousy, his fellows stood as a body and cheered him long and loudly. Those cheers and the personal conversations that had followed them still warmed him as he walked to the Holmes's house carrying his graduation papers to be shown to Hubert and his modest and valued trophy to be given to Adeline. Tomorrow he would see Scowan Perkins about a position and find a suitable room near to Adeline's home.

Chapter 8

April saw Henry in a settled pattern, days spent totalling columns of figures for Perkins, evenings visits to Adeline who was now restored to as much health as she had when he first met her and nights in his room at a small hotel on Heaton Road, above the park close to the Holmes's house. The one change to his routine was the dinner given in a private dining room of the Great Northern Hotel by Charles and Marianne to mark his graduation. They brought with them the congratulations of Nathan Stein who had expressed the hope that his advice on valuations and acquisitions had been useful to him. How much so, Henry could never adequately express or explain.

The fourth of May was Adeline's twentieth birthday and Mrs Tutt had prepared a special dinner. Henry arrived with a gift, a silver trinket box engraved with the letter A on the lid. Adeline, looking beautiful ate well and a most enjoyable evening had been spent when Adeline retired at ten o'clock. Henry made to leave but Hubert asked him to remain a while. They drank brandy in the drawing room waiting for Jane to join the company and when she had Hubert began a speech that Henry thought had been prepared and well rehearsed. Standing before the fireplace, a thumb in his waistcoat pocket, Hubert was serious, almost statesman like.

'Henry, Adeline has been the joy of my life. That I should have had that joy for twenty years, against all of which I had been warned would occur, is a tribute to the love and devotion of her mother. Mrs Tutt's skills in the kitchen here provided the nourishment she needed and avoided the foods that could have further damaged her a knowledge that Mrs Tutt possessed which is a mystery to me. Most of all I am indebted to the skill and attention of Doctor Schroeder over the years. So many times I have relied on his council and never found it to be other than wise.'

'It was his opinion that marriage might well be the end of her but when I ought to protect her and refused my consent she went into a decline from which I feared she could not recover. Your return has restored her to health. I shall always be grateful, always appreciative of that. My offer to reward you for doing so was an unforgivable insult. Indeed, I cannot help but bite a knuckle every time I think of it, which I do constantly. I ask you for forgiveness.'

Henry was quick to reply, 'At the time sir I was not talking to you, I was talking to a man with so much love for a daughter he was losing that his thoughts and words were not his own. We are both, all three of us here, overjoyed at the Adeline we see tonight and no apologies nor forgiveness come into it.'

'Well thank you for that, son. Now, Doctor Schroeder. He attributes Adeline's recovery to the sense of purpose she now has in her life. In long talks he has with her she has spoken excitedly of her planned marriage. His advice to me is that another refusal should not even be considered and that a date for the wedding should not be set so far in the future as to destroy the plans she has. Her vital signs are encouraging, her strength is as good if not better than before her decline. While marriage might be damaging to her it would be less so than withholding of the consent already given. To sum up, I am persuaded that the best course, should still be what you would wish, is that firm plans be made for an early wedding.'

Henry's heart beat fast. 'I cannot think of anything I could wish for more. There isn't anything.'

'I hoped that is what you would say and I have discussed the matter with Jane and have a number of conditions' Jane coughed and prompted him, 'Though I must say that Jane feels that I should term these, requests, not prerequisites.'

Hubert had indeed prepared and he took a piece of paper from his jacket on which his 'requests' were listed. As the bride's father, he said, it was his duty and privilege to meet all costs of the wedding. It should be a quiet affair with restricted numbers so as not to place too much strain on Adeline. Hubert and Jane would confine themselves to two guests, could Henry confine himself to four to provide balanced numbers. Hubert would want Mrs Tutt to be located in Henry's home in order that Adeline would have no housekeeping work to do and her needs for specific foods prepared in certain ways could be met.'

Henry listened intently, raising no objection, prepared to agree to almost anything for the prize of Adeline's hand. Hubert continued, they should have a home of an appropriate standard, close to Hubert's home so that mother and daughter could spend time together without reliance on transport or having to brave the dangers of the streets. Hubert would buy the house, which Adeline need not know of and in the event of her death, the house would revert to Hubert, which Adeline should not know.

At this Henry did voice his objection. 'A marriage should be based on openness and trust. This was the way my parents conducted their marriage and I know of no other way of conducting my own.' Jane nodded her approval. 'I see no shame in living in a house bought by my father-in-law if it means my wife lives more comfortably than otherwise she could. But she must be aware of and approve the arrangement.'

Hubert agreed that Adeline would be told and he would withdraw the condition that the ownership of the house would revert to him on Adeline's death.

Henry disagreed again. 'I insist upon that arrangement remaining. I want no favours from the marriage other than having your daughter as my wife. She will know that our home would not be owned by us and she will know that the arrangement was made by my insistence not yours.'

Agreements were reached and Henry returned to his hotel, his head filled with plans for a July wedding. His first call was to Thornton Old Hall to issue invitations to Charles and Marianne to be held at St. Paul's church in Manningham on Saturday tenth of July. Also, Charles, being his legal guardian, and he being shy of his twenty-first birthday, needed Charles's consent. This was given readily.

Hubert, accompanied by Henry, viewed and bought a solid detached house in a tree-lined avenue almost opposite the Holmes house. It had been the residence of a retired gentleman and still contained his furniture. This was sold to a trader with the exception of a chaise longue, which he had delivered to his office for afternoon rests. The furnishing was undertaken by Adeline and her mother with Henry affecting interest but reclining that neither of his tastes, such as they were nor his choices would have no influences on the decisions made.

On the tenth of July the emptiness of St. Paul's church was hardly disturbed by so small a wedding party but its gloom was pierced by the happiness and pride of a bridegroom and by the radiance of a joyful bride. They breakfasted in some private dining room at the Great

Northern Hotel where Henry had been hosted by Charles and Marianne just a few weeks before. Now he had his wife with him and his guests, Mr and Mrs Charles Ambrose and Mr and Mrs Nathan Stein. Hubert and Jane grinned with delight as did the other guests Mrs Doreen Sweeting, Jane's sister and Mrs Mollie Tutt.

Mrs Tutt had devised the menu and those who were aware of Adeline's condition were pleased to see her empty her plate of chicken breast and stewed vegetables, likewise with a bowl of frozen cream topped with strawberries. Gifts were presented, toasts were made to Mr and Mrs Crawshaw as Henry made a brief, humorous response in which he referred to the honour he felt for all the assistance and kindness he had had from all those present with a special word for Mrs Sweeting, Adeline's aunt. It was, he said, his longing while Adeline was away for so long in Dorset that convinced him that they should never again be separated, and never would be.

Henry cast out all thoughts of how long he would have Adeline. For that day there would be no dark clouds in his skies, only a small, wispy one. How would he explain to Adeline the raised weals on his buttocks and could he reconcile their explanation with his belief in openness and total honesty in marriage.

The first four months were everything he had dreamed of. Returning from his work to a Mrs Tutt dinner with his lovely young wife and evenings spent talking about anything and everything, just happy in being in her company; his notions of a platonic marriage proved absurd. They were two young people who had desires but Henry; always conscious of Doctor Schroeder's warnings was a gentle and considerate lover, careful, indeed anxious, that Adeline should not conceive.

Christmas at Old Hall was the most enjoyable so far. Henry was with his wife, qualified, had a position and was pre-prepared with an appropriate and comical tale to tell when called upon. He noted that Brendan Lowe who two years before had told the risqué story about a busty kitchen maid had not since been invited. Hubert and Jane showed as much pride in their son-in-law as they did in their daughter and Henry's only regret was that their pride in him was greater than his own. The company of so many successful men over three days made him assess his own position. He had been satisfied as a clerk to an accountant. Had he not been living in a provided house with provided furniture his earnings would have been insufficient to support his wife. While he had significant sums in the bank and income from the school and the farm, if he was to use his qualification and achieve financial self-sufficiency he would need to establish a profitable business.

In February, immediately following his twenty-first birthday, he visited his solicitor, Alistair Wild. There were documents to sign. Henry was released from his wardship. No longer would he need a counter signature from Charles to conduct his affairs and he felt ready now to risk his fortune without having to reveal his plans.

There were risks. He would have to incur expenses in establishing an office and there might be times when he would have to raid his reserves because he would have no assured income. He could not describe himself as an accountant but there was a specific qualification that he did not have so he would not be able to sign off accounts as audited. He could though produce accounts for small businesses whose proprietors lacked either the ability or the time to compile their own. The larger businesses employed staff for the purpose, which meant there would be no work from them.

He rented a ground floor office in a yard adjoining Piece Hall and employed a sign-writer and he would open the next day – Henry Crawshaw. Business Accounts. He had kept his plans secret from Adeline and intended to surprise her after dinner. Adeline had a surprise for Henry too, which she had kept secret until she was in no doubt. She was to have a baby. No other news could have inspired in him such joy and such fear in equal measure. Adeline, unaware of the dangers this posed said she would invite her parents to dinner the following evening and tell them they were to be grandparents. Henry was not looking forward to that.

Next morning he visited Doctor Schroeder who was concerned. The danger lay not only in the giving birth but the changes in her body in the later stages of the pregnancy. This would call for confinement to bed and the attendance of an experienced nurse at all times. In the meantime she should not be alarmed by what she might regard as any unnatural reaction or other normal conduct of those about her. Henry called upon Jane, told her the news, asked her to pass on Doctor Schroeder's advice to Hubert and to feign surprise so as not to spoil Adeline's moment at dinner that evening.

The Crawshaw office opened and in the early weeks there was a steady, albeit unremarkable flow of business through the doors. Compiling accounts of income and expenditure for small traders, even allowing for his overheads, was providing a higher income than he received as a clerk with Scowen Perkins, but he was not identifying opportunities to offer advice on how income might be increased or expenditure reduced, other than marginally.

By the date of her first wedding anniversary, in July, Doctor Schroeder confined Adeline to her bed. Two nurses were employed to ensure round the clock attention if needed. One was found by Henry and one by Hubert.

On the morning of the second of September, clients with appointments at Crawshaw's office found it closed. Henry would not be leaving home today. The birth was imminent. Doctor Schroeder was in attendance with an experienced midwife. Both nurses were in the kitchen and the night nurse determined to stay on. Hubert and Jane paced the drawing room. Henry felt sick and found himself praying.

The doctor continually monitoring Adeline's condition feared the effect on her heart from a prolonged labour but the matter moved to a swift conclusion. By noon Adeline was delivered of a healthy boy and Doctor Schroeder could detect no harm to the mother. She was to be confined to her bed for a further two weeks but the relief, prayers of thanks and joy filled the house.

Henry went to the cellar to get wine to toast the birth and, unseen watched Mrs Tutt at the kitchen table. She had arms like a drayman and wrists that could ring a bedsheet dryer than a mangle yet her fingers could fashion the most delicate pastries. There was though a sensitivity and devotion inside that forbidding frame and he saw the tears that streamed down her cheeks and fell from her chin soaking her pinafore.

Henry, back at his desk next morning considered the situation. He was husband of a wife he loved, the father of a beautiful, healthy, fair skinned blue-eyed son, who would be christened Giles and he had his own business. He felt the glow of pride and the weight of responsibility – neither out weighing the other. He must make further plans. For his home, or Hubert's house of which he was always conscious, the nurses work would seem to be done and he would employ a nursemaid for Giles. For his business he would continue to scrutinise the figures he converted into accounts, striving to identify opportunities to make investments in promising enterprises to secure a percentage interest here and there and thereby increase his source of income. Strive as he did though, a year and a half after Giles's birth he was coming to the view that his plan to build a substantial and secure income by avoiding employing others and instead by having an interest in a number of businesses that did employ others was as unrealistic as his notion had been that he could have a platonic marriage. Preparing accounts for small businesses provided a reasonable income but after almost two years it was apparent to him that it was unlikely to provide anything more.

Also the floor of his office was now as littered as that of Scowen Perkins but not with neat piles of ledgers but with bags, boxes and even a valise all stuffed with invoices, receipts and chits. Some where undated, some creased or soiled or both and some almost illegible. Henry was spending more hours in making sense and order of these than in calculating and producing accounts. He needed a clerk, someone with the patience and ability to work through bags and boxes, separate the contents of each into categories – incomings and outgoings, overheads and wages, capital purchases and revenue purchases – and present him with totals of which he could work with a high degree of reliance.

Many times he had felt compelled to make such an appointment and had always resisted it. Not only did he have an aversion to employing staff conscious of the damage that an ill-advised appointment could wreak but also he wanted to avoid increasing his overheads. He would certainly not employ a Tenpunce but might find, too late that he had employed an Elevenpunce. Moreover, with his overheads increased, unless his income was to increase commensurably, he could find himself reduced to being a servant of Crawshaw's Business Accounts rather than its master as his father had worked for Black Dyke Hole rather than have the farm working for him. He concluded that it would take quite a turn of events for him to change his mind.

Such a turn of events occurred within less than a month – two turns in fact. Henry received a letter from Bullivant Theakstone who confessed that in awarding marks for the final year paper for Valuations and Acquisitions the previous year the staff had found it necessary to accept too low a standard or fail too high a number of otherwise able students. For two years the academy had been working to a twelve month rather than fifteen month year in order that income could be increased without an increase in fees. The shorter year had meant that some subjects in the curriculum could not be explored to the same depth. This had led to the acceptance of a lower pass mark in the most difficult subject. The examination papers were not set by the college but by a body on behalf of the growing number of academies in the country. That body had expressed its displeasure at the low pass mark and hoped in future standards would be maintained.

This year it had been decided that standards in pass marks would be set and would be adhered to. As a result twelve students had been failed. All had re-enrolled but because of demands such numbers would place on accommodation and class numbers of the new final year, they would attend for one day each week and be expected to pursue private study in their own time. They would not be able to live in and their fees for a further quarter would reduce accordingly.

Henry read on. Theakstone wrote a detailed letter and it ran to several pages. It was the letter of a trained accountant, setting out the facts and the evidence for those facts before reaching a conclusion and it was a conclusion that Henry found surprising, flattering and possibly lucrative.

'My staff, amongst whose numbers I count myself, are as one in the belief that the pass standard was not set too high and that the student body has the intellect to master the subject. This leaves us having to accept that the fault lies in our inability to impart our knowledge in a way that the students can assimilate it. It is also our view that the available text books on the subject would fall well short of their needs and that your paper on the subject is superior to the published works.

Accepting that your business commitments might preclude your agreement I would wish to ask if you might be prepared to provide twelve four hour lectures to the re-enrolled students from nine o'clock each Monday from the second Monday in April. Staff members would also wish to attend. The value of your time would be fully acknowledged and payment would be by way of two fees, the one the lecture fee and the other the fee for staff training.'

The letter continued with references to the importance to the academy of maintaining a high graduation rate and high standards and concluded with a request that Henry might let him have the favour of an early reply.

Initially Henry thought that Theakstone ought to approach Nathan Stein, the master at whose feet Henry had learned both the essence and the detail of Valuations and Acquisitions that Stein taught as both a science and an art. On reflection he believed that if not Stein then certainly Charles Ambrose would not be agreeable to such distraction from the duties of the industries and estate.

But could Henry convert a six hour treatise into twelve four hour lectures and, also, what did he know of teaching. His only example was of Simon Pepper whose method was to lace instruction with sarcasm and enforce it with threats. Nathan Stein did not teach as that word might be strictly defined. Instead, he probed the gaps in his student's knowledge and worked with him to fill those gaps. Could that be done with twelve students and four teachers concurrently? His eventual decision to accept Theakstone's invitation owed less to the fees he would earn as to the pride he would feel in informing Adeline, Hubert and Nathan of his appointment.

Henry arrived early to deliver his first lecture and found the twelve students, three teachers and the Principal already in place in the lecture hall. The students were spaced along the first two tiered benches, the staff in a group on the rear tier. All were poised, pens and jotters in hand. As he took his place on the platform he held the lectern like a comfort blanket trusting that the trembling in his limbs and his attempts to control his breathing would not be evident to the audience.

The introduction to his subject, which he had rehearsed and timed at one hour, took less than half that time then he sought questions to clarify any misunderstandings or examples to which the principles he had outlined could be applied. It was, he felt a mercy that he was not left in silence. Some of the students' questions were genuine attempts at a better understanding, some of those from the teachers revealed a resentment at being trained by a former pupil and some pre-planning had gone into the mischievous traps there questions clearly were, while others from students were simply naïve.

Each question was treated with the same degree of respect with especially detailed answers supported by examples for those whose knowledge was obviously deficient. His standing in the eyes of the student body rose immeasurably when he entered into a lengthy discourse with one teacher whose question and the manner of his delivery were blatantly vexatious. Parrying, but never thrusting, Henry drew him out. He posed questions of his own, ostensibly to delve ever deeper into the question and in doing so caused his interrogator to first unravel and finally to abandon his own contention. In summing up that interchange Henry could have destroyed his question but the difficult fellow would have to continue teaching here and Henry would divest him of the students' respect beyond the damage he had done to himself.

The first hours passed swiftly. The students, with full jotters, considered it had been time well spent, both in terms of their understanding of the subject and entertainment. The Principal expressed himself pleased and asked Henry to submit his invoices weekly. The agreed fees for half a day's work were the equivalent of two day's profit from his business.

He left, satisfied with the morning and more confident about the following Monday. The students, many of them friends having worked together for two years, milled about. Most would not be seeing the others for a week. One stood apart and waylaid Henry at the gate. He was a tall, heavily built, flushed faced young man who stooped and was painfully bereft of confidence. 'Mr Crawshaw,

Sir. May I say how useful this morning has been to me the topic, calculating the unit costs of an enterprise and the factor that will cause them to rise and fall given expansion in production and the workforce was to be the theme of my attachment assignment. Sadly I failed that too and need to undertake another this quarter.'

'It is unusual to fail that paper which calls for reasoned argument and opinion based on observation. Where does the responsibility for your failure lie?'

'Ultimately with me in my choice of placement. It was at a tannery where I expected to find that the calculation of labour costs, salts, acids and overheads could be related to profits on the finished hides and skins by identifying unit costs. The owner was a fair man who gave me the opportunity but little was seen of him at the works. The manager, his son-in-law took against me. I accepted his insults and jibes as part of the attachment experience but he blocked every attempt I made to obtain the information I needed. As a consequence I did not have the material to produce a costed, well argued assignment paper and was unsurprised to be failed.'

'I am sorry to hear that and I trust you will have a far better experience next time.'

I am in some difficulty with that, sir. It is due to start immediately and I have been unable to find a position. I wondered, since you deal with so many businesses in the town, if you might suggest one or more for me to approach.'

Henry considered him. He was polite, reasonably articulate, had passed all his papers other than the two and, although anxious to return and open his office he gave the young man a little more time.

'Where was the tan house to which you were attached.'

'Wilsden, Sir.'

'And the name of the manager?'

'Mr Julian Dexter.'

'And your name?'

'George Ball, Sir.'

'If you have no success in the interim, see me at my office tomorrow and I'll think on the matter, Mr Ball.'

Chapter 9

It was almost two o'clock when Henry arrived back at his office to find an unusual character awaiting his return. He was a short, squat man wearing a faded blue three piece suit, the waistcoat of which was straining to restrain his stomach, brown boots and a black bowler hat, a size much too small.

'It's Mr Crawshaw, is it. I should have been an accountant and enjoyed long lunches like you.'

As Henry admitted him he replied, 'Then why are you not?'

'This accountancy is a mystery to me. You fellows can take two and two and get whatever answer suits your purpose.'

Henry was losing patience with his visitor's impertinence and would have terminated their meeting had the man not quickly gone on.

'It's the magic of numbers that defeats me. Now pigs' trotters, Mr Crawshaw. A different thing altogether. You know where you are with trotters. Every pig has four, although I've seen an unfortunate one with three, but I've yet to meet one with five.'

With that he laughed heartily, removed his precariously perched hat and offered his hand. 'Norman Coggins, Mr Crawshaw, a man in need of your skills.'

Coggins sat in a chair Henry marvelled at the strength of the stitches that held the buttons of his waistcoat as he listened to his visitor's story. He operated a stall in the open-air market on the three days of each week that the market was held. Prior to that, he had been a foreman overseer of backwash minder at Jowett's Mill at Laisterdyke. Henry, who thought he knew the various occupations in wool warehouses and textile productions had not encountered this one before but the pride that Coggins took in his former position, was evident.

That, though, he said, was three years ago before the dust clogged up his pipes and he was finished. Now he sold pigs trotters, cheek and snout from which he was making a fair living, but if he could rent the shop he had eyes on in Bridge Street he could make a good living. This was Henry's area of interest made flesh and he questioned Coggins on how, with increased overheads he could guarantee increased turnover and produce better profits. Coggins explained that a shop could sell for six days a week, not three, that with an oven he could sell pig parts that he couldn't at present such as lights, organs and brains and that trade needn't be ruined on the days when the rain brought the soot down on his customers and his meat.

'But from where would you get more customers?'

Impatiently, and as addressing a child he answered, 'Mr Crawshaw, there are men in this town, too many, who have neither oven nor fire. These are the people who would buy my meat because it is affordable but what use is a snout or a trotter to someone who can't boil it. If I could boil for them I'd have more custom than I could handle.'

Henry looked for flaws in his reasoning and asked, 'Are there no shops selling these cheaper pieces already?'

Coggins was ready for this, 'I've traipsed around this town to every butchers shop in walking distance of the slums. Few do and they are not shops that my customers would go into and charge prices that they could not pay.

If they all sold these pieces the slaughter houses would be selling them and not throwing them away.'

'So how can I help Mr Coggins.'?

' I came straight here from an appointment at the Bradford Bank where I was trying to get the backing for my plans but they wanted my accounts, and I don't have any, they wanted security, but didn't say what, and they wanted what they called projections of incomings and outgoings and I wouldn't know where to start on that.'

Henry, looking at the two paper sacks that Coggins had left inside his door, asked the question he had feared to ask. 'Do you have receipts?'

Coggins cocked a thumb in the direction of the sacks, 'All three years. None missing.'

'And all dates' asked Henry.

'Aye but in no particular order. I thought that was your job.'

'What amount of loan where you seeking from the bank?'

'I reckon I need seventy five pounds to get properly set up. I have forty and want thirty five. I nearly own my house. It would have been mine but my father re-married and when he died his wife found another husband and sold my own house to me. I owe only a few payments. A year or two at the most.'

'Well Mr Coggins I can produce accounts and a report in support of your application but I'll need some information about the rent for the shop and other outgoings and what they'll amount to over the first six months.' Coggins took a sheet of paper from his jacket, the movement placing further strain on the waistcoat and handed it to Henry. 'That's what I thought for one month. You'll be able to work it out for six.'

Standing and offering his hand Henry bade him goodbye. 'I hope to have your accounts and report by Friday.' Coggins was disappointed, 'I'd hoped for something quicker. Still, I'm told you're cheap and I don't expect to find I've been told wrong.' With that the hat was balanced and Coggins was on his way.

Henry's last work of the day was to prepare the long lists of figures, pounds, shillings, pence and part pence. He totalled them and noted the totals on a separate piece of paper and locked the office at six thirty. After dinner that evening he answered Adeline's numerous questions about his first experiences as a lecturer.

Arriving early at his office next morning he found a young man who had arrived earlier, George Ball and he invited him in. Henry passed the young man one sheet of figures, and took the other for himself and invited his visitor to complete timely and accurately the sum of the totals. Henry had increased his own speed significantly since the test set by Scowen Perkins. His business and income were dependent on it. For all his increased speed he had barely carried forward the pennies total to the shillings column when George Ball claimed to be finished. Checking the total against the figure he had noted the evening before and finding it correct he asked the young man how he had acquired such speed and accuracy.

Ball explained, as Perkins had done, that he calculated in rows rather than columns. It was a self-taught skill from hours of practice before beginning his course at the academy. He had felt he might struggle to keep pace with his fellow students and thought it wise to be well prepared.

Impressed, but concealing it well, Henry said, 'Mr Ball, the first three of those boxes you see covering my floor contain the bills, receipts and invoices of a boot and shoe repairer who is in dispute with the taxation officer. Under those lids you will find the history of his income and expenditure, since heaven knows when, as he was often remiss in dating transactions. If you are otherwise unoccupied for the day perhaps you might wish to see if you are able to bring some order to the cobbler's disorder.'

Without a desk at which to work, George was quickly on his knees, sorting documents and organising them into piles that soon covered every inch of floor that the bags, boxes, and Coggins paper sacks had not already claimed. Neglecting work that ought to have taken precedence, Henry was pre-occupied with the bluff market trader Coggins. Leaving Master Ball with his growing towers of documents, Henry took a walk to Bridge Street to view the shop that Coggins wished to rent. While the area was not unaffected by the smoke and dirt that pervaded the town it had few slum houses. It consisted of the well regarded Great Northern Hotel, and the offices of the Corporation and some legal practices. It was only half a mile from the areas of the worst squalor in Canal Road and Barker End but a mile round trip was a long return journey for a pig's nose if it was to be made in bare feet to an area in which the ragged people felt uncomfortable. Coggins needed to be advised.

Before returning to his office Henry visited the reading room of the commerce club to gather the factual information he would need to persuade the Bradford Bank that the projections were based on appropriate research. In two decades the population had doubled and re-doubled. Mills and factories, opening week after week, were drawing in workers from across the country and from other countries. There were already one hundred and thirty mills and thirty two collieries, belching fire and smoke, employing and killing cheap labour. The growth of the town was unstoppable, the lessons of cholera epidemics unlearned, the housing shock unable to keep pace and those whose infants survived were, in increasing numbers, living in poverty and squalor. If Coggins shop was to be appropriately located, providing sustaining food at affordable prices it was a venture that should not fail. Henry's report to the bank was half written in his mind already.

On his return to his office he found George Ball, now standing, easing the pain from his back and proudly surveying a tottering forest of documents and slips of paper.

'Mr Crawshaw. The door, quickly. One gust of wind could prove disastrous.' That done. 'The evidence is in order and accounts could be produced from it.'

Henry contained his admiration, 'Then make a start on them and let us see what you make of them, but first, this. How have you arranged the undated bills and receipts?'

George Ball, unsure whether he had acted correctly replied. 'I have interspersed them between the first dated document and the last. The cobbler hasn't placed them in time, I cannot and although my shuffling of them into the piles is arbitrary I would defy the taxation officer to gainsay my ordering. They are an honest representation over the period in question so no benefit accrues to any party.'

Henry, satisfied, left George Ball to his task and delved into Norman Coggins sacks. It was a daunting task, which he soon abandoned and made a start on a small bag that the contents of which were reasonably understandable. As Henry prepared to close his office George Ball told him that he had not completed the cobbler's accounts. Henry had not expected that he would and invited the young man he was testing to return the next morning should he so wish. He did so wish and was again awaiting Henry's arrival. He had with him a large cloth bag, fastened with a drawstring. It contained heavy pebbles, painted in various colours, which he used as paper weights on the piles of papers from which he was totalling sums and entering them in accounts. By mid-morning he presented Henry with the results of his work.

Henry trusted the totals and had no wish to check them by working his way down the towers and restricted himself to scrutinising the finished accounts. He found one fault, the purchase of a last and a file that ought to have been classed as capital purchases not revenue expenses, but that apart he was pleased and impressed and told George Ball that he was. He knew that the student's graduation depended upon a successful attachment assignment and he knew too that Master Ball was anxious for the offer of an attachment or, failing that, a recommendation, but he had another task for him.

'George,' the use of his first name would please young Ball and encourage him. 'Those two paper sacks closest to the door contain a heap of documents relating to a simple enterprise, a market stallholders trading. They should not require many categories for your coloured paperweights but because of their number and disorder they will pose a challenge. I do not wish you to prepare accounts from them, you should be relieved to learn, but I would ask you to calculate, in broad terms, the incomings and outgoings of that gentleman over his three years of trading.'

Without further prompting, George Ball was back on his knees and up to his elbows in Norman Coggins's records. His work involved little sorting and he had soon had eight tall piles of incomings and one small pile of outgoings. Some rapid totalling followed and within two hours presented Henry with two totals. The outgoings were minimal both in total and in relation to the high level of income.

'What do you make of that George?'

'Well, Sir, his only recorded expenditure is three pence a day, three days a week for the rent of his market stall. He appears to pay no wages, even to himself and there is no record of where he obtains his meat and what he pays for it.'

Although it was only early afternoon Henry told George that he had no more for him to do and that he could leave. Henry was toying with him as Charles once had with him.

'I am more than impressed with your ability Mr Ball and tempted as I am to offer you a placement here I have to accept that my business would not utilise it to the full and accept why you feel it necessary to reject my offer.'

'But Mr Crawshaw, I would not. I would accept your offer and work ceaselessly.'

'Thank you, George, but I fear you will not find the material here to produce a paper on unit costs.' George Ball was prepared to fight for this attachment, not knowing it was already his. 'If I could gain some experience of invoicing for chargeable hours I could gather all the material I could need for my paper and unit costs.'

Henry was not done, 'so tell me my valued assistant, what will you be doing on those days of the week left to you?'

'My mother is widowed. The college fees even reduced as they are, and my inability to find a paid position until I graduate are placing a strain on us. I am going to take paid work for three days a week for this quarter.'

Against all his instincts that opposed employing staff but encouraged by his plan for Norman Coggins's venture, he offered George a paid position on the three days a week available to him. Adeline was surprised to learn that her husband had employed an assistant and even more surprised to learn that he had felt able to do so on the basis of anticipated earnings from a business involving selling pig bits. Out of respect for Henry she kept her misgivings to herself and felt she should not disclose the plan to her mother during her daily visits to Adeline and her grandson.

George arrived on Thursday to find that Henry had had delivered a long table and a stool. No longer would he need to work on his hands and knees and he set about the next bag of documents in the queue. Henry was distracted and kept returning, questioning, the wisdom of investing in Norman Coggins's scheme. He was still undecided when Coggins arrived on the Friday but resolved to settle the matter once he had subjected him to some of the bluntness the butcher employed with others. Henry was, after all a farmer's son and capable of it. George, at his table with his back to the pair, heard every detail of the exchange and considered Henry to be most un-business like.

'Mr Coggins, never have I seen business accounts without invoices for stock, supplies or materials. How do you come by your pig's feet and other bits?'

'All discarded, Mr Crawshaw. Not wanted.'

'That fails to answer my question. How do you come by the meat that you sell?'

Coggins ran his fingers round the rim of the bowler hat on his knee before answering. 'I take a barrow round the slaughter houses the night before each market day, pick suitable pieces from the tips and pay for them.'

'And where are the records of payments you make?'

Coggins, clearly uncomfortable, replied as forcefully as Henry Crawshaw. 'I know just how much I paid. Six pence a visit, one shilling and sixpence a week, paid to the watchman to look the other way. You may not be aware, Mr Crawshaw, but night watchmen don't give invoices and receipts. And now you know that, you should know this – I am paying you to make out a case for me to get the backing of the bank for my shop. How I get my meat is my business and how you conjure with your sums is yours.'

'Today is market day, Mr Coggins. Who is minding your stall?'

'My lad, he's fourteen, bright and well capable. Is that your concern? What I want is my accounts and a report that persuades the bank to make the loan.'

'And I'll spare your embarrassment and my reputation by not giving you one Mr Coggins. I wouldn't want my name on it. If I were the Manager of the Bradford Bank I would not loan you one penny and would be undecided whether to report you to the police or have you committed to an asylum.' George winced. Coggins was furious but Henry was not going to relent.

'You would present yourself as a man who steals his supplies, bribes employees of the owners of the meat who connive at his crimes and who leaves his business in the hands of a child. Moreover, you expect to sell pigs noses for the staff and servants of the premier hotel in the town and the Corporation's managers and clerks who have their meat delivered to their homes by honest traders. Is that a fair summary of your application for thirty-five pounds when actually you need ninety pounds and are you really prepared to risk your house on this ill conceived adventure?'

'Fair summary or not, I take it you'll be charging me for it'

'No, Mr Coggins, I am prepared to pay you for it.'

Ball was baffled. Coggins, half risen and now re-seated, was incredulous. Henry, enjoying himself, went on.

'I have rented a suitable shop where the mills of Vicar Lane meet the hovels of the alley-ways of Peckover Street. It has cellars below and a room above that would serve as an office. At this very moment men from Dawson's Detective Agency are evicting a band of ruffians who refused to quit when I viewed the premises yesterday. The shop was previously used by a buyer of bottles and rags and, having been unoccupied some months is in a filthy state. A neighbour is gathering a gang of local women to clean from roof to cellar floor, before which the chimneys are to be cleaned this afternoon. My proposal, Mr Coggins is this. I will finance the establishing of this shop but you will be the proprietor and pay the rent. Your contribution will be only the forty pounds you were prepared to risk. I will guarantee the financial support until business is viable and for three months, which ever should occur first. In return all profits, that is all income minus all costs will be shared between us, twelve shillings in every pound to you and eight to me.'

Coggins, sceptical, regarding all accountants as shysters, thought for a while then asked. 'So I'd be working for you then?'

'Not at all, Mr Coggins. You will be the proprietor, chancing your venture but with my money. For the minor share of forty percent all the risk will be mine and the earnings from your shop and your stall may not ever repay my investment.'

'Me stall?' 'Of course, the calculations are based on its continuing and I am investing not in one shop but in the business empire to be built by Mr Norman Coggins.'

With that Coggins placed a thumb in each waistcoat

pocket. It was a strain too far for the threads on two buttons that were fired in Henry's direction.

'All these arrangements you've made, Mr Crawshaw. What made you so sure I'd be agreeable?'

'I wasn't. If you had not been agreeable I would have gone ahead without your forty pounds even though I would also lose your ability to count pigs' trotters.'

'I'll say this Mr Crawshaw, for a young man you are a hardened businessman.' 'As your competitors will discover as you increase your empire and they attempt to nibble into your market share.'

That evening Henry was at home later than usual. He had called on Hubert to ask him how he disposed of those parts of pigs that he or those who he provided a slaughtering service did not sell. Hubert told him that disposal incurred two costs – one for carting away and one for incinerating. The fat produced in burning meant that the meat could not be shovelled into the fires that heated the mills boilers and a dedicated incinerator at Bierley had to be used – paid.'

Henry told him that he had a client who made a living from selling pig parts that otherwise would be burned. Why, he asked, did Hubert not sell these himself? Hubert laughed.

'Henry, you are a graduate; indeed a lecturer in business practice, not allowing that the most precious asset any business has is its reputation. My father styled his business, and with this he wrote imaginary letters in the air with his forefinger, Holmes Butchers. Purveyors of High Quality Meats. It would damage irreparably the reputation of Holmes to have a pig's snout in its shop windows. Yes your client can sell a trotter for a farthing or a snout for a halfpenny but would need to sell a sack full for the same profit that is to be had from a shoulder or a leg. I wish your Mr Coggins well but do not fear his competition.'

'I did not mention my client's name'

'No, and you did not need to. Coggins is as regular a visitor to the slaughterhouse middens as the rats, and as well known to the night watchmen. They allow him to sort through the waste, accept his sixpence and do their employers a service in reducing the amount to be carted and burned.'

Henry proposed that if Hubert were to have pig pieces to be placed on a separate pile to save sorting he would arrange with Coggins to have these carted away on a regular basis saving Hubert his disposal costs. Hubert was happy to agree.

The second Monday lecture to the academy was as successful as the first and presented to a larger audience. A number of students of the new final year had lined the walls at the rear of the hall. How many were there to learn from Henry and how many had come having heard of the fool an unpopular teacher had made of himself the previous week, and hoping to witness his defeat could only be conjectured. On this occasion the teacher had no appetite for a joust.

Chapter 10

Coggins's shop opened on the Monday of the third lecture. Henry had appointments with clients that afternoon and awaited news from the shop but none came. At lunchtime on the Tuesday, driven by curiosity, Henry walked the quarter mile from his office to Vicar Lane and as he approached Peckover Street he realised that the crowd that had first appeared to be involved in some disorder were, in fact, crushing to maintain their place in the queue to enter the shop. Was this novelty or was this sustainable custom. Time would tell.

Friday came and still Henry had not had a visit from Coggins so he went, again, to the shop. It was lunchtime and, while there was no great crush there was a long orderly line along Peckham Street. Henry went to the shop door accompanied by muttered disapproval but no resistance as the line deferred his appearance as a gentleman. Behind the counter he saw Coggins with a woman and a boy whom he was to learn were his wife and his son Billy. All three were spreading hunks of bread with pork fat which the customers were sprinkling with salt from a tub on the counter and buying at three hunks for a penny. There was, however no meat, no trotters, cheeks, snouts. None.

Coggins drew him aside. 'Sold out two hours ago Mr Crawshaw. Got Billy to close the stall and barrow down what he had. All uncooked it went in under an hour. Billy's been out buying bread and when Tessa's dripping fats have gone we'll have nothing to sell and the weekend upon us.

Sent a cart to Holmes this morning came back empty. They don't slaughter pigs every day.'

Henry was amazed. Customers gained could be quickly lost if supplies weren't reliable. 'Hire a cart and get around the abattoirs. There are five others, which I understand you know having hunted them all. Offer to take away pig parts at no charge to the owner. If any demand payment, and the sum is reasonable, pay it until I can regularise arrangements. And try to be back before Mrs Coggins runs out of bread and fat. A closed shop on a Friday afternoon is a sorry sight.'

Coggins was off. Henry had a quick word with Billy about the price of the loaves he was cutting in to wedges then allowing for salt, labour, overheads and a proportion of the heat that created the drippings he made a rough calculation of the unit cost of a piece of bread spread with fat. Had Coggins charged half the price there would have been a profit but the queuing customers obviously considered it good value.

On Tuesday of the following week Henry received a visit from Billy Coggins bringing a bag containing lists of sales and details of his outgoings which George Ball took and began totalling. Billy, as bright as his father had described him, explained that his father had been unable to visit Henry because he was working from morning 'til night. His mother was up and boiling at five o'clock, the shop was open until eight or nine o'clock at night and still they got complaints that a slice with dripping would be most welcome when the men left the public houses if the shop wasn't closing so early. His father had got back from Griffiths slaughterhouse within the hour with a cartload of good pieces that had cost nothing but the hire of the carter.

George provided the first week's Coggins accounts. Not only did the volume of business exceed Henry's imaginings but also the profit against cost ratio was exceptional. It had been Henry's intention to give the venture three months before considering a second shop but his instinct told him that he wouldn't have that time. By then the business would be mimicked in the other poor areas around the town, and there were many – Leeds Road, East Bowling, Lower Horton, Otley Road and White Abbey were among the poorer.

Three more shops performing as well as the first and the profits would eclipse the earnings from his accounts business and he had yet to decide upon the financial involvement of Coggins in the new shops. George Ball was doing an excellent job. The floor was being cleared of bags and boxes within days of their arrival and the accounts George produced contained fewer faults and, importantly, never the same mistake twice. He would train George in calculating chargeable hours and producing invoices. This would assist the student with his assignment paper and would free Henry's time and permit him to spend more of it on his plans for more shops. If Coggins was to train one assistant a week he would have the managers he needed for the shops. They should not be hard to come by. Affable, numerate, having an affinity with the class that would be their customer, they would have a good living and the customers would have fitting affordable food.

One evening before Henry's twelfth and final lecture, Adeline tired early and retired, Henry rehearsed his presentation that would draw together all the strands of the difficult subject that he had reduced to its component parts.

There were now five shops bearing the name Coggins although Coggins himself had only a twenty percent interest in these. He had made no investment, having no funds to do so, but for his portion he was responsible for the conduct and performance of the shops and ensuring they were stocked. He had appointed a manager to his own shop and cooks to the others. Now, he worked from the office above the Peckover Street shop and wore a suit two sizes larger than he wore three months before. Also, the term Coggins had gained currency in the slums and a meal for a working man for a penny or for three infants for another. That alone would have been worth a twenty percent premium to Henry but for this portion he was also relieved of the burden of day-to-day responsibility and employment of staff. He had arrangements with all the abattoirs in the town and supplies were plentiful. With ovens and cooks in every shop the range was expanded to include steamed brains, boiled lights and chitterlings. His income had been increasing week on week and he foresaw that within that year he could buy the house from Hubert. Before retiring he thought on the love he had for Adeline and how he would provide for her every wish and he thought of his son Giles. The blue eyed boy with golden locks and a smile that lit up his face would be well educated then take control over an empire of businesses, each small but whose sum total would dwarf many bigger concerns in the town. He went to bed a very happy man.

The final lecture was fulfilling its promise of tying off any remaining loose ends. Questions were few and focused on forming all parts into the whole and would have continued in that manner had the foolish teacher, having learnt nothing from his previous joust felt the need to take his last opportunity for another tilt. There were audible groans from the students at the front and the full final year at the rear when the question sought to divert from the conclusion to an inconsequential aspect that had been fully explored a month before. Henry lost patience. This final lecture and the students remaining questions were too important to a successful examination paper to have them hijacked by a petulant teacher's ego. In a few brief, pointed and plain spoken sentences he answered the question, demolished the argument upon which it was based and queried the motives of the questioner in posing it. The teacher was destroyed and fled from the room.

Henry concluded by wishing all the students a successful paper, which they would be sitting the next day. He was thanked by a standing ovation from all present – the remaining teachers and the Principal too. A spokesman for those re-sitting invited Henry to a dinner to be held at the academy that Friday evening.

George Ball was not at the office on the Tuesday as he was re-sitting the examination and was not expected on the Wednesday as his attachment was completed and assignment paper submitted but he was back and, with his own key, was at his table when Henry arrived. The Valuation and Acquisitions paper had been equally as difficult as the students had been told to expect but there were no questions that had not been dealt with in detail in Henry's lectures and the calculations involved, as complex as they were, could be managed in the time allowed. George was hopeful. He asked that his late arrival the next day while he obtained the results of his papers be excused.

Henry did not need to ask George how he had fared. As he entered the office on the mid-morning of that Thursday he was preceded by a smile that a mortician would have been unable to remove. All the re-enrolled students had passed the Valuations and Acquisitions papers and all by a mark well in access of the pass mark. His paper and his attachment dealing with the calculating of unit costs and on expanding business had merited a special mention. He had graduated and was a little better than he had promised since his mother had been at the academy gates awaiting his news and he had taken the time to relate it in detail. Shaking Henry's hand he expressed his appreciation for the part his employer had played.

'So tell me Master Ball, graduate in business and commerce, I assume you will now be forming your own company' Henry was resigned to losing him.

'Its not that I lack ambition, but I fear that I do not yet have the experience, ability or funds for my own concern. It could be some time before I acquire them and may not acquire all three. No, I would prefer a position managing a growing concern, taking responsibility for its success and, I trust, sharing in the rewards from its growth.'

Henry asked, affecting an innocent enquiry, 'And do you know of such a concern?' George with his new confidence and a twinkle in his eye replied, 'I do indeed Mr Crawshaw and I envisage great potential in its growth. The proprietor, however, has one foot on a stool producing business accounts and the other on one that is retailing pig meat at an exciting rate. With an able assistant engaged in both enterprises I believe he will create an empire of the kind that would fully satisfy my ambitions.' 'George, I fear I am taking on a cheeky rogue as an assistant.'

The dinner at the Academy was a jolly affair. There was relief, celebration and a sense of pride all around. The staff, with the exception of the resentful teacher, attended and joined into the spirit of the occasion. Bullivant Theakstone would receive no criticism from the examining body this time and permitted himself a third glass of wine before making a speech that contained a warm appreciation of Henry's contribution. His toast to the young lecturer was noisily joined and the award of Honorary Fellows of the Academy was roundly cheered.

Happily the following day was fine and warm as he had conspired with Jane to have Adeline out walking Giles in his pram that afternoon while his early gift to mark the second anniversary of his marriage to Adeline was delivered. He could not have chosen better and Adeline's joy at seeing the piano needed no words to express it. Hubert and Jane were invited for dinner that evening and Adeline played for them. Hubert was a contented man. He had a daughter and grandson on whom he doted and a son-in-law of whom he was proud and now felt close enough to tease.

'These Coggins shops of yours are sprouting up like mushrooms. How many is it now five or six? I'm finding the competition damaging' he said with a laugh. 'There are people who ought to know better and who could afford to pay better who are eating at Coggins.'

Henry felt no need to defend his enterprise and was not going to reveal how profitable he was finding it. He did ask Hubert, though, to let him know of any Piggery that was looking for investment or even a sale. Hubert was dismissive. Pig breeders, in his experience were less intelligent than their stock and were likely to go broke before realising it had happened.

This was a worry to Henry's plans, which depended on assured supplies of pig pieces. Hubert had been jesting him but if conventional butchers were to influence the abattoirs not to provide Coggins with pig parts the business would collapse overnight. The abattoir owners themselves might decide to charge for the cartloads and reduce profits.

A certain level of charges on shops would no longer be viable concerns. The position was precarious and called for immediate attention.

He asked Hubert, 'If I was to consider pig breeding who should I seek advice from?' 'From a head doctor I'd say if the only bits you want are the cut offs. You'd never recover your money. Breeding is not the only problem, it's the selling the best cuts from a good breed sow by retail, or better by wholesale, that's the problem.'

Henry persisted, 'But you slaughter pigs, some for the breeder and some you buy for the cuts you sell in your shops and sell to other shops. Would I not have a market with you?' 'Son you are the husband of my daughter, the father of my grandson and I am as much for nepotism as the next man, but butchering in Bradford is a village in which there is gossip and there are no secrets. If your meat was not of the standard I buy or if I paid more for it than its worth then the name Holmes Butchers, Purveyor of High Quality Meats would be besmirched, nay ruined. Go into pig breeding if you wish but I can offer no promises, no favours.'

'But you can offer advice'

'And my advice is forget the idea. Pigs aren't my strong point, that's beasts, but having been in the trade all my life I can recognise six breeds of pig and there must be three times that many. Each has its own qualities. They have diseases that can wipe them out. There are boars that a lion tamer couldn't handle. A snout is a snout and a trotter a trotter. Legs and locks, shoulders and ribs are a far different thing and best left to them as understand them.'

'One question then. Who knows the pig rearing business from tail to ear?'

'You are set on this Henry and I worry for you. One disease on the farm and all stock have to be destroyed. It cannot be sold even as a Coggins. Disease causes ruination. The queues of paupers outside your shops will, I wager, have former pig farmers among their numbers. I would not wish to see you in such a queue.

'A name please, Mr Holmes. To whom should I speak.'

'Abe Grundy at Fagley produces the best pork. There is nothing about the business he does not know. Respected throughout pig dom. But Henry, I want nothing to do with this and urge you to do likewise.'

The road to Fagley passed Undercliffe Cemetery with its magnificent monuments to the wealthy dead of the town on its upper side and it's euphemistically called company graves on its lower reaches. These were mass graves into which thirty or more paupers' bodies would be piled one on the other. A descent through a wooded area and Henry's carriage halted in a clearing across which the mudded pink bodies of sows and piglets could be seen across acres of trampled fields. A long trudge, ankle deep through slurry failed to locate Abe Grundy but a hand reminiscent of Ninepunce, directed him back to his carriage and the Bluebell Inn where he found the pig breeder holding court at the bar.

Standing beside him, Henry was struck by the resemblance to his father. Grundy was a tall broad man who wore a long heavy overcoat although his had the smell of pig about it not sheep. His blunt speech and his mannerisms were similar and while his father would not have been in a public house at lunchtime both were respected as experts in their field.

Henry offered this big, gruff man a drink and introduced himself as a hill sheep farmer from the Heights and the son of one before him. He asked, politely, if he was Abe

Grundy of whom he had heard but could not disguise the softening he had brought to his accent or the breath to his vocabulary. Grundy gave a nod and Henry went on to say that he was minded to look into Pig Rearing and wondered how long it would take to learn the skill of which he, Mr Grundy, was the authority. Grundy asked his age and Henry, saying twenty six lied. 'Then you're too old to start and won't learn it all before you die,' said Grundy to laughter around the packed bar.

'What do you get if a cat is crossed with a monkey?' asked the pig breeder.

'I don't know.'

'Well you would if the wrong boar got in with the wrong sow.' This time the laughter was raucous.

Grundy, now serious, 'You don't have the look and the manners of a sheep farmer but I'll take you at your word. Have you ever had a sheep take a bite the size of an apple out of your leg or a hand trampled to death by a ram? Have you had a flock destroyed by a worm no bigger than a maggot? If not, and I think not, then your sheep farming is no preparation for pig breeding.'

More unkindly but no less accurately Abe Grundy had confirmed Hubert's warning and Henry returned to Bradford persuaded that pig breeding might prove his ruin. Yet, failing to secure supplies for his Coggins shops could also prove ruinous. Having misrepresented himself to Abe Grundy his alternative plan of buying pig parts from breeders was also jeopardised.

Henry fretted on the problem for weeks but still opened three more Coggins. On a fine warm Sunday afternoon he and Adeline took Giles to promenade in the park and while still pondering the problem, still expecting his supplies to be curtailed, a thought occurred to him. The retailers might wish, eventually would wish, to put Coggins out of business. The slaughterhouse owners would support him. However, the breeders had no interest in the matter but an interest could be created to his advantage.

Within a week a scheme had been formed, so had a company, Balls Pig Waste. A gross of sacks were ordered, boldly printed with the name Ball's. George was enthusiastic and set about identifying the pig breeders in and about the town, all twenty two of them. He visited each and offered them one shilling a sack for all pig parts that they did not require returning from the slaughterhouse, or did not sell through the slaughterhouse to wholesalers or to retailers. In return all they needed to do was to instruct their slaughterhouse proprietor to place the unwanted pieces in the sacks marked Ball's with which they would be provided and those sacks would be collected and carted away at no cost to the abattoir. George would arrange the collection of the heads, feet, lungs, organs and intestines.

Fifteen breeders agreed, within a month the other seven, seeing the scheme operating well, contacted George, to join in. This produced more product than eight shops could process and there were costs for incinerating the surplus but this kept Coggins, as they were now well known, off the market and out of the hands of the competitors.

Henry had constructed a business pyramid. He owned ninety percent of Ball's, which sold to Coggins of which Henry owned eighty percent. George was well paid from his ten percent of Ball's and his wages from Crawshaw's. Coggins was becoming wealthy from his twenty percent share of seven shops and sixty percent of one and a market stall. The poorest earners of the empire were Peppers School, followed by Crawshaw's Business Accounts, followed by Westhead Mills and Black Dyke Hole Farm.

The sale of liver and kidney improved sales and the customer numbers at Coggins, to the irritation of retail butchers but the greatest profit was realised when Henry took a fifty percent share in a family baker in White Abbey, expanded production and supplied all Coggins shops with loaves at cost plus ten percent. Fat drippings spread on good bread was a staple of the slums and sustained impoverished families at a price most could afford. Twelve shops served the town and another four on the outskirts in Thornbury, Laisterdyke, Tyersal and Shelf made up the group.

George could manage the business accounts of the whole group of shops, the bakery and Ball's Pig Waste. Henry, more particular about the business accounts he handled restricted himself to favoured clients, had more time on his hands. He had learned from Charles and spent that time well in visiting the shops and getting to know the managers and the cooks and the bakers, visiting the breeders and the slaughterhouses to ensure they were happy with arrangements and treating Norman Coggins as a valued partner, which he was. He charmed Tessa Coggins who, needlessly, still rose at five o'clock six days a week and he met George's mother who was now reaping the rewards of her son's success but was deferential to the point of embarrassment.

Chapter 11

By the time of Giles third birthday Henry was, by most measures, a wealthy man. He had appointed an assistant to prepare accounts for clients. Walter Boothman was a serious young man, not a graduate of the Academy but well educated, trained by George Ball and showing promise. George was now general manager of the Crawshaw, Coggins, Ball enterprise, and responsible for those parts of the operation that were not the province of Norman Coggins and he was fastidious in the compilation of the group's accounts.

Henry needed to be in his office for only three or four days a week but was as strict with his own attendance and punctuality as he was with that of any other. A failure to open by one shop manager had led to instant dismissal by Norman Coggins. Henry had praised his decisive action and word had spread among the other managers within the day.

Throughout the following year all the sources of Henry's income continued to prosper. Westhead Mills offered Henry two hundred pounds for the proportion of the interest he had retained in his father's farm. This was more than double the value of the portion at the time of sale but Henry declined. He was in the business of acquisitions and was becoming increasingly frustrated that the accounts being prepared by George and Walter never presented the opportunities that Henry had envisaged they would. To add to his annoyance he felt an irrational jealousy that the young men rarely needed his advice and were nurturing his business – in fact, raising his child, his creation, as if it were there own. He craved a new opportunity, a fresh challenge and now accepted that he would not find it in the accounts of carpenters, publicans or pawnbrokers.

A much more promising seam would, he believed, be found in the company of the heads of larger companies. He had twice attended functions at the Bradford Club as a guest of Charles Ambrose and now applied for membership. Proposed by Charles and seconded by Bullivant Theakstone his acceptance was assured. The club comprised meeting and reading rooms, dining rooms, a bar and accommodation for gentlemen conducting business in town. A regular attender, Henry became known to a growing circle of influential figures. The youngest of their number Henry conducted himself politely but not obsequiously with these be-whiskered, rough mannered, confident, wealthy men and they accepted him. He had substantial income that would be better employed invested rather than deposited and even the one significant purchase to make would not cause too much a depletion of his savings.

Jane visited most afternoons to spend time with Adeline and Giles and was occasionally joined by Hubert but the two would normally leave before Henry arrived home. Henry returned early on an afternoon on which he knew Hubert would be visiting. There was a matter he wished to discuss with Hubert and preferred to raise it in an informal way rather than elevate it to a topic of importance.

'Mr Holmes, without your generosity I would not have been able to provide Adeline with a home such as this. It is something of which I am ever conscious as, too, I am that it remains your property. In the five years of our marriage I have had some success in my business dealings and I am now in a position to purchase this house if you are agreeable to its sale.'

Hubert placed an arm around his son-in-laws' shoulders. 'And if I was to agree, then what would I do with the proceeds of the sale? You are master of investments while I am adverse to risk, so I should deposit the money in my bank account where it would lie dormant. It gives me pleasure to see you and your family in this house and it will continue to give me pleasure watching you employ the money you would pay me. A further sum and deposit would give me no pleasure at all and if a man's wealth is not intended to provide him with pleasure then what was the point of amassing it?'

'So this is not something on which you are prepared to think further.'

'Only in one respect. I am releasing you from your obligation to revert this property to me when the sad day we both know will one day come. I know you will not accept this house as a gift and I respect you for that so I would ask you to agree to this. Hold this property in trust for Giles until he should reach the age of twenty one. If you should choose to dispose of it in the interim, to agree to hold the value for him.'

It was only Hubert's good manners that caused him to refer to Henry's agreement. Both men knew that the arrangement could be included in Hubert's will and enforced by his nominated trustees.

Henry sat beside Adeline a week later, staring into the flames of their fire and thinking of how he had been unable to spend the money he had earmarked to establish a pig farm and how he achieved the same results for a pittance. Now he could not spend money set aside to buy this house but it could be his to use for another seventeen years. As a result of all this his deposits were awash but the money was idle and was not providing the pleasure of which Hubert had spoken.

Although his body was in the chair, although his hand was holding Adeline's, his mind was in the bar of the Bradford Club. He was making investments, increasing his portfolio, working his money as hard as he had worked himself and would continue to work himself. If only he had an outlet for the unused energy that was the cause of his discomfort.

He was roused from his reverie by Adeline's soft touch on his cheek. Her voice had weariness about it. 'Henry, I am increasingly weighed down by a tiredness that I cannot combat. My debility increases, the exhaustion is unremitting and resisting them drains what little strength I have left to me. I have never fully understood the cause of my weakness but I had thought it an unchanging condition. In recent weeks I have come to realise that my health that has been protected, at first by my parents and now in my marriage by your love for me, cannot be improved. And now, rapidly and frighteningly, it is deteriorating.'

Henry wanted to offer words of reassurance but, knowing more of the serious nature of her condition than she did herself, could not lie to her. He suggested requesting Doctor Schroeder's attendance.

'Doctor Schroeder visited this morning. There are no more potions to be taken and he says I must now have total rest and should remain, at all times, in my bed. It distresses me that you, the one I love with my whole being, should at such a young age be married to an invalid and that Giles, our beautiful son, should have a mother who cannot lift him, carry him, even hold and cuddle him.'

As Adeline wept silently, Henry took her handkerchief and caught each tear that fell. His wealth, he knew could not restore his wife's health and it could not ease the ache in his heart.

'I am resigned that I cannot survive this and do not expect to see Giles grow beyond his childhood. And I want you to know that it is my wish that you should marry again and I am comforted by the certainty that your choice of a wife will be a woman with love enough for both you and our son.'

Henry placed a finger to Adeline's lips. He could listen to no more of this and assisted her from her chair and to her bed. Sitting in a chair he saw that she was soon asleep and, being unable to sleep himself, he gazed at the golden tresses on her pillow and listened to her breathing. When morning came, Henry still in the chair awoke. Adeline did not.

The service was held at St. Paul's church where Henry and Adeline had married over five years before. It was well attended by friends and associates of the Holmes family, other than Aunt Doreen who had been left immobile by a stroke. Norman and Tessa Coggins attended, as did George Ball and his mother, Walter Boothman, and Nathan Stein escorting Marianne. Charles was absent in Huntingdon. Giles remained at home with his nurse but Mollie Tutt was there and inconsolable.

Burial arrangements were agreed between Jane and Henry. Hubert had been unable to take any part so desolate were his spirits. Adeline was a Crawshaw but, and intending no disrespect to his parents, Henry thought only briefly before dismissing the thought of the family grave at Queensbury. Those cold, inhospitable hills were no fit resting place for the fragile beauty that had been his wife. She would be interred at Undercliffe Cemetery with a fitting monument among those of the moneyed families of the town.

The monument, to be of white marble, would be a column upon which was mounted a plaque held by two angels and depicted the Madonna and child, had barely been commissioned before an addition had to be made to the inscription.' And of Hubert Selwyn Holmes, a dearly loved husband and father, May they rest in peace.'

Hubert had been found dead on the chaise longue in his office. Adeline had inherited her heart condition from her father. His being less severe but there was a weakness that could not withstand the grief at his loss of his adored daughter.

Henry visited Jane each evening before returning home. These visits became an ordeal for not only was his grief eating at his mind and spirit but Jane detained him with tales of Adeline's childhood and Hubert's life as a young man. He understood that the telling of these stories were cathartic for this doubly bereaved lady but evening after evening she would repeat the same ones, word for word, as though it was their first time of telling. Henry was concerned for her sanity and no less for his own if he had to endure many more such evenings. The one benefit he gained from the visits is that he arrived home after Giles had been put to bed. The boy's presence was a discomfort to him. The hair, the eyes, the skin – they were all Adeline's and he could not bear to look at his son.

Unless his attitude towards Giles changed he faced many years of unhappiness but, mercifully, the purgatory of his daily visits to Jane would soon end. It was six weeks after Hubert's death that her evening monologue did not consist of Adeline's first piano lessons or Hubert's proposal on a pleasure boat at Keighley. That evening she was lucid.

Either the potion Doctor Schroeder had been providing had done its work or she had stopped taking it.

'Hubert's will has been read. Your house has been left to Giles, either the property or its value, once he reaches his majority. The remainder of his estate he leaves to me with a sum of two thousand pounds to Adeline unless she should pre-decease him, In which case the legacy would revert to Giles. The only property in trust then is your home and two thousand pounds; the trustees being his solicitor Mr Barrington Hill and yourself. I was visited by Mr Hill today. He explained that he had no locus, as he put it, in any other affairs of the estate but did express his concern that since Hubert involved himself clearly in every aspect of his businesses they were now rudderless. Managers were coping, but barely, and a prolonged period of neglect could damage the reputation and value of Holmes Butchers irreparably'

Henry fully understood the solicitor's concern and, had he not been so distracted by his own loss, should have been advising Jane similarly.

He interrupted, seeking to foreshorten what could be a long monologue. 'I shall assume that he recommends the appointment of a suitable person to head the various businesses. If so I shall endeavour to find such a person for you.'

'No Henry. I had hoped that you would offer to take control'

'But Mrs Holmes, Jane if I may, I know little of the scale of your business interests but what little I did gather from Mr Holmes suggests a broad swathe encompassing abattoirs, wholesale and retail premises and scores of employees. He operated on a scale to which I, inexperienced in butchery, am unused.'

'Would you mislead me Henry? You have as many shops as Hubert, if not more and also deal in meat.'

'I have investments in shops, from interests I earn my living. I have no responsibility for the employees or the conducting of business in the shops. I have others who do that work. My skill, such as it is, lies in valuing Businesses for sale or acquisitions and that skill is, without question, at your service. If you were to authorise me to have access to Mr Holmes's business accounts I could look into each business, treating each as a separate entity and provide you with a figure to achieve a sale.'

'Henry, I am attracted to selling off the businesses. I would rather see them under another name than see the name Holmes devalued by managers as Mr Hill fears. Also I know nothing of the business. Hubert would tell me this and tell me that and I feigned an interest that I never had. Sorry Hubert.' She said with her eyes raised. 'Frankly I want nothing to do with it and I shall not be here to deal with sales and the like. I am to retire to Dorset to care for my sister. I wish to transfer all Hubert's business interests to you to either operate or sell. Mr Hill advises me that, unlike the house and the two thousand pounds left to Giles, I cannot stipulate that the businesses or their value will be held for the benefit of Giles. Still, I believe that in all conscience that is what you will do. My understanding is that I transfer all interests to you to do with as you will or I do not. I choose to do so.'

'You would need a living or a substantial settlement from the proceeds '

'I need neither. Hubert has deposits that will keep me in comfort for far more years than are left to me. Hubert used to say that you could work a pound harder than a carter worked his horse and it would be worth more than a pound when you had done with it. Work Hubert's pounds Henry, enjoy your wealth, make Giles wealthy and let him know that you share the credit with his grandfather.'

A meeting took place two weeks later at the offices of Barrington Hill. Jane was present and anxious that matters be concluded before she travelled to Dorset the following week. Also present were Henry, his solicitor Alistair Wild and the Holmes's accountant with two assistants to carry the ledgers and documents containing details of all Hubert's holdings. Documents were signed and exchanged.

Henry informed George that he would be working at his home for a few days then arranged for delivery of the Holmes's accounts there. He had assumed Hubert to be wealthy but was amazed at the scale of the wealth that even a perfunctory leafing through the accounts revealed. That wealth was now his but as he gazed through the window of his study he thought of Hubert's words in this very house only a few weeks before. 'If a man's wealth is not to provide him with pleasure what is the point of amassing it.' He missed Adeline. His misery was unendurable. What pleasure would he ever find in life again?

In that frame of mind, in deepening melancholy, he heard a discordant hammering on the keys of the piano in the adjoining room. His anger rose and he bellowed. 'Mrs Tutt.'

She came at once and Henry demanded, 'Where is the nurse.'

'Out visiting, Mr Crawshaw.'

'Not looking after the boy?'

'I am Sir,'

'Well get him out of there and when the nurse returns pay her off.'

It was irrational, he knew it but he was controlled by a temper that he could not contain. 'Without his mother's influence he will adopt an accent as offensive to the ears of an educated person as your own Mrs Tutt.'

The housekeeper, twice his age, was offended but allowed for his grief he felt and which she shared.

'And may I know of your intentions of Giles raising. Mr Crawshaw.'

'You may when I wish to share them with you. For now get him off that piano and out of my hearing.'

Henry rested his head on his desk and sobbed until he ached. He had thought he could never suffer so much as he had done when he had cried over his mother's body. This was equally painful. And from where did that pain come? – From love and loss. Should love call upon him again he would recognise it for the deceiver it was and close the door to it.

Part 2

Chapter 12

There were many daily callers to the kitchen doors of the grand houses on the avenues to the east of York. Butchers, Fishmongers, bakers and dairymen delivered orders. Hawkers and peddlers made speculative calls. Those bringing ribbons bows and buttons were particularly welcomed by domestic staff but one regular visitor was made more welcome than any other.

Fredo was a woodcutter who sold kindling at two-pence a bundle. Not only were his wares important to servants who might have ten or more fires to set and tend but Fredo would have been equally popular had he come empty handed. With his dark gypsy looks, his curly locks from which a gold ear-ring shone and his soft Italian accent he brought glamour to the staff in the kitchens he visited. He flirted and flattered, charmed and captivated. A whisper in a young servant girl's ear could prompt blushes, giggles and desires that lingered long after Fredo and his handcart had gone.

His days were well ordered. Mornings were spent cutting kindling; afternoons spent delivering his bundles and teasing servants, evenings spent in the tap-room of the Castle Tavern, where he was rarely short of female company. Fredo was equally popular with the men in the bar, rough rabble who worked the river who enjoyed his relaxed humour, admired the obvious effortless attraction he had for the girls and marvelled at his capacity for ale and rum that none could match. Firewood Fred, as he was called in the kitchens and the Tavern, was well received wherever he went.

When Fredo changed his routine, delivering both in the morning and the afternoon and never being seen in the Castle Tavern there was much speculation and gossip. He was known by some to live in a shelter in the forest south of the city, but nobody knew quite where. Some said he had a young girl, perhaps fifteen or sixteen years old, living in his shelter and she was wood-cutting while he was delivering. Others said they had seen them together in the city and that they had a young child with them.

Fredo's routine changed once more. Delivering only in the afternoon he had a young child seated on the wood pile in his handcart. At every kitchen door he was asked about this and he explained that he had provided shelter for the child and the girl who was now unwell so he was looking after the child. He would add nothing to this. More than a few servant girls had nurtured dreams of Fredo in a colourful caravan drawing up one day and of him taking them on travels and adventures around the country. Those dreams were now dashed.

Through a dark and bitterly chill winter the child appeared daily on the handcart. Dirty and poorly clad for that weather, she drew the sympathy of servants who offered some items of clothing for which Fredo was grateful. By the time spring made its late appearance Fredo's visits to the avenues, at first haphazard then stopped. No kindling, no handcart, no poorly dressed, dirty child and no firewood Fred.

The tales of Fredo having hitched his caravan and having set off with the girl and her child brought a little glamour and romance into some otherwise colourless lives. Within a few days, though, the facts became known and they were far less comedy than the fantasy.

Four local men had set out at daybreak carrying nets, snares and spades, intending to set animal traps in the forest. Startled by a rustling in the undergrowth they peered into the poor light but couldn't identify the cause. The 'animal', less than two feet long and running on hind legs was squealing like a snared rabbit. The four men fanned out and quickly surrounded their quarry.

The infant girl, still squealing, was dressed only in a knee length grubby shift. It was immediately agreed that there would be no trapping today. There was nobody in the immediate area to whom the child might belong so she would have to be taken to the authorities, but there would have to be a believable story for them being in the forest at that hour. Trespassing in possession of equipment for illegally pursuing game carried very severe penalties.

The other three were all agreed that Arthur Spink was the more articulate and with fewer criminal convictions so he should take the girl to the authorities and tell them he found her while out for a morning walk. The actual summary was, 'tha can talk a bit and tha's not too well known by t' magistrates. So tell 'em you were having a walk to get healthy so as you could get a job, you see. We'll be getting off,'

What a pair they presented at the Watchman's office in the city. Spink, a more notorious n'er do well than his friends gave him credit for, and the child, no longer squealing but rigid and terrified. The story of the morning walk was not believed but it was unimportant when set against the welfare of the child and the discovery of the whereabouts of a parent. The Assistant Watchman, a former military man and a practical organiser, quickly arranged for a team to search the forest where the child was found and he co-opted Spink to direct them to the spot.

The trek to the forest took far longer than the search on arrival. Within minutes they had found the shelter, from which it was believed the child had come. It was as unprepossessing as it appeared, it was in fact quite a sturdy structure providing a dry and functional hide. When the Assistant Watchman looked inside nothing in his military career, seeing limbs, torn off by cannon balls, intestines spilled by bayonets, had caused the degree of revulsion he experienced at the sight and the stench that met him.

Closest to the entrance was a girl who he thought to be about fifteen years old or younger. She was naked from the waist down and was dead. Also, undoubtedly dead, was the part born body she had been delivering. The baby had managed to introduce one leg to the world and there it hung between its mother's legs. The blood and tissue gathered there was covered in flies and all manner of crawling insects. Valance had to step over the sad and sickening tableau to view the third body. It was that of a swarthy man, in his early thirties, he thought, who wore a gold ring in his left ear. He was fully dressed and his left hand was swathed in rags that were blood sodden. These too had attracted armies of creatures feasting on the gore. The contortions of his once handsome features suggested a most painful death.

Valance stopped outside and addressed his small band 'one at a time. Look in and see if you can recognise the man or girl in there, but cover your mouth and nose' Then, 'Wait'. He returned inside and covered the girl's lower half with some scraps of clothing. Arthur Spink was the second in and the first to make an identification. 'The man is Firewood Fred, drinks in the Castle Tavern'. Two others agreed but none could identify the girl.

The bodies were removed to the City mortuary where examinations were conducted. Meanwhile the infant girl found in the forest was given temporary care while her malnutrition and infestations were attended to.

The medical examiner's reports concluded that the girl had died giving birth to a baby whose position was not properly presented for a birth without professional attendance. The cause of her death was uncontrolled haemorrhaging and the baby's was asphyxiation. A detailed and wide reaching investigation failed to identify the girl and the mystery of the matter was deepened by the medical examiner's opinion that the girl had not previously given birth. The foundling was connected to the shelter by the many servants who had seen her with Fredo. To whom she was related, the man, the girl or neither, could not be resolved.

The examination of Fredo's body revealed that he had amputated the thumb of his left hand and had partially severed the first finger. The probable course was a slip of a chopper while splitting kindle. The cause of death was recorded as poisoning of the blood. The girl and her baby had predeceased the man but at that time suffering from the indescribably painful and totally debilitating septicaemia, he could be of no use to them at all.

Valance reflected that evening while staring into the fire in the Watchman's office. The scene in the shelter must have been one of horror. The girl (who was she?) frightened, giving birth, in difficulties, in awful pain. Perhaps screaming but there was nobody in the forest to hear. Firewood Fred in so much pain he may well have been delirious. That would have been a release from his inability to assist the young girl, bleeding beside him. He would have been impotent and in despair while dying in agony as the poison in his blood was pumped around his organs. And the child. What a scene to witness. Terrified, cold, hungry and understanding nothing of the cries of the adults who were all she had in life.

There had been no food or drink in the shelter and the post-mortem examinations indicated that the three had died two days before the child was found. How long had they been incapable before their deaths? If God was merciful the child would have no memory of any of this as she grew older and she should now be raised in warmth, comfort, and love. He would do what he could to bring that about and tomorrow he would call on the Bishop's Secretary. Valance knew where the child would receive the affection and care she now needed and he knew those who could provide it.

Chapter 13

The church of the Blessed Virgin stood next to the school of the same name to the east of Harrogate. Between the two buildings was a covered passage, wide enough to take a coach and pair. The passageway opened onto a long driveway at the head of which was an imposing manor house. This was Bethlehem, home to the Sisters of Compassion and to sixteen girls aged between three years and sixteen years of age.

The Mother Superior, Sister Benedicta, had been visited by the Parish Priest, Father Gerard Conlan, to convey the wishes of the Bishop's Secretary, Monsignor Tetti, that Bethlehem accommodate a foundling in dire need. There were four dormitories in the home, each sleeping four children. These were called after the Evangelists with the youngest children sleeping together in Matthew and then transferring as vacancies arose to Mark, Luke and John. Vacancies arose as girls were placed in domestic service with 'good Catholic Families' at the age of fourteen or over according to their development and maturity. At that time, though, there wasn't a vacancy. So it would have remained had the request not come directly from Monsignor Tetti.

Arrangements were made for a fifth bed to be placed in John, which meant 'a promotion' and much excitement for three girls and a crush for four. There was now a bed to be had in Matthew, the child would be delivered to Father Conlan that evening and he would bring her to Bethlehem.

As was the custom the eight resident nuns and their housekeeper, Mrs Mullins, gathered in the hall to greet their new guest. Sister Benedicta opened the door to Father Conlan, a small man who looked to be about seventy years old, and it seemed had always looked about that age. Behind him hid a blonde haired, fair skinned child with wide and frightened blue eyes. Peeping around his legs she saw this assembly of strangely dressed women and screamed. She turned to run, fell over the hop step and skinned both her knees. Sister Teresa, the youngest of the nuns, ran forward picked up the child and was thanked by a piercing scream, a rigid body and a beating on her chest by two tiny fists. Quickly she put the child down again but blocked her escape through the door. Seeing Mrs Mullins, the child ran to her and hid behind her huge skirts.

While Mrs Mullins took her little charge to the kitchen and fed her with milk and biscuits, Father Conlan went with Sister Benedict to her office. 'Monsignor Tetti is aware of the special arrangements you have had to make, Sister, and he is, er, appreciative. The child's name is Firewood Her christian name is not known, she may not even have been baptised and this must be arranged at once. For now though I need to complete some records for the Bishop's office, so I shall need to have a christian name'.

The Mother Superior decided she should consult with her Sisters. The priest agreed and Sister Benedicta left. At this Mrs Mullins returned with a bottle of whisky in one hand, a tumbler in the other and a child behind her with its arms wrapped around her knees.

Having shared a short prayer to ask for the Lord's blessing on their deliberations, Sister Benedicta stated that Sister Teresa should have principal responsibility for their guest until she was settled. That being the case, Sister

Teresa should propose an appropriate name. Enthused by this the young nun immediately suggested the name of the Virgin's cousin, who the Virgin had visited during her confinement and was the mother of John the Baptist. The name she proposed was Elizabeth and the birthday should be that Saint's day, 5th of November.

Unusually, indeed almost uniquely, the suggestion gained unanimous assent. Despite the prayer and the charity that pervaded the home it was, after all, an all female household with all the tensions and competitiveness that such arrangements ferment. Yet, this time, Elizabeth it would be. The Sisters were agreed and Sister Benedicta returned to her office to inform Father Conlan.

The priest was most surprised, and no less disappointed, that agreement had been reached so quickly. He had only had one tumbler of whisky rather than the two or three his visits normally produced.

'Mother Superior, it strikes me as, er possibly, a most suitable choice. To confirm this I believe that you and the Sisters should retire to your chapel: A decade of the Rosary. The second joyful mystery, the Visitation of the Virgin. Meditate upon it, seek guidance and if that should remain your choice I should be pleased to complete the Bishop's record accordingly.'

Sister Benedicta led her Sisters to the chapel. Mrs Mullins returned to the office with the whisky bottle and with a blonde haired child peeping from behind her legs.

Father Conlan relaxed even at the pace at which nuns could sprint through their Rosary he should be able to enjoy a pleasant ten minutes. The Sisters managed it in seven minutes and they accompanied their Mother Superior when she returned. She felt that the good Father would be less likely to employ further delaying tactics, and drinking more whisky if met by a united front. Elizabeth it should be.

With a sigh he rose to leave, when Sister Teresa knelt before him. 'Father would you hear my confession. Forgive me because I have sinned. It is four days since my last confession. I am guilty of the sin of pride. I was proud. I was proud to be appointed to care for Elizabeth and to be chosen to propose her name.' The priest stood before her. His right hand was on the young nun's head, his left, holding the tumbler, was behind his back. Another was added to this by Mrs Mullins who stood behind him. Four legs protruded behind her skirts. Two were large, heavy, and wore thick wrinkled stockings. Two were short thin and pink.

'Absolutely '

'Three Hail Marys' said Father Conlan. He drained his glass, collected his hat, blessed the Sisters and bid them goodnight. Turning to Sister Benedicta he said

'Baptism after Mass tomorrow morning then please attend to the civil registration formalities.'

That first night Elizabeth slept in Matthew. Sister Teresa had permission to remove the cowl that terrified the child and she slept in a chair at the side of Elizabeth's bed so too did Elizabeth, sleeping in the arms of Sister Teresa.

Whether it had been a misunderstanding of Father Conlan's brogue, a clerical error by the civil registrar or an act of charity by the nuns may never be known, but Elizabeth Firewood was registered as Elizabeth Fairwood. Her birthday was to be November 5th and it was decided she would be three years old on that next birthday.

Within days, not weeks, she was no longer clinging to Mrs Mullins and Sister Teresa. Now clean, well clothed and amply fed she was soon playing and laughing with the little friends in Matthew and she was a frequent, popular visitor to the older girls in John in the evening. The joyful beautiful girl was soon unrecognisable as the terrified waif she had been when she first arrived at Bethlehem.

The nuns were not dour ascetics spending hours in prayer and meditation. In addition to the care of the children in their charge, each had duties to perform. Some of these involved teaching in the school and in the home. Arithmetic, reading, writing, music, literature, art, needlework, cookery and, of course religious instruction. Bethlehem was a place of warmth light and laughter.

On taking their final vows the nuns adopted new names and these rarely reflected the personality of the person they were to become. For example, Sister Piety was not the most dedicated to her devotions. Often she would be seen with a spanner or an oil can doing maintenance work about the home. By far the best pianist and leader of a hearty song was Sister Gethsemane.

This was the home, the happy safe haven, in which Elizabeth was to be raised. It is doubtful that she would for long, have any conscious recollection of her former life. There must, though, have been some residual memories. These manifested themselves when the woodman called. He had a large sided cart towed by a sturdy grey mare. A wistful look crept over the little girl's face when he arrived and twice she had been returned from the wood pile on the cart onto which she had clambered. Her fascination at watching Sister Piety split logs was, the Sisters thought one of Elizabeth's little peculiarities.

At Bethlehem, children who did not have a mother had nine; who did not have a friend, had at least fifteen. Celebrations abounded. Sixteen Childrens' birthdays, eight Sisters' birthdays. (Celebrated on the day they had taken their final vows and adopted their new name) and, of course, Mrs Mullins. Add to those the feast days Christmas, Easter, Holy Days and Saints' days, rarely a week passed, to plan, to mark, to celebrate. It was not an austere regime nor was it indulgent. The emphasis was on moral development, education, and nurturing the individual talents of each girl.

As she grew, Elizabeth had a curiosity that drove her to answer her own questions, delving into the volumes in the vast library bequeathed to the home with the house. With a bright inquiring mind, the encouraging environment in which she was being raised, and ready access to information she was achieving a level of education that set her apart from young girls of her time and her background.

It was a convention at Bethlehem that the children and girls would receive a personal gift on their birthday and at Christmas, to recognise the day as the birthday of the Saviour; the gift would have religious significance. By the age of ten, Elizabeth's birthday gifts, which had been story books and colouring boxes, were now linen, a frame, needles and threads with which to practice embroidery. It was a skill she was to hone to perfection through her young teens. Her Christmas gifts had been books of bible stories, rosary beads, simple prayer books then her favourite, the Roman Missal in English and Latin with a mass for every day of the week.

The journal she received for her eleventh birthday thrilled her. She committed to it her experiences, her thoughts, her hopes and her dreams. Her entries included some of the unhappiness that life brings. The loss of good friends who had to leave John to go into service and the death of Sister Concepta whose arthritis had at first prevented her kneeling at morning mass had eventually prevented her from leaving her room.

Each loss provided a gain, a vacancy in John, three 'promotions' and a new child in Matthew. Sister Concepta was replaced some weeks later by Sister Michael who soon played her full part in the happy atmosphere of Bethlehem Sister Benedicta would call for a full assembly Nuns and girls whenever a loss occurred. She would speak of death and rebirth and of the miracle of the Saviour and his triumph on rising on the third day. The name of Jesus was rarely used as it had to be accompanied by a bowing of the head and a striking of the breast. The use of the Saviour avoided this exertion.

In school Religious Education was normally provided by Sister Louis but, with increasing frequency she enlisted the assistance of Father Conlan to answer the more difficult questions of the thirteen years old Elizabeth.

Sister Louis would start with confidence but rarely did finish in that comfortable state.

'The Jews were bad people who murdered our Saviour'.

Elizabeth, hand raised, 'All of them Sister?'

'And the Romans were bad people who could have stopped it and didn't'

Elizabeth again, 'All of them Sister?'

'And the Christians were good people'.

Again Elizabeth ' All of them Sister?'

When Elizabeth reached full flow she could have tested the theology of a cardinal, 'was Judas a Jew or a Christian? Was St Peter a good man when he cut off the guard's ear? Was the Virgin Mary more interested in the gold the wise men brought than finding somewhere better than a stable to keep a baby in? If Jesus (head bowed, breast beaten) could raise Lazarus from the dead why couldn't he put his cousin John the Baptist's head back on? When...'

Father Conlan, now looking old and exhausted, would intervene when Sister Louis had floundered for long enough. 'It is not for us to know the ways of God whose infinite wisdom and mercy transcends our understanding.' This satisfied all difficult questions-but not Elizabeth's.

'But Father, we can't do God's will if it transcends our understanding. Can we?' These lessons usually ended earlier than planned.

Girls normally progressed to John at thirteen years of age. Elizabeth was fifteen before there was a vacancy in the senior dormitory for her. It was to be a year like no other and more significant changes in her life. Although she had enjoyed the company of Catherine Allen who was a year older they had never before shared a room. Quickly they became close, sharing thoughts and confidences. Catherine was a pretty, freckled faced girl with a well-developed body who looked for fun in every situation. Her humour was infectious and occasionally irreverent. Elizabeth found her exciting and revelled in their friendship.

Catherine was a mimic whose impersonations of Sister Benedicta and Sister Louis had her three room-mates aching with laughter. Also, and from where she gained it Elizabeth could not guess, she claimed to know about the mechanics of sex between men and women, physical differences, pro-creation and, to Elizabeth's shock and amazement, pleasure to be had when alone.

The influence of Catherine and the thoughts and feelings their whispered conversations prompted, caused her to be less frank with her journal entries than she had previously been. But there was another event that year that was to bring her emotions to turmoil.

Father Conlan, now in his mid-eighties, had been becoming incapable of performing his duties. Bishop Shaw was advised that the creeping senility was a condition from which there would be no retreat. In short, the old priest would have to be given a dignified retirement and the parish would have a priest, or at least, a curate. It was decided that Father Conlan would retain the title of Parish Priest at the church he had served for forty years and that a curate would be appointed as a matter of urgency.

The ideal situation would have been to appoint an experienced priest or a long serving curate. The parish was established, the church and the school had no debts, so there was no need for a dynamic young priest or a proven fund-raiser. The Bishop's decision was too influenced by Father Conlan's feelings and too rushed. When the old priest broke into a popular music hall song during mass the following week urgency gave way to panic measures.

Dominic Moran was the fourth son of a Northumberland land owner. The eldest was the manager of the estate; the second son was established in publishing, the third was a career Military officer. Any settlement for Dominic on his father's death would not provide a living. His choice of the church, a vocation he claimed, was a surprise to a family, albeit Catholic, that had no history of providing sons for the priesthood. There were doubts in the seminary as to his suitability but no incident or evidence, which would cause his dismissal.

Dominic himself harboured doubts about his vocation but after three years of Theology College and four years of training, he was looked to be seen to fail in the eyes of his brothers. In the month prior to his ordination he hoped that the responsibility for his failure could be had elsewhere so he sent a brief letter to the Vatican. It read 'Non Sum Dynus' (I am not worthy)'.

The reply came even briefer. 'Iomus?' (we know).

Like a bridegroom on his wedding eve, convinced he was making a mistake but who found it easier to let matters take their course than to face the unpleasantness of cancelling the ceremony, Dominic took Holy Orders.

The problem now passed to Brother Thomas, the Principal of the seminary. How was he to place the colourful and flamboyant Dominic Moran. He was clearly unsuitable for a high profile parish and lacked the discipline for an administrative position. The request from the Bishop of York for urgent assistance to an elderly priest in Harrogate gave him pause. Brother Thomas made enquiries. The parish of the Blessed Virgin had been served by a sole elderly priest. His age had meant there had been some neglect to the maintenance of the buildings, a decline in attendances, a reliance on the support of a few, elderly parishioners. Father Moran could be kept very busy and that could be beneficial to a somewhat lazy and self-regarding young priest. It would be a surprise to his contemporaries that he should be appointed to a parish church ahead of the more deserving (which all of them were) but – so be it the Bishop was informed but not forewarned.

Father Dominic Moran's arrival at the church of the Blessed Virgin that Saturday afternoon was the talk of the parish and beyond. There were those who swore that no Archbishop of York had ever made so Grand an entrance at the Minster. He had given notice that he would arrive at one o'clock but he had no intention of so doing. The congregation, some inside the church more outside, had been in place for over an hour waiting for a cab carrying a black-garbed figure. They were to be wrong on both counts.

It was almost two o'clock when a figure on a fine white stallion rode into the church grounds. wearing a full-length white riding coat and red riding boots. The young man was tall, broad shouldered and slim. His fair, almost yellow hair worn long over his ears and collar was uncovered and flowed behind him. Unmounting with a bound he bowed briefly to the welcoming party and, without a word he strode into the church. Pausing at a chair before the altar he shook the hand of Father Conlan whose eyes were glazed and whose head was lolling.

Genuflecting and crossing himself before the altar, he entered, discarded his riding coat with a flourish and revealed a russet jacket and tight cream coloured breeches that accentuated his muscled thighs. Standing in silence he awaited the entrance of those who had been gathered outside. A number of these needed convincing that they should no longer be waiting for the new priest. Father Moran had arrived.

Having led them in a short prayer and having begged their forgiveness for his late arrival, explaining that an incident on the road of which he could not speak now required his ministrations, he addressed his flock.

The front pews were occupied by the nuns, behind which were the senior lay members, the flower arrangers, those who filled the cleaning roster and those who organised the fund raising activities, the harvest festival and all those functions that make up the income of the parish that Sunday collections never could. The girls of Bethlehem, who each day occupied the second and third rows of the pews other than on Sundays, were relegated to the rear pews. The seating, normally half filled could not accommodate all those who poured in and the girls were obliged to give up their seats and stand.

The young priest stood dominant, legs apart and still carrying his riding crop. Catherine whispered in Elizabeth's ear. She replied, 'Catherine Allen, we are in church you are wicked.'

Then both shared a giggle. All were fixated on this man. His soft features, violet eyes, high cheekbones and lips of which a maiden would have been proud. In soft, deep, North Country tones he began. 'My dear children in Christ. I spent last night in prayer. Perhaps it was a selfish prayer. I prayed that I, might prove worthy to you' he paused. The unspoken response was 'you are, oh yes you are'.

He continued ' I am young and new to my calling and know that while I can never aspire to the love and esteem you have for Father Conlan, I could with grace, take his example of service and, if only in a minor way, seek to emulate it'.

There was spontaneous applause, lost on the old priest whose dementia was too far advanced but an encouragement to Father Moran to press on. 'I wish to be known not as Father Moran but as Father Dominic. I wish to be your brother and for you to be my brothers and sisters in the family of the Lord'. The older women wanted to mother him. The younger ones had feelings that were anything but sisterly. The nuns were unsure what to make of this unconventional priest. The older girls of Bethlehem were quite sure.

'There are a number of practical matters that are causing me some difficulty and although I have no right to ask anything for myself, if any amongst you could assist me in certain respects it would help, an as yet friendless soul travelling a rocky road in a strange town. This morning I had delivered some cases of wine as the bridegroom at Cana did. Unlike him I do not have the son of a guest to replenish supplies should these be insufficient. (This brought a laugh) if any would wish to meet me less formally, or any were able to offer certain assistances, I should be made to feel welcomed if you were to join me in the School Hall. Please kneel'.

Dominic blessed them with as much humility as his natural arrogance would allow; he walked the length of the aisle, out of the church across the yard and into the school hall. They would follow. He knew they would.

Sister Benedicta ushered the nuns and the girls back to Bethlehem, causing no little resentment in both groups. She introduced herself, invited Father Dominic to visit Bethlehem and left. A nun, a Mother Superior at that, drinking wine on a Saturday afternoon would be unseemly. Well, in public it would!

There was ample wine and no call for miracles. The parishioners were charmed, many in thrall to this man – no, to this representative of God on earth. A smile and a handshake here, a plea and a request there. Soon his immediate needs were satisfied. His trunks would be collected from the coaching inn in Leeds that very evening. His Stallion would be stabled nearby. The men's committee would arrange at once a room and an office in the presbytery to be refurbished to his requirements. The parish treasurers were confident that funds would provide for the purchase of new vestments, and if not arrangements could be made to make up any shortfall over time.

Dominic added two more items to his agenda from the information he had gained from his informal chats. These were soon resolved. A long standing vacancy for the priest's housekeeper, occasioned by the ill-health of Miss Ellison and filled by a list of volunteers would now be a full time appointment. Despite the dissent of some of the volunteers this was agreed. Finally, the seven o'clock morning mass should be later at eight o'clock so that any night vigils he would be holding with the sick and the dying need not be foreshortened.

By six o'clock that Saturday evening Dominic was in his room with two bottles of decent claret from his saddlebags. He was satisfied with his afternoon's work and had made satisfactory progress towards having his parish working to his likeing. One hour later, with only one half bottle of claret drunk, he was disturbed by the knocking of Sister Benedicta. Confessions were heard at seven o'clock on Saturday evenings. Borrowing a cassock, surplus and stole from the vestry he went through to the church. The numbers present would have graced a Sunday mass congregation. This would have to be dealt with in future but he could make a start right now. The seminarians were taught that there was a direct correlation between the frequency of attendance of confessions and the diversity of the penance prescribed. Tonight there would be some severe penance. And he would be in bed before some of those penitents had finished saying theirs.

There was disappointment in John that evening that the older girls had not been permitted to attend confession. Catherine was her mischievous self and said to Elizabeth, 'what would you do if father Dominic...'(and the rest was whispered in the younger girls' ear.) 'Catherine Allen! He is a priest'. Catherine was undeterred,' and what would you do if he ...' (another whisper). Elizabeth crossed herself three times, put her fingers in her ears and said 'not listening. Not listening.'

Evening confessions was a topic of conversation in the Mason's arms that night. It was after ten o'clock before Sam Long got his first tankard of ale. 'it'll be a while afore I go to yon fellow again. A decade of the rosary for what I did'. One of his group asked, 'and what was it you did,?' 'Never mind what I did, Jack Hargreaves, but I'll say this. I could have had all the nuns at the big house and not got that off Father Conlan'. This brought a laugh at the bar and he continued, 'As for you, Jack Hargreaves, if you confessed what you'd done you'd have been there 'til morning doing the Stations of the bloody Cross'.

The attendance at Sunday mass would have been exceptional had it been Christmas Day, and had Father Conlan kept records, the collection would have surprised any taken before. As he bade farewell to the last of his congregation, Dominic arranged with Sister Benedict to visit Bethlehem that afternoon. They sat in her office where, as was custom Mrs Mullins offered whisky-brandy was reserved for the annual visit of the Bishop. Dominic declined saying he restricted himself to the Saviour's drink of choice, wine. The Mother Superior acquainted him with the history of Bethlehem on how matters were ordered in the home.

Dominic suggested that it would be helpful if he was to meet individually with the Sisters and with the older girls and this was arranged for the following evening, after school and after the nuns duties of the day had been completed. At dinner that Monday evening Sister Benedicta was amused and dismayed by the attention that some of the Sisters had paid to their appearance. They had taken vows of chastity, poverty and obedience. This was known in all convents as 'no men, no money, and do what you're told!' As for the girls of John, she was alarmed. The efforts they had made with their hair and clothes were so obvious it was embarrassing.

Individual interviews were held in the library and the Mother Superior, a wry and experienced woman noted how long the young priest spent with each of her charges.

There was a pattern. The older nuns between five and seven minutes, the younger ones ten to fifteen, the four girls of John, fifteen each, other than Catherine Allen a full twenty. Mrs Mullins warranted just three.

He returned to Sister Bendicta's office, thankful for the arrangements and spoke at length of the importance he attached to personal acquaintances when providing moral guidance. The Moran magic was not having its effect with this wily old nun, he thought, but he pressed on 'Sister, Mother indeed, you are aware that Miss Ellison is incapacitated and the presbytery is in sole need of a housekeeper'. She did not respond, nor did her expression betray her thoughts. 'when suitable opportunities arise your older girls are placed in service which, for a young woman who has known no other home than this must be traumatic. While I fully understand that the time must come when these girls must leave the home, and while I cannot help them all, I could help one by offering the position of house-keeper.'

This time she did respond, affecting interest in the proposal. 'And have you Father, on so short an acquaintance, identified a person who you feel might be suitable.' Dominic gave the impression of deep thought and consideration. 'One of your young women, a Miss Allen if I remember correctly, appears suitably healthy and able and she has spoken of her fear of the fast approaching day when she must leave you and the wonderful care and guidance on which she has always depended'.

Sister Benedicta, still expressionless leaned forward. 'Placements in service are approved by the Bishop's Secretary on the basis of my recommendation. In this case I would feel it necessary to recommend that Catherine Allen needed the discipline of an ordered regime with a suitable family in order that she could gain experience of the world within the safety of a conventional household. However, Father if you would have me report to the Bishop's Secretary that it was your wish that she move from this house into yours I shall, of course, do so.'

Immediately, 'No, no. Please do not do that. The young woman's best interests are my sole concern'. After a long pause he resumed, 'in some parishes it is not uncommon for housekeeping duties to be undertaken by a Sister; might that be an arrangement with which you would agree.' Persistent fellow, she thought. As a girl her father had taught her fly-fishing and she would hook this handsome salmon.

'If such an arrangement might be agreeable with whom would the choice be, with you or with me?' quickly again, 'with you of course. With a proviso' she shot back, 'a proviso?' this would call for the full Moran charm.

'I am mindful of how Miss Ellison's health has deteriorated under long hours and onerous duties she undertook, uncomplainingly in the service of the parish. It would be unfair to inflict such a burden on a Sister of advanced years. A younger Sister would, I am sure you would agree, be far better suited to the role.'

His eulogy to Miss Ellison did not describe the woman she knew. He was hooked. should she land him or put him back. On this occasion she would put him back having enjoyed the sport. 'Father, my Sisters are the handmaidens of the Lord. They are not servants of his servant. There are in this parish spinster ladies and widowed ladies, some devout, some industrious, some both, who would be glad of a living and accommodation and an opportunity to serve the Lord. I am confident that among them you will find one who will provide for your, for your requirements.'

She rose, offered her hand and Dominec realised on leaving that it would be unwise to make an adversary of such a formidable woman.

That evening Sister Benedicta prepared a report for the Bishop's Secretary recommending that an early opportunity be found to place one of her girls. The parishes, with the exception of the Blessed Virgin, were circulated that same week and within days a placement was found for Catherine Allen in York. No urgency was evident in the Mother Superior's report but codes were employed so that the need for matters to be expedited could be unspoken yet still implicit.

Elizabeth wept as Catherine packed and boarded the coach for York. She was convinced she could never be so close to another again. How could she be so open, so intimate with anyone but Catherine. She would be lonely and friendless. There would be no more turmoil in her stomach, fear yet excitement talking of the mysteries of men and woman. There were no other girls certainly none of the Sisters, with whom she could talk of the changes in her body, in her emotions. To whom else could she admit that she could not make a full confession. How do you confess to having impure thoughts when the person about whom you are having the impure thoughts is seated at other side of the confessional screen.

The ostentatious priest spent a happy winter, the post pubescent Elizabeth spent hours in emotional turmoil. Dominic was in her thoughts and in her dreams. There was no escape from him. She was obsessed. Every opportunity to see him, especially to actually speak to him, excited her to the point of breathlessness. At all other times she sulked and was withdrawn. A frequent visitor to Sister Louis's religious education classes, Dominic did not have to deal with Elizabeth's mischievous questions. She was reduced to gazing longingly. She had no inkling how obvious her behaviour was to those who witnessed it, but the change in her was noted by the Sisters, not least by Sister Benedicta. Elizabeth though had a project and would devote her skills and energies to it.

Dominic, with fine new vestments and comfortable, almost luxurious accommodation was a queen bee around whom a court of parishioners circulated. The white stallion was a common sight hitched to the gatepost of some houses; at some more frequently than at others – which gave rise to gossip. Opinion was polarised but Dominic was oblivious to, and Elizabeth was unconcerned by, the effect their behaviour might have on their reputations.

Father Conlan, incapable now of rational thought and virtually inactive, was treated with condescension by Dominic. There was no rallying point for those who had growing doubts about the suitability of this young curate. This was to change when Father Conlan died that autumn. The Bishop was not prepared to leave such a young, and as he had been informed, flamboyant curate with sole charge of a parish while he ought to have been made aware that this had been the case since he arrived. Father Bernard Fee, a convert, late to Holy Orders and with ten years experience as a curate in a church in Hull, was appointed Parish Priest. His arrival at the Blessed Virgin had none of the theatre of Dominic's. A serious man of middle years, Father Fee listened to all Dominic had to tell him then listened to some conflicting accounts. Sister Benedicta, who was too experienced to involve herself in parish politics, and who had felt she did not have an ally, now had a receptive ear in this priest. He enjoyed the occasional glass of Bethlehem whisky, had humour and humanity, but was determined that the parish should be reunited.

Within six weeks of his arrival, Father Fee had formed a firm opinion and had requested a meeting with the Bishop. This was arranged as the Bishop felt it appropriate to involve Brother Thomas, the Principal of Dominic's seminary. The three sat in the office of the Bishop's Palace, an appropriate name for an imposing manor to the north of York.

Father Fee was invited to begin. 'My Lord Bishop since my arrival at the parish of the Blessed Virgin I have found myself increasingly unsure about the suitability of Father Moran for priest work. The stir he causes amongst parishioners, exclusively female and particularly the younger females, amounts to nothing less than idolatry.

It is as though a spell has been cast on those members of the congregation. Disputes have broken out over such matters as the rosters for church cleaning, flower arranging and continually over housekeeping duties at the presbytery. There have even been instances of violence between the women concerned. These women have lost all reason. I am convinced they are, as one, in love with Dominic Moran.'

The Bishop asked, 'and have you discussed this with him, Bernard'

'I have. He does not deny it. He takes pleasure in it'

'But Bernard', the Bishop wanted to know, 'other than some gossip and hearsay, what facts do you have for these concerns.'

Father Fee reached in to his bag and handed the Bishop an embroidered book-mark he had taken from the altar bible, measuring a foot by eight inches. It was exquisite. The needlework perfect. The detail striking. It depicted Christ on the cross and a woman at his feet wiping the blood from his wounds with her hair.

'My Lord Bishop, I assume you have not met Dominic Moran'

'It was my intention to do so as soon as the opportunity presented,' he replied.

'You will have no difficulty in recognising him. The yellow haired figure on the cross is a more accurate depiction of Father Moran than a portrait artist could ever attempt. You should know too that the woman at his feet whose breasts you will note are almost fully exposed is an equally accurate depiction of one of the senior girls at Bethlehem, a Miss Elizabeth Fairwood. She it was whose work this is and oh yes, the white horse tethered to the cross is Father Moran's.'

'Bernard, I have been given no good grounds for believing that Father Moran is guilty of inappropriate conduct with this girl or any of the women of this parish. Is this no more than a temporary case of mass infatuation, which is a not an uncommon phenomenon, that will pass.' He did not await a reply. 'Brother Thomas, Father Moran is in your charge, you recommended him for this position. What is your view'?

'When I made my recommendation it was on the basis that the parish priest was ailing, not that he was losing his faculties. The intention was that Dominic Moran would take the workload, under supervision, not that he would be able to assume full authority. As regards his intentions towards the women of the parish or the girls of the home there are certain matters, which you need to be aware. Unlike a number of his contemporaries, both in college then later in the seminary, there were never any concerns celibacy or even chastity. The fact is Father Dominic is a narcissist. This means...'

He was interrupted by the Bishop 'I am aware of the condition'

'Yes my Lord, I am certain that you are, but in his case it is not merely a case of self obsession, it is a need, indeed a compulsion, to be the focus of all attention, to actually be adored. Everything about him, his appearance, his mannerisms, his every interaction with his fellow men, and women, is fashioned to that end'.

The Bishop again 'And does this not give rise to Father Fee's concern about the forming of improper, physical relationships?' The Brother sighed,

'The other thing that needs to be known here, but not elsewhere, is that Dominic Moran is physically incapable of the sex act. He has malformations of the genetalia, in short, he is a dandy but an impotent one.'

As the two left they paused at their carriages. The old Brother shook the priest's hand and said,

'Bernard, you would have had problems with Dominic but not of the kind that you feared.'

'I would have had?' he asked.

'Oh yes Bernard, Bishops are not appointed for their godliness but for their guile and political manoeuvrings. Dominic will be out of your parish and out of his diocese before any scandal might attach itself to his Lordship's Superintendence.'

Following dinner that evening the Bishop and Mgr Tetti discussed the matter over brandy and cigars. The Bishop's Secretary, his 'Thomas Cromwell', proposed a solution. There was a town in the diocese of Leeds that was growing at an unprecedented rate with an expanding Catholic population from Ireland and Italy. The outskirts of the town had small remote parishes that could not support a curate. When priests absences occurred, as they regularly did, a heavy burden involved a deal of travelling was thrust upon the priest of adjoining parishes. It was a town in which a participating curate could be fully employed. In the town itself there were daily baptisms or funerals of infants. Some of which involved the same infants on the same day. There were marriages of swollen bellied mill girls to perform. Visiting the sick alone would provide all the exercise a white stallion could need and his travelling from parish to parish would provide little opportunity for the curate to bewitch or beguile. It was not an attractive town for an educated, well mannered or sensitive priest. It was a place for a priest from peasant Irish stock. A place that would task the vocation, even faith of a young dandy newly out of his seminary.

The Bishop was persuaded. Father Dominic Moran was to be transferred to Bradford.

Elizabeth, through her tears, prayed and prayed that God would show her the way to find her a home in that town.

Elizabeth had a fantasy on which she worked ceaselessly. She honed it during her waking hours and polished it each night as she fell asleep. It was visualised in detail. An embroidery wish, wearing a pure white habit, she was Sister Immaculate sharing Dominic's white stallion on which they rode through the night to hold prayer vigils in a squalor in a Bradford cellar. Sister Immaculate holding the hand of a dying mother, Dominic, administering extreme unction.

Her announcement to Sister Benedicta that she wished to take vows, however was not received with the joy and enthusiasm that she had seen in her imaginings. In fact, Mother Superior knew Elizabeth as well as any mother knows her daughter and, as kindly as possible, she toyed with the lovesick woman.

'How do you see your service to the Lord, Elizabeth?'

'Administering to the poor, sick and dying Mother.' 'In the missions in Africa perhaps?'

'Well, Mother, maybe where I was more familiar with the language'

'The slums of London then?'

'I did think, possibly, somewhere more local'

The old nun was tempted to suggest the town of Bradford but knew it would be crushing to a child whom she had always held dear. Instead she said to herself, silently, 'get thee behind me Satan' and walked round her desk, held the seated Elizabeth to her side and said 'Child, soon you must leave and we shall all mourn your loss. You have much to offer the world. Experience it and give it your love.'

Elizabeth had invested too much prayer and hope into her future as Sister Immaculata to have it dismissed so summarily.

'Mother, I have a vocation, as you once had.' Sister Benedicta laughed,

'Had, Elizabeth, had? I still have my vocation though sorely tested it has sometimes been. I wish you to test yours. Go into the world. Resist the three temptations – the world, the flesh, and the devil, return here in three years time and I will advise you. Be warned though that my first advice to you as a novitiate will concern obedience. This requires that you have no ambitions of your own concerning how you will serve in those places in which you will perform that service. Think on this Elizabeth. How many of the Sisters here pictured serving the Lord by serving His children who needed love and shelter! Not my will but thine be done!'

She kissed the young woman's head and Elizabeth returned to the house of John crestfallen but undefeated. Yes she would return in three years time and train to take her vows. Then, no, she would not. She would leave now, she would go to Bradford and find lodgings and a living, somehow, anyhow. No, she didn't know what she would do. She would return her prayers and leave matters in the hands of the Lord.

Chapter 14

Few girls who were placed in service when leaving Bethlehem found themselves reduced to skivvying. Kitchen under-staff and servants more normally come from younger, less educated girls. Those raised by the sisters of compassion were prized additions to the better Catholic households; more commonly employed as governesses. Elizabeth was placed in the January following her seventeenth birthday. She had been exchanging letters with Catherine Allen, who had charge of three boys and one girl, all under eight years of age. Catherine's days were long and always busy. It was a happy household, made happier at weekends when the house would be filled by teenage siblings and cousins, home from school.

Expecting similar duties Elizabeth was taken by coach a short distance to 7, Wood Villas, a double fronted, three story terraced house on the Harrogate Road north of Leeds. She was not to be a skivvy, a housekeeper or governess.

Richard and Agnes Kavanagh were childless. Richard, a stout, busy little man, a stalwart of his church, his trade association and every club that would have him as a member, was a salesman of fine cloths and threads. Agnes was an agoraphobic, and an alcoholic. He would be out and about from early each morning until late each evening making his calls, making his sales and cultivating his business contacts. Agnes would rise mid morning, take her place on the settee in the drawing room and would be drunk by early afternoon. Everything that the pair needed was delivered, groceries, a few – gin by the case.

Elizabeth's position was as companion to Agnes Kavanagh. Only fifty years of age but ravaged by drink, disappointment and shared misery, Agnes did not need, nor want companionship. She wanted to be left alone to find oblivion as early each day as her frail frame would allow. The stale gin on Agnes's breath offended Elizabeth and the incontinence from which the older woman suffered and which Elizabeth had to clean up disgusted her. 'Not my will but thine will be done' she would say, no longer believing a word of it.

That duty apart, Elizabeth had almost nothing to do. Her days were long and, monotonous and unproductive until she spoke to Richard about the piles of materials, linens, cottons and silks stacked in his office. There were cotton and silk threads of every colour and quality. She asked if she might use some samples to practise her needle work. Richard was happy for her to take and use as much as she wished for any purpose she wanted, Elizabeth was excited and set about at once to design patterns.

Taking the opportunity to speak to Agnes on one of her lucid moments, Elizabeth asked if she might make some dresses for the china dolls in the cabinet in the sitting room. That agreed, the companion could now occupy herself. Rising early and returning late she set about designing wardrobes for the china figures that had been Agnes Kavanagh's proxy children before her only hope of motherhood had been destroyed by her years.

The dresses that Elizabeth made were exquisite. Silks with lace collars and cuffs, bonnets and ribbons socks and tiny slippers. Her days, once interminable were now too short. Each creation surpassed the last. When she was ready to show her creations to Agnes she could not understand her reaction. Silent tears at first, followed by heartbreak, followed by a full tumbler of gin, drunk neat without pause. When she showed them to Richard he examined them closely, said nothing but appeared to be lost in thought. When Elizabeth rose next morning Agnes was still in a drink induced coma, Richard had as usual, left and her collection of miniature mannequins had gone.

Richard Kavanagh knew the quality of needlework but Oswald Levine was a master. His tailoring business on the ground and first floor of his premises in Park Terrace in Leeds was renowned amongst the gentlemen of the city seeking the finest attire to be had. In his basement his staff provided the most desirable gowns, particularly bridal gowns, and a Levine gown was the crowning glory of the balls and weddings of the daughters of the wealthiest of that city.

When Levine arrived at seven thirty that morning, Kavanagh, salesman first, a concerned husband a distant second, was waiting. A firm handshake, a smile and a request. 'Ossie, please look at these and give me your opinion.' Levine, Shrugged, 'so I should be selling dolls now eh, Richard,' 'the costumes, the needlework. Only an opinion, a masters opinion Ossie.' Levine put a monocle to his eye, spent time turning and returning the dolls, handling the costumes with reverence he turned to the stout, little salesman. 'That I should find a seamstress such as this. She is wasted on dolls for the sticky fingers of children. Do not sell them cheaply Richard'

The salesman persisted 'And if she were to fashion gowns not for the dolls but for young women, for older woman.' The master tailor sighed, 'Then she could dress the angels that you believe flutter, invisibly, in that church of yours.'

'So you would employ her?' 'I would want to see her working' Kavanagh saw a profit 'And how much would you pay such a seamstress?' the tailor was blunt, 'not a penny. Not a penny for one week then I would dismiss her or make an estimate of her worth.' 'Can I arrange a trial?' 'Bring her to see me Richard.'

That Friday Richard employed a fifteen-year-old Millie Bean, from his haberdashery stall in the Kirkgate Market to be a companion to Agnes. She moved in on the Sunday, Elizabeth explained her duties, lifting Agnes off the floor, placing her back on the settee, clean up after her incontinence and getting her to bed. On the Monday morning she shared a cab with Richard Kavanagh to Leeds and met Oswald Levine and the two seamstresses in the Levine basement workshop. Devina and Beattie were both in their late twenties, talented young women at whose creations Elizabeth marvelled. They both took to their new young colleague and as the week progressed, witnessing her skill with a needle and thread, they accepted her as an equal. Her only previous experience of a worldly-wise woman was Catherine Allen. These two for whom men held no mysteries, were, Elizabeth thought, fun, outrageous and an education for an innocent fresh from a convent education.

That Saturday evening Richard was anxious to hear Ossie's opinion. It was favourable. More than that, Richard detected, it was enthusiastic and after a little negotiation, while, Elizabeth waited in the cab, a deal was struck. Ossie would pay Richard eight shillings and four pence per week for the young seamstresses services. Richard did his calculations on the road to Wood View Villas. Millie Bean would be paid two shillings a week plus her keep. Elizabeth would still have her three shillings a week and her keep, even though her duties would be less arduous than caring for Agnes, and he Richard, would have a fee of three shillings and four pence a week from the arrangement. This would not be a clear profit, he felt, since Elizabeth would need fare of two pence per day for those journeys that were not convenient to the times of his own. Reconsidering he thought she should share the cost with him.

The spring and summer months of her first year in Leeds were a revelation to the seventeen year old Elizabeth Fairwood. Her Saturday evenings and her Sundays were her own, provided that she paid her cab fares, and with Davina and Beattie she experienced Leeds city life each Saturday night. When the workshop closed at six o'clock they would have muffins at a café in Queen Street then it was off to a music hall. There were Italian Jugglers, French contortionists, Spanish dancers and, Beattie's favourites, the comics, cheeky, bawdry, and some unapologetically vulgar. Did men actually do such things with women, Elizabeth wondered. Not with the woman who had raised her she thought. Did Dominic ever have such designs on any woman she pondered.

Sunday mornings were spent at St Patrick's church but the priest Father Scanlon, was old, tired and uninspiring. One Sunday she took a cab to Leeds, the railway to Bradford and went to find the parish church at which she might find the glorious, the magnificent priest, the many thoughts of whom still stirred in her that she could not, did not want, to quell.

Her first sight on leaving Market Street railway station was the drizzle, which carried the soot that settled on her bonnet and her cloak. The mud on the street might have been deeper than her ankle boots but she didn't attempt to cross anyway because she could not see the other side through the smoke and feared she might be trampled under the carriages that splashed the mud on her skirts.

The city of Leeds was she thought, malodorous. This town was foul. How would her dear gentle Dominic survive this wretchedness. Elizabeth boarded the railway carriage that had brought her.

Oswald Levine considered his tailors and seamstresses to be artists and he referred to the three workshops as studios. The reputation he enjoyed among Leeds Society would be cemented or destroyed by the wedding of Miss Persiphony Hector-Davis. Her gown was to be created by Beattie and those of her Maid attendants by Davina and Elizabeth. Persiphony, indulged by her father from infancy was known to be difficult. Her mother, the formidable Margot Hector-Davis was reputed to be hard to please. Impossible some said. Her husband had been trying all their married life without success.

The tailors were permitted to leave at six thirty. The seamstresses were to remain and await the Hector-Davis party, due at seven that Friday it was almost eight o'clock when Margot burst through the door followed by Miss Persiphony and the two maids in attendance. Mr Levine looked as these two and quickly concluded that they had been chosen to ensure that eyes would be on none but the bride. Margot, making no apology for her lateness, looked the seamstresses over and said to Mr Levine, 'There would appear to be a complete lack of industry here. Have these lasses no work to do?' She didn't await an answer but clapped her hands, 'Come on, come on, would you have me here all night?'

Levine, capable of hand wringing and fawning to a high standard, half crouched and said, 'All other work has been postponed in order that nothing should distract from the importance of the event in which we are all so proud to play a modest role.'

'Modest? Modest Mr Levine,' she barked, 'your role, as you describe it, is to ensure, in fact to guarantee, that Persiphony's beauty will be the talk of society. And reported in the London newspapers, the better ones of course.'

The bride to be smiled. Her attendants trembled, as did the three seamstresses.

'Such energy as is left to me is being poured into the many arrangements I have to make. I expect no less from you'

'Now. Enough of your delays Mr Levine. I have a number of requirements and I recommend you to note them in detail for should I fail to be satisfied in all respects then Mr Hector-Davis shall not pay you one penny. I will insist on that. Number one. Come on, come on, make notes. Number one, Persiphony's gown will draw gasps of admiration and you must supervise every stitch these lasses make.' At this she raised the back of her hand toward the three 'artists,' dismissive of them.

'Number two, do keep up Mr Levine, the gowns of her Maid attendants must compliment Persiphony's gown but must not, note that, must not surpass it in magnificence. Number three.......'

It was to be after ten o'clock when Mrs Hector-Davis swept out with her party none of whom had said a word following in her wake. The last they heard from her that night was some complaint she was making to her coachman. In the weeks to come, however, they would be hearing much more from the intimidating Margot.

The Master tailor and the three masters of the needle stood in silence. The seamstresses knew better than to speak disrespectfully of a client to their employer. Levine was not going to do so either. His staff were paid a weekly rate (other than Elizabeth whose rate was paid to Richard

Kavanagh.) and they were not paid for additional hours. Still, he was now dependent on the goodwill of these three young women. They were replaceable, though not quickly and not part way through a commission as important to the reputation of the Levine Studio's as the Hector-Davis marriage could be. Recognising that, and in view of the exceptionally late hour, and even though not one tape measure had been employed, he considered it prudent to make a gesture, rather than a comment. Each seamstress received a shilling, out they went together to spend a little of it on wine in the best room of the Midland Hotel. Davina did not have the mimicking talents of Catherine Allen but her impression of the dreadful Margot was passible and greatly entertaining.

The following weeks were dominated by the Hector-Davis commission. Patterns were drawn and re-drawn. Measurements taken and taken again. Richard Kavanagh called upon his business contacts and years of experience to procure the finest Chinese silk in pure white and cream. The threads, also of silk picked out seams in ivory and rose. An exact mannequin of Persiphony was not difficult to construct. Those of her attendants where of somewhat broader proportions all round.

The seamstresses invested all their skills into every quarter inch of these creations and Mr Levine, rarely fully satisfied, never impressed, on this occasion marvelled at the quality of the finished gowns. One evening before they were to be delivered he sat before the three mannequins. He was proud of the work, proud of the girls and proud to be the proprietor of Levine studios. Nothing should now be permitted to give Margot Hector-Davis any cause for dissatisfaction. He would spend the night at his studio guarding the gowns and he sent a message to Mrs Levine to tell her he would not be coming home.

The gowns were delivered next morning in a coach hired for the day. Levine accompanied each gown. They were protected by layer and layer of soft paper and laid full length on the width of the coach seat, which had been covered in silk. There would have to be no fold, no crease, and no wrinkle.

The wedding was to take place at Ripon Cathedral in two weeks time and the service was to be conducted by the Bishop himself. The guest list was to comprise of the nobility and upper classes of Yorkshire and a number of other Shire Counties. Oswald Levine waited anxiously for a word of complaint or, less likely, a compliment. Neither came.

There was much about the wedding that displeased Margot. Not all the flowers had the same number of petals, the bridegroom had the temerity to refer to her as mother without being invited to do so and she considered the bridegroom's mother's appearance to be 'attention seeking'. But of the gowns she basked in the compliments that were heaped upon her. The admiration of Persiphony's gown was complete and the opinions that the attending maids gowns were almost as wonderful delighted her. In fact it was the word almost that delighted her.

Oswald Levine received not a word from Margot but he did receive a visit from Mr Hector-Davis who paid in full, shook Levine by the hand and said what a rare occurrence it was to meet anyone who could so satisfy Margot. Having corrected any misunderstanding his words might have caused he left with a cheery wave.

Newspapers in all the three Yorkshire Ridings reported the wedding, as did two in London, and all described the gowns as the creations of the Levine Studio in Leeds. That information must have been imparted by Margot and that was her thank you.

Despite raising his charges in line with his enhanced reputation Levine was receiving so many enquiries and commissions that he had the luxury of choosing or rejecting them as he saw fit. Reluctant to raise pay or to award bonus payment, but fearful of losing his seamstresses to his competitors he announced that bonuses would be paid each Christmas to those who had remained in his employment for the full year. This would apply equally to his tailors whose order books were filled by the publicity following the wedding. It would not apply to Elizabeth that year, he explained, but it certainly would in future years.

On Christmas Eve, as the staff were preparing to leave, the bonus had not been mentioned, The senior tailor, Francis Baron, was deputed to raise the matter. Levine affected forgetfulness but, now reminded, he was pleased to award each of his artists- other than Elizabeth – one pound. After a quick, whispered agreement Devina and Beattie each gave Elizabeth five shillings. She protested but they pressed it upon her and she accepted with gratitude.

This was Elizabeth's first Christmas spent other than in the joy and happiness with which the season was celebrated at Bethlehem. The Kavanaghs' house was unchanged from any other day of the year. Agnes continued in her drunken stupor and Richard was absent all day, although where he found to go on such a day was a mystery. Millie Bean was no company so Elizabeth, having attended St Peters Church spent the day writing letters to Catherine Allen, Sister Benedicta, and a third unposted to Dominic.

Throughout the next year her life consisted of lodging at the Kavanaghs' where she had no role, working at the studio which she enjoyed, and evenings in the city with Devina and Beattie whose friendship she cherished and whose humour, often risqué, made her feel accepted and hinted at some adult activities that she had still to experience. Even allowing for visits to the café, the music hall and, only occasionally the best room at the Midland Hotel, Elizabeth was able to save as much as a shilling each week. She made her own clothes from Richard Kavanagh's samples and decorated bonnets with ribbons she bought from the market. Having saved a full pound, and with the ten shillings from her friend's Christmas bonuses, she believed that by next Christmas she should have, with her own Christmas bonus almost a full five pounds. A good start.

Chapter 15

The coming year had two events in store that would cause Elizabeth to have to alter her plans. These occurred quite closely together, each side of her November Birthday. On rising one morning to share Kavanagh's cab to the city she found strangers in the house. Agnes had died in the night and the agitated Richard was dealing with the undertakers staff. The conversation, as far as she could understand it, concerned his plans and budget for the scale of the funeral. A difference of opinion was evident. The undertakers were stressing the seemliness of a dignified burial in a suitable coffin with an appropriately grand memorial. Kavanagh was stressing the importance of affordability.

Elizabeth returned that evening to find that Millie Bean had been returned to the market stall that afternoon and was to return to her mother's home that evening. Funeral arrangements having been made, Oswald Levine agreed that Elizabeth could attend the funeral on the Thursday morning, with a deduction of wages of course, but she would be expected at the studios directly afterwards.

The Service was conducted by Father Flanagan who was well acquainted with Agnes but his address was brief and sympathetic, making no references to the problems, which led to her early death. Elizabeth attended the burial but as she left the priest asked her to remain while he said his goodbyes to the last of the mourners.

'What are your plans now Elizabeth?' She hadn't made any, hadn't realised that she would need to.

'How old are you eighteen?'

'Nineteen next month, Father'

'Yes eighteen. You are no longer Mrs Kavanagh's companion' Ready to tell him that she had not been a companion for over eighteen months but she decided she should not.

'And now you do not have a role in the household, and now you are living there un-chaperoned, it would be wholly improper for you to remain. Having been placed there by the church, your continued presence could be a source of scandal. You could make your own arrangements now or I could ask the Bishop's Secretary to arrange another placement. Whichever it is to be your lodging with Mr Kavanagh cannot be countenanced. Let me know what you intend but it would be preferable if you were to be accommodated elsewhere within a very few days.'

She decided to speak to Richard Kavanagh, assuming that on this night of all nights he would return home at a proper hour. He was not at all happy at her moving from his home. The cost of her keep was minimal, he retained three shillings and four pence from her wages and without having to pay Millie Bean two shilling a week, a change of arrangements would cost him five shillings and fourpence a week. Elizabeth told him that Father Flanagan was insistent and she would have to seek other lodgings.

Unsure how she would manage this on her wages of three shillings she sought the advice of her two close colleagues. They were appalled that she was paid less than half of the wages they earned and urged her to speak to Mr Levine. Elizabeth lacked the confidence to do that. Beattie did not. Levine told Beattie that his arrangement was with Mr Kavanagh not with Miss Fairwood. Beattie told Levine that he should alter that arrangement forthwith or risk losing the services of three seamstresses. That afternoon Elizabeth was informed that her wages would be eight shillings and four pence a week, but not until the following week.

Elizabeth's nineteenth birthday she would have spent alone in her new home, a room in St Catherine's Hostel for young women of good repute in Bridge Street had her two friends not surprised her with a birthday treat to the music hall. They had persuaded her that by making independent arrangements she would no longer be dictated to by the church regarding where she lived or whom she lived with.

While she regretted no longer having access to Richard Kavanagh's samples and threads she did not miss the smell of Agnes, the sour face of Millie or the company of Richard who, apart from shared cab journeys, the fare for which she paid for more often than not, she had seen little of. The room in the hostel was comfortable enough and with a little work was made quite homely. She could have stayed there happily enough and her savings should increase more rapidly now. It was in that state of mind that she turned into Park Terrace on a cold late November morning the premises were open to the skies gutted by fire, and all the staff were in tears. Oswald Levine sat on the kerb, his head in his hands, a defeated man.

The employees were to learn that it would be several weeks before the insurance claim could be assessed and, hopefully, settled. Attractive suitable premises would have to be found and stocked. New orders would need to be secured. In short there would be no employment for weeks, possibly months, possibly ever. The plan of the three young women to find temporary work together seemed feasible over a glass or two of wine at the Midland Hotel. The reality was that the only position they could find together was in the bushing and mending room of a Kirkstall Mill. The sweatshop conditions and wages less than half of those to which they were accustomed resulted in them leaving at the end of the week. They would separately seek work as seamstresses wherever they could find it but vowed to reunite once Oswald Levine had re-established his studio.

Unemployed and in the loneliness of a hostel room that Christmas, Elizabeth had a pressing problem. A condition of residence at St Catherine's was respectable, gainful employment. Her visits to the dressmakers of the city brought no offer of work nor even encouragement. She was an accomplished seamstress but her age, the length of her experience, the lack of a formal apprenticeship and surprisingly for her, employment by Oswald Levine all counted against her. The reputation of the Levine Studios had generated no little professional jealousy in the trade and there was no enthusiasm for employing his staff only until such time as Levine was able to re-establish his business.

Not a trained and qualified seamstress but well trained for the position of a governess she found a number of promising positions advertised in the daily and weekly newspaper. Her first application procured an invitation to attend for interview at the home of Mr Edmund and Mrs Sophia Fry in Armley.

They had been married for twenty four years and when Sophia gave birth to her first child only seven months after the ceremony she refused all requests from family and friends to visit the baby claiming that he was so premature that it would be some weeks before it would be known if he would survive and any illness he might contract from visitors could well be the end of him. The Midwife, respected for all her qualities other than her discretion, let it be known that the boy had weighed eight and half pounds at birth, a remarkable weight for delivery at seven months. In fact, had Sophia carried until full term it was doubtful in the Midwife's opinion that he would be no less than the size of a Christmas turkey!

The Frys' hopes for additions to their family had faded when after eighteen years of marriage, and with Sophia reaching and passing her fortieth birthday they were thrice blessed and now had sons aged six, four, and three years. They believed that the nurse they had employed could now be dismissed and could be replaced by a governess to supervise the children and begin their education. There would also be a saving to be made if the house-keeper was to be dismissed and the governess could take on some light additional duties.

In fairness to the Frys they did ask Elizabeth if, in addition to her governess duties she felt able to assist Mrs Fry from time to time with some household work. What they did not tell her was that it was intended that from time to time that she would be assisting Mrs Fry but more usually Elizabeth could be expected to do the work alone. And being, as yet unaware of the nature of the three children, Elizabeth accepted the offered position.

Edmund Fry traded as handler of goods and wares and had an office and warehouses on the wharf in Leeds from where he and his son, Jonathan, arranged transport for all manner of manufacturing goods and personal belongings by canal, wagon and railway. Chairman of the Hauliers Association, Secretary of the commerce club and a member of the Public Utilities Board, Edmund was an important man he believed. Sophia enjoyed many social occasions they attended in his various offices so more evenings were spent eating and drinking at tables other than the one in their own dining room.

Elizabeth's food preparation was usually limited to providing for the three children but her days were long and demanding. It was a large house and its cleaning could not be neglected. A daily cleaner would have been well occupied. The children were a trial. Her experience of Bethlehem, ordered and disciplined routine, the older children supporting the younger, was not replicated in the Fry household. The eldest boy was sullen and cunning, the middle one had boundless uncontrollable energy that he employed to cause disruption and the youngest, a guileless and fearful little soul was subjected to frequent nipping and slapping by his brothers who took delight in making him cry.

She saw little of the adult Jonathan, still living with his parents. Since being formally introduced barely a word had passed between them. Nor was she made to feel welcome by Edmund and Sophia. The wife's days were often spent shopping for clothes and having her hair dressed for the many evening functions they attended. Edmund had not warmed to Elizabeth. He complained to Sophia that 'She affects that accent and uses those words to make her feel our equal, our better even, and I am not having it.' He called her Betty, a more appropriate name for a servant, he felt and Sophia addressed her likewise.

Through a hot summer and into autumn she strove to fulfil her duties but, on most nights, she fell into her bed exhausted. Often she would soon be awakened by the middle boy who fought against sleep and would cause mayhem with his brothers stripping the older one's bed and slapping the younger one.

The autumn was cold and Elizabeth's room was unheated. She would sit in the evening before the kitchen fire, stare into its flames and wonder if her situation would ever improve. It was on one evening that Jonathan, home late as usually from his father's office, came in to the kitchen for milk and a biscuit. On other occasions he would leave without a word passing between them. This night he saw the reflection of the fire on her tears. He touched her shoulder lightly and asked if he could help with her unhappiness.

Elizabeth spoke to him and he drew a stool to her side. She made no criticism of his parents or his brothers but did explain that a constant fatigue and her unpreparedness for the breadth of her duties were depleting her spirits. Jonathan listened attentively and, for the first time she looked at him directly. He was tall, dark, his quiet voice softening his harsh Leeds accent. She had previously thought of him as brooding and withdrawn. Closer observation confirmed her in that view, but detected in him an underlying unhappiness.

Conversations by the kitchen fire, at first an occasional occurrence, became a regular feature of those evenings when Jonathan's parents were dining out–which could be four or five evenings week. The young couple discussed all manner of topics including their upbringing and education, but frequently they returned to each other's hopes and dreams for the future. These meetings would end abruptly, rudely even mid sentence, when the sound of carriage wheels at street level signalled the return of the Frys. Jonathan would scamper the cellar stairs like a squirrel up a tree. Not only did his father dominate him, Jonathan lived in fear of him.

Affection grew between them and they would hold hands as they talked. One evening Jonathan leaned forward and kissed Elizabeth's cheek. It was brief and touching but marred by his anxious glance to the street level skylight. Elizabeth's first kiss had not caused the emotional turmoil she had suffered over Dominic. It had surprised and pleased her. She felt loved. Not in the way she had been loved at Bethlehem or the affection her friends had shown her at Levine's Studio's. What she felt this time was being loved by a man – a wholly different feeling.

What Jonathan did next was also a surprise to her being so out of the character she believed he had. She had fed and cleaned the children and put them to bed at seven o'clock. Within minutes the room was in an uproar and as Elizabeth went to remake the beds she was stopped by Jonathan. She stood by the part open door as he spoke to his three young brothers' 'When you make a noise at night the bogey man hears you and he will come and take you away' he came out, closed the door

And the two of them listened. There was silence at first then loud, repetitive shouts from the two older boys. ' Bogeyman, bogeyman, bogeyman.' Jonathan went to the linen store, took out a white sheet, draped it over himself and re-entered the bedroom. The noise stopped, three pairs of eyes, twice their normal size, stared unblinking, Jonathan emitted a loud roar, 'Waahh!' and come out. There was not a sound in the children's room that night, nor any other night.

Back on their kitchen stools Elizabeth was both appalled and amused at what Jonathan had done. He took her hand and said, 'I doubt you would find that in the Good Governesses Guide.' Elizabeth gave his hand a squeeze as a sign of forgiveness and thanks.

Jonathan was in love with Elizabeth and she with him. The happiness they found in each other's company was a symptom, the misery they experienced when they could not meet, and the counting of minutes until they could meet once more confirmed it. In his father's presence Jonathan was reduced to trembling limbs and stuttering. With Elizabeth he was strong and confident. He proposed marriage. She accepted.

They planned their future together and it was agreed that Elizabeth should have the choice of their first child's name. Should it be a girl the name would be Teresa. Should it be a boy she would name him after her first home, Jonathan teased her saying that it would be cruel to name a boy Bethlehem. 'Not Bethlehem, Matthew.' They laughed and embraced.

Jonathan would make enquiries about arrangements that would need to be made and was distressed to find that since Elizabeth had not attained her majority she would need her parents consent to a marriage before her twenty first birthday and she was still a month shy of her twentieth.

That Sunday, after Mass at St Peter's church she asked for a meeting with Father Flanagan and explained the problem of not having a parent to give consent. He told her that until she was twenty-one years of age the Bishop was in loco parentis and she would have to write for his consent. 'Hope again' she thought

'There are certain details the Bishop will need from you. Are you with child?' Elizabeth was shocked. 'I am not, Father, not guilty of any sin of misbehaviour.'

'Is the young man in question a Catholic?' 'No but of a good Christian family'. 'And does he have parental consent?' 'He has yet to broach the matter.'

The priest did not offer any opinion as to how her application to the Bishop would be received but impressed upon her the need to include all the information the Bishop might need in order to come to a decision. She penned her letter that same afternoon, stressing that her intended husband was the son of a family of good social standing in the business community of the city.

Her letter was dealt with by the Bishop's Secretary who would need to draft the response on his Bishop's behalf. Unfortunately for Elizabeth this was not Monsignor Tetti, a pragmatic man who may well have taken the view that marriage would relieve the church of a responsibility it had carried for almost eighteen years when a foundling had been rescued from a forest in York. The experienced and wise Monsignor was now a Bishop of Norwich. Recently appointed Secretary Father McBride did not have the confidence to take any line other than a conservative one and he drafted the reply accordingly.

Elizabeth opened the envelope with shaking hands and reading the letter, signed by Bishop Delaney himself, was distraught. Her age, it seemed, was not a major obstacle but she was informed that mixed marriages rarely led to happiness and she would have an obligation to raise any children in the faith while her obedience to her husband might prevent that. It was suggested that if Jonathan was to take instruction and be suitable to be accepted as a convert to the faith then the question of consent might receive favourable consideration.

That evening Elizabeth showed Jonathan the letter. He agreed, enthusiastically, to take instruction and to convert. He would inform his father of their plans the next day. She was nervous for him and hoped their love would give him the strength to face the father of whom he lived in a terror worse than any bogeyman could induce.

Working from a small room adjoining his father's office above a warehouse on the wharf, it was Jonathan's job to process orders for collection and delivering of goods, to arrange their transfer, to issuing invoices and to ensure these were paid. It was a noisy, often chaotic environment and it was to be late morning before Jonathan could have his father's attention. Closing the door of the office and standing before his father's desk, He took a breath, put his shaking, perspiring hands behind his back and steeled himself.

'Father, I intend for Elizabeth and I to marry.' He attempted to soften his opening. 'Not immediately but after some time when I have had the opportunity to look into her religious practices.'

Edmund flushed but did not erupt. Instead he laughed. 'Don't be a fool lad. She's under your roof. Make use of her if you will but gentlemen who marry servants, and very few would, always regret it. I'm not opposed to you marrying once you settle on a suitable woman of your own class, but not a servant. I'm against it. It's not going to happen, so don't mention that woman to me again'

Encouraged by the fact that his trembling and fear were quite controlled, Jonathan continued, 'I am decided upon this, and will not be prevented and since you are so opposed to the union be assured I shall speak no more of it until I tell you that it has been joined.' He turned and left.

By noon Edmund was back at his Armley home and found Elizabeth reading to his three young sons. The two older ones were protesting about the story of the fairy in the tree. They wanted a story about the bogeyman. Fry's anger had been rising during his carriage ride and it was uncontainable when he began his tirade, ignoring the presence of the young ears.

'Whore, I take you into my home and you repay me by seducing my son. Well, I'll tell you this, whatever spell you may believe you have cast here by being so free with your favours will have no effect once you are out of sight. You are dismissed. Get out. Any references for which I am asked for will be returned with one word. Harlot. Be packed and out of this house within the hour. Should I see you or even hear your name again, you should know that I would count the cutlery, find certain pieces missing and inform the police. In prison you will not be marrying anybody and when you are released none will want you. Get out, Get out.'

Elizabeth too shocked to answer and too frightened to defend herself ran to her room in tears and packed her small trunk and her case. Now on the pavement in Leeds, too numb to think, she sat on the trunk and sobbed until she ached. Would Jonathan try to find her? Where would he look? She returned to St Catherine's Hostel but did not have the required employer's reference. Father Flanagan could not recommend appropriate lodgings but when he read the Bishop's letter he told her that, by refusing consent to the marriage the church still had parental responsibility. She could now write to the Bishop, inform him of this, politely of course, and the problem of her shelter and protection would be his, not hers, until her twenty-first birthday.

Late evening found her on Richard Kavanagh's doorstep. He was late arriving as usual and surprised to find Elizabeth there. She proposed a few nights in the room she had occupied the previous year at a sum of one shilling per night. Kavanagh agreed at once and the following morning she wrote another letter to the Bishop. Father McBride, the Secretary, was learning that a decision deferral, for whatever good reason, meant a problem unresolved. Monsignor Tetti would have known that.

A circular letter to the parishes of the Diocese of Leeds and York produced a number of possibilities. He discussed these with the Bishop who advised the option the furthest from Leeds should be preferred. Elizabeth had been at Kavanagh's home for ten days when Father Flanagan called. He gave her details and directions to her new home and the price of the carriage to take her to a village near the coast to the north of Hull. Before leaving she asked Richard for news of the Levine Studio's but Levine was still not in business.

Jonathan searched for her but could not find a clue as to her whereabouts. He traced Beattie and through her Davina but neither could help. She was not at St Catherine's and Father Flanagan claimed not to have seen her. It was in her own best interest, the priest felt, that she have a fresh start and should find another young man, and hoped he would be Catholic.

Elizabeth wrote to him both at his home and at his office. She tried disguising her handwriting in case one of her letters was being intercepted (which they were). Eventually she accepted that his father had prohibited him from any contact and he had not been strong enough to fight for her.

Chapter 16

White Cottage, rural and exposed to the winds off the east coast, was a warm and comfortable home. The lands that had once been formed from there had been sold off when Doris Churchill's husband had died ten years before. She was finding it difficult to care for herself having painful hips and ulcerated legs that ached from the strain of supporting her heavy body. Uncomplaining she accepted her condition and was appreciative beyond expression to have Elizabeth staying as a 'guest', she insisted. For her part, Elizabeth quickly learned to like the warm-hearted old lady. Doris had a wealth of tales to tell of the young men who wooed her, of her handsome young husband, her children, grown, married and settled in distant parts of the country.

The atmosphere at White Cottage was a welcome contrast to that in the Fry household. Yes, she still regretted the loss of Jonathan but, she wondered, what sort of life would she have had with Edmund and Sophia Fry as parents in law? During long talks in comfortable armchairs, sipping on mugs of hot milk and malt, Elizabeth found in Doris the understanding ear and wise counsel she had not had from her mother. She confided in Doris, her life in Bethlehem, her friendship with the irreverent Catherine Allen and the feelings she had for Dominic Moran. They giggled. She told Doris things she had told nobody before. Although embarrassed she recounted in the fantasy of Sister Immaculata sharing a white stallion as she and Dominic disposed prayer and comfort in the slums of

Bradford. Doris did not laugh at her. She told Elizabeth how normal fantasies were and Elizabeth rocked with laughter when Doris confessed one of hers concerning a one armed naval captain from Whitby who one day would kidnap her, smuggle her into his cabin and keep her for his pleasure while he sailed around the world. When she alluded to the problems that a lack of an arm would pose to a young girl, not brought up to take the lead in such matters, and how she might still be able to assist him, Elizabeth was convulsed. 'That's not fair' protested Doris, 'I didn't laugh at you on and the curate on the white horse', and both laughed until they wept.

Doris paid more serious attention to Elizabeth's account of the Frys and Jonathan and how they had never said goodbye. The old woman counselled her. 'We girls have both a mother and a woman inside of us. The mother part can love a weak man, feel a need to protect and care for him, believe she can give him belief in him self. It's no basis for marriage. The woman in her will come to despise his weakness. She will nag and against all her instincts will become a harridan. The woman in her wants a man she can respect, obey and rely on. He will fight on her behalf even when she is in the wrong and he will set lines that she will not dare to cross. Find that strong man, Elizabeth, but one who is honest, gentle and puts you before all other considerations. From what you have told me, that is not Jonathan Fry.'

Elizabeth grew close to Doris. The old woman, uneducated but wiser than many who were, was a philosopher. Her stories told had a moral and she had developed a code that had brought her a peace and contentment that her infirmities could never dent.

After fifteen months at White Cottage, where she had spent two Christmases and her twenty-first birthday,

Elizabeth had no desire to be anywhere else. She had continued to practice her needlework, though not on the scale of the Hector-Davis wedding. Cushion covers, curtains, repair were the limit of the available materials. The ulcers on Doris's legs were no longer responding to the ointments that her doctor would deliver for Elizabeth to apply. The knots in the veins on her legs were ballooning and there was no option, despite her age and the dangers posed, other than surgery to relieve the pressure before an accidental knock should lead to a haemorrhage that could not be stemmed.

Her nerves and the chill February winds from the coast caused Elizabeth to shiver uncontrollably as she watched the carriage taking Doris until it was out of sight. Unable to sit, she paced the room, twisting her handkerchief and looking out every few minutes for the doctor who had assured her he would let her know that the procedure had gone well. As his face came into view of the lamp in the window late that afternoon she knew it had not. Doris, the delightful lady, had not survived.

Archie Churchill, the eldest son, arrived from Sheffield three days later. It was not a great distance to travel but he had not visited before in the fifteen months that Elizabeth had been there. Nor had any other of her children, their spouses or her grandchildren. There was though a funeral to arrange and Elizabeth could not have done that. Archie explained that there would be some delay in finalising funeral arrangements since family from other parts of the country would need to make travel arrangements. Elizabeth would be welcome to attend the funeral if she was still staying locally but Archie needed White Cottage to be vacated so that a valuation and quick sale might be agreed whilst the family was in the area.

Where was she to go? She didn't know anyone in the Hull area, and now at the age of twenty-one the church would have no responsibility for her. Telling Archie she would pack and leave the following day, she spent her last night pondering where she might go or how she might support herself. The son returned from his hotel next morning bringing with him the cash box and documents he had taken the previous evening. Doris had not made a will but she had left a note of her wishes, the main favouring her grandchildren, some of whom she barely knew. For Elizabeth there was a bequest that Archie was anxious to settle there and then. In return for her signature on a receipt, Elizabeth received fifty pounds.

As the coach for York put the miles to Hull behind her Elizabeth's sadness at Doris's death receded and she thought instead of the old woman's happy life and her release from the pain she had suffered in her later years. It was a bright, crisp day with frost on the fields and Elizabeth's mood lightened as she considered her situation. Financially secure for now, no longer a chattel of the church and with her choices for her future before her, she felt quite the young lady.

Having taken a room at a coaching inn she went to call upon Catherine Allen and was disappointed to find she had left her position. Married, it was believed, to a Stationer's Clerk but her present address was not known. The shops of York were a delight and she decided to spend a second day. Having replaced some of her clothing she decided to attempt to find Catherine. How many Stationers could there be in York? Many. It was a centre of Law, the churches and publishing but the stationer's world is a village, as was the dressmaking world in Leeds and her second call led her to a shop in Middlegate.

She was about to make an enquiry of the woman at the counter, a broad heavy woman in the advanced stages of pregnancy when the unruly red mass that did the job of hair identified its owner,

'Catherine.'

'Elizabeth'

Not the wife of a stationer's clerk, but the pregnant wife of an assistant to the recently appointed manager. They met that evening at Elizabeth's inn where six years adventures would be told in one night. Such laughter, Elizabeth in her new clothes, shawl and shoes insisted on paying for the food and their drink. Catherine still mimicking Sister Louis with Sister Benedicta added to her repertoire. They reminisced about Dominic and Catherine, a little coarser than before was more explicit about the plans she had for him before she was so quickly evicted from Bethlehem.

Elizabeth told her of her disappointment with Jonathan Fry and Catherine's advice, rather different from Doris's was blunt.

'You look wonderful Elizabeth see him, show him what he has lost. Pin him to a wall and make him explain himself then have your way with him before walking off without a backward glance.'

'Catherine I could not.'

'I could. Anyway, forget the last bit but don't let him get away with it.'

In her room that night Elizabeth thought on this. She was undecided but with no other destinations in mind she took the coach to Leeds next morning. A room at the Midland Hotel would be convenient while she considered her options. On her walks through the city over the following days she considered possibilities, choices and opportunities. In Park Terrace there was still a hole in the ground where Oswald Levine's workshops had once stood but in Park crescent, between a bank and a solicitors office she saw a sight she had once hoped for but had not believed would become a reality; Oswald Levine's Studio's. The dressmakers room was at ground level and she looked through the large windows. Four women were seated there and two of them she knew, Devina and Beattie. Should she go in. Perhaps she would. A woman changed by her time with Doris, Elizabeth had a determination and confidence about her that she had not previously thought possible.

Oswald Levine could be seen in the basement office and it was to there that she went. He was, he said, most pleased to see her, had the highest regard for the standard of her work, would be pleased to consider her should a vacancy arise- but, if she had not been practising her skills it would be some time before she reached the same level of proficiency. In the meantime, once he was able to offer her a position it would, of course, have to be on reduced wages until she achieved an acceptable standard. She reminded him that she had worked on the Hector Davis wedding, she had worked for him for almost two years but not received a Christmas bonus and she would consider returning when he came to her, offered her full wages and the Christmas bonus she felt she should have received. She could not promise, though, that she would return. With that she left. Meeting Beattie on the stairs she learned that Jonathan had been seeking her over a year before. Plans made for a reunion of the three friends in the tea shop the following day, Elizabeth returned to her hotel, changed once more and made her plan.

When Jonathan left his office on the wharf at seven-thirty that night there was a carriage at the end of the lane, where it had been waiting for over an hour. As he passed a door was opened. 'You may get in and come with me to explain yourself or you may hurry home to your Father or we will say our goodbyes now.' They went to the Midland Hotel, where in the best room he told her of his shock at her leaving without explanation to him or his parents, leaving his young brothers unattended. He had looked for her. Her priest had known nothing of her whereabouts, nor had anyone he had asked. Her conduct had been inexcusable and he had thought her better than that.

He answered her questions, honestly no he had not received any letters, he knew nothing of any threats to have her arrested for stealing cutlery. He was disgusted that she should be called a whore and accused of having had him in her bed. Yes, he had informed his father of his intention to marry and, arriving home and finding she had fled, he had been consoled by his parents, yes his father had been opposed to the match but Jonathan had made clear his intentions.

'Jonathan, she asked' 'would you wish now that we continue to see each other?'

'Yes Elizabeth. Oh yes I would wish nothing more' He reached for her hands which she quickly withdrew. If he were to have the courage to pass the test she was about to set him, it would have to come from his own mettle not from her encouragement. Also, the lounge of the Midland Hotel was no place for such in decorousness. Jonathan studied the finely dressed, assured young woman seated before him. She bore little resemblance to the exhausted girl who had wept by the kitchen fire of his family home.

'I intend to stay here for just three more days and I will be leaving this Saturday morning. If it is indeed your wish that we should continue to see each other you will return before then to inform me that you have departed your family home and have your own rooms as an independent man of your age and standing should.'

'You realise Elizabeth, that I will lose my employment and will lack the means of supporting us.' She stood, 'Goodnight Jonathan,' and returned to her room.

The reunion in the teashop was a jolly one. There was news and gossip to share and Elizabeth learnt that the opening of the new studio by Oswald Levine had generated great excitement among local society with commissions from not only Leeds but from cities and towns across the county. Orders had been taken for balls, weddings and christenings, some over a year hence. Beattie and Devina gasped in admiration at the demand she had made of Levine.

At the desk of the Midland Hotel, Elizabeth was informed that there was a gentleman waiting for her in the lounge. There she found Jonathan who told her that he would be leaving the family home and would find suitable employment. He had already enquired about available rooms.

'And have you informed your father?'

'I will, certainly.'

'I should be happy to see you when you are able to tell me what you have done, not what you intend to do. I am here for two more days.'

With that she started to leave but turned and said 'And may I suggest that before informing your father that you take an inventory of the cutlery.'

Hearing nothing further on the Thursday and all through the Friday she set about packing that evening when there was a knock at the door of her room. 'Miss Fairwood there are two gentlemen at the desk wishing to speak with you.'

Afflicted by trepidation, her newly won confidence dissipating with every step, Elizabeth descended the stairs. On reaching the first landing she had convinced herself that the two gentlemen would be policemen set upon her by Jonathan's father. Perhaps she could glimpse them without being seen. But what then? Abandon her belongings? Escape into the night, but to where.

On trembling legs she reached the ground floor, chanced a glance at the reception desk and saw the two gentlemen, immediately recognising both. The nearer was Oswald Levine, the further Jonathan. Composing herself she strode forward,

'Mr Fry, I shall be with you soon.'

As she led Levine to the lounge, he apologised for his casual dismissal of her earlier that week. Certainly he would be pleased to re-employ her on full wages and, discreetly, passed two pounds, the bonus payment for her almost two years service. Elizabeth replied that she would keep her agreement to consider his offer of employment and he would have her decision by Monday. Levine left and Jonathan joined her.

'Elizabeth I have informed my father. His anger surpassed anything I have witnessed before and I in turn was outraged by his insulting of you and the threats he made to both of us. He denied having threatened you with a trumped up charge of theft but he was not convincing. As I expected I am as a result without employment but I have a modest sum of savings and need not starve while I find a position. I have taken rooms on the York Road from the City and I feel confident that you will approve of them. Dear Elizabeth, I have lost you once I wish never to lose you again. I will work, I will earn and I will support us. When I proposed marriage before you accepted. I am conscious that this is not the place for displaying the love and affection I have for you but I will not risk delaying another day. Elizabeth, my love, will you marry me?'

Elizabeth had been distant with him, testing his resolve but at that moment she was back with him on a stool before the kitchen fire of the hated Fry home. The feelings she had for him then flooded over her and she could deny no longer the love she had had for him and which had returned, undiminished. So long did they sit re-making their plans they had made once before that the evening had gone before she realised she had not given him her answer. When the lounge was briefly unoccupied, other than the two of them, she leant forward and kissed his cheek.

She would visit and view his rooms but appearances demanded that she be accompanied and she would arrange this as soon as she could. Jonathan would set about at once to find suitable employment and she would return to Levine's Studio's. Their earnings would keep them secure and permit some savings. Elizabeth regretted that their marriage would not be in a catholic church but the delay while Jonathan took instructions proved an opportunity for fickle fate to intervene. Once married Jonathan could, in time, convert and they could marry again this time before God's altar.

The couple spent their Sunday walking, talking and planning and the following morning found Elizabeth in Levine's office and, within ten minutes at her work-table. Beattie and Devina were delighted. The two ladies in the sewing room, Edna and Madeline, were a generation older and tended to prefer their own company to that of the younger women who, with their chatter and laughter, they regarded as flibbertigibbets.

Elizabeth's two friends were excited by the news of her marriage. She asked if one of them would accompany her to view Jonathan's rooms. Both insisted on going and that was arranged for Wednesday evening. The marriage was to be two weeks hence by the civil registrar at the offices in Bond Street. Her workmates would act as witnesses if Levine could be persuaded to permit a lengthened lunch hour. Having received an invitation to attend, which he had been unable to accept claiming pressing business, he not only agreed to an extended lunch break but also did not have the gall to dock wages.

Beattie and Devina were filled with curiosity and Elizabeth with expectation as they climbed the stairs to the second floor of number nine, York Place. It was in the centre of a terrace of substantial stone built houses and Jonathan's rooms occupied its full upper floor. Once in, the three women were given a tour, if looking into four rooms could be considered a tour, and the shared, unspoken impression was that they lacked those small but important touches that only a woman could apply. Jonathan was attentive, served tea and was clearly awaiting the judgement of his guests, that all three were too polite to offer. Elizabeth hadn't known what to expect but it was to be her first home and would have been delighted whatever she had found.

The three left enthusiastically making plans for curtains, cushions and bed linen. Beattie asked Levine if they could use the sewing room for an hour after closing each evening, with all materials provided by themselves of course. Although the employer normally remained in his office attending to his accounts for an hour or two each evening, the seamstress hadn't expected him to agree. She thought it quite out of character when he did and was convinced, as she told the others, that there was something in the wind. A familiar figure visited that same afternoon, he expressed himself pleased to see Elizabeth again and she took the opportunity to ask if he still kept a roomful of samples and threads and if so, in order that she might prepare her home for her marriage, could she have her choice of them. Richard Kavanagh agreed. The samples were now filling the room from floor to ceiling and he would be pleased to see the back of some of them. After he left, Levine spoke to Elizabeth and it was evident he was displeased. 'Miss Fairwood, while Mr Kavanagh might once have been your employer he remains one of my suppliers. I will not have my staff scrounging from my suppliers. I will let the matter pass this once.'There was no doubt that there was indeed something in the wind.

Devina was want to flirt with a certain carriage driver, Dick Budge, and she learned from him that he had taken Oswald Levine to Harewood House. That she deduced would explain Levine's desire to keep himself in his seamstresses' favour. A commission from the Earl of Harewood, even if it should be for no more than a christening gown, would surpass the Hector Davis wedding in terms of prestige for the Levine studios.

Beattie and Devina were as swept up in Elizabeth's marriage plans as the bride-to-be herself as they went with her that evening to meet Richard Kavanagh at his home. Kavanagh took a professional interest in watching the three women make their choices of materials and sewing threads. These were, he knew, people who knew their trade, and his. He was particularly impressed with Beattie who with a touch between thumb and forefinger or a brush of a cloth on her cheek was selecting and rejecting materials displaying remarkable discrimination between pelts and lengths the difference in the quality of each being no more than marginal. She was, he thought, wasted in Levine's sewing room. There were department stores in Leeds that would have paid her three or four times as much to employ her as a buyer and he and other salesmen like him would be hard pressed to slip an inferior piece past her.

Each evening for the two weeks before the marriage the three women worked on Kavanagh's materials and they fashioned drapes, covers, antimacassars, table covers and runners that would have graced a palace. It was arranged that Jonathan would be out on the Friday evening and the cleaning completed, the three set about arranging their work, transpiring drab rooms into a home of which a young bride could be proud.

Never had three seamstresses dressed so well for a morning in a sewing room as the bride and her witnesses did that morning and they set off for the registrar at eleven forty leaving behind three empty tables, an unusually genial employer and the exaggerating tutt tutting of Edna and Madeline.

Jonathan was waiting and Elizabeth felt he had never seemed more handsome. His dark curls had been trimmed to frame his high cheekbones and his suit hung well on his tall frame. Confident, relaxed and smiling he took Elizabeth's hand and led her into the office. He was unrecognisable from the man serving tea just two weeks before, fussing over his visitors and anxious for approval of his choice of rooms.

The deputy registrar raced through the formalities in a perfunctory manner and within minutes the party of four, Mr and Mrs Jonathan Fry and their two witnesses were taking the short walk to the dining room of the Midland Hotel where Elizabeth had organised tea and cakes. The bride would have been back at her sewing table by one o'clock, as agreed, had not the hotel manager served complimentary champagne. Elizabeth, he said, had been a valued guest of the Midland Hotel and he wished to mark her special day and her impending departure.

The three returned to Levine's Studio on hurried feet but it was almost two o'clock before they were back at their tables in high spirits and expecting a reprimand at the very least. Instead there was a gift for Elizabeth, a pair of matching cruets. At six o'clock, half hour before the time staff would normally finish their work, Levine asked them to put their pieces away. He summoned the tailors down from the floor above and addressed his workforce.

'Gentlemen and Ladies. For a week or more now I have been engaged in attempting to secure for this studio a commission the importance of which to all of us I cannot overstate. It is a wedding which is planned for September, just five months hence but, and this places me in difficulty, it has yet to be announced so we must consider ourselves privileged to be given fore-notice. We shall need that time to obtain the materials and to permit the creation of the mannequins, the acquiring of the materials, such materials as you will never previously have worked ladies, and the approval of the patterns. You will understand that I cannot reveal the party in question but, once the announcements have been made, you will know why. For now be satisfied that you have privileged information and that it must remain confidential.'

Beattie who had enjoyed a third glass of champagne and was still experiencing the effects was emboldened and mischievous.

'There are rumours about Leeds, Mr Levine, that there is to be a marriage involving a member of the Earl of Harewood and the tittle-tattle is that no dress-maker other than Levine's Studio's would be chosen.'

Levine, shocked but flattered still paled. 'I cannot confirm any such thing.' Then seriously, 'But if that tittle-tattle was proved correct as if any hint of such a wedding should find its way into the newspapers before an announcement is made; then this studio could lose the commission to a London Studio that is anxious for it. Our reputation could be ruined. Employment here could be jeopardised. It is your discretion that will safeguard your jobs.'

The three left together. It would be Harewood they were in no doubt and Beattie, still giggling, added, 'And Ossie is going to need us more than we need him until September at least.' Elizabeth returned to the hotel, thanked the manager for his hospitality at her wedding lunch, collected, had her cases placed in a carriage and set off for York Place to begin her life as Mrs Jonathan Fry.

Jonathan had still been unable to find suitable employment but Elizabeth was sure that the skills and experience of her handsome, talented husband would soon be recognised, and once the commission had been confirmed her earnings would be assured. That news was not long in coming. The following week she was met on the step of the studio by Devina.

'It's in the newspaper Elizabeth. Annabelle Ormesby, a niece of the Earl of Harewood is to marry the Honourable William Vanderbilt, a second cousin of the Queen and seventeenth in line to the throne. St Paul's Cathedral in September.'

The two held hands and jumped up and down in time. Levine now relaxed, told his staff that the bride was to be attended by two maids and two infants. Measurements were to be taken that coming Sunday at Harewood House. The bride's dress would be made by Beattie, the maids by

Devina and the infants' dresses by Elizabeth. He would travel with them and they were to meet the carriage at the studio no later than nine o'clock. The excitement in the sewing room was palpable, as too was the resentment of Edna and Madeline. Levine took those two aside and explained that the three he had chosen to make the dresses had proved themselves with the Hector Davis wedding and that the success with the Harewood wedding would provide opportunity upon opportunity for the two ladies to prove themselves similarly.

That evening Elizabeth was barely through the door of her home before telling Jonathan her news, and the thrill it would be to visit Harewood house and for dresses made by her to be seen on the aisle of St Paul's Cathedral by members of royalty, perhaps queen Victoria herself. Her husband's reaction was a disappointment to her.

'Elizabeth, Sunday is the only day on which I have your company. I accept your need to go but do not feel that you should view sacrificing our time together with such pleasure. This evening I must be out. I am to meet a gentleman from whom I hope to receive an offer of a position but, unlike you I take no pleasure from my absence.'

Within a few minutes he was gone and she sat to consider his words. He was right to object, she thought. He would possibly have been less hurt if she had been less excited and had expressed herself reluctant to go to Harewood but having no choice in it. Poor Jonathan, not yet employed and having lost his position because of her, he deserved more consideration.

Jonathan spent the evening in the White Hart drinking gin. If Elizabeth was going to neglect him on Sunday then he would repay her in kind and be in no hurry to return home that evening. Not only was there no gentleman to meet he had not sought an employment since leaving his position with his father the previous month. He had no experience of finding work, never having had to do it and he had no intention of lowering himself. He was the son of a man who was now the National President of the Hauliers Association as the gin took its effect he concluded that it would be unseemly for him to engage in menial work. The next morning, his attitude unchanged, he visited his father at his office on the wharf.

'Good morning Father, how is Mother?'

Without looking up from his papers Fry replied. 'As well as any mother might be expected to be when her eldest son has thrown away his future and his fortune for a slattern.'

'I shall not have you speak of her in that way. There is no basis for such insults and they insult me.'

'Then do not listen to them. You know your way out.'

'Father, I wish to return to my position here.'

At this Fry did look up. 'Then tell me you are cured of your madness for that woman.'

'We are married.'

'Jonathan, you are a fool and she has made you one. I expect that before long you will tire of her and I hope that occurs before she has every penny you have. When that day comes we can discuss your employment. Until then you can think on what she has reduced you to.'

'But I need employment now. I've had expenses in finding accommodation and being without wages my savings are all but gone'

Jonathan began to weep and his father looked upon him, thought him pathetic and felt no pity.

'There are firms along the wharf offering openings for clerks.'

'Clerks, Father. I am a transport manager with over ten years experience. You'd be happy to see me as a clerk?'

The father was losing patience. 'I'd be neither happy nor unhappy. I would not care and as for you being a manager I would, even should I be given a month, find it impossible to recall a decision that you did not refer to me. Now dry your eyes. If you have to make a man of yourself in order to keep the doxy in your bed then she will have served some purpose. Good day.'

Elizabeth arrived home that evening to be greeted by an apologetic Jonathan. He had been insensitive, he said, in not sharing her excitement over her visit to Harewood House, he had been selfish in wanting her to himself on Sunday and he had been concerned at his failure to find a position. It would not happen again he promised.

She accepted his apologies readily but felt they were unnecessary. The blame should be hers she said and she was certain that he would soon have employment.

Jonathan sat with her. 'Today I have news of my own. I received a note from my father asking that I call upon him. I was reluctant to do so but feared it may be news of the health of my mother or brothers. Instead he was merely seeking to re-employ me. I refused but did so more politely than he deserved. In truth, dear Elizabeth, I would go barefoot and penniless before working for a man who treated you the way he did.'

'Sweet Jonathan, You protect me and I love you all the more for it but I do worry for you that you might take employment below your station.'

'It is the same consideration that as so delayed my finding a position. I confess I have felt it necessary to reject offers from transport companies who know me and know of my availability. However, I have years of experience managing the transport of goods across the country by road, by canal and by the railways. There are those who would have my experience cheaply believing that I can be had for a clerk's wages. I cannot.'

'Nor shall you be Jonathan. My income is assured for some months to come and I should be happier knowing that you are awaiting the opportunity your experience and ability deserves than having you sell them cheaply.'

'Then my dear wife I shall cease demeaning myself by having to listen to such offers and I intend to make it known that I will consider only managerial posts and be prepared to wait until an appropriate one is offered.'

Jonathan, with little now expected of him, felt no pressure. This is how he had lived his life and it was a state to which he was well suited. He would be the most loving, caring and attentive husband any woman could ever want.

Chapter 17

Elizabeth was at Levine's Studio's long before nine o'clock that Sunday but was not the first there. The three dressmakers wore the clothes they had worn for Elizabeth's marriage and were a credit to Levine. He though out did them, his suit befitted a man who employed master tailors, his old valise had been replaced by a new case covered in soft leather and the carriage he had hired for the day was the most magnificent any of the women had ridden in. It was a high sprung coach, polished to perfection and pulled by a matching pair of greys. The uniformed driver was accompanied by a boy who would act as the footman and how grand the three young women felt as they were driven through the centre of the city that Sunday morning watching the heads turn as they passed by. The chatter in the coach was all speculation. Would they see the great house and, if so, would they be admitted by a servants' entrance. Would it be another case of a Margot Hector Davis and a Persiphony as it would mean even more abasing of themselves.

As the carriage entered the gates between the ornate crescent of the high stone boundary wall there was the promise of a ride down the long drive to the imposing country seat. The dressmakers were not to be disappointed and the sight of one of the finest country houses of the county, was awe-inspiring. They dismounted at the front steps, climbed between the soaring pillars and looking up were dwarfed by the height of the building then looking left and right were arranged at its span the square towers at each corner like bookends. They entered with a silence and a respect they would reserve for a church.

They were received by a young man in uniform who led them to a first floor room. Long and narrow, along its length was a table that could have seated thirty or forty at each side, they thought. The chairs were around the walls, as were five screens. Almost immediately they were joined by Lady Annabelle and her four attendants. All stood other than Lady Annabelle who brought a chair to the end of the table and invited Levine to do likewise. There she confirmed instructions he had taken on his previous visit.

Levine opened his new case and took out three notebooks, six pencils and six new tape measures, which he left on the table, then as he was about to take his leave another entered the room. It was Lord Harewood who had called as a courtesy when visitors were invited to his home. The three dressmakers were impressed and not knowing whether to bow, curtsy or prostrate themselves settled for bobbing up and down. It must have appeared quite comical but the company they were in was far too polite to giggle. Soon however there would be giggles a plenty. The men having left, the wedding party, feeling no need for the privacy of the provided screens were quickly out of their outer garments and in knickerbockers and bodices were prepared to be measured; that is apart from Lady Annabelle's infant sisters, Louisa and Clarissa, in the freedom of their underwear raced around the table, laughing as they went.

There was no Margot Hector-Davis here today and Lady Annabelle was no Persiphony. She challenged her sisters to a race under the table and with Elizabeth and Devina holding a tape measure at the far end of the table, off set the bride and the two children on hands and knees. There were squeals and loud complaints of cheating before Louisa scampered out past the tape, flushed and victorious. The tone was set for the morning and it passed in good humour and informality. Measurements were taken, checked and checked again.

The Earl had deputed one of his staff to show Levine the house while he himself had gone to examine the pair of greys that had drawn the carriage. He spent some long time with the coachman; two equals discussing a topic on which both had an intimate knowledge. The pair then examined the coach and described it as splendid.

'It is older than I am, rattles the bones, but I know I should suffer the most awful disapproval should I even consider replacing it.'

Measurements progressed and it was apparent that the three seamstresses would have different tasks. Beattie's would be the fine detail of the bridal gown upon which all eyes would be fixed, Devina would be using the most material as Alexandra and Marina were both broad in the back, hips and bottom. The result of riding from childhood thought Devina. Elizabeth though had a particular problem, how did one allow for the growth of a five year old over five months. In order to keep them still for long enough to measure them, Elizabeth made a game of it pretending her new white tape measure was a snake that crept from plump elbow to chubby wrist to dimpled knuckle but would only bite if there was any movement. The children were transfixed, fearful and delighted but soon under Elizabeth's spell. For a while she was back at Bethlehem, caring for the children of Matthew and Mark. Looking then at Louisa and Clarissa she believed that in one respect there was no difference between the daughter of the aristocracy and the daughters of the Sisters of Compassion; both recognised and responded to love and affection. She had, she was convinced, a calling for raising children. For all her needlework skills she was trained to be a governess. She had not used those skills as a companion to lady intent on drinking herself to death, as a housekeeper to a family where she was treated disgracefully or as a carer to an ailing old lady, as much as she had grown attached to Doris and would always remember her with fondness.

By early afternoon they were done and were invited to a light lunch to be taken in a smaller dining room along the corridor from the dining room in which they had been working. They had expected to take any refreshments offered below stairs but in this room they were joined by the now dressed wedding party and Levine. The table had been laid with a selection of cold cuts, breads, pastries and fruit. Louisa and Clarissa took their places and insisted that Elizabeth sat between them.

Riding in the coach back to Leeds, Elizabeth was of the opinion that the upper classes such as Margot Hector-Davis and the middle classes such as Edmund Fry could learn a great deal about good manners, behaviour and decorum from the aristocracy. Wealth, she concluded, could never buy breeding. Levine, it seemed, had caught a similar mood, even if only for one afternoon, as he instructed the coachman to deliver each of his three ladies to their doors. The first was Devina and Elizabeth saw that she lived in a shabby tenement house behind Quarry Lane. The second was Elizabeth herself and she saw Jonathan at the second floor window as she alighted from the coach and was escorted to her door by the junior footman.

Elizabeth entered bursting with the news of her day and Jonathan wanted to know every detail, urging her to re-tell her experiences and in that way they spent their evening.

Through May and June other orders to the studio came and went but the priority was 'The Wedding'. Five mannequins stood before the sewing tables, erect as soldiers but of dissimilar proportions. Before Beattie was a slim figure, before Davina two slightly taller but far broader ones and before Elizabeth two shorter, slightly chubby shapes, one two inches taller than the other.

Elizabeth fretted about the changing fit of dresses for growing girls and fretted about something else even more. She was pregnant. Her joy was tempered by having no one with whom she could share her news. She had no living relatives of whom she was aware, If she were to tell Beattie and Devina then Levine might hear of it and, although he probably would not curtail her employment while she was working on such a prestigious commission he would be likely to do so in ten weeks time when the dresses were made. What she wondered, would Jonathan's reaction be. He was still waiting for his undoubted skill and experience to be lead to a senior appointment but, without employment, he might not be ready for fatherhood. She harboured a suspicion that while his confidence was low he might feel troubled by responsibility. She decided to confine her worry to Levine; not about her pregnancy but about the extent to which the child attendants would have sprouted by September.

Levine smiled, 'Mrs Fry. It is a problem but not a new one, nor, you will be pleased to learn an unforeseen one. The bride and her two maids will have their final fits in this third week in August at Harewood House. You will not be needed for that. The two children will be unable to be there since they will be in Scotland with their father. It was planned that they would visit Leeds on their journey to London the week before the wedding but their itinerary and timetable won't permit that now. So, and here is the surprise, you are to perform the final fit and any adjustments in London on the Thursday prior to the Saturday wedding. I too shall be attending of course and since propriety demands that as a married woman, you cannot travel with me alone, Mr Fry can escort you, at the studio's expense. I would ask though that that none of this is discussed with your colleagues who will be disappointed and I need to broach the subject at an opportune moment.'

Which of her pieces of news should she tell Jonathan first. It would be the invitation to London. Perhaps he would have secured a position in a week or two and she would tell him then that he was to be a father. Jonathan at first expressed his enthusiasm for a visit to London. He had been on occasions with his father who was then the regional chairman of the Hauliers Association. Elizabeth had not been to London before and there might be an opportunity for him to show her some of the landmarks. Actually his mind was racing. Her absence might provide an opportunity he had been seeking and would be loath to miss.

August came and certain news could be kept no longer. Levine told Beattie and Devina that they would be visiting Harewood House again but Elizabeth would not. She would be travelling to London on the week of the wedding to check and allow for the growth of the infant attendants. Her colleagues were envious but not resentful; they understood the logic behind the decision. Elizabeth, four months pregnant could not protect Jonathan from her news and told him over dinner. He said how delighted he was that they were to be a family and he had news of his own. He had been approached, in confidence, to hold himself in readiness for a senior manager's position with a railway freight business. The incumbent was due to retire and Jonathan's appointment was subject to approval of directors in London. That might be forthcoming in a month or a day but he must be available to take up the post immediately it became vacant. While his appointment might not be confirmed by the date of the London visit it might be so there was nothing for it. It had to be decided now that he would be unable to go. It would be unfair to her to leave the decision any longer and to disappoint her, and her employer, nearer to the date.

'Jonathan I am so pleased for you. So pleased I cannot say. This means however I cannot go. Perhaps Beattie or Davina could attend to any finishing work on my dresses. I must tell Mr Levine tomorrow.'

'No dearest, you must go. This is your work. You must finish it as only you could.'

'But I couldn't travel un-accompanied.'

'You can with my approval and I readily give it.'

She was shocked. 'Jonathan, it is not merely a question of approval it is one of appearances. It concerns my reputation, your reputation and Mr Levine's reputation I shall not think of it.'

This would ruin Jonathan's plans but there was nothing more to be said on the subject just then. He felt instead that he should talk of the birth of their child, the joy he felt and their happiness now and in the future.

Oswald Levine was most unhappy to be told that Elizabeth could not travel to London for the final fit but told her that there might be a solution to the problem. His initial thought was that Mrs Levine might be invited to act as chaperone but Irma could be a difficult woman and even if she was agreeable to go, which she might well not be, she would, in all probability be disagreeable all the time she was there. It was, he decided, a desperate option one of last resort. He did, come what may, want Elizabeth to do the final alterations. Such dresses were creations-works-of-art and an addition or subtraction by a second artist would be evident to a critical eye.

Lady Annabelle, Alexandra and Marina had their final fit and they all gushed with unresolved delight. They were filled with admiration for the skills of Beattie and Devina. Beattie offered her sincere best wishes for the happiest of days and said she could almost picture the three of them entering the cathedral. The bride had a mischievous glint in her eye when Levine rejoined his ladies and she pretended grave disappointment. The dressmakers were perplexed and Levine was shaken, half bowing and craven.

'Mr Levine. I am given to understand that this is to our final dressing. This comes as a shock to me. As pleased as we are with your ladies' work, and we cannot find fault with one stitch, will we be so pleased in two weeks time when one of us has gained an inch, or lost an inch? I had expected a final fit along with my sisters two days before the wedding.'

Levine, now bent even lower, replied. 'But the commission, M'Lady, did not include that.'

'Then, Mr Levine, the commission is wrong. I require a final fitting and since the commission does not allow for that I shall insist that it now be included and your additional costs met. My father would want no other.'

Levine agreed at once. Arrangements would be made. Of course they would. No detail should be permitted to mar the day. Giving the impression of being willing to make every effort to accommodate the bride's requirements, whatever difficulties they presented to him, he was secretly pleased. Elizabeth would be accompanied, Beattie and

Devina would be pleased and he would not have to endure Irma's black moods. Better still all costs would be met, which Irma's would not have been.

The three dressmakers would have use of the studios after hours and on Sunday prior to the wedding to make dresses for themselves. After all, as they had persuaded Levine, the reputation of his studio rested on their appearance. What for example would prospective clients think of a cobbler whose own shoes were down at the heel?

Elizabeth told Jonathan of the new arrangements, which would mean her leaving on the Thursday and returning on the Saturday unless the Friday fitting should require last minute alterations, in which case it would be Sunday. She had been unsure of his reaction but need not have been. He hugged her, told her how pleased he was for her to be able to finish her work and assured her that she went with his full blessings.

The impression at the studio that the delivery of the dresses to London and the travel and accommodation arrangements for the proprietor and three of his staff were being organised like a military operation was confirmed on the prior Monday. A slim young man of impressive appearance and faultless accent arrived for a meeting with Levine. He was Captain Jeremy Howard, an equerry with responsibility for liaising between the dressmaker and the head of the Ormesby's London household. He was informed by Levine that the dresses had been separately crated and were already with the haulier, a man he had used before and found totally reliable. The crates clearly marked that they should not be opened by any other than a representative of the Levine Studio's and were numbered one to five, number one being the bridal gown.

The crates would be delivered to the Queen Anne's Gate address on Wednesday evening, his party of four had rooms reserved at the Belmont hotel, where they would arrive on Thursday afternoon and the final fittings would take place at nine o'clock on Friday morning. The studio's party would remain until Saturday morning in case there should be any disaster when the bridal party was dressed and would take the railway to Leeds at lunchtime, about the time of the wedding ceremony.

The equerry was satisfied and asked to meet the three ladies who had made the dresses. When he had left Davina commented to Beattie, 'You don't see many like him in Leeds.'

A carriage collected the three ladies from their homes early on the Thursday morning. Each had a large case containing their clothing and a smaller one containing the tools of their trade; needles, threads, thimbles, scissors, tape measures and a number of pairs of white cotton gloves to protect the delicate materials on which they worked their magic. They met Levine at the railway station and found him in a state of high agitation. He had received a telegraphic message from London the previous evening informing him that the crates had not arrived and another early that morning stating that four had now arrived but one had not. That was the crate marked number one, the bridal gown. Levine had been unable to locate the haulier last evening and had already visited his offices that morning but had not found him there. The dressmakers were concerned at their employer's appearance. It was apparent that he had not slept and was clearly quite ill.

Levine told them he would remain in Leeds to trace crate number one he would take the afternoon railway and expected to join his staff at their hotel late that evening. He gave them their tickets and a bundle of one and five pound notes. Beattie took these and passed them to Elizabeth.

The train left at eight thirty taking the three worried seamstresses to London. What if the bridal gown was not located they asked, then agreed that the thought was too awful to contemplate.

The train had barely left Leeds before Jonathan left York Place carrying his suitcase and arrived at his mother's door. She had never been able to refuse him and his father, who would listen to no one, had always had to listen to his wife. With Sophia he had no choice in the matter.

'Mother, I have got myself into a terrible fix. He wept and his mother comforted him. Making a great show of a manful effort to compose himself he began the speech he had been preparing and refining as events had developed.

'My father was right. It was an unsuitable marriage. She is not a bad person but, without employment, my savings have been unable to keep pace with her spending. At this very moment she is in London with friends. I had resolved to end the marriage but then learned I was to be a father. I brought my case hoping you would agree to my returning home but how can I do that? What kind of a man abandons a pregnant wife of five months? I should not have come. I will go back. Oh, mother, see what turmoil I am in.'

He wept again, longer and harder than before and his mother was won. She persuaded him to stay the night and had the housekeeper make up his room. The timing could not have been more propitious for his scheme. It was the first Tuesday of the month. His father would be at his lodge at the Freemasons Hall. His mother would not, the evening would be his.

Edmund Fry was home at six-thirty and with his regalia in his case, out by seven. He had ignored Jonathan's presence and not a word had passed between them. Over dinner his mother asked whether there was any way in which she could resolve his dilemma.

'I fear not mother. I am short of funds but my pride would not allow me to accept them from you. Anyway, they would, like my savings, be squandered. I have abased myself in applying for positions that are beneath me and still not had any success. Even my own father refuses to employ me. I accept his view that I am lying in a bed of my own making and would continue to do so if my reduced circumstances reflected on me alone but soon they will not. My father has achieved some prominence, not only in this city but, as National President of the Association, across the country. I know what others do not, and that is the not inconsiderable role you have had in this. Your support, the regard you are held in the circles in which he moves and your readiness to promote him at the various functions you attend has played no small part in building a reputation that I am going to damage.'

Sophia was alarmed. Jonathan's situation was distressing but if it was to damage Edmund, then let her dwell on this for a while and he toyed with his fruit pudding and before claiming his appetite was lost his mother wanted an explanation of his fears for his father and Jonathan was ready to provide one.

'Mother I am anonymous in this city. It is common knowledge in business circles that I am my father's only adult son, a son who gave ten years to his father's business and was dismissed. Some of the false versions of the reasons for my dismissal were as harmful to my reputation as they would be hurtful to you should they ever reach your ears. Those false rumours prevent me gaining employment.'

Sophia was sympathetic to his position but anxious to know how it might damage her and her husband. She didn't need to pose the question. Jonathan understood his mother well enough to know her vulnerabilities.

'I accept that I cannot correct the speculation about the cause of my dismissal and even if I could correct every person who harboured suspicion about me, who would accept that I was dismissed for marrying beneath myself and what would that give of a father who would do such a thing. No, I cannot and will not correct the malicious gossip, no matter the detriment I suffer for that.'

Was that it then, thought Sophia, relieved? No, that was not all and Jonathan now produced his most powerful weapon.

'I will do nothing to harm father's standing or yours and for that reason I cannot leave my wife to return home as I thought I would. My thinking was confused. My major worry, though, is that my situation is bound to harm and there is nothing I can do to prevent it. In a few short months you will have your first grandchild and it will soon become known to members of my father's Association, his lodge and the commercial community that his grandchild is homeless, his penniless father having been evicted from rented rooms for inability to pay the rent. One option would be for me to take my family to some town where I am not so well known but how shall I explain to my child in later years why he or she have been deprived of the only two grandparents they might have had. I see no way out of the fix I am in and wonder how long I can bear the worries that afflict me.'

Jonathan was in his old bedroom when Edmund arrived home at eleven o'clock, full of port and quite unprepared for Sophia's tirade. With an ear to a partly opened bedroom door he could catch some of his mother's louder complaints. Yes, he heard, Betty was the bitch Edmund and, yes, Jonathan had been a fool to be trapped by her. Now he was brought so low that she feared he might kill himself. It wasn't punishment he needed, it was help. Then certain words rung louder than the others; 'reputation,' 'the association,' 'the lodge' 'standing in the community'; Her son, she said, accepted he had been a fool, continuing in his stupidity that could be their ruination. And if Edmund thought she was prepared to be deprived of her first grandchild then he was not only a pompous idiot he was deluded.

Her parting words reverberated around the house and cannot fail to have been heard by the housekeeper and governess and possibly awakening the three sleeping brothers.

'He cannot find employment because of mischievous prattle that you have done nothing to correct. I want his problems and ours attended to or, be certain, I shall make sure you will wish you had.' Jonathan had had a most successful day, better than both Elizabeth and Levine's.

Chapter 18

Arthur Sellers, the haulier, arrived at his office that Thursday morning to be met by a worried and crying dressmaker. Sellers who knew the contents of the crates and their importance to the party who was to receive them knew at once the seriousness of the situation and he shouted, 'Pearson!' A young, gaunt man sauntered in and his employer subjected him to a detailed questioning. The five crates had been delivered to the goods office at the railway station the previous day. No, that was not early enough for the morning train they would go on the afternoon train and should have arrived last evening and been delivered that morning. He had ordered and collected fifteen printed notices, five numbered one to five, five providing the Queen Anne's Gate address and five containing the details of the transport company that had despatched sixteen crates. Each crate had all three labels securely affixed and, Pearson claimed, no blame could be placed on him other than his failure to deliver the crates in time for the morning train.

Pearson was dismissed and Levine growing increasingly unwell accepted tea and mopped his brow while a clerk was sent to the railway station to check the records at the goods office and to have a search made for a crate marked with the number one. The clerk returned and was informing Sellers that the records confirmed that all five crates had been loaded on the afternoon train the previous afternoon when another caller, another clerk, arrived. He had come from the printers office with a label bearing the address Ormesby, 5 St. Anne's Gate, London. Five such labels had been ordered and provided but one had been left behind. Levine was out of the building and headed for the railway station but still heard Sellers voice, 'Pearson!'

The goods office at Leeds Railway Station was small, busy but very efficient run by a Senior Clerk and junior clerk. They assured a breathless and weakening Levine that a crate lacking an address would be returned to the dispatch. It had not been on the night train that had already arrived at six thirty and left at eight thirty but may well be on the train due to arrive soon after noon. Levine decided to sit on a station bench and wait. He had the label he would fix it to the crate numbered one and share that train with its precious cargo to London that afternoon.

For a warm September morning the railway station was unusually cold and draughty. The dashing about, carrying his cases, the lack of sleep and the tension were taking its toll. When the London train arrived, almost an hour late, he had to be restrained from climbing into the guard's van. The senior clerk from the goods office made the search for him and informed him that the crate had not arrived but would surely arrive tomorrow. Tomorrow would be Friday, Levine could neither move nor speak. The doctor who was called to attend him diagnosed apoplexy. His brain, unable to deal with the enormity of this catastrophe, had done him the service of temporary ceasing to function. He was still in that state when Stefan Beronowski, his senior tailor collected him but he was able to give instructions before he was delivered to the care of Irma.

The morning train had arrived in London at six o'clock, far later than its due time and the three dressmakers arrived at the Belmont Hotel to await Levine and news of the missing beaded gown. The manager handed them a telegraphic message and told them that there was a gentleman in the lounge awaiting their arrival. The telegram, addressed to Mrs Beatrice Peacock was in the stop start style of the Morse code in which it had been transmitted but in essence it said that the crate numbered one had been dispatched without a delivery address. It might be found at the goods office of the station at Kings Cross or it might have been loaded on the night train to Newcastle to arrive in Leeds next morning. It should be found and a message sent from Electric Telegraphic office at Charing Cross immediately there was news to the home of Mr Levine. The telegram had been sent by S Baranowski, which puzzled the recipients. There was an addendum that merely informed them that Mr Levine would not be joining them.

The gentleman in the lounge was the equerry, Captain Jeremy Howard. Commanding and assured he gave no indication of the concern the women were sure he must have felt. Beattie handed him the telegram and he took charge.

'I expected to meet Mr Levine but now know we shall not have his company. Who would recognise the crate we are seeking.'

'We all would, replied Beattie, It was packed in our sewing room, straight off the mannequin, packed with paper and lace. It's got the look of a coffin. About that size.'

'Then I shall need one of you with me'

Beattie instructed Elizabeth to go. She would await any more telegrams, as they would be addressed to her, and if there was any work to be done on the bridal gown tomorrow she would need more wits about her than she would have if she was to spend the night hunting the crate. Elizabeth wondered if she would be similarly affected when finalising the fit of the two young growing girls whom she had not seen for five months. Yet, Beattie was her senior and she would do as she was instructed. Surprisingly as she was to think later, she had not considered the propriety in taking a carriage with Captain Jeremy Howard, whom she had already decided was a gentleman.

It was after seven o'clock when the two arrived at the goods office at King Cross. The evening clerk was a slovenly fellow and the equerry found it necessary to bring him to attention and realise the urgency and seriousness of the enquiry. There followed a long search of a list of records by this clerk whom Elizabeth felt was intent on appearing obtuse.

Howard contained his annoyance. 'Quite simply, is the article I am seeking in your store or has it been loaded on the night train?' 'Well if it has' he replied disinterested, it would be off loaded again soon. 'Its cancelled, see, broken lines, signals or something.'

Howard had had enough of him and sought out the stationmaster, unsure whether he would still be in his office at the hour but he was. The office was warmed by a good fire on which a kettle steamed. The wall clock showed seven forty and the stationmaster, elderly and smart in his braided coat and hat, took his pipe from his mouth and rose to the gentleman and lady. Captain Howard presented his credentials and the station official, a former military man came to attention and saluted his visitor.

The equerry explained his search, added that the item in question was the property of a member of the royal family and took the opportunity to give his opinion of the evening goods office clerk. Station Master Jellicoe, was offered that an employee of his station should be anything but entirely helpful to any customer and especially to consider that this one was an officer and a royal equerry. He strode into the goods office and told his clerk to do something useful, to sweep the platforms. The clerk knew better than to delay Jellicoe and, brush in hand he was gone. The Station Master knew every role in his station, he had prepared them all. Still followed by the officer and the lady he went to the goods van where he found its attendant unoccupied. The van had been loaded and unloaded when the train had been cancelled. All the goods unloaded had been taken to St Pancras for delivery to Sheffield.

'If it's in London we'll find it tonight, Captain Howard, Sir, but we'll need to hurry. The Sheffield train will be out at eighty-fifty, if it's not on there it has to be here but by the time we find it isn't it will be gone.'

They took the carriage that the equerry had waiting and arrived at St Pancras where the guard was about to flag the Sheffield train's departure. Jellicoe ordered its delay and an official of his seniority had to be obeyed despite the muttered grumbles of the driver and the fireman. The goods van was packed with boxes, packages, parcels, trunks and newspapers. Howard held a lamp while Elizabeth examined the load. She could not see the crate but could not be certain. Unloading the lot took an hour and the crate was not there. They returned to Kings Cross and searched the goods office again without success. Back at St Pancras the goods office, overstretched by the cancellation of the Kings cross train, gave up the elusive crate marked number one.

Howard gave instructions to the head night porter for it to be delivered to the rear basement doors of 5 Queen Anne's Gate. This need not disturb the household as there would be staff working through the night with celebrations so imminent. Jellicoe felt it wise to await the carrier and the equerry and the lady did too. Sheeted over, the wagon set off with Captain Howard's instructions and in no doubt as to the importance of his mission.

Jellicoe was delivered back to Kings Cross where his office wall clock showed the time to be past eleven. The clear skies that had given the warm day now gave a chill night. Pleased with the result of his work and too long without the company of an officer, the stationmaster offered mulled wine. Captain Howard, although conscious of the late hour and of his companion's long day, felt he ought to accept a cup in acknowledgement of the service that this old soldier had provided.

It was midnight before the pair arrived at the electric telegraphs office at Charing Cross. The message would be transmitted to Leeds but, unlike London, Leeds office did not operate at night. It would be received at seven o'clock and taken directly to Mr Levine's home.

Elizabeth was delivered to her hotel after one o'clock, too late to disturb her colleagues. She would sleep soundly and hoped she would not oversleep as she was expected at Queen Anne's Gate at nine o'clock. No doubt she would be more rested than poor Mr Levine who would have to wait until tomorrow to learn that the bridal gown had been found.

As she waited for sleep to come she thought of Captain Howard. She resisted those thoughts but could not banish them. His presence, his confidence, and the respect he commanded, if only her sweet Jonathan could have been born with such qualities.

Waking early, Elizabeth dressed in her new gown and was anxious to join her colleagues at breakfast and to give them the news of her evening's treasure hunt.

Jonathan too awoke early but was in no hurry to breakfast. He would not appear until his father was gone to work. Thus satisfied, he packed his case and went downstairs to his mother with the best impression of despair he could affect.

'I must leave mother. I should not have come. It is my fix and mine to get out of, though how I might do that defeats me.'

'Stay Jonathan. I am sure your father will have news for you on his return.'

He needed no pressing, had a good breakfast and spent his day in idleness.

Elizabeth's day was to be far more exciting, as she had known it would be. Even if the two young bridesmaids had not grown by one inch there would still be a deal of stitching to do as the dresses were unfinished, loosely tacked, to allow for the alterations that surely be needed.

Louisa and Clarrisa remembered her and met her with squeals and giggles. How much they had changed would be revealed by the tape measure. Two young girls given to scurrying under tables without warning could not be trusted with a filling of the dress the work would have to be done by measurement and Elizabeth had to chase them around the room as they attempted to escape the snake that would bite if they moved. It was to be some time before Elizabeth discovered how much infant girls grow in five months. Now she knew a considerable amount.

The three adult dresses had travelled well and a final fit satisfied the wearers and the dressmakers that no further work was required. Beattie and Davina's work was finished by ten o'clock and as they left to view the great building in nearby Westminster, Beattie remarked that she had never known a bride on the evening of her wedding to be less affected than Lady Annabelle. She had been as affable and relaxed as on their first meeting.

Elizabeth worked at a table in a room that provided good light. Loose tacking was unpicked and replaced by delicate silk stitches, invisible threads in seamless seams. It was work that could not be hurried and with only brief breaks to take refreshments that were regularly offered, but mostly declined. She worked ceaselessly to produce the best of which she was capable. It was eight o'clock before she was satisfied and her sewing bag was re-packed. Her colleagues had returned early that afternoon to enquire as to her progress and to offer any assistance. The two little bridesmaids had been put to bed by the time Elizabeth left but they had been brought to her work room to say goodnight and thank you which Elizabeth considered full reward for a long days work.

She was met at the exit by Captain Howard who told her that since evening had now fallen he should escort her back. He enquired whether she had dined and she told him that she had intended to have dinner at her hotel. They left Queen Anne's Gate in a carriage he had waiting at the door but entering the Strand he gave instructions to the driver who halted outside a restaurant.

'Mrs Fry, it would be my pleasure if you would dine with me and would you permit me my only opportunity to express my appreciation for the assistance you gave me last evening. This restaurant is new to me but comes recommended as being of good reputation.'

Elizabeth thought she should have declined the invitation and would have done so but this officer inspired confidence and compliance and she found herself alighting from the carriage without having answered. As they entered she saw an elegant dining room populated by well-dressed couples and parties but every table was taken. A tall man of distinguished appearance appeared. He wore a tailed coat over a starched, winged-collared shirt and Captain Howard spoke a few words in whispered tones that Elizabeth could not hear above the chatter in the room. Instantly there was a clicking of fingers from the white-gloved hand of their greeter, which caused a flurry of activity among waiting staff. A table appeared, was set in seconds and the pair were seated.

Jeremy Howard showed a tireless interest in her life in Bethlehem, her training as a governess and her self taught skills in embroidery. Elizabeth felt she should show similar interest in his military career but his replies were brief and modest. Everything about the dinner was excellent, Elizabeth thought; the food, the service, the cutlery, the crockery and, most of all, the company. She had noted the glances of some of the ladies at the tables they had passed between and wondered why some men, very few men, apparently without effort, were deferred to by other men and admired by women. She had known only two; Dominic Moran and Jeremy Howard.

Before leaving he asked if she and her two colleagues might be available next morning should any problems arrive when the party dressed. Elizabeth told him that they had intended to leave next morning but would remain a further day if required. Again in the carriage they were driven to St Paul's Cathedral and found the road closed to horse traffic. A police sergeant spoke to the equerry who presented his credentials. The police officer saluted him and allowed him through. The carriage was halted at the east entrance of the Cathedral and the captain asked Elizabeth that the three seamstresses remain at their hotel until ten o'clock, by when the bridal party would be dressed.

Would they then make their way to the cathedral and wait on the pavement at the spot he indicated. The party was due to arrive at eleven and they should be there, where he would know where to find them if needed.

Elizabeth asked if she might be taken to the telegraph office at Charing Cross. She sent a message to her husband and to Levine to tell them that they would arrive back in Leeds on Sunday. At the hotel she joined her two friends who were in the lounge resting after a day spent walking and a filling evening meal. They were not displeased to have another day in London and, although they expressed mock distress and spending Levine's money, they felt that since it was virtually a royal command, what choice, did they have.

On that same Friday evening Jonathan awaited the return of his father. It was after eight o'clock when he arrived and was obviously in ill humour.

'Sit down lad, you made a mess, as I said you would, and I have to clear it up. I've lost a days work over this and I'm not best pleased. So here are my terms.'

His wife attempted to interrupt.

'Sophia, you've had your say and I'll have mine. Right? I don't have a job for you so I have found you one. It's an under-manager's job with Archie Popplestone. He lost his to Arthur Sellers this morning. He finished his man for messing up an order. Anyway Popplestone is alright, Vice President of the Regional Association. Hopes to be president next year and thinks he may be with my support. It doesn't amount to a manager's wage but I'll come to that. I'm not having a grandchild of mine brought up in rooms. There's a decent house in Vicarage Road here in Armley, I'll rent it and you'll live in it. No rent. That should get your finances in better shape.'

'Father I'm so grateful'

'You've not heard it all yet. We'll not visit you there and you'll not bring that woman here. My grandchild is another matter and you will bring him on Sundays.'

'Yes of course I will.' Jonathan would have agreed to almost anything.

'Last thing you rein in that woman's spending.'

'I will I'm determined.' Jonathan rose to leave.

'And where are you going now?'

'Elizabeth is home today' he lied.

'So it'll do her no harm to wonder where you've been while she's been gallivanting. Stay the night. Give her something to think about and show her you're a man-and show me.'

Holding themselves in readiness at the hotel, sewing bags in hand, the three waited until ten o'clock but were not summoned. Carrying their bags they hurried to the cathedral and the point on the pavement on the east side where they had been told to wait. The throng they found there dismayed them. It seemed that the whole of the city must have gathered there. The road was kept clear but the pavement opposite the east entrance was a crush and the three women were pressed to the walls of the building behind them. They had hoped, naively, that if the bridal carriages were to pass by there, they would have a view of the women and girls in their dresses but, in that crowd they would see nothing other than the back of tall hats and wide bonnets.

Chatter in the crowds suggested that the carriages would circle the cathedral before the party alighted at the front, south entrance, so there was a hope of a sighting. As eleven o'clock approached more and more pushed on to the pavement. Some spilled onto the road and were driven back by police constables. The three at the rear were being crushed and were in fear of fainting for lack of air.

A figure appeared from the east entrance. He wore ceremonial uniform of a Captain of the Hussars. A short cape draped one shoulder and his black uniform was adorned with gold braid. Black trousers with a gold stripe the length of each outer leg rested were worn over riding boots, the tops of which vied with the spurs on their heels for which could better reflect in the morning sun. A sword in his sheath completed the epitome of the dashing cavalry officer.

He strode across the road and the crowd, although pressed, parted sufficiently for him to reach the three ladies at the rear. They had been unaware of him until those immediately in front had stepped aside but now they saw Jeremy Howard, not the urbane man but the very portrait of a young warrior. He carried their bags and led them to the east entrance where stood a solider, sword unsheathed and held vertically. The Captain placed the bags behind him and gave an order 'Guard those.' The solider, already at attention, did not reply but stiffened in acknowledgement.

The ladies were escorted to an upper gallery to the very rear where they found many others standing but the gallery was slightly tiered and they had a view of the part of the aisle and the altars. The magnificence of the architecture, the vibrations from the organ and the voices of what they estimated to be over thirty choristers combined to provide the three seamstresses with an experience they could never imagine they would ever have. In whispered voices they speculated on the identities of the members of the royal family who might be present in the foremost pews. They could not have identified any of them even if their faces had been visible, although Beattie was sure that the young gentleman at the front must have been the Honourable William, the bridegroom.

The bride came into view on her father's arm. Alexandra and Marina, erect and perfectly in step followed. Where were Louisa and Clarrisa? Spotted at last, they walked between the bride and the two adult maids. Louisa matched the strides of her sister Lady Annabelle and Clarissa, having made a number of unsuccessful attempts to do likewise, settled for skipping along. The five dresses brushed the tops of satin slippers and floated above the tiles of the aisle without touching them at any point. The dressmakers were well satisfied with their work.

It had been a long service with moving readings and uplifting hymns and Elizabeth felt privileged to have been present, she wondered though what Sister Benedicta would say if she knew that a child raised by her had been to a protestant service, or, which was just as sinful, had been married in a register office.

It was one thirty before the equerry returned to them. By then the wedding party, the guests and almost all those who, like the three dressmakers, had been admitted had left. He returned them to the east entrance where they retrieved their sewing bags and found the street outside almost empty. It had been a wonderful surprise for the ladies to be admitted, to see the results of their work, and they were left speechless – reduced to grinning. The Captain explained that he must leave them to attend to duties concerned with the evening's banquet and then, to the bemusement of the solider, still mute and rigid, he instructed them to kneel on one knee. He drew his sword, touched each on both shoulders and said, 'I dub thee The Ladies of the Gowns.' With that he spun on his heels of his boots and the three fell to the floor in fits of laughter. Their last view of him was a pair of burnished spurs descending the steps. A good dinner, a little wine, packing of cases and early to bed would cap a perfect day.

Fellow passengers on the morning train to Leeds were intrigued by the three young ladies who each addressed the other as M'lady.

Jonathan had returned home later on the Saturday afternoon to find a telegram informing him that it would be tomorrow before Elizabeth would be home. He changed, checked his appearance in the mirror and told himself that his fortunes improved by the day. Fortune, nothing, he corrected himself, the only part of his plan over which he had no control was the timing of Elizabeth's pregnancy. That it should occur within a month of their marriage was the only part that chance had played. Tonight he would toast both his plans and benevolent fortune in gin at the White Hart.

A pale and apprehensive Oswald Levine met the dressmakers on the platform at Leeds. He improved visibly when told of the success of the gowns and a return of a good proportion of his one pound and five pound notes lifted his spirits even more. Each of the three was given a one pound note and all agreed that he was still, clearly, not himself.

Jonathan was in no doubt that Elizabeth would return incapable of resisting the need to tell him every detail of every day since she had left the house on Thursday morning. He would, he was determined, show great interest and wait until she had squeezed every last tedious drop from her experiences. He would wait because it would suit him to save his news and present it casually as if there was never any doubt its inevitability.

Elizabeth, as he had predicted, gave him an almost full account of her days but she omitted any reference to Jeremy Howard by name; simply referring to him as a person charged with liaison. It was not that she had any improper thoughts about the Captain, nor was it to prevent Jonathan from feeling he had any cause for jealousy, it was that thoughts of Captain Howard forced her to draw unfavourable comparisons with her husband, the father of her unborn child, the man she loved.

When she had finished Jonathan, congratulating himself on the patience he had shown through her inane prattle, began.

'Darling I am so proud of you but I must confess I have been miserable while you have been away from me. Missing you makes me realise even more the depth of my love for you. I wish I had been able to be with you in London and could have been had I known that the position I have been awaiting would be so long in coming. But now I have It.' he slapped his knees. 'I start to morrow.'

'Oh Jonathan,' she held him and told him how pleased she was for him. 'I'm not done. These rooms are not suitable for raising our child and I have arranged to rent a whole house into which we can move quite soon. The house is in Armley, not too close to my parents' home, and chosen because it is in an area I know well and well out of the city. Contact with my parents will not be an issue because I intend that there should not be any.'

'I am delighted dear Jonathan, I truly am, but is this affordable?'

'Elizabeth, my darling, you need have no concerns about that. We have been dependant on your wages for some time now and you insisted on this so I could await an appropriate opportunity. Now I have it I shall take all responsibility for finances. It is right that I should since the rent of a complete house is an expense that would be a worry to you and you should be unworried in your condition. My wages will not reach their full worth until I am established but with yours added to them we can certainly afford the house at Armley.'

Oswald Levine was back in his office on the Monday morning. His health and spirits improved daily that week. Two London newspapers had given prominence to the wedding and both had afforded photographs to a description of the dresses, a full appraisal of them both credited the Levine Studios of Leeds. A letter received from the secretary to Lady Annabelle's father was fulsome in its praise of Levine's work, spoke of the compliments that had been showered on the exquisite gowns, told of the bride's delight and included a reference to the additional expenses that Levine had incurred in the days leading up to the wedding. His invoice, which should include all those additional expenses, would be dealt with expeditiously on its receipt.

Levine received two more letters that week, each bore the crest of Kensington Palace, and was signed by Captain Jeremy Howard and was accompanied by a covering note. The first letter commended the skill and professionalism of his three dressmakers and how they eased his task as liaison officer. The covering note asked that this be drawn to the attention of the three ladies. Levine did more than that, he displayed it in the sewing room. The accompanying note to the second letter wished Levine a swift return to full health and told him that he should treat the letter as confidential. The letter began by regretting that the two of them had been unable to renew their brief acquaintanceship and went on to commend the dedication to her work displayed by his employee Mrs Elizabeth Fry. She had, from the time of her arrival, worked exhausting hours to locate the bridal gown and to make perfect a fit for two infant young ladies in the hours before their first public engagement. They had, he disclosed, felt like fairy princesses and were disappointed not to find Mrs Fry at the banquet. He felt that her modesty might prevent her part in the full extent of the success of the Levine Studios in London being brought to Mr Levines's attention.

Levine was seeing Elizabeth in a new light and his intention to replace her in the latter stages of her pregnancy would have to be reviewed. That was confirmed when he found himself being interviewed by fashion writers from local newspapers and London publications, reinforced by the flood of commissions he was being offered when he learned that competitors were making overtures to lure his staff.

That Christmas Levine had no hesitation in awarding Elizabeth her bonus even though, once more, she had not served the full year. The sum was two pounds. She had given Jonathan the pound she had received following her week in London but she would keep this two pounds for her christening fund. She was well into the ninth month of her pregnancy, was becoming unable to travel from her new home in Armley and was finding it difficult to sit for long days at her worktable. Levine had said nothing about dismissing her but, despite her worries over the loss of her wages felt she had no option but to resign her position. Levine though would not hear of it. Elizabeth sat as comfortably as her condition would permit and Levine offered her a proposition. He would continue to pay her wages throughout her confinement upon the agreement that she would return within a month after the birth.

While this appeared to her exceptionally generous she was unaware that for Levine this was a business decision not a personal favour. The commissions for Christmas balls were all completed but his order books were filled by Spring weddings, Summer garden parties and lots of christening orders some for the full year ahead, showing exceptional forward planning.

She would have to decline, she regretted, but would not wish to leave her child to the care of another and a sewing room was no place for a baby. Levine was not done.

'For me, Elizabeth, you are a talented and valued dressmaker and I would consider you a loss; for you, well, you are earning wages that match and in some cases exceed those paid by other studios. These are wages that could provide well for a growing child.'

'Mr Levine. My husband has a senior position and will provide for us and though I confess I will miss the work I enjoy I must have time with my child. The pangs of having my baby consider a nurse maid to be its mother would be too much for me.'

'And if I was to provide a work table and deliver pieces and patterns to your home.'

'Then I should need to consult my husband.'

Unsure of Jonathan's reaction she approached the subject tentatively that evening. It had been his intention to hire a day nursemaid and have Elizabeth back in work within two weeks. He had already made enquiries and found he could secure one for no more than half the wages his wife could earn. This arrangement was better still so, having stated that his preference would have been for her to remain at home with her baby and no other work, he agreed to the proposal. When she appeared ready to abandon the idea he pressed her that she should employ her skills of which he was so proud.

The baby, named as they had discussed in the kitchen of his father's house, was born on the last day of January. Matthew Fry had a crib in his nursery room and a new baby carriage in the hall. He was warmly dressed in the beautiful clothes that Elizabeth delighted in making on the worktable that Levine had had delivered. She could not recall a time when she had been happier nor when Jonathan seemed more content.

Jonathan was indeed content. His work carried little responsibility and consisted mainly of recording orders and supervising the loading and unloading of narrow boats on the canal. It was not well paid but with Elizabeth's earnings, no nursemaid to pay and no rent to pay he was worry free. For a man who avoided responsibility and had difficulty coping with worry his situation was ideal. There was a hurdle to overcome and he would deal with it that coming Sunday.

This was the second Sunday after Matthew's birth and that morning he said, as nonchalantly as he was able, 'Would you dress Matthew please? As much as I wished it were not so, I feel that his grand parents have an entitlement to see their only grandchild.'

'But Jonathan, I fear I would not be received '

'And I would not subject my wife to any animosity. I'll go alone, consider it a duty, though what duty I owe I do not know, and that will be an end to it.'

Elizabeth was uneasy but felt unable to object. She dressed Matthew in his most appealing clothes, wrapped him warmly in his carriage and had feelings of foreboding as she watched her husband and child leave. Soon there was a knock at the door and she opened it to Beattie and Devina. Pleased to see them but disappointed that it had not been Jonathan with Matthew she greeted them and showed her two friends her new home. Unlike York Place this viewing could be considered a tour.

They had brought her a gift. It was an exquisite creation a christening gown made of silk, satin and lace made of the surplice of the London wedding. Elizabeth was overcome and wept. It was a culmination of giving birth without the support of a close female relative, her apprehension over her baby being with the Frys and the subtle changes she was detecting in Jonathan but was trying to ignore. Now here were two friends with a beautiful gift and her emotions had taken over.

'Jonathan is out walking Matthew. He is so proud of him I expect them back soon.'

She offered tea and her two colleagues wanted to wait so that they could see the baby but when noon became mid-afternoon, when conversation had stalled and the father and son had not returned silence became embarrassing. Reluctantly they would have to leave, they said and Elizabeth was saddened. She was also in discomfort caused by the retention of Matthew's mid-day feed, concerned about his hunger and was unable to understand why a duty visit should take six hours.

When Jonathan returned he was in no mood to be defensive. His parents, for all their faults, should not be denied the company of their grandson. His wife, for whom he had provided everything she could wish, was showing signs of becoming an ingrate. His mother, who having had three children in almost as many years, knew more about feeding babies than she ever would and, although he had puked and soiled his dress, he would adjust to cows milk on occasions. He, Jonathan was the head of this household and his parents would have regular visits from him and his son. The matter was not open to discussion. Elizabeth was shocked and thought so much for Sunday being our special day!

Actually, Jonathan had expected a visit of no more than an hour or two but he had been prevailed upon to remain for the day and he was now in his father's control as much as he had ever been. Edmund Fry had hoped to be able to cast doubt on the fathering of the child but he had to accept there could be no such doubt. Even at such an early age, Matthew with his dark fuzz and delicate features was as close a miniature of Jonathan to admit no such question.

Sunday after Sunday her husband took her son and she was left alone. Elizabeth returned first to her prayers and then, one Sunday to her church to attend mass. She spoke to Father Flanagan and he invited her to the presbytery to discuss her request. 'Remain aware Elizabeth that you are not married in the sight of God. He turns his face against your adultery. Your house is a house of sin and while, as a matter of urgency, your child should be baptised unless he should die and be forbidden entry into heaven, it would be preferable if your husband was to convert as he agreed, marry at the altar and I would baptise him and your son before declaring you man and wife – which you are not.'

How receptive would Jonathan be to this she wondered? Not at all she was to find.

'And this is the priest, this sinless man, who lied to me when I went to see him seeking you. Damn him and his church.'

Chapter 19

Since that day there was a distance between the two that Elizabeth was unable to cross and which Jonathan had no interest in crossing. The next week when Levine collected her finished orders and delivered her new pieces and patterns she had Matthew ready, dressed in his christening gown. She asked if she could share her employer's carriage back to the studio and when they arrived she asked the driver to wait. Beattie and Devina made a fuss over the baby boy and even Edna and Madeline were drawn from their tables and both cooed at the little bundle.

Not wishing to disrupt the work of the sitting room any longer, Elizabeth returned to the carriage and gave the driver directions to Bethlehem near Harrogate. She rode through the passage between the church and the school saw the house ahead, her home from childhood and a place to which she had not returned for five years.

The door was opened by Mrs Mullins who hugged her so well that she feared Matthew would be squashed. A commotion followed in which all the residents, other than those sisters and children engaged in school, filled the hall and excitement reigned.

At last alone in Sister Benedicta's office she looked at the Mother Superior who seemed much aged and a little shrunken but the light in her eyes was undimmed. Elizabeth told her briefly of her life and her experiences since being placed with Agnes Kavanagh in Leeds and then she came to the point.

'Mother I wish to have Matthew baptised but I am told that since I am living in sin and since my husband has decided now that he will not convert I cannot do so. The fear of my son dying in original sin and being consigned to limbo for eternity haunts my days and robs me of my sleep. Who can advise me?'

'Elizabeth my child when we make our confessions we say a prayer in which we promise never to sin again but if we kept that promise we should never need to make our confessions again and our priests would be under employed. All that our confessional prayer requires of us is that we resolve to avoid the occasion of sin, and we would if sin would avoid us.'

The old nun walked round her desk, took Matthew, returned to her seat and nursed him to her breast. 'Now don't you go telling the Bishop, but I am not a believer in Purgatory. I can't reconcile that with an all-merciful God who would deny an innocent such as this child the presence of Himself and his angel hosts. That is not to say that baptism is not important in later life. It is not, in my belief, an exemption from Limbo but it is a gateway to the other sacraments – Matthew's confirmation, his taking of communion, his marriage in church or, God forbid, his taking of holy orders. Wait here.'

She handed the baby back and on unsteady legs left the room. From the window Elizabeth saw Sister Benedicta making slow progress down the drive. Immediately, Sister Teresa was in the office, and Elizabeth chatted with her like a sister until Mother Superior was seen making her way back.

'If you would have Matthew baptised Father Daley will do it now if the sisters who are not engaged in school and the younger girls could be present too' Elizabeth stopped her 'oh yes' Sister Benedicta pleaded to be excused. Her legs could not make the long walk again so soon but readily accepted Elizabeth's offer of a ride in the carriage she had hired. Matthew was baptised, sponsored by Sister Teresa and Sister Louis and it was a relieved mother who rode back to Armley that afternoon. She would not tell Jonathan who had no interest in the matter.

The following morning Jonathan was more distant than he had been but gave no reason why until he returned home that evening.

'There has been money in your purse since Christmas and now it has all but gone.'

'I took a carriage to my childhood home to show our son at a cost of eight shillings.'

'And the other pound, Elizabeth.'

'It was a donation to the church that baptised Matthew. Would you begrudge that?'

'I carry a demanding workload and bear a heavy responsibility to provide this home and you attach so little value to the money I earn that you throw it away to re-stock a Bishop's wine cellar or to buy a jewel for a Pope's slipper.'

'And do I not earn money?'

'Your wages are a contribution to the upkeep of this home. A contribution. No more. I shall be out this evening.' With that he left.

Elizabeth's feelings for her husband were fading and she came to realize that if she was ever to have a penny for her son she would have to earn it and hide it from Jonathan. Motherhood was changing her and she was becoming more driven and confident. She had seen something of other ways of life; Harewood House, Queen Anne's Gate, a royal equerry and the respect she was shown both as a lady and for her abilities. Her husband, the man who professed his love, the man whose respect she ought to have, was showing her none.

Her long talks with Doris Churchill had offered her perspectives that she had not considered before and her recent brief visit to the Mother Superior had relieved her of her catholic guilt that had always influenced her actions. If earning money and hiding it from Jonathan were a deception then a deception it would have to be. Without evidence but highly suspicious, she believed that he was deceiving her and that she and her son could not rely on him.

Pushing Matthew, she visited furniture stores, showing samples of her work. Although she did not receive any orders she did have an interesting proposal from Hanson's Family Furnishers to produce runners, antimacassars, table-cloths and pillow cases that the store would display. They would take a commission on sales and pass the surplus to Elizabeth. Sundays became her Hanson days. Jonathan was at his parent's home with Matthew and she put the time to good use.

Some weeks she achieved no sales and some she made ten shillings and more. Even allowing for the cost of cotton, linen, lace and thread, by the time of Matthew's first birthday she had eighteen pounds secreted in the bottom of her sewing box, a place in which Jonathan had no interest nor any reason to look.

Aching to spend some of this on a gift for Matthew but knowing she would be unable to explain the source of the money to Jonathan she satisfied herself with making her son a blue silk suit with a lace collar.

Matthew's second year continued as the first with Sundays spent at his grandparent's home. Elizabeth worked six days each week for Levine and one day for her own business. There was no affection shown to her by her husband but her focus was her son and their future independence that she was certain they would need. She received no money from Jonathan and paid over all her Levine wages to him. Shopping for the house was all done at Craven's Emporium where Elizabeth would leave orders to be delivered and Jonathan would settle Craven's accounts.

It was apparent to Elizabeth that there was no shortage of money as Jonathan regularly bought suits of clothes, shoes, and shirts for himself. On the only occasion she had questioned this he told her that his appearance was essential to his success and she shared in the rewards of that success. His tone had been dismissive and she saw no point in raising the matter again.

The fact was that Jonathan was not having any success. He had been with Popplestone for over eighteen months and his title of under-manager meant little and paid little more than a clerk's wages. Yet with Elizabeth's earnings from Levine, that exceeded his own, and living rent-free he had money to spare for his appearance and the drinking he now did in the Navigation Inn.

Archie Popplestone had been angry at having failed to be elected Regional President the previous year, despite employing Fry's useless son. However the post became vacant again when the post holder, a haulier in Tadcaster was declared insolvent. In June that year Popplestone had been successful and while his duties would be a distraction from his day to day work his elevation in the world of transport would be worth more to him. Within a month, his manager retired in ill health and the assistant manager, Kershaw was a lazy, overweight fellow who appointed

Jonathan assistant manager and passed his workload down to him.

Assistant Manager Jonathan Fry, pleased with the modest pay rise but less pleased with having responsibilities, saw an opportunity. He told Elizabeth that since he was virtually running the company he would have meetings and functions to attend some evenings so it would be convenient for him to spend some nights at his club the club in question was the De Lay hotel, a cheap guest house where he would spend some one or two nights a week with Molly Shaw whose acquaintance; he had made at the Navigation Inn.

He shared a bed with Elizabeth but there was no physical relationship, something to which he had never attached much importance. With Molly, though, it was a more exciting experience. She was abandoned and adventurous, which Elizabeth had never been, he told himself. Molly flattered his abilities as a lover which, Elizabeth would without doubt have done, had she had experiences to compare, he was convinced. Moreover, it was not uncommon, he was sure, for a gentleman to take a mistress, it relieved a wife of a duty. Seated at the bar in the best room of the Navigation Inn, Jonathan felt exceedingly pleased with himself. He was wearing a good suit, had money in his pocket, a mistress, a son, parents who doted on that son and a wife who kept a good house, earned well and was no cause of aggravation to him or the life he chose to lead. He was joined by a gentleman of about his own age who offered him one of the two tumblers of gin he had bought.

'May I join you Mr Fry.'

Jonathan was suspicious of the man's motives. He was exceptually well spoken and presented, but affected, almost effeminate thought Jonathan. The gentleman however made it plain immediately that his interest in Jonathan was a business proposition.

'I am told Mr Fry that you might be receptive to a mutually profitable venture. If you would permit me to outline it to you and if you feel you must reject it or if you feel offended be it in any way then I ask that it be forgotten and we part on good terms.'

Jonathan sat in silence, inviting this stranger to continue.

'I manage a company near Bradford that has recently received a sizable contract to supply processed leather to a group of factories in Leeds which manufacture footwear, bags, gloves indeed all manner of goods. We have a haulier who conveys our raw material such as salts and acids from Manchester but I believe I could secure a most competitive price from another haulier for this new contract as it will entail many repeated orders.'

Jonathan was not pleased to have his evening interrupted by a request for a quotation and said. 'I thank you for the gin Sir. As regards a quotation, my manager, a Mr Kershaw, will, I am sure, be pleased to oblige you in business hours.'

'Which I certainly would have done Mr Fry had I not been informed that you were the power behind Mr Kershaw's over-wide throne.'

The two laughed and the visitor to Jonathan's bar continued.

'The contract for transport to Leeds is in my gift. It will be sought by a number of hauliers and I would wish to have some reward for my awarding of it. Also, I would expect to share that reward with the manager who performed the service for his employer who was awarded it.'

Jonathan, now interested, asked. 'Please speak plainly Sir, tell me what you propose and how these rewards are to be shared.'

Purchasing two more tumblers of gin, mere full tumblers not half measures, he continued in a voice that could not be overheard.

'For each twenty pounds that your company would charge you would, in a name of your choice invoice my company for twenty two pounds. One pound for you and one for me. You would pay the twenty-pound into your company who would believe that their contract was with the name under which you are operating. Both you and I would each benefit from five percent of the value of each transportation I would be rewarded for awarding the contract to you and you would be rewarded for securing business for your company that it otherwise would not have had.'

As Jonathan thought on this he saw no risk. This gentleman's company would raise no questions and Popplestone would have a new business at its full rates. 'How much do you believe this arrangement would be worth to us?'

I would be most disappointed Mr Fry if I, we, were not to make at least one hundred pounds in our first year.'

'I should mention, Sir, that Popplestone operates a quaint system whereby the insuring of each load, amounting to three percent of its value, is the responsibility of the owner of the goods and is paid in advance.'

'Quaint but not uncommon, the payment for the insurance would also have to be paid to you and paid over by your employers.'

The details were gone over then gone over again. Jonathan was guided on the preparations he would have to make and eventually, his judgement clouded and his confidence boosted by too much gin offered his hand.

'And you are, Sir.'

'Dexter, Julian Dexter. Miles Tanners and Dyers of Wilsden.'

Alone again he pondered the steps he would now take. He would need a company letterhead and a bank account in that name. But what name? He chose it with a wry smile. He would be Edward, a stronger name than Jonathan and he would be Edward Mason, to mock his father the newly appointed Grand Master of the lodge. Edward Mason Transport. The letterhead was designed in his mind and he would go ahead with the printing. His address would be the postal office from where he would collect his letters. The bank account, though presented a problem. He needed a sizable sum to deposit in order to establish solvency of the newly formed company and he did not have it.

A table in the back bar of the Navigation Inn served as an office for Barney Baines, taker of bets, pawn broker and money lender. Their negotiations were brief and Jonathan left the Inn with fifty pounds to be repaid at eight pounds each month for twelve months. Easily repayable, he felt.

The effects of the gin wore off overnight and Jonathan awoke with less confidence than he had had the previous evening. He didn't know this fellow Dexter, he wondered if he could trust him and he worried about the consequences of discovery. At lunchtime he returned to the Navigation Inn and attempted to return the fifty pounds. Baines would not have it.

'Mr Fry, we are both businessmen. We both have to project our expected income and expenses, not day by day but year on year. Our families and our enterprises rely upon it. I am relying on a return of my investment of fifty pounds by the end of one year. If you wish to offer me those ninety-six pounds now then our business is concluded.'

Jonathan could not have paid such a sum and slapped the fifty pounds on the table. 'Mr Baines, our business is concluded. That is an end to it.' Thus relieved he returned to his office but Baines was not prepared to cancel the debt. Leaving his office that evening, intent on a night at his club with Molly he was met by two men who pushed him against a wall.

'This is your money Mr Fry' said one and pushed the fifty pounds in his pocket. 'All Mr Baines asks is the first repayment of eight pounds in one month's time. Then, with metal-capped boots, they kicked his shins from ankle to knee and warned him of the consequences if he should fail to make the payments. In no state to meet Molly he took a carriage home and told Elizabeth, who had not expected him home that night, that he had fallen over a barrow. She bathed his bruised and bleeding legs and dressed them with strips of cotton.

Pain and worry conspired to prevent him from sleeping. He could repay Baines from the sum loaned but that would be gone in six months and then what? There was no means by which he would be able to raise eight pounds a month after that. Dexter's proposal or Baines's violence ? His mind was made up for him and he would order the letterheads at once and deposit the fifty pounds.

Within two weeks the scheme was operating and, despite Jonathan's misgivings, after three months it had been operating pleasingly well. Masons invoiced Miles, in advance for insurance and in arrears for transporting finished leather from Wilsden to Leeds by narrow boat on the canal. Miles paid Masons, Masons paid Popplestone and Dexter. Jonathan had made three payments to Baines and his bank account still contained fifty pounds. His old arrogance was back and he had (he smiled at his phrase) 'mollified Molly'. Once Baines was paid off he would have fifty pounds and his entire share from Dexter's contract with his company.

Masons, would be his. With patience and diligence he could amass a good sum in the following year.

But now, fortune that had smiled upon him now frowned. It was three days before Christmas and heavy snow had delayed shipments from Wilsden. The towpaths were impossible in places and the canals were frozen. Some of Mason's invoices to Miles were unpaid and Jonathan was holding payments for insurance from Miles for loads yet to be transported.

Elizabeth placed her food order at Craven's Emporium. It was slightly larger than the usual modest order and she hoped Jonathan would not object. When Craven's manager took her aside she was perplexed and when he told her that the order would not be filled until the previous month's bills had been paid she was embarrassed. She told Jonathan as soon as he arrived home and he accused the clerk at the store of being either incompetent or a thief. He would, he said, attend to it. He visited Craven's, claimed there had been an oversight by his wife and issued a cheque signed by Edward Mason, explaining it was his business account. The manager, dubious but uncertain, delivered the order.

Again Matthew's gift would be a new suit of clothes. Jonathan bought nothing for his wife or his son. On Christmas morning he told Elizabeth that he would be taking Matthew to see his grandparents. Her objections were dismissed and she watched as they left, as she always did. There was ice on the steps and she watched the toddler slip from his father's hand and strike his head on the wall.

Jonathan brought him back into the house. Matthew had a swelling on his forehead that was growing to the size of a duck egg. The skin was broken and there was blood on his new suit.

'Clean him up and change his clothes, Elizabeth, I can't take him like that.'

'Jonathan, you cannot take him at all. He is staying home today. I need to care for his injuries.'

Jonathan was in a fearsome temper and said he would not be defied. Elizabeth said he would and he raised his hand to her, something he had not done before. He lowered it quickly when his wife branded a pair of shears, his nerve having deserted him, he left alone. Although he returned that night not a word passed between them and when he failed to enquire about the well being of their son, Elizabeth decided that it was the end. With forty pounds in her sewing box basket, and although it was not a fortune she considered it would be more than enough to support her and Matthew for some time.

He left next morning, Friday, taking a case and telling Elizabeth that he would be staying at his club that night. There were letters for him at the postal office. Dexter informed him that an unusually large consignment, held up by the weather, was ready for collection. Its value was four hundred pounds and the insurance payments he had received should all be allocated to that load. Another letter was from the bank. The terms of his business account required a continuing balance of fifty pounds. The order he had issued to the benefit of Craven's Emporium, a sum of two pounds, seventeen shillings and five pence would reduce that balance below the agreed amount and would not be paid until sufficient funds were deposited. He deposited Dexter's insurance payments of twelve pounds.

By tomorrow the payment for outstanding invoices should be received and would pay the insurance premiums then. This afternoon he would send a narrow boat for Dexter's goods and tonight he would entertain Molly.

Arriving late at his office on the Saturday morning he checked that the narrow boat had left yesterday. It had and should be returning today. The Miles bills were not at the postal office and the bank was closed. Late that afternoon he was resigned to an evening at home and a day to follow with his parents. If Elizabeth should object he would overrule her, shears or no shears. Readying himself to leave he saw Archie Popplestone arrive followed by Kershaw, hurrying and perspiring. Jonathan was instructed to wait in his office.

Still in ignorance of the crisis that would bring Popplestone into the office late on a Saturday evening, Jonathan was called in. Popplestone was clearly troubled.

'Mr Fry (not Jonathan, he thought, and that was a bad sign) we have had a disaster on the canal. The tow rope of one of our boats has snagged in the entry gate of a lock and the rising water has sunk the boat. Our man saved himself but the boy drowned. Our boat is insured and Mason's load is but the boy is not.'

Jonathan was shaken but attempted to conceal it but his question was crass. 'The load was leather, finished but not yet manufactured and once dried out should still be saleable.'

Popplestone, incredulous, looked at Kershaw in disbelief and answered, 'I took the boy on as a favour to his father. The lad was nor but a child and you are concerned about the insurance company's liability. Have you ever seen a load that has been in the bottom of a canal, covered in slime and sludge. It will not be worth a penny and the insurers will have to pay Mason out, unless they can prove any liability against us. So let's get started on that. Where are Mason's works?' 'Somewhere past Bradford. His goods are loaded at Wilsden, I don't know his works. We deal with a postal office, have done for four months without a problem.'

Kershaw passed his employer a correspondence file and Popplestone became more annoyed. 'I would be interested to know, Mr Fry, why a leather treater in Wilsden utilises a postal office address in Leeds. Can you enlighten me?'

Jonathan, his mouth dry and his legs weak, replied, 'I really do not know.'

'No, and you were not sufficiently interested to wonder when you took this contract on. I doubt we shall need to inform Mason, he'll be in touch with us soon enough when he hears. For now fetch me the insurers receipt for this load.'

Jonathan left Popplestone's office, there was no receipt to fetch and he fled. His evening was spent in the Devonshire Arms on the Otley Road where he was not known and the Saturday and Sunday night was spent in a guesthouse nearby. The postal office opened at nine o'clock and he collected a letter from Dexter containing payments for the outstanding invoices, a sum of eighty pounds and he was the first customer at the bank at ten o'clock, to deposit those payments. When he asked to withdraw the total sum of his deposits and the new ones the clerk asked him to wait. Invited into the manager's office, but anxious to be out of the bank he went in reluctantly. If he was to withdraw the balance of the fifty pounds his business account would have to be closed and the new deposits of eighty pounds could not be processed.

The manager was suspicious when 'Mr Mason' said he would withdraw the fifty pounds, which he was given and watched in disbelief as his customer abandoned his new deposits and sprinted from his office.

A fugitive depends on clarity of thought fully focused on self-preservation and Jonathan was gaining it. He had avoided his home, the De Lay hotel and the Navigation Inn, all places where he might be looked for. The visit to the postal office had been a risk and, as it transpired, a pointless risk. The bank had been a lesser risk and he had his fifty pounds. It was, he realised, Barney Baines fifty pounds and he would have to be avoided too. He bought notepaper and envelopes, wrote letters to Elizabeth and his father and paid for their delivery. This would be his last night in Leeds and he intended to enjoy it. Darkness fell before four o'clock and he considered it safe to visit Molly in the kitchen of the bakery where she worked, although on the wharf it was well enough away from Popplestone's and the Navigation Inn. They spoke at the kitchen door and it was arranged that he would meet her there at six o'clock. That night it would not be the De lay hotel but another, and far grander.

Jonathan spent the two hours back at the Devonshire Arms, drinking gin and finalising the new life he would begin next morning. Molly had been busy in that two hours, she left the kitchen and went to the back bar of the Navigation Inn to provide the information she had been told to provide. She gave it not for reward but to avoid a beating.

At six o'clock, Jonathan was back at the baker's shop on the wharf. The canal side was dark, and the night was cold and ice was forming on the cobbles. The light in the shop was extinguished but Molly did not appear. A figure did approach him and even from a distance he recognised Barney Baines. Jonathan ran along the wharf but two more figures were waiting. His repayments had been made on time but he must have learned he thought, of the situation he was in and Baines would want a full repayment; a sum he did not have. If they were to give him a beating he would be unable to escape the city. It was inevitable he would be arrested and imprisoned.

The only route open to him was the loading bay of a haulier whose men were unloading a late arrived narrow boat. Baines and his thugs pursued him through the bay and up two floors to the crane platform. There was nowhere else to go and Jonathan climbed on to the spar that overhung the black freezing water below. His three pursuers stood at the hatch, issuing oaths and attracting a crowd of spectators below. Jonathan's heartbeat was rapid, he was sick with fear and when one of Baines men started to crawl across the spar towards him, he launched himself into the darkness. His best hope was to reach the water, which he did, but only after striking the bow of the narrow boat. He sank beneath the water and those on the wharf watched by torchlight but he did not resurface.

Chapter 20

Elizabeth had not expected Jonathan home on the Friday night and was not displeased when he did not return on the Saturday. He would, she was sure be back on Sunday to collect Matthew. When he failed to return she was curious but nothing more. The feelings for him were gone.

Late on Monday afternoon she was visited by three ruffians demanding to see her husband. They wouldn't accept that he was not there and brushed her aside to search the house to satisfy themselves. One of them, the leader she thought, told her 'Tell him that his problems are his concern not mine, they excuse nothing. He owes a debt and I'll take some goods while I am here. A severity if you like.'

He walked around her home making insulting comments about the furnishings but pointing out certain items for his accomplices to gather together, a baby carriage, a cot, a sewing bag and a desk. They would have taken these on the cart they had waiting until two other figures appeared at the open door. They were big men and both wore black full-length rubber raincoats. One, a balding man whose appearance was as unappealing as the first three spoke.

'Baines, get out and crawl back to the rat hole you've crept from.'

Elizabeth expected violence and held Matthew who was frightened and crying. Instead the three ruffians left without a murmur. The man who had ejected them then spoke to Elizabeth.

'I am Sergeant of Detectives Martin Leary and I wish to speak to Mr Edward Mason.'

Elizabeth told him, truthfully and convincingly, that she knew of no one of that name but was shocked to be told that a payment made on Mr Mason's account had been issued to Craven's Emporium to settle her outstanding grocery bills. He asked for her permission to search his home and being unsure whether a police officer could do that, with or without permission, and expecting it to be a cursory search for an Edward Mason, she agreed. It was soon apparent that this was to be a meticulous search of every item in every drawer.

They started with Jonathan's desk, which was locked, and they demanded a key, which she did not have. A tool was produced from a pocket and the drawer, splintered, was opened. Letter heads for Edward Mason, letters were found and shown to Elizabeth who was mystified but, as they continued examining every document in the desk she took the opportunity to retrieve her savings from her sewing bag and place them in her pinafore. They would not, she hoped, search a woman – Matthew, understanding nothing, but sensing his mother's fear, continued to cry.

The police officers took three hours over their search and gave Elizabeth a receipt for the documents they were intending to seize before telling her on leaving, 'Mrs Fry, we have more enquiries to make and would advise you that it will not go well for you if you relocate yourself without informing us. We can show that your husband and Edward Mason are one and the same, a fact that you are well aware of and you can expect that when we trace him you will find yourself in the dock of the court alongside him.'

For three days she had no interest in seeing Jonathan but now wished that she could. What had he done? Who was Edward Mason? Why was she suspected of being a compliant in it, whatever 'it' was.

A letter delivered next morning was no more enlightening.

'My dearest Elizabeth,'

There has been a tragedy on the canal and while it is none of my doing I fear the blame is to be laid on me. There have been financial irregularities, lies have been told and all so cleverly that I cannot see how I will be able to defend myself. I have been suspecting for some time that there was malpractice at Popplestone's and I was on the point of explaining it when a fraud was contrived to discredit me. The more I think on this the more I become convinced that this malpractice has been perpetrated for some years and I was appointed to be a scapegoat should it come to light.

The result of all this would, undoubtedly be my imprisonment. While I could bear that, as in just as it would be, I could not bear your ruin. Nor could I even contemplate seeing any doubts about me on your face.

My life is over and I will finish it but I do this to spare you the disgrace of seeing your husband in chains, no matter how undeserving that would be.

Raise our son as well as I know you will.

Your loving husband

Jonathan.

Elizabeth, embittered, did not believe a word of it and crumpled the letter into the pinafore pocket that held her savings. Instead of allowing herself to be defeated by this disintegration of her life she looked at her son and, drawing strength from his reliance on her, she determined to do whatever was necessary to provide for and protect him. She had played no part in her husbands crimes, knew nothing about them, and she was not going to sit about waiting to be put in a police cell and have Matthew placed who knew where, it might be some orphanage, some uncertain institution. At best but also at worse it would be with the hated Frys. She set about packing her case.

Her front door was opened by someone who had a key. Edmund and Sophia Fry came in, uninvited and Edmund brandished a letter. Elizabeth recognised the notepaper and, although Fry was shaking the letter at her she recognised the handwriting.

'Our son is dead and it's your doing. I see you're packing and quite right, I want you out of here now.'

Elizabeth was defiant. 'What right do you have to enter my home uninvited and demanding my leaving?'

'Your home, you stupid woman. It is my home and you have lived in it at my expense for over two years. Well, it is over. You could have been satisfied with living off my son and me but you are a profligate, Betty, and I had you spotted from the first. Whatever foolishness Jonathan has become embroiled in is your responsibility. Entered into to afford your spendthrift ways.'

At first shocked into silence, she gathered herself and fought back.

'Your son, Mr Fry, was a weak, vain and arrogant man. The kind of man against whom I was warned by a dear old lady who never had your wealth but who had the dignity, modesty and sense that you and your ridiculous wife, with your functions, associates and comical secret societies could never aspire to.'

Sophia was incensed. 'We had no intention of giving you a living but had wondered about a settlement, a modest one, appropriate for a skivvy, but you can forget that now. It was going to be conditional on us having Matthew. You had our son and ruined him. You'll not do the same with our grandson.'

Edmund took up the theme, 'No you'll not. We'll take the boy with us and if we have any objection you should know the alternative. Jonathan's reputation cannot be touched now so it will be no harm to him for us to swear that he told us that the scheme was devised and directed by you. We'll have Matthew with or without you in prison. It's your choice you impudent vixen.'

Elizabeth, feeling threatened but ready to respond was startled by a voice at the open door. 'And I Sir am prepared to swear that I heard you and this lady, your wife I assume, conspiring together to give false testimony.'

Fry, flushed, spun on his heels, 'You are?'

'Oswald Levine, Mrs Fry's employer.'

'Then you have no place in this Levine, kindly leave.

'You did not let me finish Mr Fry. I am also Mrs Fry's friend and I am not prepared to see a lady, a recently widowed lady, and her child bullied and threatened in this way. I find the lies you are prepared to tell on oath iniquitous.'

Edmund Fry was furious. 'Who would you expect a court to believe, the father of the deceased or a man, a maker of women's undergarments, who has been visiting my son's wife while he was absent; Ask yourself; the father or the paramour?'

Levine was unruffled. 'Repeat those accusations in public and I will have you in court where you will discover who enjoys the greater reputation amongst the society of this town, where, you should know you, are regarded as a figure of fun.'

Sophia looked to her husband but he showed no inclination to engage in a tussle. Fry pushed pass Levine to leave and said, 'we will wait in the carriage for our grandson and will not leave without him. If your friend' and he sneered when stressing the last word, 'is not out of here within the hour the bailiffs will have her in the streets where she belongs. The police have an interest in her and she will be easily found.'

Elizabeth bolted the door and she and Levine sat awhile in silence.

'Elizabeth, I came as soon as I heard. The business community in the town is buzzing with the business and I have come to see how I might assist you.'

'I am grateful Mr Levine and would ask you what is being said since this is all a mystery to me.'

'As much as I have is rumour and gossip and I can vouch for the accuracy or provenance of none of it. It is a tangled tale involving a leather processor in Wilsden called Miles whose goods were lost when Popplestone's narrow boat was sunk in a lock and a boy was drowned. Miles believed that an Edward Mason was the trans-porter. Popplestone believed that Mason was the owner of the goods. Miles' men had undervalued the value of the goods by half, so the load would not have been fully insured even if Mason had paid the insurance premium, which he had not. As a result the load was uninsured and Miles is threatening an action against Popplestone. The belief is that your husband was the fictitious Edward Mason and the police are investigating the fraud and embezzlement that has been committed.'

'Is it true that Jonathan has taken his own life?'

'There can be no doubt that he is dead in the canal but whether that was a fall, an intention to drown or an ill-fated attempt to escape some men who were pursuing him may never be known. It is said that it maybe days before the canal gives him up at the weir, unless his body remains trapped in the rubbish that litters the bottom of that rank stretch of water.'

'Is that it Mr Levine. I would wish to know it all. It will be no hurt to me.'

'That is all so far as this matter is concerned. The last is no more than gossip.'

'I would have it, Mr Levine.'

Levine sighed but went on, 'There is talk, Elizabeth, talk is all it is of indebtedness to money lenders, free-spending, excessive drinking and, I hesitate to say this, philandering.'

'I thank you for your honesty. It makes it easier for me now to put him out of my life. The Frys are intent on having Matthew and are likely to succeed in that if I should remain. Jonathan revealed nothing to me but I shall not be believed. My household accounts have been settled by a payment from Edward Mason and the police have letters in that name found in Jonathan's desk. They intend to prosecute me and have told me as much. I must leave Leeds but cannot even leave this house with the Frys in their carriage outside waiting to snatch my son.'

Levine thought quickly and proposed a plan. Elizabeth was soon packed, dressed in outdoor clothes, had Matthew similarly prepared and she was ready. The mother and child left by the rear door. She carried two cases and hurried along alleys that backed the streets where she had once proudly pushed her baby carriage. Matthew ran as well as he could to keep pace until Elizabeth stopped in the lane that led to the loading doors of Craven's Emporium.

Levine waited in the house for fifteen minutes before leaving by the front door and boarding his carriage without an acknowledgement to the waiting Frys. His carriage set off for Leeds but, with new instructions, the driver took a circular route and found his way to Craven's. The Frys had entered the house immediately upon Levine's departure and were enraged to find it unoccupied.

Elizabeth told Levine that she would most likely be sought in Leeds, Harrogate, York or even Hull. For that reason she must go west and would take the railway to Manchester. Levine advised that she should not go to the Leeds railway station as she might be overtaken by the Frys and, if they had informed the police that she was absconding, she might be awaited there instead he would take her to the train stop at Stanningly. There she could take the train to Bradford and from there to Manchester.

They rode to Stanningly in Levine's carriage and he waited with her for the hour before the Bradford train arrived. He wished her well and pressed four five pound notes into her hand.

Elizabeth attempted to return it, 'Mr Levine you have been kinder than I had a right to expect. I have money.'

'I'll have no refusal Elizabeth. You will have expenses in settling yourself in Manchester. You will be known by no one. The value of my business has increased significantly since the Harewood wedding and I am not as unaware as you might think I am of your work in London to solve a crisis that made me ill. This is not a gift, the money is well deserved earnings.'

Leaning towards him she pecked his cheek then took her son and her cases into the train stop where she boarded the train. She left it at Bradford to await the Manchester train, which was due in forty minutes, and with her cases at her feet and her child on her knees she sat before the fire in the waiting room.

Had it not been for the condensation on the window, or the steam from the engines or the smoke drifting in from Market Street she might have recognised the tall man who passed by. But she may not have realised who he was, so much had he changed. His once long yellow hair was now greying, thinning and lank. The full length-riding coat was inappropriate for a pedestrian and unbecoming on a man who once had been meticulous in the attention he paid to his appearance. Dominic Moran was exhausted and would need a lengthy period of recuperation on his father's Northumberland estate before taking up his duties as a parish priest in Whitby.

His tireless work amongst the destitute of this town had drained him. Burying infants, so many he had soon lost count, left him anguished but the greater sap on his spirits had been sitting with those children whose lungs were choked by the black filth of the air and who wheezed in cold damp cellars until their tiny hearts could no longer push the blood around their undernourished bodies. Many times he had wept but not so much as when his stallion had slipped on the human excrement that overflowed from the gutter to the cobbles of Midland Road. The crack of a bone was as loud·as a rifle shot and his horse collapsed under him. It's pain was awful to witness and release would come for the poor animal only with the arrival of the knackers man. Dominic cradled the horse neck and it lifted its head to look at him with trusting yet pleading eyes as a bolt was hammered into its skull.

Never once did Dominic rail against God. His faith had been tested and not found wanting but his health had. His seven years in Bradford had fulfilled one desire but in a way not envisaged. As a younger man he had craved admiration, adoration even. He had those now but not for shallow good looks and charisma but for unselfish service to others. He left the town with far fewer possessions than when he had arrived. Many had been sold to provide pennies here and there to families who would otherwise not have eaten that day. Among the few items in his bag were modest gifts he had received, a prayer card, some home made biscuits for his journey, and the cost of his travel home. The heaviest item in his bag and the only one of value was a marble statuette of a magnificent white stallion bought with a combined collection taken at the parishes that Dominic had been serving. As Dominic's train departed the Manchester train arrived.

Elizabeth left the waiting room but dare not pass the barrier to the platform. A constable stood there and it seemed to her that he was scrutinising the passengers as they passed through. He may or may not be looking for her and she was not prepared to take that risk.

Turning about she took her child and her cases into the mess that was Market Street. Needing lodgings for the night she took a room at the Boars Head which was a poor choice but the landlady was a kindly woman, accommodated her at the upper rear room where the noise would intrude less and she would not be subjected to the attentions of the itinerants who lodged there and next morning directed her to the principal catholic church in Westgate.

Elizabeth introduced herself as a child of Bethlehem and a former pupil of Father Dominic Moran who she was seeking to assist her in finding appropriate lodgings for herself and her son. The priest, expressing his disappointment that she should miss Father Moran by just one day, was anxious to help both as assistance to a catholic mother and as a duty to the curate whose devotion to his ministry he had grown to admire. He invited Elizabeth to stay while he went to make an enquiry on her behalf.

That evening Elizabeth and Matthew had a spacious, well furnished and comfortable room in a large house in Upper Barker End, about a mile from the town centre and above the worst of the smoke and beyond the squalor that was lower Barker End. The house comprised twelve tenanted rooms on three floors, occupied by business people and small families. It was owned by Mrs Tetley, who lived on the premises and who, as a stalwart of the church would accede to any request from a priest. Business like and correct she nevertheless was warm in her welcome of her new tenants and respectful towards this young woman who had been a pupil of Father Dominic Moran no less.

It was to be well over a year before Elizabeth had the confidence to make contact with anyone from her past but eventually in a letter to Catherine Allen she wrote.

My dear friend Catherine,

It is a full year and a half now since I left Leeds and I fear I have neglected you for too long. The circumstances of my leaving are too long to tell in a letter and must await an opportunity for us to meet. Suffice it for now that I was threatened with the loss of Matthew to my former husband's parents who threatened me with the police to get their way. It is a threat I take seriously as it is not the first time I have been so threatened. For this reason I cannot disclose my whereabouts or the town in which I am now living in case my letter should go astray and I have reverted to my former name to lessen the chances of my being traced.

Matthew is a joy to me and we room in a good home that we share with decent people, for some of whom I perform light housekeeping and I supplement my income by sewing, repairing and making up clothing and household linens for other tenants. My ambition is to be a governess and although I have applied many times for such a position I have had no success. My lack of experience, my inability to provide a reference from the experience I do have and my desire to have Matthew with me all count against me. I have not yet abandoned hope and will be writing for another post today. I send you my love and my affectionate wishes to your husband and children. As time passes the threat that hangs over me will, pray, diminish and we can meet, it is my dearest wish that we shall.

Your friend, always

Elizabeth Fairwood

It was about this time that the litigation between Miles and Popplestone was abandoned. Miles had claimed that Popplestone's was liable for the value of the lost load in that as Jonathan Fry's employer he was vicariously liable for his malfeasance. It was conceded by Miles' lawyers that an administrative oversight was responsible for the under-value of the load for insurance purposes but a premium had been paid to cover four hundred pounds of goods and since Fry had failed to pay that over to the insurers then Popplestone would be sued for four hundred pounds plus damages occasioned to the manufacturer who had ordered those goods, plus damages occasioned to Miles' reputation, plus costs.

Popplestone's lawyers were not optimistic of him coming out of the proceedings unscathed but felt his losses could be mitigated by cross-suing Miles in respect of his vicarious liability for Julian Dexter's malfeasance in entering into a criminal conspiracy to defraud not Popplestone but Miles himself. Costs were mounting on both sides but Miles's lawyers were the more confident of the eventual outcome provided Miles would make a complaint to the police of criminal conduct against Dexter in respect of his embezzlement of his employer's, Miles', company. That was a course open to Popplestone whose company had suffered no loss other than the narrow boat that was insured and the boy whose death formed no part in the proceedings. Fry was beyond the law and could not be charged with defrauding Miles.

Miles seethed with anger and frustration. He would gladly have laid a criminal complaint against Dexter, a thief who had defrauded him, but his wife and his daughter would not have it. His lawyers told him that without a conviction of Dexter his case was too weakened to pursue and that he should seek to settle by both sides withdrawing and paying their own costs. Popplestone's lawyers were against this and pressed Miles to pay both his own and Popplestone's. It was that or see his son-in-law in prison and he surrendered. His wife and daughter would not allow him to prosecute Dexter. Had he done so they would, as they threatened to make his life a misery and he knew them to be capable of that. Miles would not prosecute Dexter nor would he employ him again and nor would anyone who knew why he had been dismissed and Miles was determined that would be everybody.

The final casualty in the affair was Edmund Fry. Archie Popplestone challenged him for the position of National President of Association of Hauliers claiming that Fry had foisted on him a son who was a thief and who, probably, had dismissed the son for the same reason but was prepared for him to prey on a fellow member. Popplestone won and Fry lost his presidency and his reputation in the world of hauling and transport. It was scant consolation that he narrowly survived a vote of confidence at his lodge as he and Sophia were consumed by a need for vengeance. Irrationally, they attached little blame to their son who they accepted was easily led. Their spite was to be vented on that woman who had corrupted him. They would have their grandson and the law would have her.

Having completed her letter to Catherine, Elizabeth wrote another.

Myra Shay
Upper Barker End.

'Mr Henry Crawshaw, Sir,'

I write in response to your invitation, published by the Bradford Chronicle for application for the position of governess. This is a role for which I have had several years training and have gained practical experience. It would be my pleasure to attend you at your convenience

I am, Sir,

Mrs Elizabeth Fairwood.

Part 3

Chapter 21

In the months following Adeline's death Henry's spirits did not improve, his grief was not relieved and his behaviour became increasingly bizarre. He complained to Mrs Tutt that he heard the piano played in the night, although it was locked and she had the key. His dreams were haunted by his dead wife's voice and his days by his memories and her scent that he detected every time he entered his home and he accused Mrs Tutt of sprinkling it to disturb him. His housekeeper doubted his sanity and would have left his service had Giles not been so dependant upon her. When Henry announced that the house was to be closed up and they were to occupy the Holmes house on Manningham Lane, she was compliant but her worries increased.

Henry's days were spent with George Balls and Walter Boothman, with whom he was never less than professional and, in denial of his depression, was always affable and encouraging. Too many nights were spent at the Bradford club were he would retire with doses of laudanum to banish his memories and aid his sleep. He became a stranger to his son who had become to regard Mrs Tutt as his mother.

Young, wealthy but damaged he was in need of advice but Mrs Tutt was reluctant to incur his wrath and he avoided Charles and Marianne, excusing himself from repeated invitations and never issuing one in return. The jolt he needed was to come from an unexpected source, a blunt spoken older man who was not given to pussyfooting around sensitivities – Norman Coggins.

'It's your business, Henry, your ownership but it's our living, mine and Teresa's, and it's stable enough but not growing any more. A year ago you'd have been like a rat out of a trap for the opportunities we've had but your head is not on it anymore. We could have been selling sacks of baked pigs' ears to the kennels of the hunts but Walker's have got the contract and the pig bits we are buying are coming with the ears cut off – including the one's we buy from your slaughter house. We've all had every sympathy for your loss, me and Teresa, your manager and your clerk, but while you're counting your money we're missing our chances to make any.'

Henry was affronted. 'I'll not have you speak to me that way.'

'Well someone needs to and it may as well be me. There's no telling you owt but you need to be told. Your slaughter men are taking meat out of the back door and you've got managers in your butchers' shops, not Coggins's mind, who are taking more than their wages. George Ball won't tell you but I will, that he is turning down offers because he thinks he owes you. That won't go on for ever unless you get hold of yourself.'

Angry but seeing sense and concern in Coggins's admonishment Henry could foresee the decline of the Holmes's business concerns. He thanked Coggins for his frankness and told him that he would find out for himself how much of what Coggins had said was true. If there had been any loss of opportunity or loss of profit he would attend to it.

Henry accepted that any changes were needed both in his business and in his domestic arrangements. He would deal with the second first. Adeline, his dear lost wife, would expect no less than that her son now almost five years old should be properly raised and that Henry should employ his skills to increase her father's legacy to the benefit of Giles. He would devote his energies to Adeline's memory and aspirations not dissipate them with claret and sleeping draughts.

He placed an invitation in the Bradford Chronicle for applications for the position of governess. Giles was almost five years old and he would gain no reading or writing skills from Mrs Tutt. What he was gaining from her daily company was an accent that Henry had striven to improve. This was not a question of snobbery it was simply that the Bradford accent suggested, unfairly as it was, a lack of education and a lack of intelligence.

Having placed his advertisement he visited Holmes's Slaughterhouse, intent on looking into Coggins's allegations. The manager, Stanley Grace, had been with Hubert for thirty years and Henry had been content to leave matters in his hands until he was ready to re-organise the Holmes's businesses, which he still planned to do. Grace was surprised to see his proprietor, a rare visitor, and expressed his pleasure but it was apparent to him from Henry's demeanour that his employer was displeased. At one end of the midden in the yard were sacks marked 'Ball's' and Henry opened one and found the pigs' head had had their ears removed.

'Where are they Mr Grace?'

Grace indicated another Ball's sack. Standing separately, Henry opened it to find it filled with ears and turned angrily on Grace.

'You are selling my property to my competitors and providing him with my sacks. How much are you being paid for your theft?'

Grace was equally angry and outraged that he should be spoken to in such terms by this young upstart who knew nothing about butchering beyond trotters and snouts. Tempted to be equally insulting in return and to suggest Crawshaw had acquired the business by seeing his opportunity by marrying a woman without long to live he thought better of it and controlled his fury.

'Mr Crawshaw, I have not been paid a penny. You have been paid a shilling a sack by Walker's for bits that Coggins had no use for. Every month the sales are invoiced, paid and the records are delivered to your offices, not as ears for Walker's granted, but under miscellaneous income. Mr Ball will vouch for that. As for your sack, one is loaned each week and returned when the next sack is collected. It was business done for your benefit as I always did for Mr Holmes.'

'Would you enter into arrangements without Mr Holmes's approval?'

'That would never arise Mr Crawshaw since, unlike you, Mr Holmes would be here for part of most days, not on just an occasional visitor.'

The two now stood toe to toe, neither prepared to yield. Grace was only an inch or two taller than Henry but in his gumboots, overalls and hat, all blood spattered, he presented a more formidable figure. Henry would not retreat and, had he been able to reach would have gone nose to nose with Grace.

Now with voice raised, Henry went on. 'How many of my employees are leaving this place with meat they have not paid for, and do you number among them?' Grace too was capable of raising his voice and unafraid to do so. 'It is a practice introduced by Mr Holmes that all staff may purchase, once a week, a cut of meat at half price that would be charged to the retail shops. For some, for a special occasion, this might mean a modest size joint of beef, more usually it would mean a neck of mutton or a few pork ribs. Yes, I benefit from this too. As Mr Holmes put it, this is a prerequisite of employment.'

Henry and the slaughterhouse manager were now shouting. Work had ceased and they had an audience who expected the two to come to blows. They needed to be separated but none was prepared to become involved. A loss of employment could quickly lead a family into poverty.

'Those men who are getting meat at less than cost are full time employees who draw full wages while there are families in this town surviving on scraps and you consider it acceptable to reduce your employer's profits to fill the bellies of men who can well afford to fill their own. More than that you connive at this embezzlement so that you can share in the benefits.'

'This is not my practice, Mr Crawshaw, it is Mr Holmes and if you showed any interest in this business other than your profits you would have been aware of it and could have amended or discontinued it had you so wished. These men are loyal employees, many since they were boys. They work in the noise, stench and the flies, in conditions that you do not have the stomach to walk through, and you begrudge them tuppence off a bag of tripe. You find those tuppences in your accounts as well.'

Henry's need to walk away with his authority, if not his dignity intact, said loudly for all present to hear. 'No more ears for Walker's I'll have Coggins inspect the contents of every sack and you'll account for any pig's head that does not have two ears attached. Also, every piece of meat that leaves this slaughterhouse will go, at full cost to the wholesale retailer. The slaughter men can buy from the shops like everybody else, my-self included, has to do.'

Grace, increasingly angry, yet relieved still to be in employment for now, said no more and Henry mounted his carriage, instructed the driver and left. His own anger subsiding he began to regret his instruction that his employees could not buy at a discount. He considered that he ought to have amended the practice to permit a sale at cost price but only in quantities that would not encourage selling on. Then his mind turned to the day he accompanied Charles Ambrose to distribute gifts to ex-employees or their widows. Not a discount, not at cost, but a gift. It was good management that instilled loyalty in a workforce and Henry felt ashamed. He did not have, nor, he was convinced, would ever have the skills and temperament of either an employer or a manager of people. His skills lay in valuing investments and taking his from the returns. In time he would disassemble Hubert Holmes's group of businesses.

George Ball confirmed the receipts from the slaughterhouse that confirmed the payments from Walkers for the ears and from employees for their purchases. Perversely, Henry, wished that Grace had not been innocent of his delegations. Turning his thoughts to the other slaughterhouses that supplied Coggins, Henry gave George Ball his instructions.

Ball was to visit those slaughterhouses and remind them that the agreement was for pigs' heads and trotters. He was to inform them that a sack containing a head that did not have two ears attached would not be paid for. After that he was to visit Walkers and inform them that an agreement for the supply of ears would have to be reached with Henry personally.

Two days later Albie Walker was at Henry's office and he was not pleased.

'Mr Crawshaw, I have contracts to supply some hunts with baked pigs ears for their packs and I have other hunts showing interest and now I can't fulfil my orders or take on any more. I had a gentleman's agreement with five slaughterhouses and all have now gone back on that.'

'Mr Walker. A gentleman's agreement is made with other gentlemen, it is not made with companies that have existing agreements with me. In breaching those agreements they showed themselves not to be gentlemen so you could not have had a gentleman's agreement, even though you thought that you had. I do wonder, though, why you didn't question why the ears were supplied in sacks all bearing the name Ball's, which is one of my companies.'

'Aye it did seem strange. I thought perhaps they had all bought a job lot. Anyway, I didn't know the contents were yours and I apologise for that and since you appear to me to be a gentleman, Mr Crawshaw, perhaps we could have an agreement.'

This is what Henry had expected and he was prepared to negotiate a deal. 'Gauging from the supply you have been getting from my slaughterhouse, Holmes' in Stuter Lane, and the comparative volume of slaughtering at the other slaughterhouses, you have been taking about eight sacks a week'

Walker was coy but admitted, 'About that, I'd say.'

'And you have been paying about a shilling a sack'

'About that.'

'So, having baked them, an expensive process, you are selling them for what, may I ask?'

Walker was uncomfortable, 'Nay, hold on. That's confidential. It's my business'

Henry held the upper hand. 'And without ears you have no business. If we are to reach an agreement there needs to be honesty between us, so let me show you my honesty. I can honestly say that by visiting one or two hunts of my acquaintance I can discover from the keepers of the hounds how much they are paying to you and thus discover your honesty.'

Walker, resigned and defeated, replied. 'All right. It's about eight sacks a week, sometimes less, sometimes more, and I'm paying a shilling a sack and I'm selling them at three shillings but there's the baking and then I have to deliver them.'

Henry had discussed with Coggins the question of baking the ears for sale in his shops but the ears that could be chewed for hours by a hound could only be sucked by the toothless children and the elderly. There would be no sustenance in them and no sales. So the question was whether to bake the ears and supply the kennels or let Walker do the work and take some profit from it. His instincts were against employment and he preferred the latter option.

'My offer Mr Walker is to supply you with the ears at one shilling a sack but I shall incur costs in removal of the ears from the heads and in the packing for collection by you, so the charge will be one shilling and eight pence per sack. For that you get a guaranteed supply and a monopoly on pigs ears in and around this town.'

Walker was not happy but had little choice but to agree and said so. Henry was not finished 'It will not be a gentleman's agreement, it will be a written, binding contract. This will not prevent you from obtaining supplies from further a field but any sales of your other supplies will incur a premium of eight pence a sack to me.

Walker left resentful but still in business.

Henry's priorities now were the valuation of Holmes' various businesses and the selling of shares in them, which would occupy him for some months and the appointment of a governess for Giles that he hoped to achieve quickly once all the applications for the post had been received.

Chapter 22

Enquiries of members of his club suggested that he would have a dozen or two applicants to choose from with regards to the advertisement he had placed in the Chronicle. Within two weeks he had, but they were not all of a calibre he was seeking. Many were from women currently working as nurse-maids and had neither the training nor experience for the position. Some were brazen enough in their letters of application to state that they had had enough of disturbed nights by infants and wished to work with older children to enjoy unbroken sleep.

Settled on just three applicants he invited them to attend his home on consecutive days at two o'clock. The favoured candidate was a primary school teacher and he would see her first to establish a standard against which he could judge the other two. Propriety was a consideration, he felt and he asked Mrs Tutt to sit in, but not participate in the interviews. Giles could be relied upon to play unsupervised and if that proved not to be the case he would have to be brought in and the applicant's reaction to him could be informative.

The first applicant was the schoolteacher whose experience meant that she had the credentials to educate Giles. However, her accent, although softer than Mrs Tutt's, was still lower class Bradford and, in her late twenties, given her good looks it was inevitable that she would have suitors and be unlikely to remain long. Giles needed some continuity, he decided, and this lady would not provide that.

His second candidate was Elizabeth Fairwood. Like the teacher the previous day, she was seated well back from his desk in order he could have a full view of her and Mrs Tutt was seated in a corner behind and out of her sight.

Henry studied this applicant. A well presented woman in her mid-twenties, about his own age and although he would have preferred her not to bare any resemblance to Adeline he could accept her blonde curls since there the similarity ended. Both were attractive but this woman did not have the luminous fair skin or frailty of his dead wife but had stronger features, though no less beautiful, and had a confidence about her that Adeline could never have carried.

Satisfied with her training, impressed by her vocabulary and keen that Giles should adopt the pleasing tones of her accent his initial impression was more than favourable doubts arose though as he questioned her more deeply.

Her appearance was quite acceptable. Her dress, obviously not new, was clean and well pressed and complimented by a cape and bonnet in almost matching colours. Her cotton gloves with lace cuffs were appropriate and if that lace had been repaired the needlework had been undetectable. The only item of apparel that was obviously new was the ribbon attached to her bonnet. The lilac satin slippers showed signs of having walked from upper Barker End to Manningham and were not up to the job but her choice indicated the efforts the lady had made for the day. What was it then that was causing Henry's concern. He would delve until he found it.

'It is Mrs Fairwood. What is your marital state?'

'I am widowed, Sir, eighteen months now.'

'And your family?'

'I was orphaned as a child, raised by the Sisters who trained me for the post of which I now apply. My sole family is my son, Matthew, who will be four next birthday.'

'So your arrangements for his care should you be successful in securing this post?'

He watched as she tensed slightly and breathed more deeply before replying. 'it is my hope Sir, to find a position in which I might have my son with me.'

'And if I was to offer you the post but not accept your child?'

'Then I could not accept the post'

An honest answer thought Henry, but he had not considered taking in another child and was not disposed to do so, but he had not given up on her. 'You will have references from the Sisters who trained you?'

'I can obtain them.'

'Mrs Fairwood, I would prefer to do that. Is there any one reason why I should not.' He watched her reaction and saw it and her attempts to disguise it.

'I moved to this town and I did not wish my whereabouts or those of my son to be known. Similarly, if we were to reside here I would not wish them to be known. The experiences I spoke of in my letter of application was at the home of my husband's parents who, following his death, were determined to raise my son. I fear that if my whereabouts became known they would seek to take him from me.'

Henry had heard enough. He was not going to complicate his life, Giles's life or his household with this women's problems. Intending to draw the interview to a conclusion he made a statement, attempting to temper it as well as he could.

'To sum up Mrs Fairwood, you come here without references of either your training or experience, making your acceptance of the post conditional upon the acceptance of your child and if you were to reside here I should have to conspire with you to keep your presence confidential to protect you from a custody struggle that I neither understand nor have any interest in, but it seems strange to me that you are widowed with neither a living nor even a settlement.'

Her response shook him as much as a simultaneous crash of summer thunder shook the house. The sky darkened and the rain beat on the windows enough to break them. His applicant stood, looked to the window and said, 'I must leave now. The reason for my situation is that I was not accepted by my husband's parents. I was unapproved of for being of low birth. Whether I am or am not I may never know but even if I am I have worked diligently all my life to acquire skills.'

This resonated with Henry. What she said next affected Henry deeply.

'My son's grandparents, the only two he will ever have, are lost to him because I am regarded as unsuitable. They had higher ambitions for their son than that he should take a wife such as me. Good bye Sir and thank you for considering me.' She left.

Her words stung him. 'Higher ambitions, he was brought back to the Miles's back doorstep, having the same words and the pain in his buttocks returned. Standing to relieve the discomfort he went to the window and saw his applicant at the gate taking a dark haired boy by the hand and walk into the curtains of rain that swept one after the other along Manningham Lane. Her cape was around the child and her parasol over his head it was an inefficient umbrella and collapsed as if melted. Up to their ankles in mud and water the two were lost to his view.

'Damn cheek if you ask me Mr Crawshaw' offered Mrs Tutt.

Henry distracted, had not heard her clearly but asked 'Mrs Tutt?'

'She comes here to care for your son and expects you to care for hers. Damn cheek if you ask me. But, only seeing as your asking mind.'

Henry was disturbed by thoughts, images and sadness he thought he had left behind. The sight of the two figures struggling through the rain, ill dressed for the task, was a reminder of the desolation he had felt walking home with his mother from his father's inquest; aching from his loss, disgusted by the lack of respect from the fools around the bar seething at the giggling of the Ogden brothers. He needed the laudanum and he would have it. Perhaps the morning and then the third candidate would raise his spirits.

Miss Constance Devlin came with impeccable references, many years experience as a professional governess and qualifications as an educator. Her latest charge had progressed to boarding school and she was seeking a new position. Henry considered her ideal in all respects but one. She was a middle-aged woman of severe countenance who spoke too often and at too great a length of the need for discipline. Henry had learned to discipline himself, knew its value in achieving ones aims and favoured it for boys approaching manhood. For a five year old, deprived of a mother's love it was, he felt entirely inappropriate. Miss Devlin would not do.

That evening he wrote four letters; One each to the first and third candidates thanking them for their attendances and informing them that they had been unsuccessful in their application and one to Elizabeth Fairwood to inform her that no decision had been made but, while she remained under consideration, should another opportunity arise she should take it. His fourth letter, which he would hand deliver the next day was to Donald Dawson, the detective, asking him to make enquiries into the character and background of a Mrs Elizabeth Fairwood of Myra Shay, Upper Barker End.

Dawson himself visited Henry's office two days later to provide a verbal report.

'Well Mr Crawshaw, there isn't much to tell. Been in the town about a year and half, her and the child. Does some cleaning for other tenants – capable enough but doesn't have the wrists for it that a bigger woman does. Her needlework is very good and although she doesn't let on about her past she did let slip that she worked for one of the most famous studios in Leeds. To sum up, she conducts herself as a woman of good reputation. Is temperate in her habits and doesn't keep unsuitable company, or any company at all, in fact.'

'That is it, is it Mr Dawson? That is what you would call a report into a person's character and background? You are telling me what one of your men could have learned in five minutes knocking on her neighbours' doors. Find the studio in Leeds and you will find the key to the information I am seeking. I will accept your invoice only when I am satisfied you have done your job.'

George Ball and Walter Boothman had grown accustomed to their employer's dark moods, though they had never been subjected to his temper, but the tone of his voice he had adopted with Donald Dawson knew new depths in his anger and impatience.

Dawson knew Henry to be a respected member of the Bradford club and appreciated the damage that could be done to his agency's reputation if it was to be disparaged in such company. Thus motivated he undertook to investigate

Elizabeth Fairwood personally and he left for Leeds that day. He would not be knocking on the door of dressmakers premises he would be visiting other private investigators. Investigators in other towns were not regarded as competitors but as sources of information and assistance on a quid pro quo basis. His first call directed him to the agency that could provide the answers he was seeking. Inhabiting an insular world the private detectives thrived on gossip and exchanging snippets. The Fry fraud and the disappearing widow were not forgotten in the village that was Leeds private enquiry agencies.

It cost Dawson a good meal and two bottles of wine, taken with a senior investigator of Anderson and Anderson, to gain enough to satisfy Henry Crawshaw's requirements and a day later Henry had a written report. From this he learned that Elizabeth's husband had died when he either jumped or was thrown into the canal when he was chased by a moneylender who had not been repaid. There had been a police investigation into a fraud but the injured company referred to issue a complaint and Elizabeth Fry, as she then was had fled the town in the mistaken belief that she would be implicated when there was no reason to suspect her involvement. She had been a highly regarded seamstress who had worked for a titled family and was regarded by all who knew her, other than her dead husband's parents, of being of unimpeachable repute.

Henry, satisfied and accepting Dawson's invoice, wrote to Elizabeth asking her to attend a second interview and asked that her son accompany her. What Dawson had failed to tell Henry was that the Frys had retained Anderson and Anderson to trace their grandson, that the source of his information had been Anderson and Anderson or that he had revealed that the client interested in Elizabeth Fry was Henry Crawshaw, a compiler of business accounts in Bradford.

At two o'clock on the appointed day Henry watched from his window as Elizabeth and Matthew entered his gate. The weather was kinder and he saw that they were dressed as before, although their clothing was once more clean and well pressed. The mother no longer had her parasol but did have a new length of ribbon on the bonnet that had survived the drenching remarkably well.

He was still ambivalent about appointing this applicant and wondered if, in offering a second interview, he was seeking good reason to reject her while salving his conscience; though why he should feel any responsibility for her situation he did not know.

There were two chairs well back from his desk and the boy had to clamber on his own and, having done so, his legs dangled a good foot above the carpet. Mrs Tutt was again in the corner. Her disapproval was unspoken but her expression was itself a tirade.

First to Elizabeth, 'thank you for attending again Mrs Fairwood,' then to the boy, 'and what is your name?'

He glanced at his mother before replying, softly, 'Matthew Fairwood.'

'Well Master Matthew Fairwood, can you recite the Lords Prayer?' Again a look to his mother who prompted him, 'The Our Father.'

Matthew began. 'Our Father who art in heaven, hallowed be thy name. Thy Kingdom come, thy will be done on earth, as it is in Heaven. Give us.........'

Henry stopped him. He had heard what he had wanted to hear. The child placed all the aitches in the right places and none in the wrong ones – something which Henry, from his Yorkshire farm upbringing, had taken some years to master and something which he feared that Giles, whose model was Mrs Tutt, might never master. To Mrs Tutt next, 'Please introduce Matthew to Giles, observe them while they play together but kindly leave the door to this room open.' Then to Elizabeth, 'provided you are not discomforted by that arrangement' Elizabeth had no objection.

Now alone, 'Mrs Fairwood, do you play the piano?'

'I do not, Sir, would it be a requirement that I did?'

'No, it would be a requirement that you did not.' Without explaining his statement he went on to ask a number of questions that Elizabeth satisfied. She was, she told him, in good health and had never suffered a serious illness. The appointment would be for as long as she was needed and she promised satisfactory service. No, she was not in any personal relationship and was not seeking one. Her priorities were her son and practising the training she had undertaken since her own childhood. Yes she had taught reading, writing and arithmetic to children at Bethlehem, taught them still to her son and felt confident of her ability to teach and raise Giles in accordance with his father's preferences.

When done he asked Elizabeth what questions she might wish to ask. She had two. They seemed concerned whether her son would be accommodated and what would be the extent of her duties. Henry did not answer directly, instead he made a lengthy statement.

'Mrs Fairwood, my son has been motherless for two years and I worry for his upbringing, his education and the lack of affection he has in his young life. Mrs Tutt does what she can but what he requires is not her forte. I am anxious to make an appointment because the reorganisation of my business is about to place increasing demands on my time and my energies. Yet for all my anxieties to settle Giles's needs, I will confuse him if I make inappropriate appointments that have, too frequently, to be replaced. I will confess that I have misgivings about offering this appointment to you. It had not entered into my reckoning to accept another child into my house, however it may be no bad thing for Giles to experience such company. Such uncertainties as I have though are minor compared with a situation of having a governess whose whereabouts may not be known, who is unable to provide references and who masquerades under an assumed name Mrs Fry.'

Elizabeth rose to his bait. 'Mr Crawshaw, Fry is the name of a man who dishonoured himself, his wife and his child. It is the name of his parents whose threats cause me to live in dread. It is a name I have disowned. Fairwood is not an assumed name and I resent that description. It is my birth name. I have no shame of it indeed it would be Miss Fairwood if that title did not raise questions about my son's legitimacy. In conclusion, may I say Sir, that I appreciate your asking your housekeeper to withdraw so that we might resolve this matter privately.'

Henry could not but admire this woman's mettle. There was more of his mother, the solid Yorkshire-woman, about her than the pliant femininity of an Adeline or Marianne and though he was more attracted to the latter's traits he was not seeking a wife but a governess. He thought for a while then decided.

'I make my living investing in probabilities and after I have obtained all the information I am able to ensure, as far as possible, that the investment will be profitable. I make an offer, I do not negotiate. The offer is either accepted or rejected. It works well for me and I will now make you an offer. You are invited to take this appointment for a trial period of one calendar month during which you can demonstrate the talent you claim. At the end of that period should I decide that you are not suited to the appointment or should you decide that you find the appointment unsuitable then that shall be an end to it. I would not have you homeless so I would pay the rental for your lodgings to keep them for you for that month. You will have rooms and keep for yourself and your son, your pay will be seven shillings a week and your duties will be confined to raising and educating Giles. I am well provided for in terms of housekeeping, cooking and cleaning and, I am sure, Mrs Tutt would not welcome any interference in her duties. Such time from your duties will be agreed with Mrs Tutt.'

Elizabeth did not attempt to negotiate. 'I accept, Sir, and I am available to start at once. I shall return to my room to pack.'

'I'll have Mrs Tutt make up your rooms and she will summon a carriage. A member of my household should not be chancing the squalor of the town unnecessarily. The carriage will return for you tomorrow to collect your cases and Mrs Tutt will settle the charges.'

Elizabeth and Matthew left Myra Shay at noon the next day and arranged for their room to be kept for one month. They had been left no more than two hours when two men from Anderson and Anderson came seeking them, to be told she had left and did not know for where.

Henry spent the next two nights at his club and on both occasions he was followed through the fog of Piece Hall Yard and Piccadilly by two men. On the third night he took a carriage home. The two men also took a carriage but fell behind in Manor Row and lost their quarry. When the carriage they had followed returned to the rank in Kirkgate, the driver was given a florin and they had Henry's address. Next morning the agents of Anderson and Anderson returned to Leeds.

Chapter 23

Setting about his plan to restructure the Holmes's empire, to divest himself of responsibility for employment while retaining an income, Henry cursed his own impatience. He had seventeen separate but interdependent enterprises to untangle, slaughterhouse, wholesale distributors, retail shops, a hide and skins business and two knackers yards. There were also interests in one sheep farm and two piggeries to either increase or sell off. They should have been tackled one at a time but he had chosen to deal with two simultaneously; the slaughterhouse, the most valuable of the wholly owned concerns and the hides and skins business, the least.

It suited him to be away from home while the housekeeper and the governess settled in their respective duties and reconciled the tensions that would inevitably arise and he was pleased to be able to devote his energies, as depleted as they sometimes were, to his major project. He returned to the slaughterhouse, expecting and receiving a chilly reception. He met the manager, Stanley Grace, in what had been Hubert's office.

'I owe you my apologies Mr Grace, I had reasons for my conduct but I find that they do not amount to justification so I shall not offer them and offend you no further. You have invested your working life into the Holmes' abattoir and know more of the business than I ever shall, nor I concede, would wish to. I value this business at two thousand pounds and would invite you obtain an independent valuation in confirmation of that. My offer to you is a forty-nine percent interest for one thousand pounds. In return you would still draw your wages, have control over the management of the business, and would benefit from forty-nine percent of the profits.'

Grace needed time to consider the offer he had been made. Both excited and frightened he made no response other than to thank Henry for his apology and to accept it. They would meet again in two days time. Those were long days for Stanley Grace who had long discussions with his wife, with his brother, a lawyer who expressed an interest in taking a share of the investment and his bank manager about the cost of a loan and the value of his home. He could offer eight hundred pounds.

At their next meeting Henry offered a loan of two hundred pounds at the same rate as interest charged at the bank, but Grace was worried about affording the repayments so Henry told him he would have George Ball prepare projections of expected profits based on current business. To that Grace, should add his earnings.

With that information, and after further deliberation, Grace agreed and the deed was done. The two men shook hands and Henry told him, 'Now, Mr Grace, the question of supplying meat to employees at cost is one for you. If you supply it below cost, that will come from your profits. How do you see it now?'

Grace smiled, 'There'll be no meat leaving here at less than full price.'

Content, Henry returned to his office to receive news from George Ball. The manager of the hides and skin works was not interested in investing in the business. He was ready for retirement and, as Henry directed, George had advertised for an investor and part owner. He had had a response from a Julian Dexter who wished to invest the required two hundred and fifty pounds for a forty-nine percent share. It was a name known to George but he thought it would not be recalled by Henry who surprised him with his reaction.

'Write to him George, inform him as briefly as you are able that his application has been unsuccessful.'

After three weeks of Elizabeth and Matthew's presence in the Crawshaw household Mollie Tutt's animosity had melted. She admired Elizabeth's skills with Giles, was heartened by the boy's obvious happiness with his governess and his friendship with Matthew and she marvelled at Elizabeth's talent with a needle and thread. For her part, Elizabeth asked Mollie if she could watch her cook and fashion pastries. The housekeeper had never had such attention and praise.

Anderson and Anderson had not been idle. Edmund Fry had been informed of his grandson's whereabouts and he wrote to Edgar Miles asking if he would instigate proceedings against Elizabeth on condition that his son-in-law Dexter would be kept out of the matter. Miles, stung by and sickened of the whole affair, refused. Fry, undeterred, employed Anderson and Anderson again and two men called at the Crawshaw home.

The door was opened by Mrs Tutt who claimed, innocence that there was no Mrs Fry at that address but the conversation was overheard by Henry who ushered the men into his office. All introduced, Henry addressed himself to the senior of the two, Richard Anderson.

'So tell me directly Mr Anderson, the purpose of your visit to my home.'

'I am retained by a client, whose name I may not disclose, to inform Mrs Fry that should she not surrender the custody of her son to my client, who will provide the boy with a more financially secure future, failing which her whereabouts will be disclosed to the police who are seeking her for fraud.'

'Then take it that I shall do that on your behalf and you may consider your work done and you can return and collect your fee.'

'There is an expectation Mr Crawshaw that we will return with the boy.'

Henry was adamant, 'Know this, Sir, as a member of my household the boy and his mother enjoy my protection and shall continue to do so, threats or not. Inform your client, Mr Fry, accordingly.'

Anderson and his colleague rose to leave but Henry asked them to remain. He was impressed by this young detective who was, to his mind, far more professional in his appearance and conduct than Donald Dawson.

'Now your duties to Mr Fry, it is Mr Fry is it not? are done.'

Anderson did not reply.

'And now that your duties to your client are discharged I would wish to retain your services. I require full history of Mrs Elizabeth Fry, a full history of the business concerning her husband and the alleged fraud and, suspecting as I do your ability to obtain information from clerks in the offices of accountants and the taxation authorities, full details of Edmund Fry's business and financial standing. It is my expectation that you will be as discreet in protecting my identity as you have with your client and demonstrated to me today.'

The efficiency of Richard Anderson amazed him. Within five days he had a written report of a full twenty pages and knew all there was to know of his governess, the child found in a forest, her misfortunes and her successes, her ill-advised marriage and the arrogant bully who was Jonathan Fry; a moneyed and articulate version of Joe Ogden. He would confirm Elizabeth's appointment but not yet.

They agreed a further two weeks trial and her rooms at Myra Shay would be paid for and kept for her. Henry did not tell Elizabeth of the visit of the two men or the reason for it. Mrs Tutt had told her of the men seeking a Mrs Fry but did not know the reason for it. Elizabeth was apprehensive and thought that the visit was reason for the extension to her trial period. For Henry, it was an opportunity to finalise the matter before entering into a long-term appointment.

Edmund Fry received a letter on Coggins headed notepaper proposing a visit to discuss a business matter and it was arranged for the following Friday. Henry took the train to Leeds and the short walk to Fry's warehouse and office on the wharf.

'Good morning Mr Coggins. I understand you wish to discuss the transporting of your goods.'

'From where you gain that understanding, Mr Fry, I do not know but it is a false understanding. The name is not Coggins it is Crawshaw and I have come to meet the man who had the temerity to send enquiry agents to my home. My home!' and he shouted these last words.

'So, Mr Crawshaw, you are the fool who that woman has marked as the next for ruin. You may not be aware that she was the cause of my son's ruin and death.'

'I am fully aware of the facts. Your son's ruin was caused by his weakness and avarice. As for his death, he would have been well gone with his stolen money had he not wanted one last night with his doxy and had he not put himself in the clutches of a shylock. Were he not now dead he would be in prison for fraud. Accept that Fry and let his widow alone.'

'You speak of temerity, Crawshaw, while you a seller of pig-meat to paupers feel free to employ a subterfuge to come here to lie and to insult my son. I could have that woman in prison and I could ruin you, at a whim. So if you want to keep your living, as poor as it must be, and if you want to keep the woman in your house and, no doubt, in your bed the course still open to you both is to hand over my grandson for a better life than you could provide.'

Furious, but determined to maintain his composure Henry replied, quietly but firmly.

'Before I came here I did, as I always do, make every enquiry to be sure of my facts. Had you done the same in respect of Crawshaw rather than Coggin's you would have more knowledge of whom you were dealing with than to issue inane threats about ruin. I shall not boast about wealth, but be aware it is substantial. Let me instead give you an insight into what my enquiries about you have revealed. Since you were jettisoned by your Association, that back slapping coterie of carters and canal boat labourers, your fortunes, never significant, are severely diminished. I was at first puzzled as to why you should rent rather than buy the house you bribed your son with until I discovered you could not have afforded it.'

'Get out, Crawshaw, now. I demand it.'

'I am nearly done. Even had there been any suspicion that Mrs Fairwood, a name she now prefers, had been complicit in your son's crimes, which there was not, Miles has no interest in a complaint that would see his own son-in-law in prison. Your threats are as hollow as your accounts.'

'Leave now, Crawshaw, or I'll have you thrown out.'

Henry rose, reached the door and turned. 'Should I or Mrs Fairwood ever hear from you again I shall buy up every one of your customers, sink your failing business and see you and your wife in the gutter, I would consider it money well spent and may do it anyway in response to your having sent enquiry agents to my home and your disgusting implications concerning my relationship with my son's governess. You may offer an apology before I leave.

He saw that Fry was trembling. He had bluffed and lost. 'My cause was not with you Sir. I apologise for any insult and would wish to have an end to the matter.'

'Your apology, begrudging as I consider it to be, is accepted. Whether I shall agree to this being the end of the matter is something I shall think upon.' Henry left.

George Ball dealt with all correspondence other than one letter marked for the personal attention of Mr Henry Crawshaw and that awaited him on his return that afternoon. He read it.

'Dear Mr Crawshaw,'

I must ask you to review a decision by your clerk, Ball, to reject my husband's application for part ownership of the hides and skins business. There is nobody with more senior experience of the processing of these materials and the two hundred pounds investment you need presents no difficulty.

May I remind you of the kindness I showed you when you were friendless at the social afternoons. This was at no little expense to my-self in terms of the scoffing of my own circle. I would ask that you recall this.

Sincerely

Alice Miles Dexter.

His reply was brief, penned immediately and dispatched.

'Madam'

I see no reason to intervene in the eminently sensible decision taken by my Senior Manager <u>Mr</u> George Ball.

As regards matters that you would have me recall, what I do recall is a letter stating that there should be no more correspondence between us, I have abided by that and would be obliged if you would do likewise.

Henry Crawshaw.

In poor humour from his annoyance with Fry he was tempted to add a postscript and had mentally written it. 'If I was ever to find my-self in need of two hundred pounds I should find it from a source where I could be confident it had been obtained legally! Deciding against that, he sealed the letter and hoped to hear nothing more of a Fry, a Miles or a Dexter.

At six o'clock that Friday evening, Henry returned home, tired and unable to free himself of the dark mood that too often over took him. On entering he saw Giles and Matthew, giggling and squealing, racing up the staircase pursued by Elizabeth on hand and knees.

'Mrs Fairwood we will speak in my office.'

She followed and he continued, 'If I had wanted my child entertained I would have hired a clown at half the cost and with none of the attendant distraction and aggravation I am caused. Explain yourself.'

Elizabeth had seen little of Henry since assuming her duties but had seen enough to know that he was a young man who appeared burdened with cares that were weighing down upon him and depleting his spirits. She had formed an early affection for Giles and had great hopes for the promise he showed and did not wish to jeopardise her position, or her home and her own son's security. However, if she were not to stand her ground she would be prevented from fulfilling her duties and would prefer to return to Myra Shay than be cowed by this young man who was showing signs of becoming a tartar.

'Mr Crawshaw, the children are given a sum appropriate to their ability and must calculate it by the count of five. If unsuccessful they can save themselves a tickling by reaching the top of the top step before I catch them. This is fun, a lesson in arithmetic and exercise. All done without equipment and expense.'

Henry felt he was being lectured and asked Elizabeth to bring Giles' workbook. Examining it he accepted that the improvement in his son's lettering had improved immeasurably in just five weeks but did not say so. He asked for Matthew's compared the two and questioned why the younger boy's lettering was superior.

Matthew has been practising for a year. 'Giles will soon over take him in all disciplines because his thirst for knowledge and his eagerness to please. He will be ready by Christmas then, with access to appropriate books, of which there are none here, his ability will take him as far as his curiosity will carry him.'

'And what are those pinafores they are wearing?'

'They are smocks I made to protect their clothes from the paints they use. I have provided paint boxes. Nurturing talent and teaching involve far more than can be gained from books and study.'

He was being lectured again. 'Thank you Mrs Fairwood, you may go.'

Henry sat at his desk and beat his fists on his head. Why, he asked himself, could he not reserve his bile for Fry and Dexter and not feel he need to vent it on Stanley Grace and Elizabeth Fairwood. He missed Adeline but knew it was irrational to put up barriers to all other human contact. That would not return her to him.

But was the governess correct to say that there was more to learning than books and study? Hadn't they served him well? Yes he had learned lessons in life at Black Dyke Hole, Old Hall and the Academy, some useful, some painful but all, he had to admit valuable. After dinner he asked Elizabeth to see him again.

'I would like to confirm your appointment as governess so you may give notice to the room you have been reserving'.

Her response was not the grateful thanks he expected. 'You have told me that you do not negotiate and you have told me that at the end of my trial period we must both be agreed and my suitability for the post. I am pleased that you are satisfied with my suitability and I need now to be assured of the suitability of the post for me. I will not attempt to negotiate, knowing that you prefer not to but will state my conditions.'

He watched as she sat without being invited.

'Firstly, as long as you remain satisfied with the results I am achieving with Giles you will not interfere with the methods by which I achieve those results. There might even involve a walk in the park to feed the ducks, he might return home with skinned knees from chasing a hoop or climbing a tree to collect leaves, it might even involve something so strange as seeing him racing up the stairs to avoid a tickling. Secondly, it is essential that I am able to acquire books, some of which you may approve and some of which you may not. These will include the life of Jesus and the Bible stories, the geography of other countries, the history of Nations and some picture stories read for the sheer pleasure and joy they offer.'

Henry found her infuriating. Not once since his mother refused to let him leave school and work the farm had he had a woman tell him what he might or might not do. Mrs Tutt could express disapproval with a drop of her jowls but she would not dare express it. The woman sat before him was challenging him to accept her terms or dismiss her.

'Is that it Mrs Fairwood?'

'The time will come, and come soon Mr Crawshaw, when you will wish to place Giles in a school. Everything to which I have referred is a preparation in order that he will almost certainly match and, I intend, surpass the boys who have benefitted from private tutors, each an expert in a particular field would you settle for anything less?'

Feeling he was left with no argument and contrary to his instincts he heard himself saying. 'My son's education and achievements in life are of the utmost importance to me. In agreeing to your terms I am placing a great deal of trust in you. I shall remind you, should the time come that I have need to, that your terms included my continuing satisfaction with the results you achieve. For now I shall set up an account at Templeton's booksellers. Any published work not in stock but is obtainable quite quickly you may order freely. May I take it that we have an agreement on your appointment? You should know also that you will hear nothing further from Edmund Fry and his threats of the police were groundless. They have no interest in you.

Chapter 24

Even in his darkest moments, Henry was sufficiently rational to realise that he needed help, that sleeping draughts and wine were not providing. He rejected his initial thought of consulting Doctor Schroeder. Drugs left him dull in thought and lacking in energy. Instead he wrote to Charles Ambrose to solicit an invitation and it was immediately forthcoming.

Charles and Marianne received him warmly and introduced him to their houseguest. 'Mr Henry Crawshaw, please meet Miss Celia Lawrence.' Celia was a three year old with auburn ringlets forming a freckled face. She shook Henry's hand, gave a little curtsy and ran off to play. Charles explained. 'She is Marianne's sister's child and her father is the Reverend Bertram Lawrence. They are off to a mission in Africa for two years and felt, quite correctly, that the climate and conditions might be harmful to a child.'

He had spoken the word 'Reverend' with mock gravity and Marianne chided him for it. 'Charles disapproves.' Charles smiled, 'Not at all dear. We all seek our own route to heaven and it is a delight to have Celia here with us.'

It was both a delight and a joy for the childless Marianne, the gap in whose life was temporary filled. Henry made full use of his stay, unburdening himself to Charles and Marianne, concealing nothing, confessing everything of his difficulties as an employer, a manager, in fact as a person who could not fully engage with his fellow man. He told Charles that he could not have dealt with Simon Pepper and the Ogden brothers as Charles had done without a loss of temper and a raised voice. The way he had addressed Stanley Grace at the slaughterhouse and his subsequent embarrassment were revealed. Finally he disclosed that the governess he had appointed, an able and good woman who was deserving of the opportunity, irritated him because of her lack of deference.

Charles did not make light of Henry's distress. Each of his concerns, taken singly, was easily remedied but taken together and heaped upon a young man who was in depressed spirits called for a studied response. Charles proposed that Henry should extend his stay. Nathan Stein would be taking a carriage to Bradford the next day and Henry could join him, give his instructions to his staff and inform his household that he would be at Old Hall for a stay. Henry's reply was sad.

'Thank you Charles, I should like that. I'll inform my office, although it operates well enough without me and I shall collect more clothes. As for my household, I am convinced it is a happier place in my absence.'

As Henry left Old Hall next morning to join Stein in his carriage he saw him in conversation with Charles seeing his approach Charles said hurriedly to Stein, 'We know how he bristles at criticism or advice. Prompt him to question himself.'

During the journey Henry was animated telling Stein in minute detail of his plans to divest himself of the Holmes' employees and the capital that would release. They parted in the town, met again, called briefly at Henry's home and set off back to Thornton.

'Henry what are your plans for the capital you will release from selling off shares in your companies?'

'Are you suggesting I am wrong to do it?' Henry was clearly sensitive.

'Of course not. Raising capital for a promising venture is good business practice. Reducing profits to leave increasing balances in banks may not be, that is all.'

Withdrawing into himself, Henry, arms folded and head low let the rest of the journey pass with no further conversation.

Charles had re-arranged his week to allow as much time as he could for Henry but there were some commitments that had to be honoured. On those occasions he enjoyed Marianne's company and, he was surprised to discover, the company of Celia just as well. The child was irrepressible. Without warning she would launch herself on him as he sat, insist on sitting on his lap and demanded a story. Not only was he charmed by her, she distracted him from his troubles. With no stories to tell her, he invented tales and was so pleased with his ability to do so and her open-mouthed amazement that he looked forward to more opportunities to entertain this charming little girl.

For part of each day he rode with Charles. The discomfort in his buttocks was a relief from the aching in his heart and the pain that came with his thoughts. He waited for Charles's advice but it didn't come. Instead, Charles would tell him of instances when he had himself been angry, frustrated and had felt temper rising. He had learned that these clouded thinking, and he had learned to control those emotions.

'How did you do that Charles because I confess that I can not.'

'When too weighed down by responsibilities, when too impressed with my own importance I put them both in the balance against my blessings; my wife, my father's raising of me, the respect of those who rely upon me for their living and lastly, but not the most important, my wealth. My blessings always outweigh my concerns even though there is one I have and you do not and one you have and I can never have. You do not have the love of a wife, although you may yet again. I do not have a child and may never have one, yet, here we are back at the Hall and I will be greeted by Celia, whom I shall have for two years to come. What, I ask myself, are all those compared with the transient pleasure of shouting at a grasping school teacher or two inadequates?'

After a week at Old Hall he was settled in his mind. He had enjoyed and benefited from the company of Charles and Marianne but, more than either, it was Celia he would miss. He could make her smile, laugh and dance with delight at the stories he had rehearsed in his room each night. She had no interest in his balances, his business, his wealth or his ambitions. She wanted his company and his stories nothing more.

He was to share Stein's carriage to Bradford again but Stein had no business here that day but was acting on Charles instructions, 'Now Nathan you can criticise I feel sure he is ready.'

Stein was prepared and the criticism would be brief and brutal. 'I have heard of the success you have had with Coggins. What do you actually do for the impoverished in the hovels near where you have located your shops?'

'I feed them at a price they can afford. Otherwise some might starve.'

'Commendable, I'm sure but why are they unable to feed themselves better?'

'They are without employment.'

'Of course Henry, and your plans for the Holmes' group of businesses means that those businesses will not be able to offer new employment again. Not as they did when Hubert was their proprietor.'

'Please speak plainly Nathan.'

'You make the managers a non-negotiable offer to raise the funds to pay you half the costs of their place of employment or lose their employment. Having raised those funds they have no means of expansion so no means of offering others employment. In fact Henry, the plan upon which you are embarked is a greater threat to employment in the town than Cholera.'

'I know you are attempting to goad me and I know from past experience that you do so not from viciousness but for my interest. So, advise me.'

'Henry you are a fellow of the Academy, an expert in valuations and acquisitions and you are reduced to valuing your own assets and selling them off, for no better reason than an aversion to employing. Employing creates wealth some of that wealth will be spent in your businesses. You benefit, the impoverished benefit and the town benefits. We are nearly at your office so I will finish by saying this. The pursuit of wealth for its own sake creates a sickness of the soul and that, I believe, is the cause of your illness.'

'Nathan, unless I am mistaken you have no business in the town today and you intend to return to Thornton, so would you ask the driver to take me home. I am grateful for your advice.'

'That being so, and since we are to share the carriage a while longer I think you ought to examine your aversion to negotiation. Preparedness to negotiate need not denote weakness it can be time consuming but time well spent. In negotiation concessions are not only made, they are often gained and the other party who has even one, even a small advantage will feel better about the deal they have struck and are less likely to feel resentment towards you. This makes for happier relations in the future and keeps open opportunities for co-operation in other enterprises.'

'Thank you once more Nathan, it is a policy that might bear revisiting.'

Henry found his governess in the workroom with the two boys. 'Elizabeth, if it is not too much of a disruption to your programme may I have some time with Giles and Matthew. I have some stories they might enjoy.'

Elizabeth was enjoying the longest substantial period of happiness and contentment of her life. She had had happiness before; in her first home with Jonathan until he sold himself back into captivity with his father, her work at Levine's studio and the triumph of the wedding at St Paul's Cathedral were happy memories too. During her stay with Doris Churchill at White Cottage she had been content and had learned much from the jolly old lady. Here though, and her first year in her post now completed, her fears of discovery were gone, her son had a secure home and was being educated with a boy with whom he played as a brother. The change in Henry had been remarkable and she and Mollie Tutt had speculated on what might have occurred at Old Hall to bring about such a transformation but they could not think of what that might have been.

Programmes for the day, the week and the month were flexible enough to permit days in the park with Giles and Matthew and two half days a week for Elizabeth to visit the shops and stalls in the town. Templeton's had a reading room where she would spend an hour or two indulging her own passion for reading and drawing inspiration for future lessons. Mollie Tutt had a budget for Giles clothing and footwear, which Henry had doubled to include Matthew's needs. Uncomfortable with this responsibility the housekeeper had asked Elizabeth to take responsibility for managing the money and Elizabeth did it well. She bought remnants, off cuts and any other suitable material offered at a good price by the drapers on the market.

Evenings spent practising her skills provided soft furnishings and bed linens for the bedrooms of the boys, Mrs Tutt and herself. She made gowns for Mrs Tutt but the lady, pleased as she was, always wore the same one on her monthly visits to her sister-in-law at Bierly. It wasn't done to appear too grand.

Henry was about the house more frequently and for longer periods; his presence no longer brought gloom and the boys would run to the door to greet him each time he arrived home. Although he now called his son's governess by her christian name their relationship was quite formal. Elizabeth was pleased that he had not, even once, interfered with her methods of teaching but he had asked for progress reports and evidence of improvements and had always declared himself satisfied.

Elizabeth was satisfied too with the progress of her two young charges but, working and playing with them day by day, it was obvious to her that there were differences in their ability and attainment that could not be explained by the disparity in their ages alone. Giles was now eight years old and Matthew seven. Looking at them bent over their workbooks she studied Giles. Slim and slight, of golden locks, blue eyes and soft pale features, he bore no resemblance to his father and must have inherited his physical appearance from his mother. There was a trait though that she suspected had come from his father; Giles was quick of mind and wit, competitive and driven. No subject defeated him. No mistake was ever repeated.

Considering her son, Matthew, she looked at the stocky boy with dark tousled hair and mischievousness in eyes that he made no attempt to disguise. Matthew was intelligent enough but used his intelligence to do just enough to complete his work and nothing more. He did not have the love of learning that Giles had but he had a love of life. In the park, Giles could name the species of birds and waterfowl, Matthew was more interested in how far he could throw pieces of bread into the lake. While Giles could name the trees from the shape of their leaves, Matthew's interest in trees began and ended in whether or not they were climbable. For all that, and setting aside that she was mother to one but not to the other, she knew that of the two Matthew was, by far, the most lovable.

Over the following year, Henry's enquiries about the boys' progress became increasingly frequent and on those evenings in his office when the topic became exhausted their conversations would roam more widely. They would talk of their life experiences, their successes and disappointments and their hopes and plans. These evening meetings became the norm and relocated to the drawing room where Henry, tentatively at first, then quite openly discussed his business affairs. He told her of the history of his inheritance of the Holmes' group of businesses, how he had intended to sell off half shares but had been advised that his partners without the funds to expand would have been unable to offer increased employment.

Elizabeth did not need to feign interest. She was fascinated by the world of business, and would think she had only glimpsed in her sales of household linen to Hanson's Department Store in Leeds. Encouraged by her promptings, Henry told her in detail of how he had dealt with the Holmes' businesses. The reservations he had when revealing himself to men did not constrain him with Elizabeth. It was easy as talking to his mother, to Marianne or even to his dear Adeline.

He had, he explained, kept a half interest in each business and had sold a share that the manager could comfortably afford up to a maximum of forty percent. The balance, which in some cases was ten percent and in some as much as thirty per cent, he set aside. These were funds that managers could draw on to expand and provide employment opportunities. Elizabeth pressed for more. Henry told her that a manager owning a twenty percent share drew a wage and twenty percent of profits. If funds were needed to expand, and if these amounted to ten percent of value, Henry would advance half of that and the manager would then have twenty five percent of profits, some unemployed would be in work and the wealth of the town would increase.

Elizabeth admired his business ethics and was not shy of saying so. She was also growing to admire Henry the man, the farmer's son who, she was convinced, would have amassed wealth with or without the Holmes' inheritance. The Coggins business, was, she felt, inspired and said so. It now comprised of twenty shops spread between Halifax and the township between Bradford and Leeds.

Curious about what he had done in business since selling off shares but cautious not to intrude too far she hoped he would reveal it. When he had not done so, and taking advantage of his exceptional good humour one evening she touched on the subject. Without hesitation he told her and she was to learn why he had not volunteered the information.

'Substantial deposits were being added to almost daily until the sums were becoming an embarrassment to me as a person who witnesses the misery in which so many live in the town. Also, for a businessman, such sums, left unemployed, amount to negligence. I have taken shares in the railway companies. These will provide branch lines and stops so that more can live out of the town but travel in and enhance the wealth of the town. I have shares in the Gas light company. Extending lighting to streets in the poorer areas will reduce crime, violence and deter prostitution. I sit on the boards of those companies, which consumes some of my time.

'You must take some pride and satisfaction from that?' She asked.

' It is not purely altruistic Elizabeth, a town with transport, streets, houses and businesses well lit and ever improving employment is a wealthy town; a town in which to do business. Also, the value of my shares in these companies far exceeds the income I would have received from bare deposits. I have listened to advice about social responsibility and found it to be both good for the soul and, financially, highly profitable.'

'Do you have any plans now?'

'I am making contributions to a clean water system. These do not provide a monetary return but the benefit to health in this town will be immeasurable'.

That was it she thought. His modesty prevented him volunteering what she had drawn out of him.

'For my other plans Elizabeth,' he fell silent and she saw a tear forming in his eye, 'once my son is grown I intend to do something about my loneliness. Please excuse me I must retire.'

Henry had balance in his life, his spirits where high as were his energies. A regular visitor to his club but rarely staying the night he enjoyed the esteem in which he was held by the business community. He continued to visit Old Hall, attended the garden parties and made a call on one of the Christmas days, but did not stay. He had his own family with whom to celebrate the season. While he would have liked to have Elizabeth accompany him he realised that that could cause ill-informed gossip about the nature of their relationship. For the same reason he was reluctant to entertain at home. The governess was an attractive, articulate young woman and false inferences might be drawn.

His journeys to Old Hall were spent wracking his brains for a new story for Celia. How many ways, he wondered, could he weave stories of fairies, witches and giants? But every attempt was a pleasure. Always pleased to find her still there he was curious why a two year stay had extended to five and eventually he felt able to broach the subject to Charles. 'Their church has heard nothing of her parents since they arrived in Africa. I console Marianne with the thought that people have emerged from that continent after longer years than theirs but she is not convinced. It is rumoured that there have been instances of violence in that area, a thought too awful to contemplate, but I am resigned that we shall not see them again. Marianne is too sweet a person to celebrate the swapping of a sister for a daughter but there is too much mother in her not to want to raise such a lovely child.'

As a member of the boards of the railway companies, the gas lighting company and the water company, Henry occasionally had fellow members visit his office off Piece Hall Yard for minor matters of casual business and he was becoming ashamed of his business accommodation. He relocated to a new building in Hallings Road on the better side of town. On the third floor he had four offices, a conference room and a reception desk. George Ball was appointed Managing Director of the Crawshaw Group of Companies, Arthur Coggins the Managing Director of the Coggins Group, Walter Boothman, the Accounts Manager and a personable young man, Robin Price was appointed as a clerk and receptionist. Henry would be the chairman of all concerned.

Mrs Tutt excelled herself in preparing the special tea for Giles' tenth birthday. Her cakes and pastries were almost too delicate to handle and it seemed a sin that they be demolished. The five members of the Crawshaw household sat around the table together, a rare occurrence reserved for occasions such as this and Christmas.

Once the boys were in bed and Mrs Tutt, tiring more easily as she aged had retired too, Elizabeth found Henry in the drawing room. 'Mr Crawshaw, I have to tell you that I have taken Giles as far as I am able and he is ready for school where, I am confident, he will acquit himself admirably. Should you delay that, I fear it will hold him back and he will, later, be disadvantaged.

'What of Matthew?'

'I cannot be sure when he will be ready. He does not apply himself as fully as he ought and I suspect he will struggle, despite my best efforts.'

'Would you object if I was to place them both in school? You could review their days work each evening and prepare them for their following day's lessons. Give Matthew his chance and I would raise no objection to you withdrawing him if you felt he was unable to cope.'

Uniformed and fully equipped the two boys joined the junior department of the Boy's Grammar School. Henry, unbeknown to them had positioned himself with a view of the school drive and was touched to see them enter the building holding hands. Elizabeth's evenings were spent reviewing and helping them prepare their work. The standard was not taxing Giles. Matthew's work improved significantly. His teacher's criticisms had more effect than his mother-tutor's and the impetus he gained was producing results.

With empty days, Elizabeth returned to her sewing. Some provided clothing for the boys, some pieces were practice samples to return her skills to their previous high levels. She wrote to Catherine and they began a regular exchange of letters. She wrote to the sisters at Bethlehem and was saddened to learn of the death of Sister Benedicta. Elizabeth knelt and said a prayer. Sister Louis was now Mother Superior and she sent Elizabeth the love of all there who remembered her with affection. She wrote to Oswald Levine and his staff. Levine took the time to pen a long letter. Beattie was now a buyer of materials for the principal department store in town. Devina was now his Senior Seamstress and his business had never looked back following the London wedding. He wondered if she might be interested in employment, even if conducted from Bradford. She declined politely but promised to consider it if her circumstances changed.

Chapter 25

A year passed quickly and happily. Henry building on his successes, Elizabeth taking pride in the progress of both Giles and Matthew. The situation was destined to change when Henry received a letter from the headmaster from the grammar school requesting a meeting. Some parents were invited to a meeting at the school. The affluent, certainly a fellow of the Academy and a member of so many boards, warranted a visit to his home. Elizabeth, as the tutor, was asked to be present and she was apprehensive that there might have been some misbehaviour; and if there were it was more likely that Matthew would be the culprit.

The headmaster, Pearson Rhodes, came directly to the point. 'Mr Crawshaw, Sir, your son shows outstanding academic ability which is a tribute to his raising and his tutoring.' He nodded at Elizabeth. 'If his full potential is to be realised then he needs to play a fuller part in the life of the school. Education is about more than books and learning.'

Henry recognised these words and glanced at Elizabeth who had the grace not to react. 'I would recommend that you place him as a boarder. Monday lunchtime to Saturday lunchtime. The progress he will make will be unimaginable; I have seen it so many times.'

'But Mr Rhodes, he is still a child.'

'A child with a thirst for knowledge and a mind to accumulate and relate that knowledge, deny it now and he will lose it. Trust me, Sir.'

Henry pondered. He paused. 'What of Matthew?'

'Master Fairwood is a little young. Not yet ready. If pushed beyond his current abilities he might well revolt and be lost to academic achievement.'

The boys should not be separated, should not be differentiated, thought Henry.

Negotiate, seek concessions. Obtain a deal and arrive at an arrangement acceptable to both parties.

'In a years time, perhaps, Mr Rhodes?'

'Given acceptable progress I cannot see why not but there can be no guarantee that he will make that progress and reap the benefits of boarding. There is pressure on our boarding accommodation and we become oversubscribed. To address this there is a qualifying examination for boarders. Your son would pass that, without question. I do doubt though that Master Fairwood will pass with another years work.'

'Thank you for your frankness Mr Rhodes. Allow me to propose an arrangement. My son's education is important to me but no less is Master Fairwood's. I accept Giles should not be held back and I accept that Matthew is too young and too unprepared for boarding. Here is my proposal. Both boys will sit the boarding qualification examination in twelve months time. Their tutor, Mrs Fairwood, will visit his tutors and obtain details of the syllabus for this coming year and ensure that he is stretched beyond the day boys in his year. She will also learn what Matthew needs to achieve in order to pass the examination. Can we agree on that?'

'I can agree on that far, Mr Crawshaw, even though it is an unusual arrangement. What I cannot agree is that in twelve months time the acceptance of one is dependent upon the acceptance of both.'

'Nor would I ask such a thing. If, after one year, Giles is successful and Matthew is not then I shall agree to Giles attending as a boarder and Matthew as a day boy.'

The two men shook hands and the agreement was made. Stein's advice had stood in good stead many times in reorganising the Holmes' companies. Negotiate, be prepared to make concessions and you will receive concessions.

So began a most difficult year for Elizabeth. Excited at thoughts of Matthew obtaining an education better than she could ever have provided but still saddened that her little boy would be living away from her on most nights of each week, it was her job to make her fears a reality. Presenting herself at the grammar school as agreed she was introduced to the year head of the first boarding year, Dermot Shay, and his animosity was palpable. Without explanation, he loaded her arms with notes, textbooks, and some sample examination papers from previous years. Her reception by the head of Matthew's year was no more welcoming. Once more without explanation she was presented with two piles of assorted notes, and a pile of books and no guidance on the standard required for the boarders examination. She would have to work from the sample papers she had. It took three journeys to carry the materials home and she was convinced that she could expect no co-operation from the school.

The boys' workroom was littered with piles of books and notes for each and Elizabeth set about an initial reading to gauge the difficulty of the task that faced her. Matthew's work, although at the boundaries of her own knowledge would be manageable for her and, she hoped for him. To take Giles to the level he would have been expected to attain in his first boarding year, however, was, she knew at one reading, beyond her. The subject that would defeat her was a mathematic syllabus. Not only could she not attempt any answers to the questions on the sample paper, she could not even understand the questions. She must learn, she told herself, Henry and Giles were depending on her. It was a role for which she was employed.

Elizabeth's days were spent preparing lessons and the evenings spent in teaching but the boys were to be taught at different levels so could not be taught together. This entailed working long hours. Her nights were spent studying the mathematic textbooks she had been given but for all her efforts each new page read like a foreign language, foreign to the page before and foreign to the page that followed. She made no mention of her difficulties to Henry but he was missing their evening talks and noting her obvious exhaustion felt the need, eventually to ask her if the task was becoming too difficult.

'Elizabeth, you advised me over a year ago that you had taken Giles as far as you were able, I have placed an unfair burden on you by asking you to take on the role of a specialist tutor on a range of subjects. What assistance can I offer, the employment of tutors perhaps?'

Elizabeth, more fatigued than she had been in the Fry household and touched by Henry's concern could contain her emotions no longer and wept. Henry placed a gentle hand on her shoulder to offer comfort but quickly withdrew it and waited until she had collected herself.

'I believe I am capable of taking Giles through his missing first boarding year in all subjects other than mathematics. The sample paper makes no sense to me and for months now I have attempted to teach myself from the text books but they do not bridge the gap in my knowledge of arithmetic and the starting of the books.'

Henry picked up the textbooks and studied a few pages. His expertise lay in calculations and he felt he might be able to guide Elizabeth but page after page was filled with algebraic formulae as indecipherable to him as a scientific theory. He read through the sample examination paper and could make no more sense of it than Elizabeth. 'May I borrow these, I insist now that there be no more study for you tonight. Please go to your bed and rest. I am not a teacher but I do hold a respected qualification in calculation and these books make no sense to me. I intend to find out why.'

The next morning Henry was back at the Academy and in the office of Bullivant Theakstone who received him enthusiastically.

'Mr Theakstone, Sir, I am seeking a service might I ask your opinion on this examination paper.'

Theakstone read it through quickly and answered, 'I recognise it. Set two or perhaps three years ago. A standard paper on the subject.'

'This is a standard for a twelve year old seeking entry to a grammar school boarding class?'

Laughing, Theakstone replied, 'Certainly not. This is the second year university paper for students of higher mathematics.'

Henry handed his old Principal three textbooks.

'Yes these are the current texts for the second and third years. There should be another book, which introduces all the principles developed in the other three. That is a reference to each formula and without it the three are unintelligible.'

Less than half an hour later Henry was in the office of the headmaster of the grammar school.

'Mr Rhodes, I would be grateful for an explanation as to why my son's governess has been given this sample to prepare Giles for his first year as a boarder. I wish to know whether this is the standard achieved by your first year boarders or if it has been provided in error or whether there is mischief afoot?'

Pearson Rhodes studied the paper and sent for the year head, Dermot Shay. He handed him the paper and asked for an explanation. Shay said that he could not understand how such a mistake could have occurred. Possibly the lack of notice he had been given and the urgency with which he had had to gather the material was the cause. It was after all, he added, most unusual to provide a governess, who was not even a qualified tutor with the school's material.

Henry was not satisfied and was annoyed by the arrogance of the final, unnecessary, comment. He produced the three textbooks, deposited them on the headmaster's desk more heavily than needed and asked Shay.

'Am I able to ask, to accept that in your urgency to provide the required materials you inadvertently included three text books, books which I will wager are not in use in this school, text books provided without the introductory reference volume?' Feeling his voice rising he remembered Charles's advice and moderated it.

Rhodes turned to Shay, his face stern and his words clipped.

'Explain yourself Mr Shay.'

The teacher was unabashed. Defiant even. 'I should not be asked to explain myself to a parent even in a school in which the wealth and status of parents is held in higher regard than the talent of their progeny' and without permission he left.

Embarrassed and angry the headmaster started into a lengthy apology but Henry interrupted him.

'Mr Rhodes, you will understand why I see no prospect of placing my son as a boarder here when I suspect he will be subjected to petulance by that man.'

'Mr Crawshaw, Sir, I will tell you in confidence that since Mr Shay was unsuccessful in his application for the deputy headship he has been disaffected and unsupportive. He claims to have another position to take up but will not decide until term end whether to take it up. I have now made that decision for him. Your son will not find him here again.'

'Then Mr Rhodes, this is what I would have you do.' He stated his requirements and Rhodes was anxious to agree. That afternoon a messenger from the school was sent to collect all the materials with which Elizabeth had been working. She was to have a week of shorter days and earlier nights in bed. The materials that were returned at weekend where in a vastly different form.

Matthew's work was of no less volume but it was in indexed sections with schedules and lesson plans with a readily understandable outline. It was accompanied by a note from Matthew's year head, apologising for the previous haphazard assembly of the materials and an explanation that he had been given little notice of the need to prepare and provide the notes.

Giles study materials were now reduced to just a quarter of the mass that had overwhelmed Elizabeth. They too were indexed and supplied with schedules and lesson plans. Apprehensive, she turned first to the mathematics lessons and saw, with relief, that they were well within her understanding and would not call for long nights and spent with textbooks in her room.

The boarders' entrance examinations were held in June and the results were announced in July before the summer break. As predicted, Giles passed with high marks in every paper. Elizabeth had been doubtful of Matthew's prospects, knowing that he had no wish to board and doubting that he would give of his best in the examinations in order to avoid boarding. Matthew, though, for all his mischief and aversion to effort had an especially close bond to his mother. Sensitive enough to see her suffering when she was lacking sleep to teach him and Giles, determined not to disappoint her, he had stretched himself to qualify. He could not know that she was torn between her ambitions for him and the wish to have him with her. Matthew too had passed, a tribute to application over innate ability as the headmaster's letter had put it, prompted Henry to fund a celebration and the five members of the household dined at the Palm Rooms, the best restaurant in the town. The boys felt so proud and spent the meal grinning at each other and patting each other on the back.

Elizabeth was busy arranging uniform, sporting clothes, nightwear and equipment, knowing this would probably be the last work she did for Henry Crawshaw. She would miss him; his friendship, his support and she wondered if she would ever find another position that would suit her so well.

It was a week before the beginning of the boarding term and she had expected Henry to raise the subject but, since he had not done so, she would have to prompt the conversation.

'After Giles is boarding, and it is now just a week away I shall need to find another position. I shall not have a role here.'

Henry was not unaware that the subject would arise but had hoped that by avoiding it his loss of Elizabeth might be delayed. He did not want to be parted from her, he had feelings of affection and though he would not permit himself to think of love, if he was to love again it would be a woman such as her. She was intelligent, so very attractive and he took so much comfort and pleasure from her company that he could not imagine his life or his home without her. 'Negotiate, Henry,' he told himself.

'Elizabeth I am surprised and saddened that you would wish to leave. I understand that there are concerns as regards appearances if you were to be here without a role but I do have a role for you. Mrs Tutt is now aged and would retire to her sister-in-law in Bierly if she could afford to do so. I intend to provide her with a pension to facilitate that. It would be an insult to you if I was to offer that post and I already decided to appoint a housekeeper with cooking skills. What I will need is a head of household and it would please me if you would accept that position.'

Despite her wish to remain she could not see how that could be achieved with propriety. 'The role would not be understood by the others. The situation would be damaging to your good name and to mine. My reputation has been traduced before and, mercifully, Matthew was too young to understand. Now with both our sons at the grammar school any scandal, no matter how false the premise it be based upon, would attach to them. We cannot permit it Mr Crawshaw.'

Henry, desperate now, treated the situation as a negotiation. Offer a concession in return for one. It was a clumsy, cold hearted approach to make an offer such as he was about to make. 'We could satisfy your concerns, avoid the scandal you fear, protect your reputation and secure your stay in this house if we were to marry.'

As he said the words he cringed at the lack of warmth in them. They were no better than he would have used to sell a ten percent share in a street corner butcher's shop. He attempted quickly to recover the situation but his confidence and ability to express himself had for once, and on such an important occasion, deserted him.

It was little better and he was well aware of it but a more effusive expression of emotion would, he felt, be a betrayal of Adeline.

Elizabeth thanked him for his proposal in a voice she might have used when offered a cup of tea but told him she was unable to accept. In her room her emotions were in chaos. She had feelings for Henry, deep feelings that she knew could become feelings of love. He would be a fine husband and she could be, she knew, a respectful and loving wife. Why had he not spoken of his feelings – if not of love then at least of affection. There had been no mention of either, just a business arrangement. She had lived in a loveless marriage and could have done so again but she would not, again, live in a marriage bereft of affection.

Henry spent the following day in his office, cursing his clumsiness, still determined not to lose Elizabeth but knowing he could not repair the damage he had done. He formed a plan and invited Elizabeth to join him that evening.

'I have a business proposition for you.'

Elizabeth, thinking that his proposal the previous evening had been no more than a business proposition, was tempted to say that but her manners stopped her.

'I have a house nearby that would provide a good home for you and for Matthew. It would make a spacious workroom if you wished to return to your practice of dressmaking. For me it would represent a good investment for you a home, a business and your independence.'

'Provided that it was on a business basis, not a charitable one, I would indeed be interested in a partnership.'

'Elizabeth I would have it no other way. I hold the premises in trust for Giles to either retain or dispose of for value on his behalf, I may not let it so the rental is not an issue. The only value of the business would be goodwill, of which until it is established, there would be none. There would be costs in respect of worktables, materials, thread and the like which you would have to acquire and we could share the costs according to the portions of the business each of us is to own. You should know though that the house has been closed for nine years, it was my marital home, and there will be costs involved in opening up, cleaning and converting certain rooms. Since the property will not be yours, unless in the coming nine years you are able to purchase it, the costs will fall to me.'

Elizabeth visited the house alone and was in no doubt as to its potential to be both a good home and a place of business. Excited by the possibilities it presented she would agree a partnership with Henry provided that it would be an equal partnership. She had savings of twenty four pounds and would need to equip the workroom for forty eight pounds. That was ample she was sure and asked Henry for twenty four pounds, a half share partnership and the right to draw twelve shilling in wages each week before any division of profits.

Henry agreed but there would be one condition. As equal partner she should, from now, refer to him as Henry.

After two weeks the team of cleaners were done, the piano had been removed and sold and the worktables and initial tools and materials were delivered. Both Matthew and Giles spent their weekends there, although Giles visited his father each Saturday evening. The boys had both settled as boarders better than Elizabeth could have hoped and Henry, at first reluctant to visit the house seemed happier to do so when it was redecorated and converted. His visits, ostensibly to show interest in his investment, became more frequent and they soon settled into a routine of regular evening conversations about dressmaking, the boys and any topic he could conjure up to prolong his stay.

Elizabeth visited Oscar Levine. He had a contract to supply finished goods to a good class department store newly opened in Bradford. In order to maintain the prestige of the name Oscar Levine's Studios, these were supplied under the name Park Terrace and Levine offered to sub contract some of this work to Elizabeth. It proved to be highly profitable and, as the orders increased, she took on an assistant, Daisy Mellor, who was both adept with a needle and thread and good company.

Henry had a new housekeeper, a woman younger and more personable than Mrs Tutt, and Elizabeth was annoyed at herself for feelings of jealousy. The two boys had got on well as boarders for the first two years but when Giles was transferred to the senior department and senior dormitory their relationship changed. It was common at the school that some seniors would bully some juniors; to establish his credibility with his senior colleagues Giles had attempted to bully Matthew. The younger boy, stockier and better physically able, retaliated and fought Giles and beat him. It was a humiliation that Giles would never forgive.

Elizabeth was summoned to the school and informed of the incident. Matthew was warned about the consequences of a repetition and Giles would no longer stay with them. Distressed that Giles, whom she had raised as a son, and loved just as well, would no longer stay with her and concerned that Matthew might be jeopardising his education, Elizabeth discussed the situation with Henry. He was to visit Old Hall for the weekend of the garden party next week. He would take both boys and have them make their peace.

Appreciative of Henry's generosity but feeling guilty that it should continue in those circumstances, Elizabeth, now earning well, proposed that she should take responsibility for Matthew's school fees. Henry would have none of it. She also proposed buying out his half share of the business and he would not have that either.

During the journey to Old Hall Henry admonished both boys. Giles expressed his sincere contrition, said that while there had been fault on both sides, he accepted full responsibility for his part and promised there would be no recurrence. He offered his hand, which Matthew accepted, but felt suspicious of Giles's claim that the matter was forgotten and would not be referred to again. Celia was pleased to have company of her own age and encouraged the boys to ride her pony. Matthew was all for it and fall after fall from the saddle did not diminish his enthusiasm. Giles would not subject himself to such indignity and sought out the head gardener to identify trees that were new to him, spent time in the stables wishing to know the names, size and breed and age of each horse and missed no opportunity to ingratiate himself with Charles.

Celia had such a jolly day that she asked Marianne if the boys might be invited more frequently. Although the motives differed, both boys never missed an opportunity to visit Old Hall, which they continued to do throughout their school years. Giles became distant from Elizabeth. He was no longer dependant on her for her tutoring, his affection for her as a surrogate mother was dissipated as he grew and she became of no use to him and, comfortable with his affluent friends whose intellectual snobbery he shared, he considered himself superior to her and far superior to young Fairwood, as he referred to him in school. Reliant on his father, he feigned respect and Henry, on more than one occasion, detected that his son was patronising him. For two years Giles was rarely at home on Sunday nights. He had friends in the choir and they gave concerts at churches and other venues around the town.

A continuing visitor to Old Hall, Giles grovelling and embarrassing to Charles, and barely acknowledging Marianne, he explained to Charles that his interest in the choir was not merely a diversion. He had, he said, been relieved to rid himself of all traces of his Bradford accent, inflicted upon him from childhood by an unsuitable housekeeper, but since he intended to practice law he had needed to lower his higher tones by a notch or two. In that he had been assisted by his choir master, Bruno Saville, who had taken a personal interest in him. His praise of Bruno was so long and so fulsome that Charles considered it excessive. As Giles left on one occasion Marianne regarded this tall, slim young man. His fair hair she thought too well groomed, his clothing too well co-ordinated and his self-absorption suggested a young man on the verge of becoming a dandy. She had commented to Charles, 'Do you not think him a little too, er, delicate?' Charles smiled, 'You are too charitable. A less kindly soul may think him effeminate.'

'What of Matthew? How different they are for two boys raised together.'

'Giles has much of Adeline about him and little of Henry. I know insufficient of Matthew's parentage to offer an opinion but I do believe that he has the makings of an officer in the military. Of Giles? perhaps a clerk to a clergyman.'

'Oh Charles, Giles is exceedingly clever, brilliant it is said.'

'Yes, my dear, but such brilliance if not properly directed, can lead a man into devilment. I would wish he was more influenced by Henry than by this man, Bruno, with whom he seems too enamoured.'

Chapter 26

Elizabeth, in business now for seven years, had established her reputation, built an impressive client list and expanded in the manner she had learned from her partner Henry. He had matched the savings she had made from her share of the profits, she had bought out Oswald Levine's Park Terrace label and was operating as Fairwood Studio. Daisy Mellor had responsibility for Park Terrace and Elizabeth employed another seamstress, an older and more serious woman than Daisy but an accomplished dressmaker who could match Elizabeth in the quality of her work.

Henry received a huge windfall when the Borough Corporation purchased the gas company and he received a ten-fold return on his original investment from which he made a substantial contribution to the town's clean water scheme that was coming on a pace. He took vicarious pride in Elizabeth's success and even though he would have been incapable of sewing a tassel to a nightshirt, he felt he deserved some credit for the reputation of the Fairwood Studio. The local newspapers were scoured for reports of weddings in which the name of the gown designer might be mentioned and it was while so engaged that his eye was caught by a report on a case in court.

'At Leeds Assize Court today, Mr Justice Armitage directed that Luke Ogden of Halifax was unfit to plead to a murder charge on the grounds of his insanity. The case followed the death of Mr Barry

Throop following the fight over the ownership of a
dog. Evidence was given against Luke Ogden and
his brother Mr Joseph Ogden by reliable witnesses.
Luke Ogden was committed for life to an institution
for the criminally insane and Joseph Ogden was
sentenced to death by hanging.'

Pearson Rhodes, the headmaster, visited Henry by appointment. It was his recommendation that Giles, now eighteen years of age, should attend university. Giles had he said, a fine mind that would have no difficulty with the intellectual rigours his studies would entail. Rhodes informed him that Giles's ambition was to practice law it was realistic and should be encouraged.

Henry was not displeased (as he would have been had his son wanted to pursue his interest in music) and stated that he would support his son through his studies.

'What of Matthew Fairwood, Mr Rhodes? I would wish to treat them equally.'

'Then you would do no favours to him or to yourself. Master Fairwood is not unintelligent but he achieves his results by plodding application rather than inspiration and his interests and abilities are too narrow for the demands of university where the motivation has been self generated, not imposed.'

'Does Matthew have any discernable strengths Mr Rhodes?'

'But of course, we all do. Master Fairwood has an uncommon facilitate with numbers but a degree in higher mathematics would, I fear, be a stretch too far. Even if he were to succeed I do not think his spirit would be satisfied as a teacher of mathematical theories to a room full of boys over half of whom were wishing they were elsewhere.'

Giles, delighted, was to go up to Cambridge in October. Henry discussed options with Matthew who favoured leaving school, finding employment and making his own way. Expressing gratitude and ever respectful, Matthew still rejected each of Henry's suggestions – an apprenticeship in accountancy or a two year attendance at the Academy of Commerce, now in new premises in Clarendon Terrace, where a qualification from there was becoming regarded as an equivalent to a degree in business studies. Henry was not prepared to offer a position in his own group of companies as that was not likely to be well received by his managing directors or his managers who would suspect nepotism.

He visited Elizabeth, as he did almost every evening. His loneliness was now relieved but his clumsiness of his proposal to her seven years before still annoyed him. As her business had grown, so had her confidence and independence. So too had her attraction for him. What finer wife could he ever have had. Now, though, friends and companions for too long, an expression of affection would, he thought, be quite impossible. More difficult still for him was that his affection had grown and he was in love. Elizabeth did not share Henry's determination that Matthew should remain in formal study. Where Giles might be suited to it, Matthew was not. He had energy and a spirit that would not find their satisfaction in lecture rooms and books.

When next at Old Hall, Henry discussed Giles and Matthew with Charles, his past protector and mentor he respected the older man's counsel.

Charles did not comment on Giles but referring to Matthew said, 'He is a most pleasant young man. Unpretentious, companionable and adventurous, I would have no concerns about his ability to equip himself well in any venture he undertook. Let me make a suggestion, not on the basis of our friendship but on the basis that I find Matthew so likeable. My father is ageing quickly. He will not contest his seat in Parliament next time. Within a year, perhaps a little longer, I shall need to locate myself in Huntingdon. To prepare for that I am grooming Nathan Stein to step up from business manager to estate manager with far more autonomy than he currently enjoys. Why do we not suggest to Matthew that he be apprenticed to Nathan. He will learn a great deal and I wager leap at the opportunity.'

'You appear most confident of this Charles.'

'Cousin Henry. His ever frequent visits here, as welcome as I find them are not to see me or Marianne. Do you want to take the wager?'

'No Charles. Celia has blossomed into a charming and beautiful young woman. I shall keep my coins in my purse.'

Nathan Stein, elated at the prospect of the post to which he would eventually be elevated was, nonetheless, resentful at having his assistant foisted upon him. It was an appointment he had expected to be able to make. That did not prejudice him against Matthew, whom he had met on occasions and found likeable, he would give him a fair opportunity. Soon his misgivings were banished by the bright, attentive and industrious young man. There was none of the introversion that he had found in Henry, who had been the same age as Matthew when Stein first met him. The young apprentice was up early, always prepared to work until late and was popular with Charles and Marianne who both were generous in their attention to him. They noted, approvingly, the attention he gave to Celia and that she gave to him in return.

Henry visited the Academy in its new premises in Carleton Terrace and met with his old principal.

'Mr Theakstone, Sir, I have had it in my mind for some long time now to take certain action but have been constrained from doing so by the possibility that either my son or a young man I have raised as a son might seek a place here. I am in no doubt that my action, if taken earlier, would have had no influence whatsoever on your decision to admit one or the other or not. However, there are those who might have interpreted it so. Now it is no longer an issue. Neither will be seeking a place here and I seek your approval to establish a scholarship to pay the fees each year of one entrant who does not have the support of a parent; I would wish the entrant to be chosen on merit by competitive examination and interview.'

'That is most generous Mr Crawshaw. I would need to seek the approval of the Board of Governors but, if I may say, given your status both in the town and as a Fellow of the Academy, I foresee nothing but enthusiastic approval. I, though, will not be here to oversee it. We are in our new premises, we have expanded our intake and it is an opportune time for my retirement, which will take effect at next year's end. May I suggest you address your proposal to Councillor Clarence Jowett and be sure I will give it my full support.'

'I fear Mr Theakstone you may need to declare an interest and, consequently, disqualify yourself from participating in the decision. I have had some degree of success in business but have always been aware of how close I came to destroying my opportunity through foolishness and greed. It would have been easier for you to dismiss me than keep me but you did not do so and I would have you know how I have continued to appreciate that.'

'You had a most eloquent advocate in Mr Stein, if I recall. He provided a service to us both.'

'I have made my thanks to Mr Stein and wish to make my thanks to you and the Academy. I do not wish my name to be associated with the scholarship and would have it known as the Bullivant Theakstone Scholarship, with no student ever knowing which of their fellow colleagues was the beneficiary.'

His donations to the clean water scheme and his establishing of the Scholarship had confirmed the wisdom of the advice he had been given as a young man, that a pound well spent could provide more pleasure than a pound saved.

Giles's first letters from Cambridge dealt mainly with his settling in and made only passing references to his finances. Later letters were concerned with little other than the inadequacy of his allowance. He pursued that theme when he returned home for Christmas and pointed out that since his father had not attended university he could have no understanding of the costs involved and the standards that one had to maintain to avoid being regarded as impoverished and being excluded from the company of the better fellows. Henry agreed a substantial increase.

Charles, conscious that it might be his last Christmas at Old Hall, had drawn up an eclectic guest list. Celia was insistent that Matthew should be invited and Charles, who could deny her nothing, relented despite the convention that employees were not invited. Henry and Giles would be invited and Marianne wished to invite Matthew's mother whose reputation for the design and creation of magnificent gowns had been the talk of Marianne's circle for three seasons. Charles concluded that he could not invite Matthew without inviting Nathan Stein and Mrs

Stein; not only because Stein was Matthew's senior but because he would, sooner or later be the manager of the estate and needed to be accorded the respect that the position commanded.

The three days, thought Charles had been a success. He had found Giles to be an irritation, continually attempting to monopolise his company and being embarrassingly obsequious. The ladies who danced with him were generally of the opinion that he was odd and far too self regarding. Those same ladies however were keen to make the acquaintance of the Principal of the Fairwood Studio. There was a certain social prestige to be had from this.

Henry danced with Elizabeth. It was the first time he had held her and he had wished the dance would never end. Later, as Giles watched his father dance with Marianne, Charles with Elizabeth and Matthew with Celia he was displeased. It did not suit his plans that there should be a Fairwood – Ambrose alliance nor that his father should be a party to it.

At the entertainment evening on Boxing Day, Giles sang, unaccompanied, a long choral piece. He demonstrated a remarkable range and an equally remarkable lack of empathy with his audience in that it seemed to them that his performance was interminable. The applause he received owed more to relief than appreciation. Resuming his seat he said, silently to himself, 'let's see young Fairwood match that.'

Matthew did more than match it. He first coached and then led the audience in a rollicking sing song in which the ladies sang a line and the gentlemen replied in the words of the following line. The mix-ups that ensued had his audiences crying with laughter.

Giles's letters made no further complaint about his finances throughout his first year, nor had he any cause to, given the generosity of his allowance. He returned home late for his summer break and returned to Cambridge early. That same October Charles received less notice of his need to relocate to Huntingdon than he would have wished and in circumstances that he would not have wished. Sir Isaac had died before he could retire. Matthew and Celia were devastated at their impending separation. They had grown close, were now romantically involved and had reached the stage of discussing a future together. Now she would have to leave.

There would be no Christmas celebrations at Old Hall that year. Matthew would have two days at home with his mother. Giles wrote to inform Henry that he would not take the break but would remain in Cambridge to continue his studies. Henry invited Elizabeth and Matthew to Christmas dinner and Elizabeth, with her resentment of the housekeeper's presence in Henry's home, as irrational as she knew it to be, could still not do other than to admire her ability as a cook. She noted that Henry's relationship with his housekeeper was less formal than it had been with Mrs Tutt and, while piqued by it, attributed that to the fact that Henry was now a happier and more relaxed person than the one she had first met.

As Easter approached Giles wrote to say that he would not be home for the break, although he would dearly love to do so, but some 'chums', as he termed them, were planning a break in Paris. Now accepted into the best circle of his year he did not wish to risk exclusion by not accepting such a sought after invitation. There would, however, be costs involved and he requested an additional sum of twenty pounds.

This was the second break during which his son had found a reason to absent himself from home and Henry was suspicious. While he had not, as Giles had reminded him, attended university, he could not accept that a student would need funds, that his son was spending to support themselves through their studies and to attend appropriate social functions. He asked Richard Anderson, the Leeds investigator, to visit him.

Henry outlined his concerns and the nature of the investigation into his son's activities that he wanted. Anderson explained that he did not have agents sufficiently proximate to Cambridge University to undertake the detailed enquiries required but he did have a reciprocal arrangement with one of the better agencies in London. With Henry's consent he would convey his requirements to Simon Whitney of Whitney & Son of Paddington who would report directly to Henry.

Whitney's reports came promptly and frequently and Henry offered the invoices by return. Some of the reports contained information that Henry found perturbing and some distressing. It was not only the content of the reports but the fact that he was being provided with some correspondence between Giles and another, obviously intercepted that convinced Henry that the documents could not remain safely in his home. They needed to be in a bank vault; but not the vault of his own bank.

He asked Whitneys to enquire into the average sum that a student at Cambridge University would need to live comfortably each year and found it was less than a tenth of the sum that Giles was receiving. He wrote to inform his son that his allowance was excessive and in future he would be paid double the average sum on which his colleagues were subsisting. Giles was furious and in his fury he wrote to his father in ill-considered and intemperate terms.

'Dear Father,'

You can imagine the vexation you cause me by your meanness. I attempt to make allowances for your ignorance of university life but need, now, to acquaint you with certain facts.

My set comprises the brightest and best of their generation, amongst whose number I am included. They are the sons of gentlemen of wealth and social standing. My inclusion in their circle will provide me with contacts to enhance my legal career. I admire your rise above your low beginnings and I am striving to emulate you by rising above my raising in the squalid town to which my birth condemned me.

You should know that I am associating with and accepted by the sons of peers, judges, industrialists and landowners. I merely ask that you accept that their fathers breed in them expectations that a dealer in pigs feet could not understand.

You have spoken often of your hope that I would qualify as a lawyer and practise in Bradford to provide services to your business interests. I have higher ambitions. I will qualify but it is my intention to practise at the bar in London and to that end, I have already formed the connections necessary to achieve that aim.

As I approach my final third and final year it would be nothing less than iniquitous if it was to be derailed by your parsimony and I must ask you to reconsider your savage reduction in my allowances.

Your son

Giles.

Henry seethed at the insults and ingratitude of the arrogant popinjay he had fathered. Tempted to reveal what he had learned of his son's activities and associations in Cambridge but anxious not to alert him to the fact that he was being observed and reported upon, he satisfied himself with a measured response.

'Dear Giles,'

I am saddened that you condemn your birthplace and the business that has provided your education. Are your friends so shallow that you have to buy your way into their acceptance? If so, such friends are worthless and when you look to them to advance your ambitions you will find them gone when you no longer amuse them.

I suspect that you have accounts with tailors, wine merchants and restaurants that are nothing less than extravagant for a twenty year old who has yet to earn a penny; whether that be from pigs feet or any other such respectable enterprise.

I have enquired into a sum that is reasonable for your expenses and have doubled it. There will be no increase.

Your father.

A reply arrived.

'Dear Father,'

I expected better from a father who owes his wealth not to his own efforts but to the achievements of my grandfather and the generosity of my grandmamma. Do not expect me to come to you again for funds. Having done so, having explained their importance to me and having found you miserly, I will not prostrate myself again.

Next year I shall attain my majority. Until then I shall borrow against my inheritance, which I know from grandmamma to consist of two thousand pounds and my mother's house in Manningham I shall need the cash to set myself up in London but the value of the house should more than clear the debts that I intend to incur in my final year.

Had you not bestowed your largess so freely on the Fairwoods you might have been in a better position to support your own son.

In less than twelve months I shall come into my inheritance. In preparation for that I require you to have Mrs Fairwood out of my mother's house, convert it back from a work room to a gentleman's residence and make it readily saleable.

Giles.

Matthew pined for Celia and she for him. They had been apart for nine months and their letters were no consolation to either but the most recent of these lifted Matthew. It was an invitation to a weekend at the Ambrose Huntingdon estate to mark her eighteenth birthday in September.

Henry was also invited, as was Giles but Henry feared the animosity between the two would be evident to their hosts and sour the occasion. He sent his apologies and a gift.

Although he had not been totally neglectful of Jane Holmes, Henry had corresponded with her regularly over the years, but now her sister had died, she was alone, and despite the hazardous journey to Dorset, he undertook it. Jane was thrilled by his visit, grateful for the company, anxious for his news but he sensed an underlying concern. It did not surface until the second evening when she passed him a letter she had received from Giles.

'My dear Grandmamma,'

I wish my studies and my circumstances would permit me to visit you but they will not. I am about to commence my final year at Cambridge, following which I have,I am sure, secured a pupilage with a prominent chambers in London where I shall seek admission to the bar. It may be that in years to come, should God bless you with a long life that you will visited by Giles Crawshaw Q.C. or K.C. depending on the longevity of our beloved Queen.

It is not a matter with which I should trouble you but my plans are jeopardised in that I might not be able to finance my final year. My father is refusing to support me through it.

In less than a year now I shall come into the inheritance so generously provided by you and my grandfather but he holds that in trust and will not release it so I fear I may have to abandon my studies. I had thought of taking loans to see me through this year but the repayments would erode the value of

*what you have provided for me and I could not
countenance my grandfather's lifetime efforts for
me being handed to some moneylender.*

*If I was to obtain a loan of just six hundred
pounds I could complete the studies that I have
been labouring over for two years. That would be
repayable from the sale of my mother's house but
I am doubtful now if I shall benefit from that. My
father has housed a woman there and I suspect he
has designs on her.*

*I would be most grateful and ever appreciative
for your advice and any assistance that you might
afford me. With my father having distanced himself
from me, you are now my only living relative.*

Your loving grandson

Giles.

Jane did not invite a response but Henry gave one. 'This
letter is a mixture of the misrepresentation, half-truths
and blatant lies. I am aware of Giles's lifestyle and I will
not shock you with it but assure you that it is one of which
you would disapprove. Further funds will draw him deeper
into the disreputable behaviour that my reining in of his
profligacy is intended to discourage. I would urge you not
to advance him any money.'

'Henry, I have clearly done so, the full six hundred
pounds.'

'Then I fear that neither you nor I will hear from him
until he wants more.'

Chapter 27

On the eve of Celia's birthday celebration Matthew had a long, hard day at Old Hall in preparation for his three day absence. His travel that Saturday morning was a difficult one involving two carriages and two railway journeys and he arrived at the Huntingdon Manor in the late afternoon. Bathed and changed he met Celia and her guests, neighbours and friends of Charles and Marianne. Giles was already there and attempting to charm the gathering. Matthew had hoped to travel with Henry and was disappointed that he said he had sent apologies of a pressing business commitment.

Sitting for dinner beside Celia he could not have been more content and they dared to squeeze hands below the table. There was little opportunity to spend time alone but tomorrow they would have that.

Few guests stayed the night and Matthew retired at the same time as Giles who proposed a drink in his room. Matthew needed to sleep but Giles persisted, provided a bottle of claret and the two sat by the fire in the elder's room.

They reminisced about their grammar school days, exchanged news of the two years gone by and Matthew felt his eyes growing heavy. At eight o'clock next morning he awoke in his own bed still fully clothed, with no recollection of having found his way there. The insistent knocking on his bedroom door had roused him and a staff member informed him that Mr Ambrose awaited him in his office.

Still drowsy and dishevelled he went there at once and Charles, behind his desk was not welcoming.

'Master Fairwood, at two o'clock this morning my housekeeper was awoken by one of my under maids, Jenny, who was in distress. She complained that you entered her room, attempted to join her in her bed and sought to force yourself upon her. My housekeeper spared me this unhappy event until seven o'clock when I questioned Jenny and was convinced by her account. I have questioned Giles who confesses that the two of you did not retire but stayed late in his room and drank too well until you left him about two o'clock.'

Matthew bemused but with no memory of the night, attempted to protest but Charles stayed him. 'Jenny has no reason for such an invention. She is seeking nothing and wishes to leave my employ today. Her claim is verified. In order to deter your unwelcome attentions she scratched your cheek. You bear the marks. Do not deny it and add lies to your crimes.'

Touching a hand to his cheek the stinging of wounded flesh shocked him.

'You will leave now and consider yourself fortunate that I do not see you prosecuted. Your attentions to Celia will cease and you will not be welcome at my home again pack and leave now.'

Shocked, still drowsy and unable to defend himself, Matthew felt destroyed. Charles Ambrose was in no mood to hear any denials even if he had any to offer.

Henry knew nothing of what had occurred for two weeks when he received two letters. One was a report from Whitneys enclosing another intercepted letter from Giles to the person the nature of whose relationship with his son induced nausea in him.

It read *'I would far rather have weekended with you but my stay at Huntingdon proved great sport and young Fairwood ruined such ever chances to ingratiate himself with Ambrose. I shall tell you the tale when I visit at month end.'*

The second letter was from Charles Ambrose.

'Dear Henry,'

There was an unfortunate occurrence at my home on the occasion of Celia's birthday celebration. I shall not recount it but leave it to Mr Fairwood to provide you with the unpleasant details. Suffice for me to say that he will no longer be welcome at my home nor will I permit any further communication between him and Celia. You, of course, will always be a welcomed visitor here.

I have written to Nathan Stein to require Mr Fairwood's dismissal. He will not have it and since he has full responsibility for the management of Thornton Estates I shall not undermine him but I am unhappy about it.

Your cousin

Charles.

Henry, outraged, went at once to visit Elizabeth. He handed her Charles's letter and asked if she was aware of what had occurred at Huntingdon. She told him that Matthew had acquainted her with the allegation and had explained why he had been unable to defend himself.

'Did you not feel Elizabeth, that I should have been told at once. Your son was raised in my house from infancy and in dishonouring himself he dishonours me – and you. Why did you not inform me?'

'Would you please sit, Henry, and cease to harangue me and I shall tell you. Matthew was, indeed, raised in your house but you could never know him as completely as I do. I am his mother and know every facet of character. He is incapable of the charge against him. It is concocted and, although I have never laid a wager in my life, I would wager now that the hussy who has besmirched Matthew's name has had a payment from Charles to prevent her making a complaint to the authorities.'

Henry asked, 'Who is the accused and of what is he accused?'

Elizabeth stood, indignant. 'You come here knowing nothing of the allegation but speak of yourself being dishonoured. You employ clarity of thinking in your business dealings that you remain incapable of doing in personal relationships. I anticipated your reaction and that is why I did not inform you of the matter. It was my hope, a worthless hope, as I should have expected it to be, that you would enquire into the facts before reaching a conclusion to my son's disadvantage. Have you not considered seeking Giles account of what occurred?'

'For reasons entirely unrelated, Giles and I are estranged.'

'Until this sorry affair is resolved, or until you are prepared to look into it with an open mind, you should consider that you and I are similarly estranged. Charles speaks in his letter of you being welcome in his home. You are not, though welcome in mine. I do not have the means of unearthing the facts of this fabricated charge but I am confident that, if you were sufficiently interested, you could do so. Until then, Henry, we must say goodbye.'

Henry, angry with Elizabeth, was not inclined to intervene on her behalf or on behalf of her son. Hadn't Matthew's father been licentious and might that be in the son's blood, he reasoned. Charles Ambrose was not a man given to rash action and must have had compelling evidence. Why couldn't Elizabeth realise that? Why does a woman who is otherwise rational become a snarling lioness when her cub is threatened? Can a woman never see the faults in her child that are apparent to others? He considered her reaction to his visit to be that of a shrew. Still, he loved her and would miss her.

Their separation saddened him and his loneliness returned. After two weeks he became anxious to renew their relationship but remained of the opinion that Matthew was at fault. If he was to investigate the matter, as Elizabeth wished, and if he was to establish her son's guilt, then that might mean an end to any hopes he had for a relationship with her. If he was to do nothing the result would be the same.

Henry arrived, unannounced, at Old Hall and found Nathan Stein occupying a lodge house as both his office and his family home. Stein's position entitled him to rooms in the Hall but, since he was not a family member, the rooms would be in the staff wing. He preferred his privacy and to distance himself from the domestic staff. Matthew was living in the Staff wing, the rest of the Hall having been closed up.

It would be late afternoon before Matthew was expected to return and Henry took the opportunity to discuss the unhappy affair with Stein. He was particularly interested to know why Stein had defied his employer in refusing to dismiss Matthew.

Stein told him of the accusation; that Matthew had

attempted to force unwelcome attentions on a maid. He, Stein, had not, and would never believe a word of it.

'Mark my words Henry there is a conspiracy here. The girl has been rewarded for agreeing to lay no complaint. Rewarded by Charles, no doubt, who will have acted with the best of intentions and out of loyalty to you.'

'You speak of conspiracy though. Who do you suspect to be involved?'

'They are just that, Henry, suspicions and I have no evidence to support them. For that reason I dare not lay myself open to an action for slander and I shall be drawn no further on that. As to why I would not dismiss Matthew, there are two reasons. Firstly the facts are unconvincing. A girl of such lowly station would lack the wit to devise and carry out such a scheme. Matthew's room was not in her wing of the house so she would need to know from another person that Matthew had retired to his room before she awoke the housekeeper and made her complaint. The one person who could inform her of that was the person who told Charles that Matthew left him about the same time that the girl was supposedly attacked. A little investigation is all that would be required to get to the truth of the matter. So I refused to dismiss Matthew because I am in no doubt that he is the victim of a fabrication. My second reason is, as I informed Charles, because I am either managing this estate or I am not. For as long as I am, such decisions will be mine.'

'Nathan. I do not know sufficient of the details to be aware of who it was who supported the girls story that Matthew was about, alone at the time she was attacked.'

'Look in to it Henry but be prepared for what you will discover. While you are about it consider this; would Matthew, smitten as he is with Celia, jeopardise that for a fumble or a role with a menial under the same roof. If he was capable of such behaviour he has had ample opportunity in the Hall for almost a year and you may be assured that he has done no such thing I would have been made aware of it before the bed was cold.'

When Matthew returned late that afternoon, Henry questioned him relentlessly well into the evening. Matthew recounted everything he was able and expressed his frustration of his vagueness. He had been tired that night but not exceptionally so. He had drunk but not drunk to excess. The two combined, he believed with the heat from the fire in Giles's room and he had felt light headed. He had never seen the girl in question, would not have known how to find her room and would have had no desire to do so.

Henry listened and detected no guile. In summing up he said.

'The girl claims that she was attacked about two o'clock. You agree that you left Giles about that time?'

'Yes'

'How can you be sure of the time you left Giles?'

'I have no recollection of leaving. I know it was that time because Giles recalls it to have been that time.'

'You accept Giles's account unquestioningly, Matthew?'

'As you are the only father I have known and Giles is my only brother. We have had our differences, as brothers do, but I have never known him to lie. He would not lie about a matter as serious as this. If he was capable of lying he would have had to say that I remained with him after two o'clock. He was not prepared to lie to spare me this shame so he would certainly not lie to my detriment.'

'I shall look further into this.'

'I should be grateful because I cannot. I am sickened by the scandal that touches me and feel my only support is from my mother and Mr Stein. I am distressed by the dishonour I have brought on you. Not least among all this my heart aches from my separation from Celia.'

Henry knew that feeling. Adeline's long absence in Dorset had been a torture to him and he had felt a void inside him that nothing could fill. He had had some consolation from the letters but Matthew was denied even that.

It was to be another month before the letter he had written to Charles to solicit an invitation was answered. Charles's reply was apologetic for the delay but his explanation was unconvincing and his tone other than warm. He did however have his invitation and he travelled to Huntingdon.

Charles received him politely but Marianne did not join them. It was obvious to Henry that his host was trying but failing to disguise how vexed he felt in having to repeatedly recount the incident. Charles was annoyed to have his judgement of the complaint called into question and he bristled when Henry asked if he had made any payment to the girl.

In a short statement intended to draw this unwelcome inquisition to a finish Charles said, 'Henry, I fully understand your distress, your wish that this had not occurred and your desire to exonerate Fairwood, as futile as that is. Had you been in my place that morning you could have arrived at no conclusion other than the unpleasant one on which I had to act. Fairwood's appearance was disordered, his account disjointed, and, I am in no doubt, still drunk. His cheek bore four scratches and the maid's nails had his skin and his blood under them from fighting him off. She did not ask, nor did she receive, one penny. She wished only to leave forthwith, which she did, and I have heard nothing from her since. I had hoped I would hear nothing more of Fairwood but you have been insistent that I should.'

Henry left that same afternoon but did not return to Bradford. He travelled to London, took a hotel room overnight and early next morning found the Paddington offices of Whitney and Son. He was surprised to find that Simon Whitney was a younger man than he had imagined and told him that he had thought he had been corresponding with the principal of the agency.

'I am the son in the 'and Son', my father being retired and I am most pleased to have the opportunity to meet with you Mr Crawshaw. I trust the work my agency produces is satisfactory to you, allowing for how upsetting some of our discoveries have no doubt been.'

Henry assured him that he was fully satisfied and now required a further, although not necessarily unconnected, service. Whitney made detailed notes of Henry's requirements that the truth of the affair at Huntingdon be discovered.

'The key to this, Mr Crawshaw, lies with the under-maid, Jenny. You know nothing more of her I take it?'

'I do not.'

'No matter. Visits to the inns in the vicinity of the estate will remedy that. I shall let you have my report as soon as I am able and may I take this opportunity to express my appreciation of the dispatch with which my invoices are settled. Would that all our clients were so prompt. Will you be remaining in London some time?'

Henry said that he would not but might well need to return at some time to confront a certain person for purposes that Whitney would fully understand. Riding back to Kings Cross he instructed his carriage driver to take a detour and stop in a mews off Kings Court where Henry stared at the three-storey building where his son had been spending nights – too many nights.

Back in Bradford, his first call was on Elizabeth to tell her of the investigation he had put in progress. She was more impressed by that than his declaration that he doubted Matthew was guilty of the accusation that had been made. He then spoiled that by telling her that there was an aspect of the case, the scratches on Matthew's cheek and the blood under the maid's fingernails that would surely convict her son of the matter, having been resurrected, was to result in a prosecution. He was not invited to stay.

Having walked less than a few paces he turned and was back at Elizabeth's door. They sat in silence for a while until Henry was satisfied that he was properly prepared.

'I have been to London from where I returned just this afternoon. If the man I have engaged cannot get to the truth of this matter, I fear no one can. Whatever the outcome I shall never believe Matthew to be guilty and if others do he will always have my support. He is my son in everything that term means to me. I have not told you why I am estranged from Giles, nor shall I, it distresses me too much, but the shame he brings on himself and on me is a thousand times greater than any shame I would experience from Matthew being wrongly convicted of this trumped up charge.'

Elizabeth listened. She did not answer but looked at the sadness of this good man who had taken her and her son in, protected them when she was falsely accused, educated Matthew, established her in business and had never been other than generous and caring.

Henry stood before her chair, took her hands in his and said, 'Dear Elizabeth, we have spoken of the dishonour that our sons, in one case innocently and in the other gratuitously, have visited upon us. I wish now to speak of honour and the great honour you will do me if you were to be my wife.'

She waited.

'I do not wish to wait until all these troubles are resolved before proposing marriage. For good or ill they will be resolved and all the better for us facing them as husband and wife'

Still she waited.

'Elizabeth. Dear Elizabeth. I love you, without you I am miserable. All I have achieved is meaningless. You will make me complete and I will be a good and dutiful husband. I thought once that I could never love again. With other than you I would not have. My love for you is true. Will you consent to be my wife?'

Had he said such words, so many wasted years before she would have consented. They had now been said. He was, she knew, sincere. She stood, they embraced and they kissed, a long, sweet and loving kiss. They separated and stood awkwardly before kissing again.

The wedding was arranged for three weeks hence and they would be a very full and busy three weeks for both. Elizabeth created her own gown and Henry was measured for a fine, well-tailored suit. Their plans and arrangements were hectic. Elizabeth would have a marriage before the altar that her first marriage had denied her. She would live in Henry's home but retain her present home as a studio and continue her business. Henry, concerned about his future wife's security arranged a valuation of Elizabeth's home and sold it to her, at value, for five hundred and seventy five pounds, funded from profits and a gift from her husband.

Henry wrote to Giles. He did not inform his son of his wedding plans but did inform him that the house had been sold. The proceeds, five hundred and seventy five pounds had been sent to his grandmother together with twenty-five pounds, which would be deducted from his inheritance. Giles, he hoped, would be pleased that the money he had scrounged from his aged grandmamma had been repaid.

His hopes that the investigation into the allegation against Matthew would be completed before the wedding were dashed by an interim report from Whitneys.

The tracing of the maid was taking longer than anticipated.

Henry's invitation to Charles and Marianne was declined by Charles without explanation. His invitation to Celia was declined by Charles. He would not invite Giles so he would have no relatives at his wedding. Elizabeth had only one relative, Matthew. They discussed inviting employees and while that might be an option for long serving employees to supplement the attendance of family members it would be most unconventional for a wedding such as theirs to consist solely of employed guests. Too many years had passed for Elizabeth to be contacting Catherine and ex colleagues like Beattie and Levine.

The wedding took place in the parish church of St Patrick in the town. It was inappropriate, Henry felt, he marry again at St Paul's in Manningham. There were just two witnesses, Matthew on behalf of his mother and a now infirm Mollie Tutt, conveyed to and from the church, on behalf of Henry. Giles's absence had to be explained and he told the two witnesses that mid-term final examinations prevented Giles absenting himself from Cambridge.

The ceremony was followed by a restaurant lunch, after which the bride and groom travelled to Scarborough where Henry had reserved the grandest suite of rooms in a hotel overlooking the bay and the promenade. There was little of the awkwardness Henry had feared when they undressed for bed. The urgency of Elizabeth's lovemaking encouraged and energised him. Elizabeth was not a frail, inexperienced young Adeline. She was a confident forty three year old woman who was uninhibited in expressing her love for her husband.

Their mornings were spent in the hotel lounge, talking and watching the waves in the bay. Each afternoon they walked the sea front promenade and their evenings, after dinner were spent in each other's arms. During the four days of their stay, Henry outlined his plans for the future and made minor amendments to those plans at Elizabeth's suggestion. He had plans for their home, re-structuring of his businesses and proportion of his time he would in future, be devoting to them and the terms of his will which he would now re-draw. Elizabeth was puzzled at his plans to totally disinherit Giles but this was one matter on which Henry was not prepared to either compromise or explain.

Their honeymoon passed too quickly they felt and agreed that a few days on the coast should be made an anniversary event each year. It was with a greater enthusiasm for settling the problems concerning his two sons and to taking a new approach to his business and social responsibilities, that Henry returned to Bradford

Whitney's report, which he had been anxiously awaiting, arrived the following week.

'Mr Henry Crawshaw'

Sir

The under-maid, Miss Jenny Booth, has been traced. Her statement, to which she has appended her mark, has been written and witnessed. It will be delivered to you by personal courier since mail entrusted to the postal services does not always reach its intended recipient. (Henry smiled at this disguised reference to letters posted by Giles and diverted by him.)

Miss Booth's statement has been recorded verbatim and her Norfolk accent and use of colloquialisms renders her account virtually unintelligent in places. To assist your understanding; there follows a summary of the contents of her statement.

She states that she was not attacked and believed at the time, and still so believes, that she was employed to play a part in a prank between two university friends who have a long running game of outdoing each other with tricks and jokes. During a previous visit by the two young men she met only one of them, Master Giles, who suggested the trick to her then. She had refused fearing she might be dismissed.

She was pregnant to Arnold Ramsbottom, an agricultural labourer, Ramsbottom had told her he would marry her but was too young to be given tenancy of a tied cottage and did not have a bond to rent his own cottage. She told her story to Mr Giles and asked if he still wanted her to play his joke. If so she would play her part but would need ten pounds in order to leave afterwards to marry her young man, Arnold. The plan was agreed, his friend was expected next day and Master Giles, she believed, travelled into Huntingdon that Friday afternoon to withdraw money from the bank.

On the Saturday night she waited in his friend's room and fell asleep in a chair. It was far into the night when she was awakened by Mr Giles who carried his friend and laid him on the bed. She was told to scratch the sleeping man's face, told he was called Mr Matthew and she must remember him if she had to identify him. Her first two attempts at scratching the face were feeble and Mr Giles was angry with her. He told her the man would not wake up and he took her hands and applied the pressure to ensure that the marks on the man's cheeks were not mere scratches but gouges. There was blood on her hands.

She was told to go directly to the housekeeper's room, claim to have been attacked and to repeat that to whoever should ask her. Mr Giles gave her five pounds when she had finished her part and was ready to leave the house. After that, he assured her, he would tell the story, everyone would enjoy the jape and it would be the talk of the university within days.

The housekeeper believed her story but would not disturb Mr Charles before morning. Mr Charles questioned her and she felt she might not be believed. When she packed to leave she did not see Mr Giles, he did not seek her out and she never received the second five pounds.

Her misfortune did not finish there. She gave the five pounds to Ramsbottom and did not see him again. He left his employment and neither his mother nor his employer has heard from him since. Now, obviously heavily pregnant she is a barmaid back in her home-town in Norfolk.

My agents visited the apothecaries in Huntingdon to examine their registers for the Friday of that weekend. They were unsurprised to find the sale of a sleeping draught to a man who called himself Mr G Bradford. He was described as a slim, fair-haired man of pale, soft features.

I trust you will be satisfied by the success of my agency's investigations as distressing as the conclusions might be to you and, adding as they do to the distress and other reports of your son's conduct.

I remain at your service

Simon Whitney.

Henry, by now beyond distress or even disgust at his son's behaviour and chosen life, received Jenny Booth's statement and agreed he would have found it difficult to understand without Simon Whitney's summary. He took both documents to Manchester where he found a document copier. Any nearer to home risked him being identified. It took the writer until late afternoon to complete the work and Henry arrived home late that night.

By noon the next day a courier was en-route to Huntingdon. Henry had sent Charles the copy documents with a brief letter asking his cousin to consider the evidence gathered by a highly reputable London agency and to allow that the investigation revealed that Matthew had been falsely accused.

Giles would have to be dealt with. There had been a conspiracy even though one party to it was illiterate who had been duped; but Charles, understandably, would not want the scandal of the matter being made public. Nor would Henry, It had been Stein's clarity of reasoning that had identified the conspiracy. Again Stein had been proved correct; had he ever been proved other?

As a married man he should, as a priority redraw his will and he visited his Solicitor, Alistair Wild by appointment, later that week. Wild noted his wishes, expressed some surprise at the extent of his generosity to certain people but cautioned him against fully disinheriting his son Giles. It was explained to Henry that failing to include any reference to his son might prompt a contesting of the will on the grounds of an oversight. That could be avoided if he provided a legacy; even a token one. Henry, reluctant to leave Giles a penny, proposed a solution that Wild, bemused, noted.

A week after receiving the documents from Whitney they were still in Henry's desk rather than in the vault he had rented for the earlier reports. Aching to tell Elizabeth that Matthew, her son, their son, had been exonerated by evidence he had secured but knowing she would not be satisfied with that he agonised over the matter. She would, rightly, want to know why, how, who, when and where but how could he tell her without exposing Giles. It was not that he wanted to protect Giles but that he was shamed by him. Still, Elizabeth had shared Giles's raving as a child and would not blame Henry. Eventually he saw no other course.

His wife's joy at knowing that Matthew was exonerated was tempered on learning that Henry had kept the news from her for a whole week. She was only partially placated by his explanation that he had immediately informed Charles, the only one to his knowledge who believed the accusation, and that he had hoped before informing her of the evidence to be able to tell her that Charles had accepted it. When the next day a letter from Charles arrived seeking an invitation for himself, Marianne and Celia to visit, with a hope that Matthew would be present. Henry was forgiven.

Elizabeth set about immediately to make improvements to the house which had become shabby during her years in Oak Rise. With no time to make new soft furnishings, she visited Brown and Muff's department store and added cushions, bed linens, pillows and towels. New lamps completed her order. The housekeeper was given ample money to procure sugars, flours and fats. She would be given free rein to fashion her pastries and she would select the best fruit and vegetables she could find. Henry's task was easier. His manager at the Holmes's shop in Ivegate would provide the finest most select cuts of beef, pork and lamb. Flowers in profusion, ordered by Elizabeth, were delivered on the day.

The Ambrose party arrived on the Friday afternoon and after dressing they were treated to a dinner that would match the esteem in which Henry held them. Matthew nervous, Celia excited and Charles thoroughly ashamed at having been duped all spoke at once. The fine wines provided with their meal were enjoyed in quantity and the tensions were soon gone. Twice Henry felt the need to ask Charles to stop apologising. The case as presented to him at the time, allows no other interpretation but it was done.

Anyway, offered Henry, beyond the hearing of others, his own shame at Giles conduct was by far the greater.

By the time Mrs Boyle presented her sugared, fruit pastries to gasps of admiration, the party of six were confirmed in their renewed friendships and all were in high spirits; none more than the young couple who were reunited. The ladies having withdrawn left the three gentlemen talking in the dining room, Matthew nervous, stood. 'Uncle Charles, on the morning following Celia's birthday I intended to seek your permission to announce our engagement to marry. We were agreed on it and we have spoken again this evening and we are no less agreed.'

Henry interrupted, 'Matthew, Charles. Perhaps I should leave?'

Charles, brandy in one hand a cigar in the other, raised his hand to stay Henry and Matthew said, 'no father, I have always valued your counsel and on this matter I would value it all the more. Uncle Charles, I hope I am not taking advantage of your presence here or my invitation, but to make my request this evening as I am unaware of your plans for morning.'

'My plans for tomorrow are to travel on to Old Hall. Staff have been instructed to open up the family rooms for the weekend. It is my intention to invite your parents and you to join us for two days. I hope you will all agree to join us there. As for your request for my permission for Celia to marry – he paused – I will let you have my answer before we leave Old Hall.'

The weekend at Old Hall was enjoyed enormously by all. Elizabeth and Marianne had time to become more closely acquainted and each found the other most likeable. Henry rode with Charles to visit employees, both current and retired. Matthew and Celia rode together around the estate eagerly awaiting Charles's decision. Dinner that evening came and went without it. Sunday was passed as Saturday and Matthew had to restrain himself from approaching his uncle a second time.

As the Crawshaw family packed on the Monday morning Charles called Matthew into his office.

'Matthew you require your parents consent to marry.'

'May I ask my father while you are still here?'

'In law, Matthew, it is your mother's consent that you require but I am aware from her conversations with my wife that she would not withhold it. So there remains the question of my consent and I will confess that I have discussed the matter with your father. Any misgivings I might harbour are tempered by the debt I feel for so badly misjudging you, so I shall not withhold my consent.'

Matthew offered his hand, his thanks and his promises of the care and love he would always have for Celia.

Charles stopped him. 'I shall not withhold my consent to an announcement of an engagement between the two of you but I feel I need to attach conditions which must be fulfilled before that consent extends to marriage. Please sit. It would be unfair to you both to conduct your engagement at such a distance but I would not be content for Celia to be here. Nathan speaks highly of your abilities with staff. You do not have his business acumen but then neither do I, nor any others I know. As a manager, though, you have a talent to engage with people.'

'Thank you, Uncle.'

'It is a talent I can employ at Huntingdon. I am well past my sixtieth year and lacking the energy I once had to devote my attention to staff. The Huntingdon estate is spread far wider than this one and the travel tires me. I wish to employ you there, see for myself the abilities that

Nathan claims for you and satisfy myself as to the role with which you might be entrusted once a member of the family. This will present you an opportunity to be close to Celia, for both of you to test your feelings and aspirations. After a year we will discuss the matter further.'

Elizabeth rode home in deep content. She was settled with a loving husband and she was secure. Her son was exonerated, accepted by the Ambrose household and was more happy than he was able to express with his new position that would allow him to remain close to Celia. Henry, too, was content that the weekend had been such a success. He had been indebted to Charles Ambrose since his youth, he had been wounded by his cousin's coldness on his visit to Huntingdon and the only threat to his future, he believed was his son Giles. His son, would, he was convinced, continue to be a source of insults and vexation. These he could combat but he worried that if Elizabeth had to face him unsupported she would be no match for the mendacious, arrogant, fop Giles had become. Henry also regretted feeling unable to tell Matthew of Giles' part in the accusation against him. Believing that Matthew would accept that the maid had drugged him and acted alone, he then discovered that Charles had told him of Giles' involvement. Matthew had not understood why his father would mislead him but he had not confronted him with his concerns. That apart, Henry was in good spirits when he arrived back home but a letter awaiting him would sour his mood.

'Father,'

A letter from my 'brother' has acquainted me with recent events. He expressed his sorrow that my studies had prevented me attending your wedding to his mother. When I am less busy I shall write to him to tell him that you lied and I was never offered an invitation.

I must say that I was disappointed, but not wholly surprised, that you are reduced to marrying the hired help. It is rather shabby of you to attempt to make a present to her of my house. While it was uncommonly generous of you to settle my loan from grandmamma, I shall consider that to be an unexpected windfall, entirely unconnected to the ownership of the house.

You will be pleased to discover shortly that, despite your unfounded suspicions that I have spent my time here in revelry, I have devoted myself to my studies, so the education you have funded, as inadequate as I have found those funds, was not wasted and I am about to demonstrate my knowledge of the law. You may consider it a wedding gift.'

Giles.

Henry, refusing to be provoked, chose not to reply.

A second letter, less than a week later, did call for a response.

'Father,'

I have received a letter from Uncle Charles, which contains a foul allegation against me. Was it he or you who paid the trollop to invent these lies about me. I doubt it would be young Fairwood. For all his fancy title in a job you had to find him when he was unsuited to any profession he would have had neither the money nor the intelligence to engineer his own acquittal. While he is back in favours rather than in gaol, I have my name blackened.'

The defamation I have suffered is actionable and both you and Uncle Charles will have no one to blame but yourselves when I sue for and am awarded, exemplary damages. You should expect that a consequence would be Fairwood's prosecution for his attempt to rape.

The Fairwoods have ingratiated themselves with the Ambroses'. It will be interesting to see how durable the relationship is when Charles comes to appreciate how his dalliance with the lower orders has dragged him down.

Giles.

Henry had felt that Giles could not have infuriated him any more than he had done previously but now his son was taking his feud beyond his own family and into the Ambrose house. This would have to be stopped and he would need to pay careful attention to the words he chose to do that. Late that evening he sat at his desk to write his reply. It would be pointless to appeal to Giles's common sense he showed no evidence of having any. His words would need to threaten his son's self interest. He took no pleasure in doing this he had avoided it for so long but he could not risk a court case that would expose Charles to public scrutiny or Matthew to prosecution if the court came to a perverse verdict in favour of Giles.

'Giles,'

You need to be protected from the self-destructive course on which you are embarked. Be aware that the apothecary in Huntingdon can identify you as the purchaser of the sleeping draught with which Matthew was drugged. The maids betrothed can verify that she had the five pounds that she will say was paid by you. (This was Henry's invention). It will not be the maid's word against yours because there is corroboration of her account and none of yours. You did not even have the decency to pay her the balance of the promised payment so you cannot expect her to be well disposed towards you.

I am in possession of a letter sent by you to another but, and I know not how, delivered to me. Perhaps you should write your envelopes whilst sober. In this letter you speak of the sport you had that weekend at Huntingdon and the court will, I am sure, take a view on your meaning.

As the expert on matters legal, that you claim to be, you will know that in the action you are considering, the question of the character of the parties will be an issue. Matthew, of course, has had a blameless life and Charles Ambrose is a man of unimpeachable integrity. Could you stand these in such confidence? You could not and I shall tell you why.

Since the Easter of your fourth term I have had you under investigation. I have evidence that you did not visit Paris with 'chums' but with one 'chum' whose identity I can reveal. Your unnatural practises disgust me and I have ample evidence of them. Should you continue with your threatened actions, be aware that I shall, without compunction, expose you and the criminality of your 'chum.'

You need to not await your twenty-first birthday, an anniversary that no longer has any meaning for me. I shall, at once, transfer your grandfather's legacy to your bank. This will be the two thousand pounds less the two hundred and fifty pound added to your mother's house and paid to your grandmother in settlement of your debt.

That concludes the business between us and I expect to hear nothing further from you.

Henry Crawshaw.

In reply, Henry received a telegram.

'Father.'

Expect to take delivery of your wedding gift within days'.

Giles Crawshaw.

It was in fact over a week later when the letter arrived. It was from the Superintendent Registrar of Lord Tithe to inform Mrs Elizabeth Crawshaw that an interim injunction had been sought and granted to prevent her registering her ownership of 5 Oak Rise, Manningham, Bradford in either her first application in the name of Mrs Elizabeth Fairwood or subsequent amendment in the name of Mrs Elizabeth Crawshaw. She should seek legal representation should she be minded to defend her title in the property.

Alistair Wild, Henry's solicitor, advised him that the action had no prospect of success. The terms of Hubert Holmes's will were that Henry would hold either the property or its value in trust to the benefit of Giles. He had done that and had disposed of the property at value, as he had been entitled to do so. They would enter a defence accordingly and Wild would attend the preliminary hearing.

The injunction had been obtained by a barrister's chambers in London on behalf of the client Mr Giles Crawshaw but the application at the initial hearing wrong-footed Wild. It was for the transfer of title to be held in abeyance until the sixth of September the following year when the applicant would achieve his majority. As a minor he was disadvantaged since his father, his legal guardian, was the husband of Mrs Crawshaw.

The court directed that the cause would be held in abeyance until Mr Crawshaw could act independently of his father but, until the sixth of September, Mrs Crawshaw should continue to have full enjoyment of her occupation of the premises. Wild told Henry that in his opinion, the action amounted to nothing more than mischief and, come September, it would most certainly fail.

Chapter 28

Annoyed, at having been distracted from the plans that he, and Elizabeth had formulated during their honeymoon. Henry now addressed them with vigour. Norman Coggins had expanded his shops into Keighley, Halifax and Leeds. William Ball had expanded the Holmes's group of shops, acquiring failing and retiring independent butchers across town. Henry's balances, already swollen by his sale of his shares in the gas company were increasing week by week from the industry of his managing directors. He needed a use for the money that would satisfy both his interest in social responsibility. A substantial share holding in the electricity company met both his needs and assured him a place on the board.

During the first two meetings he attended, he contented himself with listening and learning. The Chairman was Alderman Hector Owen, the founder of Owen's Textiles. Henry had him marked as a man puffed up with self-importance with no interests other than profits. By the third meeting Henry was ready and asked him why electric street lighting was being provided in the roads and streets of the better houses in the town but not elsewhere. With exaggerated displays of impatience, Alderman Owen addressed him as if he was a child.

'Mr. Crawshaw, Sir. The generating stations and the sub stations represent a significant investment. The Borough Council's payment for street lighting will not provide a return on that. However, once the electricity wires are in place they can be used to feed private houses whose owners will be keen to have their homes lit by electricity. It does not have the smell or noise of gas; it does not produce the soot that oil lamps do. They will be prepared, and importantly, be able to pay for electricity in their houses. It will be convenient and will increase the desirability and value of those houses. Who, in the slums, could afford to have the electricity from the streets to light their homes – such as they are.'

Henry expected that answer and hid his annoyance at the manner in which he had been addressed. Alderman Owen was also a member of the Watch Committee of the town police force and Henry worked this to his advantage.

'Mr. Chairman, I understand from your senior police officers and from representatives of the newspapers, who are here today, that crime in the slums is rife. Prostitutes, bookmakers, robbers and thieves ply their trade – such as it is' (He emphasised these last words to mock the Chairman's final words). The Italians fight gang wars over a share of the ice cream trade, the Poles tax casual workers and share of their day's pay – those who won't pay don't get taken on. Illicit alcohol is sold in the streets, it is injurious to health. Your police officers tell me that illumination of these streets, at least the thoroughfares, will flush out these undesirables. The other benefit to be had is that an improvement in the town will encourage trade and investments. Given increased wealth, steps can be taken to clean our water and prevent another cholera outbreak. Eventually we may be able to reduce the foul smoke and soot that falls from the hundred or more chimneys of our textile mills.'

The final words stung the Chairman, he took it as a personal slight and opposed Henry, but other members appeared to be more receptive. Later meetings were always followed by Henry providing interviews to newspaper reporters. The support he was gaining from the Board members and the Chairman's embarrassment over the conflict between his Watch Committee responsibilities and his preference for profits for investors led eventually to the Board agreeing a commitment. A small proportion of electric street lights would, over an extended programme, be located on the corner of thoroughfares in the poorer areas. The programme would take several years to come to fruition but the principal had been established.

The plans he and Elizabeth had agreed upon to undertake a modern refurbishment of their home had been revised. The impending visit of the Ambrose's had caused them to view their home through the eyes of others. In the years since Elizabeth had left for Oak Rise, Henry's home had shown increasing signs of neglect. The planned modest refurbishment would, instead, be a thorough renewal; roof to cellar, inside and out.

In March they removed along with the housekeeper and staff to Oak Rise. The Villas house was emptied; stripped of carpets, curtains, furnishings and lamps. Floor boards were lifted and work began to prepare walls and ceilings so that the electric cables and wires would be concealed. Henry's misgivings that living once more in the house where he had been haunted by the smell of scent and the phantom pianist proved groundless and he and Elizabeth passed a happy summer there. She and her assistants continued to conduct their business as dressmakers and overseeing the conversion of the Villas house occupied what free time she had. Henry took the view that his wife's eye for design, colour and co-ordination made her the better qualified for the task and Elizabeth was happy to agree.

Henry would deal with tradesmen and building supplies and be responsible for financing the project. Given his wealth, this presented him with no difficulty.

Elizabeth was unconcerned by finances; either for the work on the house or for her own business. Following her marriage the accounts of the Fairwood studio were administered with those of the whole Crawshaw/ Holmes/ Coggins Group. Her materials were purchased through the group and her invoices, albeit on her own headed notepaper, were issued from the Bradford office. The agreement relieved her of the administrative burden, the aspect her business she least enjoyed, but it was an arrangement that was about to prove a mistake with serious consequences.

On the fifth of September Henry met with his solicitor, Wild, who reminded him of the action by Giles to prevent the ownership of 5 Oak Rise being registered to his wife. There would however, be no requirement for Henry or Mrs Crawshaw to attend since he, Wild, had received fore notice that Giles Crawshaw would withdraw his objection to the registration. His barrister had been provided with a copy of the terms of Hubert Holmes's will and it would have been obvious to him that the cause was bound to fail. Wild reminded Henry of his initial opinion, that the application for the injunction had been nothing more than vexatious. Cost would have to be borne by Giles and Henry, Wild assured him, could put the matter behind him.

Riding home one day along Manningham Lane in the failing light Henry watched the labourers, working by gas torches, digging trenches in readiness for the electricity cables from the generating station which was under construction on the site of the worked out quarry on Westgate. He thought of his son and the joy and relief he had felt at his birth twenty one years ago. His thoughts then turned to the man that son had become and how tomorrow he would have costs to pay for a doomed adventure that could have had no purpose other than to aggravate and provoke his father. What he wondered, had corrupted a nature that was not inherited from either of his parents?

Arriving at Oak Rise and alighting from his carriage he expected Elizabeth to be home. Instead she was delayed at the Villa house agreeing designs for carpets with the manager of the textile company that had gained the commission.

The air in Oak Rise hung heavily with the smell of lamp oil and when Henry opened the front door of his temporary home he found the source. The house reeked. He was barely across the threshold when he was struck from a violent blow to the back of his head and he fell. Too stunned to move he found his face in a pool of lamp oil and he was aware of a figure standing behind him in the doorway. The figure did not flee, as Henry expected, but lit a taper, which he dropped in a pool of oil. It did not ignite. He then lit a lamp he took from a table in the hall. Horrified at what was to happen but still incapable of moving he saw the lamp smashed on the floor in front of his face. The oil ignited; it exploded and the upper half of Henry's body was in seconds, a screaming candle.

Neighbours and passers by, alerted by the explosion and the screams came quickly to his assistance and dragged him out by his ankles. They beat at his burning head and clothing but it took time and a lot of effort to extinguish the flames since his clothing, soaked in oil, proved to be a most efficient wick. As they worked the house was rocked by further explosions from every level from the cellar to the roof void.

The fire tenders were first to arrive but had to confine themselves to dousing the adjoining properties to protect them; the house was beyond saving. When Elizabeth, who had become aware of a commotion across Manningham Lane and had seen flames lighting the evening sky, hurried to Oak Rise, Henry was already inside a hospital wagon and was being carried away at speed.

She found him at the infirmary in a dim windowless room. The plain brown walls added to the sense of gloom. Seated on a hard chair to the right of the bed she saw he was in a frame designed to prevent the sheets coming into contact with his skin. In removing his clothes they had removed the flesh from his torso. The fire had destroyed his features. His hair, ears and nose were gone; his left eye was a blackened hollow and the right one was a burnt crust that was nothing more than a slit through which she could see the movement of his eye. Elizabeth longed to hold his hand but the blisters were like balloons and some had burst and were weeping.

The doctor, a young Scot, whom Elizabeth found inappropriately cheerful informed her that he felt sure that her husband was capable of surviving although he would be hideously deformed. She wouldn't care, she told herself. Deformed or not she would nurse him, love him, feel blessed to still have him; and she prayed more earnestly than she had done since she was a child at Bethlehem. In a later conversation with the matron, a woman who was the epitome of busy efficiency, Elizabeth was told that she should not raise false hopes. It was the matron's opinion that if the pain did not kill him then the quantities of morphine being administered to control the pain would. The weeping wounds would admit infections and if he were to live it would be no blessing. There would be damage not only to his body but also to his mind. She had seen it too often as a young nurse treating casualties from the wars.

Elizabeth had clung to the hope the doctor had given her but had been dashed by the matron. Who to believe? The young doctor, medically better qualified or the experienced nurse. It had been her experience in life that the counsel of an older woman was usually more reliable than that of a younger man. She now prayed that death would release her beloved Henry.

Before dawn the parish priest of St Patrick's church gave Henry the last rites. A year ago, this same priest had married them. Elizabeth asked him to hear her confession, which she made at Henry's bedside, unconcerned that her husband might hear. She had never deceived him or had nothing to reproach herself for.

It was difficult for her to tell when Henry was conscious but late that afternoon; he raised his right hand to beckon her close. He looked at her through his one, part open eye and tried to speak. She leaned closely to his face, the smell that permeated the room was offensive enough but at such proximity it was a nauseating stench that no one who loved him less than Elizabeth could have stomached.

Intelligible speech was impossible for him. His tongue, black and twice its normal size was immobile. There were no lips to form the words, they had been burnt away leaving a grinning rictus. A once possibly handsome face was a horrific mask. Such sounds as he could make came from a parched throat and Elizabeth laboured to translate those sounds into words. Time after time Henry attempted to say the same short sentence but the first words were always inaudible and all she could make out were the words 'Benny's fault,' and she was unsure of those.

Henry wept from his eye. The pain, the frustration at his inability to advise Elizabeth, and the realisation that his life was lost were overwhelming him. It was then that the doctor entered, saw Henry's distress and administered another dose of morphine; a significant dose and Henry, temporarily without pain drifted into reverie. Memories of his mother first, then of Adeline, then of Elizabeth, and finally of his father. He was a child again, holding the rough hand of the man he had idolised, and, now back in his hospital bed he was struck by the irony of his imminent death. His father had suffered a blow to his head, however occasioned, and his body had been frozen. He, Henry, similarly injured had been burnt. Those were his last living thoughts. He died on the twenty first anniversary of his only son's birth.

Elizabeth, preparing to leave, was visited by James Broughton, an inspector of detectives. The fire was out, he told her, but the house was a shell. Fourteen drums that had once contained lamp oil had been found in the ruins. Neighbours had seen a carter deliver them shortly after she had been seen to leave that morning. The smell had been apparent throughout the afternoon so it was evident that the intention had been more than arson. There had been an intention to harm her or her husband, or both of them. Broughton said, that having been informed of Mr Crawshaw's death, he would undertake a murder investigation.

Elizabeth stood on the steps of the infirmary. It was already dark and she was chilled by the autumn night. There was nothing more she could do for Henry beyond arranging his funeral and she now had to think about herself as a widow. It was then that she was struck by the situation she was in.

The Manningham Villas house was uninhabitable and the Oak Rise house burnt to the ground. She had nowhere to go and even had she had somewhere to go she had no money to get there. The clothes she was wearing were the ones she had worn for two days and they were the only clothes she now owned. To add to her misery at her husband's death and her own sad situation was the realisation that she was, that night totally alone. She could not recall a time in her life when she had been so destitute. That was because she had no recollection of the time, as an infant, when she had been a foundling in the forest.

Part 4

Chapter 29

A carriage appeared from the murk and stopped outside the infirmary. The man who alighted was no taller but far heavier than he had been when he and Henry had first met. He waddled from the kerb to the low wall where Elizabeth had been sitting and trembling uncontrollably, for over an hour. Norman Coggins had learned of the fire that afternoon and had come directly from his work to enquire after Henry's condition. Elizabeth's state of shock made any enquiry pointless.

Distressed at the loss of his partner and friend, Norman Coggins soon recovered himself and set his personal grief aside. Practical Coggins took over and Elizabeth was immediately in his carriage and on her way to his home. This home was not the modest house he had once struggled to buy from his dead father's wife but a fine family home in Heaton, on the hill, overlooking Manningham. Before a good fire, one of Tess Coggins's shawls around her and a mug of hot milk in her hands, the shivering from cold subsided, leaving only the trembling from trauma.

Tess Coggins was solicitous. Her husband was a kind, honest man but sensitivity was not in his nature. He was a hard headed businesslike man and his wife cringed when he set about Elizabeth to order her thoughts.

'All due sympathy and respect Mrs Crawshaw, but there's things that need to be attended to. I need to know what they are and I'll do the doings. I can't do that until I know what's what.'

Elizabeth was not offended. His directness, she knew, was a kindness and Coggins, pencil in hand, made notes and then re-wrote them into an order of priorities. Her room prepared, Elizabeth retired not expecting sleep to come but her loss of rest the previous night and the draining of her emotions combined to have her in a deep and restful sleep from which Tess had to rouse her early next morning.

The Coggins' took her into Bradford and they were at the Bradford Bank when the doors were opened at ten o'clock. Estimating the cost of her immediate need for clothing, the likely cost of a funeral and allowing for all the incidental expenses she was bound to have overlooked, Elizabeth arrived at a figure to withdraw. Norman Coggins urged her to double it.

Elizabeth's day was spent at Brown Muff's department store and George Thorpe's drapers store in Tyrell Street. Her mind was not on her purchases but Tess, even though twenty years older, led her through some good choices that were appropriate for a widow in mourning and one for a widow to attend her husband's funeral. All the purchases, shoes, coats, underclothes, bags, capes and bonnets would be delivered to the Heaton house that evening.

Norman Coggins had not been idle. Telegrams had been sent to Matthew, Charles, Giles and Jane Holmes. The undertaker who was favoured by the wealthier families of the town was retained; announcements were placed in local newspapers. He couldn't register the death without a doctor's certificate and he could not have that until after the inquest. His final task was to visit Elizabeth's assistants and to inform them that it might be some time before the Fairwood Studio could be re-established.

It was six o'clock when the three, exhausted, returned to the Coggins home. Bathed and freshly dressed Elizabeth was lifted slightly and began to feel a degree of control. The undertaker, said Coggins, would need notice of her intentions for the burial and Elizabeth thought of little else that evening. Should it be in his parents grave on the Heights or in his first wife's grave at Undercliffe. He had, she conceded, been married to Adeline for three years and to her only one. Yet, she and Henry had known each other for seventeen years, she had been his wife when he died and if she chose one of the two options she had been agonising over, that would mean that they would never be buried together. Her mind was made up. The burial would be at Scholemoor, a terraced hillside between the road to Thornton and the lower of the two roads to the Heights.

A messenger called. Charles and Matthew would be arriving the next day. Detective Broughton called and wanted Elizabeth to account for her movements on the day of Henry's death. This she could do having been engaged with the builders, decorators and the carpet designer throughout the day.

'Mrs Crawshaw, did Mr Crawshaw speak to you before he died?'

'He was incapable of intelligible speech. He made several attempts at some words but I could not understand his meaning. I believe he said Benny and the word 'fault' but I cannot be sure.'

'And do you know, or did Mr Crawshaw, know of anyone by the name of Benny or Benjamin?'

'Not that I know of. May I ask when the inquest will be held Inspector?.'

'It need not be delayed. We have identified the store from which the lamp oil was purchased and the carter who delivered it. They both describe a swarthy man of rough appearance, perhaps a quarry worker. A man in his middle years. Do you know of anyone of that description?'

'No'

Charles and Matthew arrived the following afternoon and Elizabeth was invited to stay at Old Hall. She expressed her gratitude for Norman and Tessa Coggins' help and hospitality and asked Norman if he would continue to make the funeral arrangements.

Over that weekend Elizabeth felt isolated and uninvolved but there was nowhere else to go. As thoughtful as Charles was and as pleased as she was at Matthew's presence, she needed female company and there was none to be had. The inquest was held on the Monday. It was a brief affair and the verdict of unlawful killing had been expected. Now the funeral could be held and it was arranged for Thursday. The costs would be significant but she politely declined Charles's offer of assistance. Before she left Bradford she visited the Bank again and withdrew another large sum.

The funeral service was held at St. Patrick's church in Westgate where their marriage had taken place. The Church could not contain the numbers wishing to attend and the streets around the church were thronged with spectators who added to the chaos caused by the scores of carriages. All the Crawshaw businesses were closed and every employee was in attendance, many with their wives and families. There were representatives from the electricity company, the clean water scheme, the Commercial club, the Academy and the Borough Council. Every newspaper had a reporter there and carriages were provided for Elizabeth's assistants; Mrs Boyle and a now arthritic Mollie Tutt.

The eulogies were long and fulsome. Charles Ambrose and Bullivant Theakstone were articulate. Norman Coggins's description of the young man he had first met and his praise of the successful, man of business Henry had become moved many to tears.

The cortege was as stretched as any seen in the town before. The rear carriage had barely left Westgate before the coffin arrived at Scholemoor. It was fortunate for the mourners that it was a clear September day that still had some warmth in it. Elizabeth, on weak legs, was supported by Matthew and she looked across the valley that lay below the cemetery. This had been Henry's town. It had become her town but there would come a time, when Oak Rise would be rebuilt and Manningham Villas was completed, when there would be nothing to keep her here. Her son was settled in Huntingdon. And Giles? Well Giles was not a consideration. He had not responded to the telegram nor attended the funeral. After what he had done to disgrace Matthew she would be happy if she was never to hear from him again.

It was a wish that would not be fulfilled because Giles attended the reading of the will at Alistair Wild's office just two days later. He sat to one side at the rear and avoided eye contact with all those present.

The will was as detailed a document as might be expected of a man with so many interests and properties and Wild read each word slowly with pauses to assist understanding. Giles feigned a yawn of boredom and tapped his palm on his open mouth. Matthew was provoked and Charles held his arm to stay him.

The first bequests were incidental and included donations to the water scheme, a sum that would secure the long term financing of Bullivant Theakstone Scholarship and a further and substantial bequest to a scheme investigating whereby the smoke and the soot pouring from the chimneys of the textile mills could be reduced. He increased the holdings of his three managing directors and his shop managers to forty-nine percent, at no cost to them and, finally, Wild came to the personal family bequests.

'To my son, Matthew Fairwood, the sum of five thousand pounds. To my wife, Mrs Elizabeth Crawshaw, the residue of my estate, my personal deposits, my properties and interests and the income accruing from them, to use, enjoy and dispose of as she thinks fit.'

Wild paused and Giles seemed jubilant. He had, he thought, not been mentioned and a contesting of the will on the grounds of oversight could now be proved. But Wild continued.

'Mrs Elizabeth Crawshaw will retain in trust the sum of five thousand pounds to the benefit of my son Mr Giles Crawshaw. Of this, three thousand pounds is to be paid on the occasion of his lawful marriage and the remaining two thousand pounds is to be paid should that marriage remain extant after a period of five years.'

The gasps of those present were stilled by the crashing of Giles's chair as he kicked it across the floor before flouncing out.

Charles was to leave the following day and proposed that Matthew should remain to support his mother, at least for a short time. He offered Elizabeth the use of Old Hall for so ever long she needed it but expressing her appreciation, she declined. She needed to be local to Bradford, to the Oak Rise house that had to be re-built and the Manningham Villas that had to be made inhabitable again. The fire had destroyed completed gowns, part completed gowns and stock. Customers needed to be informed, advances and deposits had to be repaid and an insurance claim had to be pursued. It was fortunate that her accounts, invoices and correspondence were held at the Hallings Road offices. Had they been lost in the fire her problems, difficult as they were, would have been far greater. She needed a location near to Manningham and Charles offered her the services of Nathan Stein. Elizabeth accepted gladly.

Displaying his usual efficiency, within a week Stein invited Elizabeth to view a suite of furnished rooms on the first floor of a good sized house in tree lined Park View. She considered it ideal and, together with Matthew, moved in the following day. The rental was not cheap but the value placed on the residue of Henry's estate, bequeathed to her, was thirty-three thousand pounds so the cost of her rooms was not a consideration.

Elizabeth and Matthew visited the Bradford Bank to make a withdrawal. The clerk asked them to wait and then they were invited into the manager's office. The manager informed Elizabeth a high court writ had been issued on the accounts both personal and commercial and had been frozen. He advised her to take legal advice and she and her son went at once to Alistair Wild's offices. They were kept waiting for a good hour before being shown into Wild's office and he made neither explanation nor apology for the length of their wait.

'I received a copy of the writ yesterday, Mrs Crawshaw. The effect is to freeze personal assets and the assets of companies in which Mr Crawshaw held a controlling and substantial interest. The definition means the writ will not affect the Illingworth School, the farm at Black Dyke Hole or the electricity company but it does prevent your benefitting from earnings from those sources. All other companies are affected by this order.'

'I am confused, Mr Wild. What does this mean? Who has done it and why?'

'Mr Crawshaw's will is to be contested. The interim order is to prevent the assets being raided before the matter is decided, and that may take months if not longer. The effect is that none of the companies may trade; payments may not be made to suppliers, to employees or to you. This, though, is just an opening salvo. I have instructed counsel to represent you at the high court in Leeds this afternoon to make an application to continue to trade. It is not in the interests of the other party that the business should fail and my application will not be resisted, I am sure.'

Elizabeth rose to leave, saying 'had I not called today when would you have seen fit to inform me of this matter and spare me the embarrassment of being turned away at the bank counter?'

'I intended to inform you once I had the outcome of this afternoon's hearing. The matter should be clearer then and I felt you would find it more understandable.'

'And I take it the other party to whom you refer is Giles Crawshaw?'

'It is and I am unsurprised. He is exceptionally well represented and has a case.

I practise business and this case is headed for Chancery, an altogether different discipline and you will need a solicitor who has the experience to brief council. You may also need a solicitor who practices criminal law.'

'Mr Wild. I am shocked at your news and no less shocked at what I consider to be your casual attitude to me and to this case.'

'Mrs Crawshaw. I saw this coming and so did your husband. When he left me on the afternoon of the fire he was exceedingly annoyed that his son had dragged out the injunction to prevent the registration of your house in your name. As I expected, Giles Crawshaw represented himself at the hearing next day in Leeds, withdrew his cause and accepted responsibility for the costs. But returning to the previous day, Mr Crawshaw said, and I recorded,' Wild consulted his notes, 'should Giles contest me again he will wish he had not. I have documents and correspondence that would ruin him. They are securely held, readily accessible and I will, without hesitation, use them against him.'

This registered with Elizabeth but so too did the knowledge that Giles had been in Leeds on the morning of the sixth of September and so had probably had to travel to Yorkshire the previous day – the day of the fire. She raised this with Wild but he was dismissive and she and Matthew left.

They went to Henry's Hallings Road offices where Elizabeth wished to explain the situation to the three managing directors but George Ball was not expected to be back before lunchtime. It was important to her that the three be told together so she went with Matthew to the tea room to pass an hour.

Matthew confessed that he had not fully taken in what Wild had said but offered, 'Mother, this it would seem, is going to take some time to sort out. I am quite happy to forgo my five thousand pounds and would be glad for you to have it.'

Elizabeth looked at her son, full of love for him but knowing for all his qualities his affability, his loyalty and his generosity – the impart of Wilds' words had been lost on him. She would not expose his lack of understanding but instead, thanked him and said she did not expect that she would need his money. He was missing Celia that was obvious. Waiting for Charles's consent to the marriage was telling on him. As gently as she was able she suggested, that since, as Wild had said the matter might take months or longer to be resolved, he should now return to Huntingdon. He needed no persuading.

The three managing directors around the table in the conference room listened attentively and respectfully to Elizabeth. She hoped that by late afternoon she would have news for them.

Still with Matthew, Elizabeth returned to Wild's offices late that afternoon seeking news of the counsel's application to the court in Leeds. Wild was impatient. 'I will not be badgered Mrs. Crawshaw. Once I have news, you will have it.'

She was shocked into silence and Matthew said nothing in protest. Wild would not have spoken to Henry in that manner; she knew and felt in need of a hero. Henry had presence and a brusque manner that did not invite opposition, but he was lost to her. Oh for a Jeremy Howard, a man with authority and command who accepted deference as a right.

Matthew packed that night and left next morning. Elizabeth waited all day for news from Wild; a messenger, or a telegram but nothing came. She had one caller that evening Nathan Stein.

'I trust that I am not intruding Mrs Crawshaw but Mr Ambrose has charged me with inquiring that any concerns you have are attended to. While it is a duty it is also my pleasure since I have known Mr Crawshaw from boyhood and I admire the man he became. May I ask if you are content with your rooms or if there is any improvement you would wish to have?'

'Mr. Stein, I am more than content here but there is a matter that is distressing me.'

She told Stein of the developments of the past two days, of how she had not heard of the outcome of the application to the courts the previous day and how she had found Alistair Wild dismissive of her. She believed that his attitude toward her was coloured by his attitude to having to do business with a woman. Stein assured her that he would look into the matter and was at Wild's office early next day. Admitted at once the two took tea. Wild could not have been more obliging, explaining in great detail the merits of Giles Crawshaw's case and the excellence of his counsel, Mr Lionel Swan QC. Mrs Crawshaw, he told Stein, needed to be realistic and attempt to come to a compromise.

'Alistair, we have known each other for, what, over thirty years? I first introduced Henry Crawshaw's business to you. I accept that it was, at first minor interests in a school and a farm but how those interests grew. One of your more valued clients I would have thought and deserving of the best representation for his widow.'

Wild became defensive. 'And you think I am providing less than that!'

'I have never known you so ready to yield to an adversary and I wonder if you are over impressed by the reputation of Giles Crawshaw's counsel.'

I am breaching confidentiality in telling you this Nathan but I shall do so rather than damage the relationship that I value so much. I warned Henry Crawshaw that the condition he attached to Giles's inheritance was provocative and would give rise to suspicion about his, er, nature. It was tantamount to defamation. He should, as I advised, have bequeathed to an amount greater than the amount bequeathed to his wife's son and should have done so without conditions. He had even intended to disinherit his own son completely. I often found him stubborn and only agreed to his strange request as a compromise.'

'It was always my understanding, Alistair, that the lawyer advises and the client instructs and having accepted instructions the lawyer does not, through petulance, display his annoyance to the client's widow. Now, what was the outcome of the application to the courts.'

'Lionel Swan agreed to the companies continuing to trade subject to the appointment of an independent administrator to oversee all receipts and to approve all outgoings. An accountant, Theo Hayden, of Leeds was acceptable to both sides.'

'And the detail, Alistair. What sums need the approval of the administrator?'

'All sums. It remains at the administrator's discretion but he is empowered to require all sums to be authorised.'

'Why have you not sought an amendment to that. It is unworkable.'

'Your experience is in business. Mine is in law. Lionel Swan is renowned in his field. I was pleased to have the businesses operating again without delay that would be occasioned by not antagonising the adversary.'

Stein was having difficulty hiding his annoyance. 'When did you intend to inform the chairman of the group, Mrs Crawshaw?'

'I shall write to her today.'

'Perhaps if you showed a quarter of the respect to Mrs Crawshaw that you obviously have for this man Swan, who you apparently consider to be some superior being, you might be better entitled to the earnings you have had from Henry Crawshaw for so many years. I now have a better understanding of why you allowed Giles Crawshaw's injunction against the registration of Mrs. Crawshaw's to fester for so long. It was a pointless and vexatious cause that you might have exposed had you so wished. As for

Giles being defamed you must have realised that the man is dissolute and deranged. It is said that a man who represents himself has a fool for a client. So too, Lionel Swan. So tell me, why should Mrs Crawshaw need the services of a criminal lawyer?'

'Ask yourself, as the police have been asking, who would benefit from Henry Crawshaw's death. The answer is in the will.'

'You do not like Mrs Crawshaw do you Alistair?'

'It is not a requirement of the services I provide.'

'Well do not be surprised if you are not providing them for too much longer.'

Stein made further calls at offices in Bradford that morning then met with George Ball at the Crawshaw offices. He explained to Ball that he would need to travel to Leeds, probably on a daily basis to have all incomings and outgoings approved. These included any personal withdrawals made by Mrs Crawshaw which would only be approved if they were for modest and essential housing costs and purchases.

He then outlined a strategy to Ball that would soon have the administrator more than anxious to agree a variation in terms.

Theo Haydon, a well established and respected accountant, had a profitable practice. The fees for his work as an administrator, payable by the companies he administered, were not significant but ample for an hour or two's work a week and the appointment gave his firm some status. He was to find that administering the Crawshaw group of companies might prove to be less than lucrative taking into account the hours he would be required to devote to it.

George Ball arrived at ten o'clock next morning accompanied by Robin Price who was assisting him to carry the cases of files and accounts. Hayden was still engaged with Ball four hours later approving and signing off invoices for single sales of pig's ears at two shillings a sack. Ball insisted in explaining, in stultifying detail, the purpose of each payment and each receipt.

When Ball and his assistant returned next morning with a similar number of accounts, Hayden groaned. Another three hours and sack after sack of pig's ears trotters, snouts and cheeks; separately accounted for and all explained, intermittently, by George Ball.

By the third day Hayden had had enough. His principle business interests were suffering while he was spending three and four hours a day being bored by George Ball and his stories of buying, cooking and selling bits of pigs. The final straw for Hayden was two accounts of personal expenditure by the chairman, Mrs Crawshaw; a card of buttons of one penny and a yard of elastic at a penny half-penny. As if this was not enough, Ball launched into an invented explanation for the need for a button. It involved an undergarment and offended Hayden's Methodist sensitivities. The purpose to which the elastic was to be put finished him.

Hayden proposed varying the terms of the order, as he was entitled to do, to a requirement to seek approval for expenditure of ten pounds or more. Ball agreed that this would reduce the frequency of his visits to perhaps no more than three a week. A figure of twenty pounds or more could reduce that to one short visit a week. Hayden quickly agreed, as Stein had predicted that he would.

Stein then detailed the second part of his strategy. Wages would be accounted for per shop or business, not as a whole for the group. In this way the twenty pound limit would not be breached. Suppliers would be asked to submit invoices in multiples of less than twenty pounds, so they would not need approval. This also meant that Elizabeth could make any drawings she needed, or wished, provided they did not exceed nineteen pounds, nineteen shillings and eleven pence per occasion. This Stein explained to her, was per occasion, not per day, or the number of occasions she withdrew that sum each day would be a matter for her.

The action brought by Giles might have disabled the businesses and reduced Elizabeth to a state little better than penury but Stein's strategy, immaculately executed by Ball, had circumvented that. Attention could now be turned to defending Henry's will. First, though another problem arose. The Domestic and Commercial Insurance Company's attempts to evade responsibility for the cost of rebuilding 5 Oak Rise. Alistair Wild wrote to Elizabeth to explain the insurance companies ground.

The house had, initially been insured by Henry Crawshaw who had never been the owner. At that time the owner had been Giles Crawshaw in trust. When it was sold to Mrs Crawshaw the change of ownership had not been notified. Following his marriage Mr Crawshaw insured the premises in a joint policy with his other commercial concerns while 5 Oak Rise had been a domestic dwelling. To complicate matters further the Domestic and Commercial Insurance Company had learned from the General and Legal Insurance Company that the premises had been insured a month prior to the fire by Mr Giles Crawshaw in anticipation of the courts confirming his ownership.

Wild's letter had been concluded by his view that pursuing the claim would be an expensive fool's errand.

Elizabeth was outraged at Wild's lack of interest in the claim but no more than was Stein when she showed him the letter. He proposed that Wild be sacked. He had already taken soundings of a highly respected firm in the town who could provide lawyers well versed in business practice and also a solicitor who had the experience to brief counsel for a case in the court of chancery, where the disputed will was headed. Stein would not advise Elizabeth to pursue the insurance claim through legal channels just yet though. He felt it might be resolved sooner and at less cost.

He spent almost the whole of the next day with George Ball, studying accounts and making notes. At the close of the day he visited the offices of the publishers of the daily and weekly produced newspapers and collected clippings. His request for an interview with a senior member of the Domestic and Commercial Insurance Company at their head office in Wakefield was answered by return of the postal service and he and Ball went there the following Monday.

Ball introduced Stein as a consultant on business insurance matters. The chief clerk they met, a ruddy faced man with a thin moustache, appeared unimpressed. He was as small as his desk was tall and nothing below his starched wing collar could be seen.

After brief opening pleasantries Stein was into his presentation but the clerk showed no interest.

'Mr Stein. This claim is in the hands of our legal advisers. Your legal advisers should be having this conversation with them.'

'And you are content, are you, that your legal advisers will compensate your shareholders for the loss of business you are likely to suffer from this?'

The clerk was answerable to his Board and the Board to his shareholders. Stein had his attention. 'Mr Crawshaw has insured with you since he first established a business over twenty years ago. In those years, unless your records are more complete than Mr Balls's here, he has made only two claims; one in respect of a chimney fire at a shop in Bierley and one for a shop that was wrecked during a riot by weavers sacked by a local mill. The cost of both claims was recovered by your company in the form of increased premiums.'

The clerk continued, 'Standard insurance practice, Mr Stein and completely irrelevant to this claim.'

'This is the first significant claim made in over twenty years. And, as substantial as you may consider it to be it amounts to less than the premiums to be paid in the next quarter for the insurance of the group of the Crawshaw companies.'

The clerk was unmoved. 'The one does not touch upon the other. Insurance is not a savings scheme that can be drawn upon at will on the promise of future deposits.'

Stein persisted, 'And if the Crawshaw Group should take it's insurance to one of your competitors?'

'I will not negotiate under threat or duress. That is the choice of the Crawshaw Group. The loss or the gain of a customer is a daily occurrence in insurance.'

Stein had a final card to play. It was not a trump card, it was a bluff, but it was all he had.

'Mr Crawshaw was a highly respected leader of the business community in Bradford. He was an influential member of the Bradford Club and the Commerce Club. Please take a few moments to study these.'

He passed the clerk the clippings of the Bradford newspaper's reporting of the funeral of Henry Crawshaw. The tributes were of little interest to the clerk but the attendees were impressive. There had been a member of parliament, the Mayor, councillors and, more significantly, thought the clerk, members of the board of the electricity company and the proprietors of a number of textile mills. The names were known to him and the names of their companies; many insured by his company.

'You are not suggesting, Mr Stein, that these persons would take their business away are you? I consider it most unlikely.'

Stein was quick to reply. 'I do also, some may, a few may but I consider it unlikely too. I note that you recognise the names of some persons and some companies in those newspaper reports and it may well be that most or even all will be content to trust their mills and there stock to an insurance company that seeks to wriggle out of a claim as minor as Mrs Crawshaw's. No, my purpose in showing you those reports is to confirm that the proprietors of the Bradford newspapers, as a man, hold Mr Crawshaw in esteem and will be most interested in an opportunity to demonstrate that esteem by vilifying the insurance company that seeks to rob his widow. They will need no persuasion to advise their readers that the insurance of their homes is safer in the hands of an honest company. I shall obtain the names of each of your shareholders and send every one of them copies of those newspaper reports to which I shall append a note to inform them that you, Sir, had an opportunity, at little cost, to avert this damaging publicity but lack the nonce to do so.'

The clerk was flustered. 'It is a claim I shall have to refer to the chairman.'

'Then I suggest you do that with all due haste. If we have to take this matter to law we have an unarguable case and the publicity will be more damaging than that which I presently have in mind.'

The first delivery of post on the Thursday brought a letter to the Crawshaw office that George Ball took, at once, to Elizabeth's home. The Chairman of the Domestic and Commercial Insurance company informed her that an offer for the full claim on 5 Oak Rise had been issued to her bank and an additional sum of fifty pounds had been added as an ex gratis payment in respect of her distress caused by the company's misunderstanding of certain facts.

Chapter 30

Lionel Swan QC sat on a red leather sofa in the drawing room of his mews house off Kings Court. He wore silk pyjamas and a satin dressing gown, identical to those worn by the young man who reclined his head in Swan's lap. With a tumbler of whisky in his left hand and with his right hand gently stroking the long blonde curls of his companion, Swan was happy and relaxed.

'What news of your grand mama's will, Giles?'

'There were no properties, nor interests, just deposits and they amounted to more than a thousand pounds. She has left the lot to a hospital looking into the treatment of heart disease, the miserable crone. Had it not been for my father's uncalled for intervention I would have had no need to repay her loan to me and I might well have benefitted from her will.'

Swan's stroking of Giles hair was now a comforting tap. 'Dashed bad luck, eh?'

'My great grandfather laid the foundations of a number of businesses which my grandfather built. They saw the money to be made from keeping filled the beer-swollen bellies of the masses. Yet grand mamma dies with little to show for it. How grandfather came to marry such a stupid woman I shall never know.'

'Your contesting of your father's will should be progressed, don't you think?'

'On the contrary, dear Lionel. Those managers, working for wages, believing that they are to benefit from a half share of profits, will be toiling harder than ever before. They are worker bees, filling my hives with the honey that I will drink and they shall never taste. I would be an idiot to rush while profits and value of the estate that will be mine continue to increase.'

'Giles my love, please do not bristle, I intend no criticism but merely wish to gain an even greater insight into your brilliant mind. You seem so confident that you will win your case and have your father's estate, every penny of it, you may well do so but you withdrew your contesting of the registration of your mother's house and you did not carry out your intention to sue your father and great-uncle over their defamation.'

With a sigh of bored irritation Giles explained himself.

'There was never any prospect of my preventing the eventual registration of the house since the terms of my grand-father's will permitted the sale provided that I benefitted from the proceeds. I might have been content with that had my father not made a gift of my mother's house to the woman he had move in there and was, I am sure bedding. It was his pretence that there had been a sale that provoked me and I obtained the injunction to annoy him. When he paid the value of the house to settle my debts to grand-mamma I was greatly angered. If his solicitor had been worth his salt he would have applied for and obtained a dismissal of action.'

'But still you paid a premium to insure the premises in your name'

'I was toying with the thought of challenging the transfer of the house on the grounds that there had been no sale of the kind the will had intended. The will permitted 'disposed for value'. It was my intention to argue that Mrs Fairwood's favours did not represent value. The insuring was done to bolster my claim and, to be frank, to needle my father but, I suspect he did not become aware of it.'

'You withdrew your case the day following the fire.'

'I had decided to do that some days before and my father's solicitor was duly informed. Tempted as I was to have Mrs Fairwood in the witness box and question her about her relationship with my father, the fact I could not get past was that she had been conducting a small business for some years and might have been able to establish that she had had sufficient funds to buy the house and paid them over.'

'Then fate played its part and the house was destroyed.'

'Fate Lionel, fate.'

'You never disappoint me, dear love, be assured, but it was, I suppose, a surprise that you did not prove the defamation of you by your great uncle. I would have prosecuted the case and found no difficulty in clearing you of the malicious charge laid against you. The maid would not have coped under examination and the apothecary would have been shown to be unconvincing. The Fairwood boy, lacking, as you have informed me, in mental activity, could not have recovered his earlier admission of having no recollection of the event. Indeed, I feel confident that I could have extracted a confession from him.'

'Leo, my magnificent lion, you could, I know, have done all that but my father threatened to expose me. I would not have expected his allegations to be admitted since they were not relevant to the case but I was unsure quite what he had and felt the risk was too great.'

Lionel, the lover of the young man was alarmed and alerted. He was now thinking as a QC. 'Expose you, Giles? Expose what?'

Giles noted the change in tone and did not intend to tell Swan the truth of his father's threat.

'My father had my finances investigated while I was at Cambridge and judged me to be extravagant. He claimed to have evidence of my spending and would produce it to raise a doubt in court that my action was not to clear my name, but was intended to gain damages in order that I could continue what he considered to be a profligate life. Furthermore, he would contend that I had engineered the whole business to that end.'

'Giles, please answer me truthfully, as I know you always do. Did your father have any suspicion of you and me?'

'Oh Lionel, no,no. It was only my spending, nothing more. You can be certain of that.'

'And it will not touch upon your contesting of the will?'

'In no respect will it. Anyway, my father is dead and his disapproval of my spending died with him.'

'Giles, speaking now as your advocate, and not as your lover, I would advise you to bring your case to court. You run the risk of Mrs Crawshaw's solicitor bringing an action for dismissal on the grounds of your failure to prosecute your action. I need to draft the grounds on which you contest the will and I do not know what they are.'

'Dear Lionel, how serious you can be you little worrier. I have asked you before that you refer to the respondent as Fairwood but I will let it pass this time. Be assured that the grounds I will present for you to draft will be incontestable. She cannot succeed and you will learn why that is when I am ready to tell you. In the meantime, there are butchers all over Yorkshire toiling away for my benefit. I will present my case when I am required to do so and not before and you can expect a surprise.'

'My beautiful boy, you constantly surprise me.'

'I trust that is not all I do for you.' And saying this Giles raised his head to offer his lips to Lionel Swan's mouth.

Swan did not sleep well that night and was awake before Giles went to his own bed in the adjoining room to ruffle the sheets before the arrival of Swan's housekeeper who, each day, prepared breakfast for the lawyer and the pupil who lodged with him. There was little conversation over breakfast because Swan was preoccupied. For all his obsession with Giles if that threatened his career then it would be the young man and not the career that would be sacrificed. Could he be sure that it had only been his son's spending that the father had looked into? He would not jettison Giles just yet. Not only was he enjoying him but by keeping him close he would be forewarned if his own reputation was threatened. Should that occur, he would attend to his own best interests and Giles Crawshaw would be discarded.

Chapter 31

Nathan Stein was again at Elizabeth's temporary home. 'We have the registration of the Oak Rise property resolved, the insurance for the building and its contents paid and the worst aspects of the businesses being subjected to administration have been ameliorated.'

'You have done that and I am most appreciative, Mr Stein.'

'But now the contesting of the will has to be dealt with. Since our last discussion I have arranged for a long established and highly respected firm of solicitors, Hartley and Spencer, to conduct the legal business of your companies and Alistair Wild will have no further involvement. Hartley and Spencer have expertise in business law, criminal law and, importantly, Mr Jason Hartley, a son of one of the foundling partners, Mr Sheldon Hartley, now long dead, is an expert in wills and the chancery that can follow the contesting of them. I have arranged for you to provide him with an initial briefing.'

Elizabeth met with Jason Hartley. She had never known his father but if she had she could not fail to recognise the showmanship that the son had inherited and who, now in his late fifties, was an accomplished Sheldon Hartley impersonator.

He also possessed his late father's knowledge of the law and attention to detail. His interview with Elizabeth took a full day and left her exhausted. Hartley questioned her responses.

'Now Mrs Crawshaw, see yourself in the witness box and all eyes upon you. The audience in that daunting theatre is not only listening to your words but watching your expression and looking for clues for how you hold yourself and whether your voice is now operating in a higher register. Are you ready now? Here is a question to which you will be required to respond.'

Elizabeth waited and Hartley paused for effect.

'Mrs Crawshaw. The conditions, those strange conditions, that your husband attached to his son's inheritance, a minor sum and a proportion of his total estate, but an inheritance, nonetheless; why did he attach those conditions and what should one assume from his having done so?'

Elizabeth replied without hesitation, 'My husband never discussed the terms of the will with me and the conditions to which you refer were unknown to me until the reading of the will.'

'Please answer the question Mrs Crawshaw. What can one assume from your husband having attached these conditions?'

'They should assume, Sir, what they would wish to assume. If you were to ask what I assume then it would be that my husband wished to see his son, his only son, in a long and happy marriage that would produce heirs and wished to encourage that.'

'A clever answer, Madam, but might another assumption be that your husband attached these conditions to cast aspersions on his son's nature knowing that they would not be complied with, that the inheritance would, therefore, not be claimed and that the son would not dare contest the will for fear that the smear implicit in the attachment of the conditions would subject him to public censure.'

'Such an assumption never occurred to me.'

This line of questioning was pursued relentlessly until Elizabeth was wearied and Hartley was satisfied that he had a witness with the resolve to withstand a sustained badgering.

'Before leaving Mr Hartley would you explain chancery to me. It is a term with which I am unfamiliar.'

Hartley was on his feet and on his stage. Hands clasped behind his back he paced the floor.

'Chancery, Division of the High Court. Realm of the Lord Chancellor, no less; he who soars above criticism. The court of chancery is an arena which only the foolhardy or desperate enter. Guilt and innocence have no meaning in this court. It is, ostensibly, concerned with equity; that is with fairness. Neither party may win. The victor is declared to be the one who lost the least.'

'A rather strange justice, Mr Hartley.'

'Ah, but chancery and justice are strangers to each other. In thirty-four years practice of law I have never known one decision in that court that has suited either party. Cases will, typically, run for months; some for years and costs can swallow up the wealth of both. An example, Mrs Crawshaw, an example. You have a claim against me for a thousand pounds and I resist it. After many hearings and adjournments we await judgement. It is decided that there is merit in your case but also merit in my defence and I am ordered to pay to you five hundred pounds but each of us is ordered to pay our own costs of one thousand pounds each. You are the victor since, although neither of us has won, there being no winners in chancery, you have lost less than I. We both leave court poorer but wiser.'

'Do you know, Mr Hartley, that when his son chose to study law my husband had hopes that he would be a lawyer for the Crawshaw group of companies. Mr Crawshaw had an aversion to lawyers and would have been pleased for the companies to have their own. He told me once that I should never permit myself to fall into their clutches because my own lawyer would suck my blood then pick my pockets and then share the spoils with his brother lawyer who had opposed me.'

Hartley sat again, 'A jaundiced assessment of an ancient profession but not, sadly, completely unjustified. When we are faced with having a little blood sucked and a pocket picked, by neglecting to defend ourselves, to having our opponent's lawyer open our veins, drink our blood by the tankard, raid our deposits and seize our properties what are we to do but put ourselves in the clutches of lawyers as your dear departed husband considered legal representatives to be. We do not turn to lawyers from choice but from necessity, in the way we turn to undertakers. Finding ourselves in need of either is rarely occasioned by our own actions but from circumstances in which, through no fault of our own, we find ourselves.'

'So, and let me be clear about this, you are telling me that if I defend this action the likelihood is that I shall certainly lose some of my husband's estate and, possibly, all of it. Also the costs involved might bring me to ruination. If I fail to defend the action I will avoid the costs but have to hand everything over to Giles and just as surely be ruined. My dear Henry was right to caution me against lawyers and he would see the irony in the situation in which I am placed. The lawyer he had most cause to fear was the one he raised, and educated and supported through his studies; his own son. Tell me my best course, Mr Hartley. Advise me. Do I place myself in the hands of this unjust court or do I attempt to escape ruinous costs by capitulating now?'

'Neither, Mrs Crawshaw, neither. The Court of Chancery is the end game in this chess match that is only just beginning. The aim is to reach a resolution before the end game. Your opponent's opening move was the action to contest. You must now counter by requiring him to state his grounds. He must provide them but only in outline. You will require what are known as more and better details. There will be dissembling and obfuscation designed to withhold information which your opponent considers favourable to you and which he intends to surprise you with in court. Once you can be satisfied that you have all the grounds that are to be had we enter the middle game. In this, the aim is to identify the compromise to which both parties will agree. He may want everything while you may wish to give nothing but you will both be advised by senior counsel, experienced in the workings of chancery and both of you will reach an agreement rather than risk all on the turn of a chancery card.'

'Then Mr Hartley, discover Giles Crawshaw's grounds. I expect to find that there is more malice than justification in his action.'

Hartley's associate, Victor Irvine, who now acted for the Crawshaw business secured the agreement of the administrators that the sum paid by the insurers in respect of the fire was not subject to the order freezing company assets. Elizabeth owned the property in her own right and had done so prior to her marriage. She knew she would need substantial funds to defend her case so only sufficient of the insurance claim to demolish the shell of 5 Oak Rise and clear the ground was employed. The rebuilding would have to wait and, if she was defeated, that would be beyond her means.

Jason Hartley applied to have Giles's cause struck out for lack of prosecution. He had not told Elizabeth of his intention since he felt it pointless to raise her hopes when he knew his application would not succeed. Instead, the court ordered that Giles provide details of his grounds within twenty eight days or attend court to provide good reason why he had not done so. Failure to do either might result in the cause being dismissed.

Hartley had what he wanted. A request to Giles's lawyers might be ignored or a response might offer details some long time in the future. The court's order would put a fire under the opposition. There was now a time limit and a sanction for a failure to comply.

Lionel Swan accepted the service of the court order and was excited by it. Giles was nonchalant.

'Lionel, please, do not take on so. I shall dictate my grounds and you will draft them in your inimitable style. She has, I assume, sacked Wild but this man Hartley's drafting of his application for dismissal suggests Mrs Fairwood has chosen no better representation than before. Hartley will be no match for you. They will have the grounds, though not yet the evidence on which I will destroy them, but they will have to wait until the eleventh hour. And you, dear Lionel, will have to wait until the tenth.' Giles then gave a perfunctory kiss to the balding head of his QC pupil master.

Elizabeth, agitated and distracted, had a miserable month of inactivity. Giles, though, was in high spirits and these were not dampened by Swan's insistence that the details must be provided. It was the Tuesday of the week that the order required Hartley to be provided with the details by the Friday. Swan was anxious to draw up the response that evening but Giles would not agree. He claimed to be too tired but might agree should he feel differently the following evening. Swan would have allowed no other to treat him so dismissively but his infatuation with Giles robbed him of both his pride and reason.

The next evening Swan sat down at the desk in his study, his pen poised. Giles reclined on a chaise lounge and began to dictate his grounds. The writer was a distinguished lawyer, an expert in his field and a master of his craft but he felt the need to choose his words carefully when suggesting to his young lover how the document might be better phrased. Giles would react irrationally if criticised but a legal document was no place for bile or gratuitous and unsubstantiated insults.

'While I agree that it is pertinent, and quite clever of you, to give the court reasons for why your father would, perversely, so favour a wife of twelve months to the detriment of his only son and heir I think your reason might be better phrased. I do not favour this woman inveigled your father into her bed while he was still a grieving widower and you were a child! What is the basis for this assertion?'

'If I have to justify myself at every juncture we shall be at this for hours. My assertion is self evident. Why else would a man accept as his own child of a member of his staff, he educated him as he educated me and never differentiated between us. The court will draw conclusions from that. He set her up in business, spent more evenings with her than he spent in his own home and made over my mother's house to her. In what way was she re-paying his generosity over so many years?'

'But did you, Giles, witness the two of them sharing a bed?'

'My recollections from childhood are foggy but I am sure they will be clearer when I am in the witness box.'

'Next then, that Mrs Fairwood, is not a fit person to be

chairman of so many businesses that she will ruin them and ruin the livelihoods of all the employees.

All that is relevant, but needs to be supported by evidence. Your contention that she plundered your father's account when the doors of the bank were opened on the morning following his death may be factual but it is unnecessarily emotive.'

Giles was annoyed. 'That woman is uneducated, qualified in nothing, inexperienced in business and good only for embroidering pillow covers. Had her losses over the years not been covered by my father she would have been broke. Anyway Lionel, you are irritating me. If you loved me as you claim to do you would write as I wish you to write, not seek to impose your outdated views on me.'

'Giles, my love, my advice is in your interest. Gratuitous insults will not advance your case. You will forfeit the sympathy of the court.'

'I shall have no need of the court's sympathy. She will beg to settle on any terms you will see. I have not yet revealed to you or to her the grounds that will sink her. So sure am I of her rush to settle, so convinced that she will not want this matter in court that I can afford to be emotive, as insulting and provocative as I wish. Listen carefully now Lionel, for I am about to tell you something that will surprise you. It is possible from public records and the testimony of a man with no interest in the case and no reason to lie. It is the result of months of investigation for which I have paid too much but will prove to have been an investment. My discovery will surprise you but it will shock Mrs Fry.'

'Who is Mrs Fry?'

'I am about to tell you my doubting lover.'

Chapter 32

It was a more serious and businesslike Jason Hartley that Elizabeth met on the next visit to his office. He was accompanied by a woman of severe appearance whom he introduced as Mrs Wilmer, a secretary.

'Mrs Crawshaw I have received the response, the grounds on which Mr Giles Crawshaw contests your deceased husband's will. It is, as I led you to expect, a flimsy document consisting of little more than a list of grounds with no supporting evidence. Some of the those grounds, however, touch upon matters of an intimately personal nature so I have invited Mrs Wilmer to be present on behalf of both of us. Do not feel you have to respond to any matter that offends you. When we have more and better particulars you may then decide whether you do or do not wish to respond. I must advise you strongly not to respond to matters that allege criminal conduct if your response has to constitute an admission. In those circumstances I would be unable to continue to represent you.'

Elizabeth had feared that Giles would be spiteful and churlish. Hartley's introduction caused her to fear the worst.

'It will be best dealt with if I was to list his grounds in full before we explain them singly.'

With that he began and Elizabeth suffered shock after shock at the sullying of her name and this by a man whom she had raised from childhood with the same love and care she had shown her own son. She had, according to Giles, been in an adulteress relationship with Henry Crawshaw, her influence over him caused him to accept Matthew Fry as his own, to house him, raise him and educate him. He had housed her in Giles's mother's house to hide but continue the relationship and had subsidised her failed attempts to conduct a business as a sewer of cheap materials. She had conspired with her son to conduct a charade at a house party in Huntingdon to disgrace Giles Crawshaw and to bring Matthew Fry into favour. The police were investigating the murder of Henry Crawshaw and had been unable to identify anyone who would benefit so much from his death as Elizabeth Fry had. She had married Henry Crawshaw under an assumed name to which she had no entitlement in law and had assumed that name as fugitive from justice while suspected of fraud. Henry Crawshaw had made a new will immediately upon his return from a four day stay in a Scarborough hotel during which she had been his only influence she had used her influence to secure ownership of Giles Crawshaw's mothers home, left to him in trust and so kept until he was about to inherit it. Her first act on Henry Crawshaw's death was to withdraw a large sum from his deposits. Giles Crawshaw had petitioned the court to curb her plundering

But she had employed a device to circumvent the will of the court enabling her to withdraw sums daily, on occasions more than once daily. She had diverted the insurer's payment for the re-building of Giles Crawshaw's home to her own ends and had not set the work in progress. She had.....

'Stop, Mr Hartley, please stop. This is nothing but lie upon lie I cannot bear to hear anymore.'

'Mrs Crawshaw. There is another ground upon which all else hinges and I must explore it with you. Did you register the death of your first husband, Jonathan Fry?'

'Circumstances prevented me'

'Have you had contact from or heard from him since that day?'

'I have not'.

After seven years of his absence and silence you were entitled to have him declared dead in law. Have you done that?'

'I was unaware that I could or that I needed to do that.'

'Well Mrs Crawshaw, the pivotal ground of Mr Giles Crawshaw's contesting of his father's will is that your marriage to Mr Crawshaw was entered into bigamously during the lifetime of your legal husband Mr Jonathan Fry. If that is established, then you have no case. All the other grounds are irrelevant and you face prosecution.'

'Mr Hartley, the other grounds comprise nothing but lies, insults and a misrepresentation of the truth of many matters. This final one, though wounds me deeply. I was unable to have my first marriage sanctified before the altar and for three years I bore the guilt of living in sin. I will not have my marriage before God snatched from me. When I came here today I was minded to foreshorten what you call the middle-game and I was prepared to offer Giles a settlement that you thought reasonable and that you would negotiate. Not now though, not now.'

'Do you wish to instruct me on all or some of the grounds that I have put to you?'

'No, Mr Hartley, I do not. I wish to instruct you to draw out this game for as long as you are able. Request more and more and more particulars. Demand better and better and better particulars. If the time comes when you have to get into the middle-game then make offers, increase them in penny increments, promise anything that is not binding.'

'I will, of course follow your instructions but you need to be aware of how your costs will mount; and what, may I enquire, will that buy you?'

'Time Mr Hartley. It will buy me the time to expose these lies. If that means travelling to the ends of the earth I will do it and, should I fail, I am determined that Giles Crawshaw will be at least as damaged as he is attempting to damage me.'

Elizabeth awoke next morning wondering if her defiance of the previous day had been born of a bravado that would desert her overnight. It had not and her determination was as strong but now needed direction. There were two with whom she wished to speak and went first to St. Paul's church in Manningham where she knelt, alone, and said a prayer to the Virgin Mary. She followed that with a request 'Mother Mary. I have not led a sinless life as you did but I have tried. Twice I have experienced great happiness, once on my first marriage and the birth of my son and once for the year that my second marriage lasted. Each was followed by fear, sorrow and misery. I do not doubt or rebel against God's greater purpose but I now feel that the difficulties visited upon me are a punishment but I do not know for what it is that I am being punished. You had to seek refuge on the birth of your son but then had many years of happiness and security with your son and your husband Joseph. I have, so many times, had to seek refuge in rooms, hostels, hotels and other people's homes and I am, once more, renting rooms that soon I may not be able to afford. You know I am not guilty of the list of accusations laid against me yesterday and I ask you, as my mother to guide me in how to prove my accusers wrong. I ask this through Jesus Christ, Our Lord. I am, Mother Mary, Elizabeth, your child.'

From the church she rode to Scholemoor and visited Henry's grave. He would have had a Marble Monument, as impressive as the one he had provided for Adeline if the administrators had not deemed the cost excessive and she felt it demeaning to Henry that his grave should be marked so humbly. It was a small oblong of local stone and there was a budget for the inscription that permitted a few letters. It read, 'Henry Crawshaw. Aged 44 years. Safe in the arms of the Lord.'

Elizabeth spoke with her mind but not with her lips. 'You were a good man Henry. I loved you and I say my prayers for you every night. You are in my thoughts every day. I know you are in heaven but do not know if you are permitted to intervene in my difficulties here on earth. All you worked for is at risk and I am searching for ways to counter the vile accusations that besmirch both our names. You were a most persuasive man, an accomplished negotiator and now you are in the presence of God, his angels and his saints, would you employ your skills to intercede? I do not wish to profit but neither do I wish to see evil prevail. You never did.'

The widow stood in silence for a while. She recalled the introverted young man who first employed her then the confident business man he became. Happy memories of their marriage were overtaken by the pictures in her mind of the man cruelly burned beyond recognition and she heard the only words that came from the blackened hole in his face. 'Benny'? Was it Benny? Who was Benny? His injuries, the manner of his death, had robbed her of the opportunity to speak with him for one last time. That privilege had gone to Alistair Wild who, she felt, had been so casual in his dealings with her; so dismissive.

She dwelt as she so often had on Henry's word to Wild that he had ammunition that he would use against Giles should the need arise. It was secure, he had said, and accessible. Accessible yes, if it had been in the drawer of his desk in the study but secure? Not from the fire. As she stood thinking of this her eyes were on the headstone's inscription. 'Safe in the arms of the Lord.' Had Henry made his evidence against Giles safe? Henry's desk had one drawer that could be locked and the key was kept in an unlocked adjoining drawer. Would Henry have risked that? She asked him. Although she received no reply, she became filled with a belief that he would not. It was elsewhere. Still secure. Still accessible. She must find it. She mouthed the words, 'Thank you, Henry' and returned to her carriage.

The driver was directed to take her to Old Hall at Thornton.

'Mr Stein, forgive me for arriving unannounced but I am in urgent need of advice. In your opinion, where might a businessman keep securely, and safe from prying eyes, documents of a deeply personal nature?'

Stein was too professional to raise an eyebrow and too polite to enquire as to the contents of the documents in question but, thought for a while before offering a list of suggestions.

'An old hat box in the roof space of his home, under a floor board, a hole in his garden, in a safe with his accountant or a strong room at his bank or a jeweller. There are companies that provide storage services. Such documents might even be left with a trusted friend. The options are endless, Mrs Crawshaw but the conventional choice would be a safe deposit box at his bank.'

'Thank you Mr Stein, I shall begin with the conventional and work through the other possibilities if I am unsuccessful. May I ask if you know of any person whom Mr Crawshaw might have known who was called Benny or something similar?'

'The name means nothing to me but should any possibility occur to me I will, at once, let you know.'

Elizabeth was at the Bradford Bank later that day. The manager confirmed that her husband had a safe deposit box but he felt unable to permit access to it without the consent of the administrators of her deceased husband's estate. She went immediately to Joshua Hartley's offices and asked him to seek the administrators consent to her examining the contents of the box and she asked the Crawshaw Groups' legal adviser to search his records for documents that were unconnected with business matters.

At the Crawshaw offices George Ball was able to assure her that there were no personal documents in either of the two office safes. There was not a piece of paper in either that he was unaware of, he told her, and he had an inventory of every document the safes contained. Elizabeth asked him to enquire of the accountant who now held all the Crawshaw audited accounts, Scrivan Perkins and the solicitor Alistair Wild whether they held documents, other than business documents, on behalf of her husband. Ball provided the Chairman's letters of authority.

'I am grateful Mr Ball. Could I now ask if you will search your memory for any person known to Mr Crawshaw as Benny or a name similar to that and will you ask Mr Coggins on his return to do the same. I will return tomorrow morning.'

It was a far more positive Elizabeth who went to her bed that night. That was not for what the day had achieved but because having set enquiries in motion she felt she was controlling events rather than allowing herself to be buffeted by them.

The next morning however, brought no useful news. Wild no longer held any documents and Perkins had none other than records of audited and taxed accounts. As for 'Benny' there was nothing of use. There had been a Benji Arbuthnot, dismissed from the East Bowling shop for pilfering but long since gone to sea and not heard of since. Norman Coggins recalled a night watch man at Coulson's Slaughterhouse, Barmy Benny, dead for years now.

Tempted to re-visit the offices of Hartley and Spencer to discover the progress of the examination of Henry's documents, she decided instead to wait for that news and to wait for the administrator's consent to her examination of the safe deposit box at the Bradford Bank. It was to be a long and frustrating wait. The administrator Theo Hayden, fearing he might be occupied for days while piles of documents, detailing pieces of pigs, were scrutinised delayed his response. Realising eventually that he had no choice but to agree, subject to conditions, he replied to Jason Hartley and Hartley wrote to invite Elizabeth to a meeting at his office.

'Mrs Crawshaw, this consent has taken longer in coming than I expected but it is given with conditions that I did expect. You may examine the contents of the box but you may not remove any. Mr Hayden will have a representative present to ensure compliance and the bank is required to have a senior member present as an observer. A copy of this letter has been sent to the manager of the bank and arrangements have been made for eleven o'clock on Monday of next week. I suggest that you are accompanied by representation from these offices.'

'As regards your suggestion, Mr Hartley, I am not wholly impressed by the service of your Mr Victor Irvine, it is two weeks now since I requested a search of my husband's documents and have heard nothing since. I regret to say that I feel no better served than I was by my husband's former solicitor who I found to be less diligent to my needs than I would have wished.'

Hartley felt affronted. 'Mrs Crawshaw, I shall show you the mass of documents held here on behalf of your business. All have been examined that could be examined and a Herculean task it has proved to be. It was concluded only late last evening. The bulk comprises contracts with suppliers, customers, managing directors, managers and associations and organisations with which Mr Crawshaw was involved. There remains a few parcels and packages of documents that are sealed. To break those seals demands the presence of a senior partner and the principal, in this case you, Mrs Crawshaw, to attest to the re-sealing without amendment or interference, we can do that while you are here today.'

Excited by this news, Elizabeth readily agreed. These could be the documents she was seeking. Hartley and Footit accompanied her to the strong room in the lower cellar level of the building. It had a smell of its own; not unpleasant but a mixture of dust, damp and ageing manuscripts. Two metal cases were placed on a reading table outside the door of the vault and Hartley placed a candle, sealing wax and the company seal beside it. As each package was opened, Elizabeth held her breath in anticipation but disappointment followed each revelation; a contract for shares in a farm; with a textile manufacturing company, a contract for shares in a school with the owner, another with his successors, another with their successors. There were share certificates for the electricity company and title deeds for the Manningham Villas house and shares for more shop and business premises. The documents that Elizabeth believed might protect her were not there. The packages that had been opened were re-sealed and duly attested before Jason Hartley invited Elizabeth to re-join him in his office.

'Your instructions to delay the progress in the case of the will are proving far easier to comply with than I imagined. It is most strange. I have concentrated on the central plans of their case, the existence of Mr Jonathan Fry at the time of your marriage to Mr Crawshaw. My first request for the identity of their witness drew a curt reply they only told us that he was a man of unquestioned integrity. A request for more information was met with a one line reply that he was a man of standing in his community who had held national office. My last request for this person's identity has not yet been graced with the courtesy of a response.'

Chapter 33

That same morning, as the QC and his pupil walked the few yards to their chambers the elder said to the younger, 'I would be happier if I was responding to the requests for additional information.'

'Dear Lionel, I try in so many ways to make you happy and if that was the only purpose for which I was placed on this earth then I would unhesitatingly permit you to draft those responses. Yet, that solicitor, Hartley, is not precise in asking his questions and plays into my hands. The Crawshaw worker bees are still stocking the Crawshaw hives and as the only living Crawshaw those hives are mine.'

'But Giles, your responses might be regarded as inadequate by the court and that will count against you.'

'It will never reach court, Lionel. She will surrender. You will see.'

At Elizabeth's request, Nathan Stein accompanied her to the Bradford Bank that Monday morning. This was her best chance to find what she hoped was the information Henry was prepared to use against Giles, she thought, and she was trembling with anticipation when she was led to the strong room. Haydon's representative was there. He was not the senior clerk that Elizabeth had expected but a youth and an obviously gormless one at that. The bank was represented by a senior cashier.

There was one metal box and the cashier had the key. Stein sat alongside Elizabeth and carefully opened packages and envelopes. The youth, who had introduced himself as Footit, peered intrusively over their shoulders but soon grew bored and was seen wandering around the vault aimlessly. The cashier, a more professional man, stood a little distance off and observed. Stein scanned document after document but took the time to engage Footit in conversation. From this he learned that the youth was not a clerk or even a junior clerk but merely a messenger employed by Hayden. This information was stored by Stein who would take an interest in how Hayden described his 'representative' when he billed Crawshaws for his employees time. In business, as in law, leverage always had a value.

Elizabeth's hopes faded with every document examined. Stein explained that, in the main, they comprised side agreements to contracts. These were documents, signed by both parties, that amended, clarified or interpreted terms in original contracts or, in some cases consisted of agreements as to how one party or another might breach the original terms, and to what extent they might do so without incurring penalties. Without Stein she would have been unable to understand them but she would still have known that they were not what she was seeking.

As they left, Nathan Stein shared her disappointment. He was desirous as she to find what she sought; whatever that was.

'Mrs Crawshaw, I do not wish to pressure you but I do want to offer any assistance I am able. May I ask if the information you seek is in connection with the contesting of the will by Mr Giles and, if so, whether it is information concerning him. No, I should not have asked but permit me to offer this. If I am not incorrect then I suggest you contact Mr Ambrose. I understand from Matthew that Mr

Crawshaw provided certain documents to Mr Ambrose that had the effect of exonerating Matthew. If those documents are still available to you, they might assist you.'

With all other avenues now closed to her, Elizabeth decided to visit Huntingdon on the pretext of a courtesy call on her son and his fiancée. She was met by Matthew at Cambridge to be taken to the Ambrose estate in Charles Ambrose's carriage. Matthew asked about the progress of her defence of his father's will and Elizabeth, not wishing him to know the sordid allegations made against her told him only that the case was progressing slowly.

The son had news for his mother but kept it until dinner that night when he announced that his great-uncle Charles had consented to his marriage to Celia. Charles and Marianne looked on proudly and Celia beamed. Elizabeth expressed her delight but seeing the opportunity to speak to Charles alone said that she would need to discuss the planned arrangements with him.

In Charles's office that evening Elizabeth confessed that both her visit and the need to discuss arrangements, as pleasurable as both were to her, were, nevertheless, a pretext. She told him, in detail, of Giles's challenge to the will and of the allegations he had made against her.

'Elizabeth, I am furious. That haughty, pampered young man should be thrashed. I had wondered why Matthew had not come into his inheritance. Now it is explained. In what way can I assist you, you need only ask.'

She went on to tell him of Henry's conversation with Wild concerning information regarding Giles – information that she had been unable to locate and asked him about the documents Henry had provided to him that persuaded him of Matthew's innocence.

'It consisted of a statement taken in the vernacular from the under-maid. Although it was made by a document copier I have kept it should the business again raise its head. It contains the names of two agents but not the principal of the agency. The other document, Elizabeth, again a copy, was a report by the principal of the agent. I have destroyed it. To be frank I was embarrassed to have been so easily duped and did not wish to have that report seen by others. It may well be that any other information received by Henry was from the same agent. An enquiry of that gentleman might prove well worthwhile.'

'Can you recall who that was?'

'I was very impressed by the company's professionalism so, before destroying the report I noted the name of the agency and it is in my desk. The company is Whitney and Son of Hounds Row, Paddington and the report was compiled by Mr Simon Whitney. Would you wish me to make enquiries of him on your behalf?'

'Thank you Charles, but no. I am set on doing this myself.'

'Well, if you intend visiting London then please take Matthew to escort you.'

'There are things said about me, as I have just told you, that a son should not hear said of his mother, even though they are lies. I will go alone.'

'If determination will resolve this matter for you I believe you will resolve it. But let us have the pleasure of your company for a day or two before you travel on. I have to say though that I am not entirely happy at having you in London alone. If you were prepared to delay your journey for a week or so I could re-arrange my commitments and escort you.'

'I am touched by your concern Charles but I'll not inconvenience you and I intend to travel on in two days time.'

When Marianne found Elizabeth in the garden the following day she made a request, Elizabeth detected Charles's hand in it, it was a request she felt unable to refuse.'

'Elizabeth, we understand that you are to travel to London. Celia wishes to visit London to select her trousseau and I had agreed to accompany her, but now she knows of your intentions she has asked if she might approach you to assist her

Like me, she has spent too many years in the country to have garnered any understanding of fashion, style, sympathetic materials and colours and garments appropriate for a honeymoon. You are an expert and she is excited at the prospect of having a professional like you to guide her through a process that she finds daunting.'

'You clever man, Charles Ambrose' thought Elizabeth. How could she refuse a request to employ her expertise to the benefit of her future daughter in law. It would though provide an opportunity to know Celia better and she would have a companion in London. It was agreed and the two left early on the Friday morning. That afternoon they had their rooms in the Belmont Hotel, the only hotel in London that Elizabeth knew. Her first action was to write a note seeking an early meeting with Mr Simon Whitney and she had it delivered by messenger. The messenger returned quickly with a reply. Mr Whitney was in the country for the weekend but would be pleased to see her at ten o'clock on the coming Monday.

Saturday was spent visiting fashion and gown shops and stores, not buying but comparing quality, value and suitability. Elizabeth provided Celia with a lesson in judging design, hang, stitching and combinations of colours and materials that complimented and enhanced each other.

Celia showed herself to be a quick learner and the questions she posed early in the day and the observations she made as her confidence improved evidenced an inquisitive mind and a retentive memory. They dined in their hotel that night exhausted from their long walk and happy in each other's company.

Elizabeth wishing to re-live her memories of her last visit to London, twenty years before, and wishing to share those memories with Celia she hired a carriage.

She pointed out the house in Queen Ann's gate where she had worked on the infant attendants' gowns and they visited St Paul's cathedral where Celia was amazed at Elizabeth's adventure and her attendance at the wedding for which she had worked. Before they returned to their hotel they called at the restaurant at which she had been dined to reserve a table for dinner. Elizabeth did not believe that she would be able to arrive unknown and without a reservation and still be admitted as Captain Jeremy Howard had done.

While dining that night, Elizabeth told Celia of the dashing young Captain, of their treasure hunt for the missing bridal gown, of his gaining a table in that very room as if it was his right and how the ladies' heads had turned to admire him. When she painted a vivid picture of the Captain in his ceremonial uniform, with such detail as the number of buttons on his tunic, Celia burst into fits of giggles 'Mrs Crawshaw, you were smitten by him admit it. Do'

Elizabeth, flushed and flustered, protested, 'Celia I was a married woman. I was carrying Matthew.'

'How sad for you.' And Celia giggled again.

Elizabeth attempted to claim she was affronted. 'My head was not turned, certainly not.' Then, sensing that

Celia was considering herself reprimanded she softened. 'Though if a young girl's head could be turned or her emotions juggled with then Captain Howard was the man to turn and juggle.' Both laughed so well that they had to control themselves or risk drawing the attention of the other diners to their table.

Now, completely comfortable with each other, the topics of their conversation ranged far wider. Elizabeth's opinion of Celia soared. Her suspicion that her son's fiancée might be no more than a cossetted country girl, raised behind the walls of an estate where she had passed her days reading poetry and practising pieces on the piano was dissipated. Celia had been personally taught by a qualified teacher on four mornings each week. She had supplemented that with private learning from the volumes in the extensive library at Old Hall. Although Celia did not boast about it, Elizabeth gathered that Celia and Charles frequently had discussions, some heated, about their differing views on politics, the law, religion and the unfairness of the taxation system. Elizabeth left the restaurant with a new respect for Celia and increased pride in her son in that he could attract and retain the affection of such a confident, and accomplished and highly attractive young woman. She hoped that the following morning would bring an end to her search for whatever would combat Giles. If it did her weekend would have been an unalloyed success. So close she felt to Celia that she confided in her every detail of the quest on which she was embarked.

The next morning found them both at Simon Whitney's conference table. Courtesies and pleasantries were exchanged and the smiling, handsome man seated opposite did not press Elizabeth to raise the purpose of her visit. He offered his condolences on the death of her husband, of which he was already aware, and waited for her to begin.

'Mr Whitney, you have done certain work for my husband and I am unable to locate the results of your enquiries. These would be of great assistance to me in defending a malicious action that has been taken out against me. May I ask if you have retained copies of the materials you provided to my husband and if I might have access to them?'

'You may indeed ask Mrs Crawshaw but, and please be assured I am not unsympathetic to what you are seeking to achieve, I may not provide you with the answers to your questions.'

'Could you confirm that you have undertaken certain enquiries on my husband's behalf.'

'Mrs Crawshaw, I wish I could assist you but I cannot. If Mr Crawshaw had been a client of this company, and I cannot tell you if he was or was not, then we have a duty of confidentiality that we may not breach. My father built this company on our reputation and confidentiality and integrity. We are famed for it. One breach and we might as well lock our offices today.'

Elizabeth regarded this as the end. Celia did not.

'May I pose a hypothetical question? If I was your client and you had provided me with reports of investigations I had commissioned but had lost these in, say, a house fire, could you provide me with copies?'

Simon Whitney smiled. 'I am afraid that I would have to inform you that this agency does not keep any copies of materials that it gathers or creates. All are passed to the client.'

Elizabeth could see no way in taking this any further. Simon Whitney would not even confirm that Henry was his client and even had he done so he had no documents that would assist her. She was preparing to end the brief meeting when Whitney added.

'I am aware from a company in Leeds a company which we have reciprocal arrangements of the contesting of Mr Crawshaw's will and the grounds on which the contest is based. It is a matter for regret to me that I am unable to assist you. Permit me though to use a hypothetical situation. (He smiled again at Celia). If your husband had employed this company over three years ago to investigate a certain individual and that individual was now bent upon damaging you and if certain materials delivered to your husband might, in the hands of experience council, defeat that individual you would do well to believe that such material existed. You would do well to use every endeavour to locate it.'

Celia considered that her introduction of hypothetical situations had made a contribution and she felt encouraged to make another.

'I assume Mr Whitney that you would accept Mrs Crawshaw as a client. She is in need of an investigator who operates with such integrity and whose diligence in investigating false allegations against my future husband so impressed my guardian, Mr Charles Ambrose. Yes, we knew that you acted for Mr Crawshaw and you knew that we knew but yet still you would not compromise your principles. I share my guardian's respect for your company. May we have the tea you kindly offered and which we declined on arriving and may Mrs Crawshaw and I speak together briefly?'

With Whitney gone Celia suggested a course of action that Elizabeth had considered before but felt would be unnecessary if she located the materials she was seeking.

'Mr Whitney, I wish to retain your services for two investigations. One is to attempt to establish that my first husband, Jonathan Fry, is dead and was dead prior to my marriage to Mr Crawshaw. The second is to delve into my background to discover any person called Benny or a similar name.'

'I would be most happy to investigate for you Mrs Crawshaw but I will need a full day with you to draw out every fact I shall need before we begin. I cannot cancel my arrangements today but could do so tomorrow and propose a meeting here at eight o'clock in the morning.'

Elizabeth and Celia would be staying for two more nights and sent a telegram to Huntingdon to tell of their plans to return on the Wednesday. They spent the afternoon examining sample bridal gowns in studios and Elizabeth was critical of the quality. Oswald Levine would never have allowed one stitch of an uneven size to another to leave his premises and Beattie would have been scathing of the materials that some of these studios were foisting off on their customers.

The Tuesday at Whitney's Paddington office was a very long day that was almost a short one. Simon Whitney told Elizabeth that some of the work would be undertaken by a Leeds agency and she objected.

'If that is Anderson's I do not want it. They worked against me on behalf of my husband's father.'

'If you were to know, but I cannot confirm it, that Anderson's worked for your husband to his complete satisfaction you might have a different opinion, Mrs Crawshaw. Also, if they have acted for Mr Fry senior, as you believe, then they have background information that could open other lines of inquiry. Be confident that if at any time I believe that locating my own agents in Leeds will progress matters then I shall do it.'

Elizabeth relented and Whitney began his questioning. He was meticulous in his probing and every answer prompted question upon question. On occasion, Celia suggested to Elizabeth that she should include what might be inconsequential details that she had learned from Elizabeth until all the facts had been told and re-told to the point of exhaustion.

The final evening in London was spent in the dining room of the Belmont hotel. Elizabeth made an offer to Celia, while adding that she would not be offended if Celia had other plans. The bride to be did not have other plans and was overjoyed at Elizabeth's efforts to create a wedding gown to Celia's own design. Not only would she have a beautiful, unique gown she had a reason to spend some time with Elizabeth – not in Huntingdon, she hoped, but in Bradford. Celia's favourite reading was mystery novels and here she had a real life puzzle. It intrigued her and fascinated her. Before the accusation levelled against Matthew she had had little liking for Giles, on learning that Giles had orchestrated the affair she had nothing but contempt for him and would relish the part she would play in his downfall.

Elizabeth accompanied Celia to Huntingdon but had not envisaged that Celia would be accompanying her to Bradford two days later. While Elizabeth expressed her anxiety to return and discover the progress her solicitor was making, Celia expressed her desire to have some preliminary designs done and to see some of the work in Leeds that Elizabeth had been praising so highly. It would give Celia, she said an opportunity to visit Old Hall and she was very persuasive.

They arrived at Elizabeth's rooms to find a letter from Jason Hartley preparing an early meeting but it was Friday evening and that would have to wait until Monday, so next day they took a carriage to Old Hall. Nathan Stein, pleased to see Celia again and always pleased to see Elizabeth welcomed them warmly. 'Mr Stein. All I have learned in London is that if the documents relating to Giles can be found, they should be found. Celia reminds me that documents far less sensitive than the ones I seek were lodged with accountants, solicitors and a bank.

For this he was prepared to pay a fee. It is logical that he would have been equally prepared to pay for the safe custody of these elusive documents. I have every confidence in George Ball but there may be a clue in the accounts that he is overlooking. There have been times when I have examined and re-examined my own stitching but the fresh eye of a colleague has found a defect that I have failed to see because of my over-aquaintanceship with my own work.'

Stein knew that a request was about to be made and Elizabeth paused before making it.'The period in question is three years. Could I ask you to cast a fresh eye over the company and personal accounts to see if you can detect a clue.'

'Mr Ball is a conscientious and able man and, I trust he will not be offended by my intrusion. I do not expect to find what he might have missed but I will be at your offices early on Monday.'

The two women spent their Sunday afternoon walking in the park that Elizabeth's rooms overlooked and their evening sketching options for the design of the wedding gown. Elizabeth was enjoying Celia's company and could scarce believe that it was just the previous Sunday that Celia's teasing over Jeremy Howard had so warmed their relationship. She would have been proud to have had Celia as a daughter but she was going to have her as a daughter-in-law. The date for the wedding had not been set, Elizabeth felt, it would be held before there was a resolution to her difficulties.

When they had been in the restaurant off the Strand the previous Sunday evening they had been a short walk from the mews house where the Q.C. and his pupil sat in silence, an obvious tension between them. Lionel Swan was deeply unhappy at the response that Giles had sent to Hartley's last request for further details. The Bradford solicitor wanted to know the identity of the witness who could speak of Jonathan Fry still being alive. Swan had been alarmed at the rudeness of Giles's reply. He worried that Giles's arrogance would damage his case and that he, Swan, could be compounded by Giles's recklessness. He dare not criticise his young lover for fear of provoking his fury but needed to take some action. He would take it that next morning.

Jason Hartley was not expecting Elizabeth to bring a young companion with her but introductions made he told them of developments.

'It is strange, Mrs Crawshaw. You will recall that I requested the identity of the person who could attest to the continuing existence of Jonathan Fry. Unlike the earlier curt replies, this one is nothing short of outrageous. It states quite simply that the information will be provided when and only when the contester chooses to provide it. This is unprecedented. Even stranger is a second letter I have received. Also posted in London but on un-headed notepaper and unsigned it advises me to apply for a dismissal of the cause for lack of co-operation. I am inclined to do that and need your instructions, Mrs Crawshaw.'

'Is there any possibility of such an application succeeding?' asked Elizabeth.

'None. None at all. Failure to co-operate at this stage, and on only one of the stated grounds, would not result in the dismissal of the whole cause.'

Celia spoke. 'Then would it not make sense to respond to the contester, as he chooses to term himself, and threaten such application in the event of non-compliance.'

Hartley, annoyed by what he considered to be impertinence, replied not to Celia but to Elizabeth.

'Tell me, Mrs Crawshaw, what might that achieve. Is your young friend unaware of your strategy to delay developments?'

'Actually, Mr Hartley. I see the logic in this course. If the threat does not have any effect, then the application your anonymous correspondent advises, might be submitted. More time will be bought. If, on the other hand, the evidence of Jonathan's existence is forthcoming, that will foreshorten an investigation I have commissioned.'

'You have my advice, Mrs Crawshaw.'

'And I value it Mr Hartley but would have you write to Giles's legal representatives, express your outrage and threaten an application to discontinue.'

Elizabeth and Celia visited the Crawshaw offices where Elizabeth soothed George Ball's discomfort at having Nathan Stein scrutinizing his accounts. Ball accepted that a fresh eye might make a discovery and promised full co-operation.

Having paid a courtesy visit to Stein in the conference room, where he sat surrounded by a mountain of ledgers and accounts, Elizabeth and Celia took the railway to Leeds. Elizabeth wanted to show Celia the quality of work being provided in the studios.

She was sure that Oswald Levine would be long retired but expected his successor, possibly Stanley Beronowski, would have maintained standards. Failure to do so in a town with so much competition would result in ruin. Elizabeth reasoned that if the Levine Studios were still in business they would be able to show Celia work of the highest standard and that would be their first call.

Levine had not retired but could be seen through the window seated at the desk in his office. Elizabeth thought that her old employer must now be in his late seventies and she wondered whether the desire to continue working was fired by love of his work or a reluctance to spend more time than was necessary with the formidable Mrs Levine.

As they entered his office, Levine was on his feet and greeting Elizabeth like a long lost daughter. He was proud to show Celia gowns that were in preparation and she marvelled at their magnificence. If that studio was in London, she thought, none of those she had visited could have competed. Elizabeth told Levine of her plans to make Celia's wedding gown and he made her a most generous offer. He would procure the materials to Celia's specification, provide a work-space in his studio for Elizabeth and construct a mannequin – and all at cost. Elizabeth was excited at the offer and Celia was thrilled. When Levine examined the preferred sketches, proposed minor improvements and suggested an over-layering of silk on satin, Elizabeth knew that his brilliance had not deserted him.

He would inform her once the mannequin was ready and the materials obtained.

Chapter 34

The week passed uneventfully for Elizabeth and her young guest. She expected Celia to be anxious to return to Huntingdon but it was clear that she was not. They received a caller on the Friday afternoon. Nathan Stein had news, he told them, but until it was checked, it should not raise hopes too high.

'The clue lay in the precision that George Ball applies to recording transactions.

A bank customer, in this case Mr Crawshaw, has to pay a fee to his bank in respect of transfers made to others such as suppliers, accountants, solicitors and, in this case you will be interested to know to Whitney's investigation agency. There were more than a score of payments over three years. Also, it is not uncommon when a large company, such as Crawshaw's in dealing with small businesses that the contract, or a side-agreement such as those you saw at the Bradford Bank, will stipulate that the large company will accept responsibility for the transfer fees charged by the smaller business bank.'

The two women listened intently. Celia had a thirst for knowledge and was taking in every word. Elizabeth knew Stein was not a man given to long, unnecessary monologues intended to boost his own importance as some men were.

'For these reasons Mr Crawshaw paid fees to all the Banks in Bradford, not only to the Bradford Bank but to the Bradford Old Bank, the Bradford Savings Bank, the

Yorkshire Penny Bank, the Bradford District Bank and the Commercial Bank together with many beyond the town including banks in London and Dorset. Almost all of these fees, but not every one of them, was recorded in the ledgers as 'Transfers.' But the holder of a bank account also has a fee to pay for the bank opening and conducting the account. Those payments were recorded as 'Services.'

Both 'Transfers' and 'Services' are claimable against taxation liability by a business but are not claimable against personal expenditure. I therefore went to the taxation declarations and compared each 'Transfers' and 'Services' entry with that year's taxation claim. This is why the search has taken me so long.'

Both Elizabeth and Celia had shifted to the edge of their seats. Stein was, they knew, about to reveal his findings.

'For each of the past three years there have been just three payments of fees recorded as 'Services' that have not been included as a claim against tax. Two each year were to the Bradford Bank, one in respect of the rental of a security deposit box, the box that you and I examined, Mrs Crawshaw. The remaining payment each year was made for 'Services' to the Yorkshire Penny Bank: 'Personal 'Service' and not claimable against tax liability. I have examined the relevant invoices and they relate to the rental of a safety deposit box.'

Elizabeth was elated. 'We must go at once.'

Stein checked his timepiece and said it was too late that day. They must wait until Monday and he agreed to accompany Elizabeth again.

The post on Saturday morning brought Elizabeth a letter from Giles, delivered to the Crawshaw offices and brought to her rooms by a messenger.

'Mrs Fry.'

When you sacked that fool of a solicitor, Wild, I had hopes that you would appoint someone whom I would respect as a worthy adversary. Instead, your second appointment is no better than your first. I have received a letter from Hartley and it contains no more than hollow threats.

I was prepared to indulge you and permit you to have the representative of your choice but my patience is becoming worn threadbare. The fees you are paying Hartley are coming from my inheritance and my money is being squandered on a cause that you cannot win.

This case is not providing me with the sport I thought it would and I am tiring of it. Before I have you in the Court of Chancery, with the ruin that you will surely face there, I will give you the opportunity to get out of your fix. Throw in your hand and I will consider a payment of a few hundred pounds.

I make this offer 'without prejudice,' a term that even a solicitor such as Hartley should be capable of explaining to you.'

Giles Crawshaw

Elizabeth was not upset nor even provoked to anger. Rather, she was confirmed in her resolute to fight Giles to the last and she passed the letter to Celia without comment.

The Sunday morning found Lionel Swan in a low mood. It was the day of the week when his housekeeper did not come in and Giles, as was his practice chose to remain in

Lionel's bed until noon. The master had served the pupils breakfast and Giles lay there pleased with himself. Lionel however had risen early and was at his desk, his head in his hands wondering how he might extricate himself from this situation. He was in despair at Giles's scatter-shots approach to the case; a case that had been launched by Swan's chambers. This could be damaging to Swan's professional reputation. After three years the eccentriatics of the young man in his bed, once endearing, were now increasingly annoying and Swan still harboured a fear that Giles's father had investigated more than his son's spending.

How, though, could he discard this young man who was now boring, irritating and, he feared, endangering him? How does a man free himself from a mistress who threatens to expose him to his wife? Pay her off? Kill her? Swan shook his head. This case must be brought to a conclusion, he decided. He had pressed Giles as hard as he dared and the result had been a childish letter to his father's widow. No, Swan must intervene and he wrote a letter to Jason Hartley, again anonymously, intending to achieve an early resolution.

Celia was keen to join Elizabeth and Nathan Stein at the Yorkshire Penny Bank on the Monday morning but Elizabeth dissuaded her and asked her to wait at the Crawshaw's offices. She suspected that the box, if it was to contain what she was seeking, would contain material not suitable for young woman's eyes. This would be the day she thought, when her search would be over but, as on so many other occasions, it was not to be. The manager, aware of the action against the Crawshaw estate, but being unsure of whether the court order extended to the box in his custody, required the approval of the administrator before permitting access to the box.

Elizabeth felt she was being baulked at every turn but Stein, now at her offices, asked her to write a letter to Theo Hayden, seeking his agreement to an examination of the box. It would, he assured her not mean the lengthy wait she had experienced on the previous occasion. By noon he was in Hayden's office and presented the letter. The administrator was not, at first, very receptive to the suggestion of immediate approval. He would, he said, have to spare a representative and that might take two weeks or more before he could spare a representative for the task.

'Tell me, Mr Hayden, will this representative be the senior clerk for whose hours at the Bradford Bank you billed Crawshaw's and who I was most sorry not to have met. Or would it be your messenger, Master Footit, who I did meet. We should be happy to have Master Footit, again provided that you can arrange that for ten o'clock tomorrow and that there should be no bill on this occasion.'

Hayden, frustrated and embarrassed, changed his attitude immediately.

Elizabeth and Stein were at the Yorkshire Penny Bank the next morning and presented the administrator's letter of authority. Footit was there and the manager, rather than depute a senior clerk as the manager of the Bradford Bank had done, provided a junior clerk.

At a table in the vault Stein took the key from the junior clerk and turned the lock of a green metal box which measured two foot by two foot and was a foot tall. Elizabeth trembled with anticipation as the lid was opened and Footit, leaning on Stein's shoulder groaned audibly on seeing the box was stuffed with documents. He was resigned to it being a long day. The junior clerk started by standing attentively at the end of the table but soon tired of that and it was not long before the two young men were at the far end of the vault discussing the competing attractions of the music halls in Leeds and Bradford.

Stein worked methodically scanning report after report from Simon Whitney to Henry Crawshaw. They all concerned a student at Cambridge University who was not identified by name but referred to as 'the subject of our enquiries.' There were reports of debts to bookmakers, money lenders, tailors, wine merchants, restaurants and Hotels. Other reports referred to another man who was only identified as the visiting lecturer. Stein read far more quickly than Elizabeth and the reports he passed to her soon formed a pile of those he was investigating. Should these reports go astray in the post Whitney would be protected from actions for libel and defamation as not one person was identified.

Also in the box were letters. original letters. These clearly identified the writers and the recipients. The reports made no reference to these letters or to how they had been obtained. All were either from Giles to Lionel or Lionel to Giles and the envelopes that contained them left no doubt as to whom Lionel and Giles were.

Stein questioned whether they were too explicit for a lady's eyes and suggested to Elizabeth that she might wish to spare herself the reading of them but she was set upon it even if she would need to steel herself. She did not read them all nor even every word of the ones she did read but read enough to gain an understanding of the nature of Giles's relationship with the older man and an understanding of the conditions Henry had attached to Giles's inheritance. Although she had been twice married, Elizabeth was unaware, and happy to be unaware, of some physical practices that men and women indulged in. To see such practices between men detailed so explicitly and shamelessly in writing disgusted and nauseated her. She could read no more and was relieved that she had not permitted Celia to accompany her that day. The Sisters at Bethlehem had taught her that innocence was a state once lost could never be regained.

There was a further item in the bottom of the box and Stein guessed its contents from its dimensions. While Footit and the junior clerk were discussing whether the Incredible Rubber Man was indeed made of rubber Stein slipped the package into his bag. The reports and letters were replaced in the box.

Walking from the bank to the Crawshaw offices, Elizabeth asked Stein if their find would defend against Giles's action. He was unsure this was a legal matter and one that would need very careful handling. Celia was delighted that Elizabeth found the documents that Henry had stored and wanted to know what they revealed. Elizabeth restricted herself to saying that they revealed Giles to be a spendthrift, which was of little relevance to the case but they also revealed an unnatural and unlawful relationship with Lionel Swan, Giles's barrister. She expected Celia to be shocked but she appeared not to be. Elizabeth questioned her.

'Mrs Crawshaw, if, like me, you have been raised in the country you would have seen rams mounting rams and farm hands dismissed for the same. I was taught to politely look the other way and put it from my mind. The reason I am not shocked is that I am not surprised. Giles has a softness about him that men of a certain kind might be attracted to and he has the guile to take full advantage of such men.'

Elizabeth was amazed at Celia's maturity and knowledge of life but worried that she was accepting of such conduct.

She would not visit Hartley today but go home and order her thoughts. Before leaving she was invited into the conference room by Stein who had opened the package he had found in the box and confirmed his belief that it contained five pound notes, fifty of them. He handed these to Elizabeth, told her that it was not uncommon for a business men to keep sums in cash for emergency purposes and suggested that she should not disclose the source but use the money to defray the expense of the cause on which she was embarked.

She arrived home with Celia and found a letter from Anderson's to Whitney's that Whitney had forwarded to her.

'Our enquiries reveal only three persons from Mrs Crawshaw's background who are or were known as Benny or a similar name. Concepta McCall entered the Order of the Sisters of Compassion at the age of twenty-two and adopted the name Benedicta. She has been deceased for many years. Bernadette Faux remains in that order where she is now known as Sister Teresa. Mrs Crawshaw's past employer Oswald Levine was originally named Osbaldiston Benjamin Levinsky. He continues to manage a fashion studio in Park Terrace, in Leeds.'

Celia said, 'Well that need not concern you now.' And Elizabeth expressed her puzzlement.

'When I was at your offices this morning I knew an hour before you returned from the bank that you would certainly find what you were seeking there. Business men, like lawyers, doctors, like all professional people I suppose, speak in a kind of shorthand or code and I have been interested to listen today. When Mr Coggins arrived he asked Mr Ball if Mr Stein was still there. It was Mr Ball's reply that told me that you were looking in the right place.

He said, 'No he's done. He believes that the information to save our business will be found in the Penny's vaults. Pray God he is right.' You were at the Yorkshire Penny Bank and the words, the shorthand, the Penny's vaults were so similar to Mr Crawshaw's last word's to you, Benny's Fault, that I was confident that this was what he was saying.'

Elizabeth was convinced too. Again with Celia she was at Jason Hartley's office the next morning ready to inform him of the ammunition that her husband had been ready to use against Giles but Hartley had news of his own. 'I have received another letter form my anonymous correspondent in London and I shall read it to you.'

'Evidence that Jonathan Fry was alive when his wife entered into a bigamous marriage with Henry Crawshaw will be sworn to by his father, Mr Edmund Fry. He is a man of integrity who has led a blameless life and was recognised by his peers when he was elected to be National President of Transport and Hauliers Association.

His son found it necessary to flee the country when he was falsely accused of involvement in a fraud perpetrated by others and, since then, has travelled between Italy and China trading in silk. He had a background in such threads and clothes and had set his wife up in a business producing garments.

Mr Edmund Fry will give evidence that he receives regular, albeit infrequent letters from his son Jonathan and will attest to the handwriting and signatures on those letters. He was unaware that his son's wife had illegally remarried because he had been unable to maintain the contact with his daughter-in-law, which he would have dearly loved, as he had been threatened by Mr Henry Crawshaw with whom she was co-habiting.

The last letter he received from Mr Jonathan Fry post dated Mrs Fry's unlawful marriage by eight months.'

Hartley put down the letter. 'If the facts of this letter are true, and we have no means of refuting them before Mr Fry senior steps into the witness box, then your case is lost Mrs Crawshaw.'

Elizabeth was undaunted. 'There are a number of misconceptions in that letter and knowing Mr Edmund Fry, as it was my misfortune to have known, I would not accept a word he says. He has previously threatened to perjure himself about me and I have a witness to that.'

Celia added her comment, again to Hartley's annoyance. 'I note, as I am sure you do Mr Hartley that there is no claim that any of these supposed letters have been kept and can be produced. The silence on that point is telling.'

'Mrs Crawshaw. I admire your determination and praise your optimism but from where do they spring?'

It was Elizabeth's turn and she told Hartley in as much detail as was proper for a lady, of the contents of the safe deposit box. Hartley's reaction disappointed her.

'In addition to the other crimes alleged against you are you prepared to admit to being in possession of items stolen from the postal service?'

'But wouldn't the threat of disclosure work to our advantage Mr Hartley. Both Giles and Lionel Swan have committed criminal offences.'

'My dear Mrs Crawshaw, please understand this, if we were to threaten disclosure the effect would be the withdrawal from the case of Mr Lionel Swan QC and his replacement by another. Evidence against Mr Swan would be deemed inadmissible. Also, since Mr Giles Crawshaw was under twenty-one years of age at the time of his alleged behaviour he would be regarded as a victim, not a perpetrator and his conduct would also be inadmissible as it is irrelevant to his claim.'

'Then it is worthless, Mr Hartley? Is that what you are saying?' Elizabeth was angry and Hartley was thinking.

'Not entirely worthless but how this information is best deployed in your defence takes me into realms in which I have never before been. My father would have known but he can longer be consulted. A suggestion, Mrs Crawshaw I did not see any need to advise you to appoint Senior Counsel until the case came to court and it has always been our intention to settle before that sad day. Now, though, the middle game has changed. The black king is exposed but if the white queen, you, was to mount an attack she could be lost. You need a knight who is equal to the black king, Lionel Swan QC. And I suggest we attempt to retain him.'

'Do you have such a man in mind, Mr Hartley.'

'When I was in training my father made a new appointment. He was a personable young man who did not settle here for long but we have followed his career with interest. He is now a leading barrister and the head of his chamber in London. If we can get him, and you can afford him, you should have Mr Carlton Devereux QC.'

'Then use your best endeavours to retain him, Mr Hartley.'

'I shall require a retaining fee, say fifty pounds, it will take me at least one week to draft a brief of these most complicated grounds and of documents you have unearthed. How I shall explain your entitlement to possess those letters I do not know. Thereafter, and provided that Mr Devereux agrees to represent you, he will need to take instructions from you personally. However, protocol demands that a solicitor be present. I know you well enough to be confident that you are capable of articulating your instructions without the need for an intermediary but in law what protocol demands protocol must have. I tell you all this so that you will not have unrealistic expectations of any early progress. It can be some weeks before there is any progress of note.'

'Thank you for your frankness, Mr Hartley. Before I leave, may I make some notes from the anonymous letter you have received it may be of interest to the investigation being conducted on Jonathan Fry's death.'

Celia prepared to return to Huntingdon. She would travel on Friday Elizabeth cautioned her that she must not lose or gain a pound before the day she wore the gown that Elizabeth was going to dedicate her time to creating. She returned from her good-byes at the railway station to find two letters. One was from Oswald Levine informing her that the mannequin was ready and her workplace had been provided. Her work could begin.

The second letter was a report from Anderson's to Whitney and Son. 'The body of Jonathan Fry was never recovered from the canal in Leeds. It is extremely unusual but not unheard of that bodies have failed to resurface. The bottom of the canal is littered with wreckage and debris that could keep a body on the bottom. On one occasion when a length of the canal was dredged the remains of a horse were found, trapped in weeds.

All this said, enquiries of men who have worked the canal all their lives and some who knew Jonathan Fry drew a common response. It is their view that he did not die in the water and if he had it is almost certain his body would have come up. Fry is described as a trickster in life and a trickster in his supposed death. It is not evidence but strongly suggests a detailed, far reaching investigation might prove fruitful. Neither his death or assumption of it have ever been regretted in Leeds.

A note from Simon Whitney asked whether Elizabeth wished him to undertake a wider search, the cost of which might prove to be substantial. She wrote back urging him to continue without delay and informed him of the anonymous letter, while telling him why she would not believe a word of anything Edmund Fry might be prepared to say.

Chapter 35

Elizabeth packed her cases on the Sunday afternoon. From then until the gown was finished she would work at Levine's studios for six days each week and stay at the Midland Hotel. What memories, she wondered, would be revived from returning to that routine. She planned to return home on Saturday afternoon each week to deal with her correspondence. Recently she had been waiting day to day for the arrival of the postal delivery. Now she would have to wait a week at a time.

Her first week passed quickly. Comfortable and at ease in her room at the Midland Hotel she was not haunted by the ghosts of her previous stay when she was preparing for and nervously anticipating her marriage. The studio lacked the fun and gossip she had before and enjoyed. Beattie and Devina were gone and the young seamstresses, accomplished and full of fun did not include Elizabeth in their little circle. She recalled that she had had a similar attitude towards Edna and Madeline. Being excluded did not offend her. Her stay was too temporary and she did not want any distraction. After a few hours on practice pieces her needlework was as faultless as ever and as she worked her love for Matthew and the deep affection she had for Celia were woven with her threads into every hem and seam of the exquisite fabrics that Levine had acquired.

There was only one letter awaiting her when she arrived home but it was one that she was happy to receive and she replied to it at once. It was from Celia who thanked her for her stay, for the work she was doing on the gown and she pleaded to be kept informed of every detail of Elizabeth's struggles to defend herself. As difficult as she found it to keep her promise she had not told Matthew of the grounds for the contesting of the will but she hated deceiving him. Her Uncle Charles had not questioned her about it. One paragraph of Celia's letter caused Elizabeth to smile:

> 'I have visited the apothecary in Huntingdon and lingered so long I feared I might be drawing attention to myself. While there I learned that a customer purchasing certain draughts and tinctures is required to sign a register. If you were to obtain one of the letters from 'Penny's Vault' the handwriting could be compared with the register.' Dear Celia, she thought.

The second Saturday home had news for her in two letters. The first was from Jason Hartley to inform her that Mr Carlton Devereux QC had consented to accept the brief but wanted a clerk from his chambers to examine and take notes from the documents in the safe deposit box. Elizabeth could be present but did she not wish to be she should write to the manager of the bank authorising the examination. She did that at once. The second letter brought depressing news. It was from Simon Whitney.

> 'Dear Mrs Crawshaw'

> 'Our enquiries have discovered that three days after Mr Jonathan Fry's supposed death in Leeds, a man of that name took a passage on a trading ship from Liverpool to east Africa. I have put enquiries in hand with the authorities at the port of disembarkation and will keep you informed of developments.'

Your servant

Simon Whitney.

The third weekend did not bring any news and by the Thursday of her fourth week in Leeds, Elizabeth's work was done. She gazed at the gown on the mannequin and was so proud of it that tears formed in her eyes. When the young seamstresses stood and applauded the tears flowed down her cheeks.

She asked Levine if he would arrange the packing, crating and transporting of the gown to the Ambrose estate in Huntingdon and to add the cost to the sum she owed him. Levine would only accept only the cost price of the materials. Everything else was a tribute to her talent. It would be his pleasure to arrange the transporting. It should be regarded as a wedding gift to the charming and beautiful young lady to whom your son should be proud to have as his wife.

Elizabeth pecked his cheek and had a joke with him.

'I trust you will not be employing the haulier who once had me searching London at an unearthly hour?'

Serious now Levine said, 'I have, since then, employed no other. When a business or a person makes a serious error they are, ever after at pains to ensure that the error is not repeated. A business that has never made such an error has not learned the lesson so is far more likely to make one. And I promise this, if the gown is not delivered I will walk from here to there on my hands and knees searching ditches and hedgerows until I find it.'

He smiled, and returned her kiss and she left with the good wishes of all those she had worked amongst during the last month. On her journey back to Bradford she wondered what news might await her and this made her question her morality. For all that Jonathan had been a deceiver of her and others he must have loved her once and he was, and he always would be, the natural father of the fine young man her son had grown to be. She had for years, seventeen or more, believed Jonathan to be dead and now that there was a possibility that he might not have died in the canal, probably did not die there, what right did she have to wish him dead. Yet, if he was alive he would be more ruinous to her than he had been before. As her train passed a small parish church in Pudsey she wondered if she should pray that he was alive or that he was dead. Some things, she concluded, were just not fit subjects for prayer.

Whitney had more news for her and she read it at once.

'Dear Mrs Crawshaw'

Our enquiries of the port authorities have been answered far sooner than I could have hoped. This is because, on disembarking, the man called Jonathan Fry took employment with that authority recording loading and manifests. He amassed some considerable debts while gambling in card games during his short stay and left after only three months on the S.S.Minerva bound for America.

Following his departure it was discovered that a large sum of money had been stolen from the company's offices and Mr Fry is suspected of having been responsible. The records of the S.S.Minerva show that Mr Fry embarked but there is no record of him having disembarked. However a Mr Edward Mason disembarked in North Carolina but there is no record of him having embarked in east Africa.

Mr Fry had compiled the passenger manifest for the voyage.

The names employed, Fry and Mason, leave little doubt that the man in question was your husband.

I am having enquiries made in the Carolinas and await further developments.

Your servant

Simon Whitney

Elizabeth pondered on her situation. It seemed to her that the position was hopeless. Giles had offered, or said that he would consider offering a few hundred pounds to withdraw her defence. Would he, she wondered, agree to meet her costs too? Probably not, he was malevolent and would not be satisfied with defeating her. He would seek to humiliate her, rob her son of his inheritance, exploit Henry's partners and employees and pillage his companies and properties. No, she could not surrender. There were too many others relying on her fortitude. She could not abandon them to Giles Crawshaw's better nature. He did not have one. She must fight. Henry had seen value in storing information about Giles's conduct and, despite Jason Hartley's misgivings, she owed it to Henry's memory to capitalise on these documents the contents of which must have caused him much heartache.

Another letter arrived that afternoon, delivered by a messenger. Jason Hartley informed her that Mr Carlton Devereux QC would wish to confer with her at his chambers in Parsons Walk in London at ten o'clock on Monday week. A London solicitor would attend on his, Hartley's behalf.

She ought to arrange for a stay of perhaps a few days since it was Mr Devereux's hope that matters could be settled through negotiation and her continued presence would be essential if that was to occur.

Elizabeth spent the following week rehearsing and re-rehearsing the details that Mr Devereux would need. She prepared her clothes, some she cleaned and pressed, some she bought. Should she go alone or should she invite Celia? No, she would go alone. She would not inform the managing directors at her offices and raise their hopes in case she would later have to dash them. They would need to know where she could be contacted though and so too would Simon Whitney in case any further information should come to light. She would stay at the Belmont Hotel from that coming Sunday and would inform all those whom would need to know.

She had access to the remainder of the insurance payment from the fire and the money Nathan Stein had recovered from Henry's box. While she had no concerns about her immediate financial needs, if she had to pay Hartley, Devereux and Whitney out of a minimum settlement she feared that she would be unable to do so.

The last letter she received before leaving for London contained a request from Celia for Elizabeth to visit Huntingdon for an extended stay to assist her and her Aunt Marianne to prepare for the wedding on the second of August, just two months hence.

Elizabeth looked from the window of her room at the Belmont Hotel and saw it was a fine late May Monday morning. She chose her dress for the day, mid-blue, feminine yet business like. For the negotiation day, which might be the following day or the day after that, she would save the red jacket and skirt, fiery and defiant.

At Carlton Devereux's chambers she was met by a shy young solicitor, Ephrain Grant, who would be her representative on behalf of Mr Hartley. Shown into Mr Devereux's office she was impressed by its size, and the great desk inlaid with leather and the carpet into which her shoes sank. Lined with bookshelves and with chairs around side-tables in studied disarray put her in mind of the Bradford Library.

Devereux rose, came around his desk to shake Elizabeth's hand and chatted amicably to put her at ease. She did not wish to be at ease. She wished to be alert and determined but appreciated the barrister's intentions. He had a relaxed manner and a ready smile, a full head of hair and an exquisitely tailored suit. Devereux oozed confidence. Tall, slim and by now in his mid fifties he could have passed for a forty year old. For all his charm, though, would he, wondered Elizabeth, prove a match for Lionel Swan.

He had Hartley's brief before him and a report from his clerk who had examined the contents of the box at the Yorkshire Penny Bank.

'Now, before we begin Mrs Crawshaw, would it offend you if I was to smoke? I find it an aid to concentration.'

'Not at all Mr Devereux, I enjoyed the aroma of my husband's cigars.'

With a foot long Cuban cigar in his left hand and a pen in his right he began.

'I had hoped you might be accompanied by a lady since I have some questions of a delicate and personal nature that I must put to you. Would you wish to have me arrange the presence of a lady.'

'That will not be necessary Mr Devereux. You must ask what you must ask.'

'I must insist though that, unlike your interview with Mr Hartley, you do not choose the allegations you are prepared to discuss and those you are not. My task is to gauge the extent to which the Court of Chancery would find merit in Giles Crawshaw's grounds. Having done that I must seek to secure a better outcome for you in negotiation that I would anticipate you obtain from the court and spare you the costs of contesting in that place. Arrangements have been made for negotiations to commence tomorrow so we must make full use of today. That requires full, frank and honest responses to my questions.'

'I understand Mr Devereux and I have no intention of responding to your questions in any other way.'

'We shall see. The theme that runs through each of many grounds of the contesting of the will is the nature of your relationships over many years with Mr Henry Crawshaw and the extent to which that influenced him to favour you and your son over his son and heir and eventually to him marrying you. So, Mrs Crawshaw, when and where did the first intimate physical union between the two of you occur and, before you answer, picture yourself in the witness box, having sworn on oath and facing imprisonment should you perjure yourself.'

Elizabeth fighting her discomfort at discussing such a personal matter, replied, 'It occurred in our honeymoon bed in Scarborough the night following our marriage.'

'Before that, when were the first occasions of intimacy which stopped short of a physical union, say, touching and exciting?'

'Mr Devereux. Sir. Is this necessary?'

'Madam, the courts will be curious as to why Henry Crawshaw took in your child, educated him at considerable cost and housed you, rent free, in a property which he was holding in trust for the contester in this case. The court is hardly likely to conclude that Mr Crawshaw's motives were entirely altruistic.'

'I will answer your questions, Mr Devereux, but may Giles Crawshaw be damned for putting me through this.'

So began one of the more difficult days of the many difficult days she had experienced in her life. Her ordeal was not relieved when questions turned from matters sexual to a forensic probing of her finances, her ambitions for herself and her son, her acceptance of a house and a business from a man who owed her nothing and her lack of self esteem in accepting the roll of a kept woman. This theme came full circle when he asked to refute the allegation that Henry Crawshaw was prompted to propose when she withdrew her favours and the transfer of Giles Crawshaw's home to her ownership was a condition of her acceptance.

After a brief break for refreshments at lunchtime the questioning started again. It concerned her first marriage and whether the court would, on balance, conclude that Jonathan Fry was alive when she married Henry. When it appeared to Elizabeth that Devereux's interrogation was about done Elizabeth spoke.

'I have been placing great store in the value of the documents that, I understand you have had examined, yet you have made no mention of them. Do you see no value in them at all?'

'On the contrary Mrs Crawshaw, as the case presently stands I believe that our opponents would be less unhappy at having the case in court than we. However, our possession of the information that you did so well to discover, will dissuade them from that course and render them as keen as we are to reach a settlement. The keener we can make them the more the settlement will favour us. For now though, it is imperative that they remain unaware of our possession of those documents. It is our power and as Cromwell urged his troops 'place your trust in God and keep your powder dry'.'

'What should I expect tomorrow Mr Devereux. What do you consider to be the best outcome for which I could wish for?'

'If you mean how much will I offer or accept, then that will be subject to your approval. There will be bids and counter bids. For some I will want to present, for others I will want you nearby. I shall be gambling in a card game that calls for bluff and a gambler does not approach the table with a sum in mind that he is prepared to lose. He approaches it intending to walk away with the total pot and that is my intention Mrs Crawshaw.'

Elizabeth spent the evening in her hotel room. She had no appetite for dinner and wondered how she would face Matthew and her managers if she failed them. She would have to trust Carlton Devereux's advice. If that advice was to settle, even on very poor terms, it would be foolhardy to reject it and risk everything to chancery.

Chapter 36

Nearby, and close to Lincolns Inn, stood an impressive detached building that had the appearance of a gentleman's residence but was Browns, an exclusive club the membership of which comprised the luminaries of the legal fraternities of the city. Membership was by invitation and while some judges were excluded for reasons they were never permitted to know some esteemed solicitors were admitted. It was a place in which private conservations remained private.

There was a convention, never spoken of, never admitted to, but religiously observed that competing barristers would meet there on the evening before pre-trial negotiations. On occasions such negotiations were settled by the third glass of brandy and the second cigar but, more usually, the purpose of such meetings was to draw up battle-lines, examine the enemy's deployment of his cavalry and his artillery and to probe them for weaknesses.

It was eight o'clock that Monday evening that Devereux arrived and found, as expected, that Lionel Swan was there.

'Carlton, old chap, how good to see you.'

'And you Lionel. Shall we take a chair?'

Seated, served brandy and cigars by a uniformed, white gloved steward, they engaged in inconsequential pleasantries that ranged from the uncommon warmth of the day to the progress of Devereux's twin daughters at Oxford.

'Medicine, not the law, I understand Carlton'

'Influenced by my wife who greatly respects doctors but rarely displays such respect for lawyers., Well for this one, certainly.'

Both laughed politely and waited to see who would break first. It was Swan.

'I do believe we are to meet tomorrow. Some family squabble about a will.'

'You know, Lionel, you remind me that we are, robbing a poor grieving widow of her living, if I recall correctly. Not something I feel you would be comfortable with nor something the court would wish to do.'

'If the widow was indeed the testator's wife and she had led a blameless life that might well be the case. Since neither applies to this avaricious woman, the court will have no more sympathy than I.'

Devereux had tested Swan's front line and would not probe his flanks.

'Your client is also your pupil, Lionel. A unique situation in my experience. Also he is something of a strange cove I am told.'

Swan took the bait, 'Strange? In what regard pray?'

'The highest achiever in each of his three years at Cambridge by a distance and, I will add here, you have done well for your practice to secure his pupilage, but an isolated figure. Not universally popular with his contemporaries. Quite the opposite I am told.'

Swan smiled. Was this the best that Devereux could offer? He drew on his cigar, gazed into the blue haze that rose above his head and set about fortifying the flank that Devereux had made a weak attempt at exposing.

'Giles Crawshaw has a brilliance that borders on genius Carlton. My respect for you knows no bounds but contest with him in court and you will need to be at your best.'

'There has never been a genius yet who wasn't without flaws.'

'An exceptional mind operates on a higher plane. Impatience with those who cannot match their speed of thought might be regarded by some as arrogance but because those few who are gifted have done much to achieve in life, so much to offer others, their intolerance of criticism is a defence against being distracted from their greater purpose.'

'Deservedly, you hold Mr Crawshaw in high regard, Lionel. I look forward to meeting him to morrow. I must be away now and re-acquaint myself with the facts of this case. It is clear that my client has a formidable adversary.'

Devereux left, satisfied that his evening had been well spent. In attempting to shore up his flank Swan had revealed its weakness. So, Giles Crawshaw was arrogant and intolerant of criticism. Swan was enamoured of him so the relationship revealed in their letters was extent. He had a basis on which he could construct a strategy, Devereux's daughters would be home from Oxford on Thursday and he wanted to have the case finished and be home out of the city by then.

Elizabeth was preparing for bed when she was startled by a tap on her door. A maid, apologising for not noticing earlier, had a letter that had been left at the reception desk. It was from Simon Whitney.

'Dear Mrs Crawshaw'

I have further news of our enquiries. The man called Edward Mason who disembarked in North Carolina has not been traced but Jonathan Fry, who is without doubt one and the same as Mason, went from there to Virginia where he lived a life of idleness for a year. This was funded by the exchange of African currency for American dollars.

He formed a relationship with an Elvira De Velt, the widow of a tobacco plantation owner and they married soon after. They lived together for four years, during which Fry spent or salted away the bulk of her wealth. He supposedly went on a hunting trip to the mountains, did not return, and has not been heard of since. It may well be that he is still alive and he may, contrary to your disbelief now be trading between China and Italy. However, Elvira Fry, as she then was wished to remarry and seven years after Jonathan Fry's disappearance she applied, successfully, to have him declared dead.

This declaration of Jonathan Fry's death by the court of Virginia pre-dates your marriage to Mr Crawshaw by at least three years. Whether this declaration applies in this country is a matter I would take up with your legal representatives.

We are unable to advance this investigation any further but if there are other services you require I should be pleased to provide them.

As before

Simon Whitney.

Elizabeth met Devereux at Swan's chambers as arranged at nine o'clock the next morning. The solicitor Ephraim Grant was there but had played no part the previous day and seemed to have no role that day. Protocol demanded the attendance of a solicitor but protocol didn't pay the solicitor's bill, she thought. Carlton Devereux studied Whitney's report then amended some notes he had prepared for the negotiations.

Lionel Swan's office was as spacious and as well appointed as Deveroux's but Elizabeth noted little touches, lamps matching the upholstery on the chairs that softened the overall image. Swan sat behind a desk that was in every way as grand as Devereux's and Giles Crawshaw sat to his right. Elizabeth fought to banish from her mind the images of the two that their letters had created for her. The two barristers' informality of the previous evening was absent.

'Mr Devereux, for reasons we both know well, it would not be to the advantage of either party to subject itself to the lottery that is chancery. The value of the Crawshaw estate, as significant as it is, would be reduced significantly by the costs of a lengthy and unseemly squabble in that court. My client, over generously I feel, offers your client the sum of five hundred pounds to abandon her defence of his action.

'And costs incurred to date, Mr Swan?'

'Both parties should be responsible for their own costs.'

'Our offer to your client Mr Swan' he paused and Elizabeth held her breath, 'is five thousand pounds willed by his father to be paid in instalments and on the conditions stipulated.'

'Is that it Mr Devereux?'

'No, Mr Swan. From that five thousand pounds, Mrs Crawshaw may deduct her costs of defending this vexatious challenge.'

Swan was too professional to display his annoyance. Giles was not. 'Mr Devereux, would you please desist from referring to your client as Mrs Crawshaw. It insults my father's memory. I will accept only Mrs Fry.'

'Then let us dispose of that issue right now. Jonathan Fry was declared dead to the law over three years before my client and Mr Crawshaw married.'

Giles reacted, 'and do you intend to ship over here some toothless, chewing hillbilly, who will be accompanied by his nine year old sister who is also his wife to testify to that?'

'My, my Mr Crawshaw, you have been a busy little boy, making the same enquiries that my client has made.'

Swan was rocked. He had been told nothing of this.

Devereux continued. 'It is only one hundred years ago that America was one of our colonies. Now independent it has adopted our Status and procedures. Just as a marriage solemnised there is recognised here, so too in a declaration that a person be regarded as dead in law.'

Swan was unsure. He would want to check but did not have the opportunity and, anyway he thought, Devereux would have had this information for some time and would be sure of his facts. Or was it a bluff. Giles was not countering so it probably was not.

'It would not be the resident of Virginia whom you are so ready to disparage but the State Court who will provide the proof. Do you wish, Mr Crawshaw, to counter with a man who will claim that a wastrel son who could not safely convey a load from Wilsden to Leeds is now trading Chinese silk in Italy? A man, who has previously threatened to give perjurer evidence to the detriment of my client?'

Giles would not retreat and Swan sat there helpless as his pupil chose, most unwisely Swan knew, to joust with Devereux.

'Alive or dead. Drowned or travelling. It is irrelevant. The fact is that your client entered recklessly into a marriage not knowing or caring which and employed subterfuge when she married my father. She assumed a name that was not hers in law.'

'Usage, Mr Crawshaw. The common law is replete with cases stated on the subject. A person may adopt any name they wish provided that it does not imply a qualification or a title to which they are not entitled and they do not use it to gain an unlawful advantage.'

'On what cases would you relay to justify a Mrs Fairwood who was a Mrs Fry choosing to be a Mrs Fairwood which she was not and never been.'

'Quickly Devereux replied, Polkingham v Polkingham, and Rex v Monpassant are but two.

'I am fully familiar with the two you cite but I fail to see their significance to Mrs Fry – Fairwood's right to adopt an alias.'

Devereux provided Giles with a brief outline of the facts and findings in each case and his contentions as to the relevance of those cases to his client's case.

'I remain unconvinced Mr Devereux. Please elucidate for me.'

Elizabeth was fascinated by the exchange and wished Celia could have witnessed them.

Devereux provided the details of the facts and the findings in each case. They were long and detailed explanations. Swan realised that Giles was being defeated and felt he had to intervene.

'Mr Devereux', said Swan, 'The extent to which these cases are applicable is for the consideration of the court, where this case is headed.'

But Giles would not be stilled. 'No. The facts of those cases are not in dispute but the extent to which Mr Devereux considers them applicable to the hopeless defence of my case interests me. So. Mr Devereux, enlighten me, do.'

Here it was. Giles's arrogance thought Devereux and he provided an articulate argument.

'Mr Devereux, I am no wiser.'

'But that would be beyond me, Mr Crawshaw, content yourself with knowing that you are better informed.'

Swan had to stifle an appreciative chuckle at his brother barrister's ability so easily to deflate the haughty Giles. Swan had, he thought, Giles's agreement to remain mute in the conference in order that his pupil's superior intelligence would be employed in a telling fusillade in the final stage of the negotiation. Giles had not stuck to his agreement and the fear he had that the inexperienced young man would be no match for Devereux was already manifest.

Giles was pricked by Devereux's put down but did not learn from it. He engaged once more with a comment designed to show his contempt. 'If that is your reading of the law, Mr Devereux, then perhaps I should burn my books.'

Devereux rejoined, 'If you remain intent on a career in law I would recommend you read them first.'

Giles shook with rage. He struggled for a riposte but did not have one. His shaking turned to trembling and he burst into tears and fled Swan's office. It had been Devereux's intention to exploit Giles inability to accept criticism and he prepared to do so later in the negotiation. Devereux surprised, but not displeased, at how Giles had laid himself open to attack so early in the meeting and then had reacted so irrationally to what was merely a flesh wound not a deathblow. He turned to his client and her solicitor.

'May I ask you to wait in the ante-room?'

Swan was reduced to perplexity and sat in silence. Devereux, realising that he had breached his flank thought he may not have to deploy his big gun so he attempted to achieve a victory through the likely outcome in court alone.

'Lionel, you should know, and please believe me on this, I have tested Mrs Crawshaw's responses to a degree that no judge would ever permit you to do, indeed, you would not even contemplate an examination of the most private areas of her personal life that I, to my shame, felt I had to do. Even should you be allowed such latitude she would show a stead-fastness and a resoluteness of purpose that I am confident would not be undermined.'

Swan did not respond. He sat with his hands joined as if in prayer, his fingertips to his lips, silently inviting Devereux to continue.

'Mr Crawshaw, on the other hand, has provided us with a demonstration of how he will, so completely be, destroyed. I do not wish to be unkind but it seems to me that there is a defect in his personality that he cannot repair or disguise. You cannot prosecute his contesting of the will without calling him to the witness box and you cannot call him to give evidence without the danger that he will destroy his own case.'

Again Swan did not reply, so Devereux went on.

'The contention that Mrs Crawshaw's marriage was bigamous and that she was not entitled to style herself, Mrs Fairwood, is lost. The other grounds are either vexatious, malicious, insulting, added for padding or just, plainly irrelevant taken together with the dismissive and obstructive responses to the application from Mrs Crawshaw's lawyers for more and better details. Forgive me, old friend, but I am driven to the conclusion that you have been over influenced by your client, your pupil, in the draftings.'

Swan flushed. 'What compromise do you propose?'

'None, Lionel. My client wants a complete withdrawal of this cause in order that her deceased husband's wishes are not interfered with.'

'My client will not even consider such a cause. It was his great-grandfather who laid the foundations on which his grandfather built a successful chain of businesses. They were given to Henry Crawshaw, at no cost to him, and they represent the bulk of the wealth that Mrs Crawshaw will have, despite the fact that she has made no contribution whatsoever to the creation of that wealth. Giles Crawshaw will give evidence that his grandmother gave all the assets to Henry Crawshaw in the belief that he, Giles, her only living relative, would one day be the beneficiary. She told him this and, if she was still with us, would testify to that. The court is going to give him a portion, a substantial portion rather than the petty amount to which is attached an insulting insinuation. There is no prospect of him withdrawing.'

Devereux was left with no option but to deploy his most destructive weapon. 'Lionel, what I am about to tell you is told in friendship. Soundings for suitability for the Bench are being taken and your name is among those under consideration. Your potential for being a fine judge is well recognised by those who are taking these soundings. There could though be a complication that would, I fear, disqualify you. Giles Crawshaw's father had his son's years at Cambridge investigated. Amongst the information the investigation gathered were a number of letters from Giles to you. They are explicit in revealing an unlawful physical relationship.'

After a pause, during which he watched Swan drop his head into his hands in despair, Devereux continued. 'How these letters come to be diverted into the possession of

Henry Crawshaw, I do not know, nor does Mrs Crawshaw but, to your advantage, they were never delivered to you. They could be passed off as a juvenile fantasy of a sexually confused young man who was fixated upon his visiting lecturer and never intended for your eyes. Some would accept that assumption but others would not, particularly since he now lodges with you. Be advised, Lionel, distance yourself of the danger that this unstable fellow poses to your ambitions.'

Devereux, seeing Swan weeping silently, left the meeting saying, 'Let us resume here at nine o'clock tomorrow and conclude this business.'

That night, before retiring, Elizabeth added another prayer to her nightly ritual. It thanked God for having looked into her heart and answering prayers she had not voiced. She had not prayed for Jonathan to be dead and now he may still be alive but without the damage to her case that it might have meant. She had hoped for, but not prayed for a hero, but she believed that she had one in Carlton Devereux.

Swan had refused to talk with Giles at his chambers, wanting time to order his thoughts. At his home that night he confronted him. Giles, embarrassed at his easy defeat by Devereux was unusually subdued.

'It's over Giles. Do not interrupt for my mind is made up. I will no longer represent you in this case. You may pursue it with another barrister but not one from these chambers. Be advised though that you will be defeated and your reputation so destroyed that you will never find a position in law in any place where the city's writs run. Withdraw, totally or perish. You will find your own rooms forthwith. If you resist me in any way you will leave my chambers. If you do not, you may remain but not under my pupilage. I shall appoint another.'

Giles was shocked. 'Lionel, my love, my heart, I do not understand.'

'As soon as I saw the conditions that your father attached to your inheritance it was obvious to me that he suspected the inclinations of your nature. When you informed me that he had had you investigated I was not convinced that he had looked only into your spending. I now know that your opponents have letters sent by you to me that, should they come to light, will ruin us both.'

Giles fell to Swan's feet and hugged his knees. 'I love you Lionel. Together we are unbeatable. Do not cast me aside, I beg of you.'

'Tomorrow morning I am back in conference with Carlton Devereux. Your presence will not be required. Before then you will instruct me to withdraw unreservedly or I will attend that conference to announce that you are not represented by me and will be instructing another. If you choose the latter former course you will be out of my home and my chambers by the close of the day's business. I'll discuss this no further.'

Devereux entered Swan's office alone next morning, leaving Elizabeth and the solicitor Grant, in the anteroom.

'We can foreshorten our further negotiations Carlton. Will Mrs Crawshaw be agreeable to increasing Giles's inheritance to ten thousand pounds and to removing conditions his father attached?'

'I cannot answer that without the need for further consultation with her. The contesting must be withdrawn and her husband's wishes realised in full.'

'I anticipated that and have prepared the application to withdraw.' He rang the tiny silver bell on his desk and a clerk entered office. 'Those papers I gave you. You may deliver them now to the clerk to the court.'

Then to Devereux, 'So is it over then?'

'Other than the questions of costs,' replied Devereux.

'Each party to meet their own, of course. What else?'

'Giles Crawshaw, I suspect, faces no costs, supported as he has been by you and your chambers. Mrs Crawshaw though has the significant costs of two solicitors, counsel and an investigating agency that has been pursuing enquiries in various parts of the world. Add to that the damage and disruption to her businesses and the hurt occasioned by her inability to mark her husband's grave as she would have wished and the costs, both calculable and incalculable are enormous. She would, I am sure, be content with the legal costs of her defence and the cost of employing the investigators. It would be invidious if she was left with these from a fight she never sought.'

'Be realistic Carlton. Giles does not have the means to meet those costs. If she was to sue he would muddy the waters with allegations from the claim he has now abandoned. And even if she was to be awarded cost against him, he would be unable to pay.'

'I accept that he is a man of straw but you, Lionel, are not and could meet those costs, and put this whole business behind you and anticipate your future on the Bench.'

'Meet the costs? Why should I wish to do that? They are not my concern. I shall not even consider your proposal. It is preposterous.'

'Giles's letters to you are explicable, as we discussed yesterday...'

Swan interrupted. 'She has played that card and cannot expect to be paid twice for playing it again.'

'Allow me to finish, Lionel. It is not the same card. As I was saying, Giles's letters to you are capable of exploration by you while other letters she possesses, letters from you to Giles are in a far different category.'

'Is your client aware of how serious are the penalties for diverting mail entrusted to the postal service, for possessing stolen goods and for blackmail?'

'She may not be as aware as you and I, but she does not know, while we do, that the penalties are no more severe than those for buggery, particularly when that offence is aggravated by having been committed against a minor. The greater penalty to my mind is the damage to your reputation and the loss of you to the Benches of the higher courts, which I know you would agree.'

'You know your client Carlton. I do not know. Would she, for the sake of a few hundred pound or a thousand pounds, be so vindictive as to have me prosecuted and destroyed?'

Devereux did not answer that question directly. 'We know that the courts have little appetite for prosecuting these cases unless they come to public attention, a charge having been laid by a person with a right to grounds to complain, and amount to bringing into disrepute the law, medicine, the church, the military or the aristocracy. It is antiquated to make criminal the nature of people but the statute survives because of the influence the church wields in parliament. I would wager that within a generation or two such conduct will not be prosecuted but that is not the situation at present. Even when the statute is removed there will be those in society who will disapprove and the stigma will remain.'

'Mrs Crawshaw is no relative of Giles. She has no entitlement to lay a complaint.'

'Try to see this from her perspective Lionel. She raised Giles from the age of five and considers that he has been corrupted by you. Her view, not mine Lionel, but if she was accused of vindictiveness she would feel justified in seeking revenge.'

'I did not corrupt him and I object to the word. The fact is that his nature, his preference, was revealed to him by his choir master at grammar school and it was he who seduced me.'

Hardly a defence, Lionel, he being a minor and even if the charge against you never came to public attention if the suspicion were to gain currency in our circle that you had used your pupil as your catamite then you would be finished. Your greatest critics would be those hypocrites who conduct themselves similarly but will attempt to cloak their own activities by condemning yours.'

'Advise me Carlton. I am too close to the problem to see it clearly. How should I proceed?'

I asked yesterday for an agreement that Mrs Crawshaw's costs would be deducted from the five thousand pounds she holds in trust until Giles Crawshaw marries. If you have sufficient holds over him to obtain his consent to that, there is one solution. If you are unable to persuade him I would advise you to meet Mrs Crawshaw's costs and be done with this.'

'If I was to do so could it be made conditional upon the destruction of the letters?'

'Mrs Crawshaw would still need the defence they provide if Giles were to be foolish enough to mount another challenge. I would take possession of them, seal them securely and undertake never to allow them to be used against you provided that you did not mount another action against Mrs Crawshaw.'

'And if Giles did so independently?'

'Then only his letters would be used and I could contend that they were his fantasies about you. Nothing more.'

'On that basis you may inform Mrs Crawshaw that the matter is withdrawn and, in one way or the other her costs will be met.'

Swan rose and shook Devereux's hand. 'I trust none of this will effect our friendship'

'It will not, Lionel, and I trust I may look forward to addressing His Honour Judge Swan before too long.'

'Thank you, will you take tea with me before you leave?'

Elizabeth and Grant's tea was served in the anteroom where they were when Giles came seeking Elizabeth. Disregarding Grant's presence he stood above Elizabeth with fury etched into his once soft features.

'You have tangled with me, and emerged unscathed madam. Should we ever tangle again, and we may, you will find that when you play with fire you will get your fingers burned. My father would confirm that were he able.' With that he was gone.

Devereux joined Elizabeth and informed her that her husband's intentions in his will would be realised. The contesting was withdrawn and the costs of her legal representation and investigation would not fall to her. He would, however, require the letters from her bank for her future protection. The accountant who had acted, as administrator would no longer have a locus standi and both he and her banks would be so informed later that day. Relieved and elated she thanked him sincerely.

'Mrs Crawshaw,' said Devereux, 'I had no reason for recalling this other than because it was my first occasioning as presiding as a coroner but I wondered if there was a family connection with a Mr Crawshaw, a shepherd, whose suspicious death on his farm above Bradford, was a family member?'

'He was my husband's father.'

'Then I did have the pleasure of meeting your husband and I am doubly pleased to have performed a service for him as well as for you. And now, my week's work has been completed sooner than I anticipated I am going to my country home in Stafford to join my wife and await the arrival of our daughters from university. What are your plans may I ask?'

'This evening I shall dine at my favourite restaurant. Tomorrow I shall return to Bradford.'

'To a life less busy than that you have endured recently.'

'Not at all. I shall have a meeting with my managing directors and my managers to implement my husband's wishes regarding their greater share of their endeavours. Thereafter I have a monument to order, a house to build, another house to convert and a part to play in the arrangement of a wedding.'

'But now this case is behind you, you can put Giles Crawshaw behind you too?'

'Would that I could Mr Devereux, and that had been my hope and my intention but he has just made a comment to me that makes that impossible. I would not have him behind me but firmly in front of me. He has committed crimes, and I do not mean those revealed in the letters. He has committed a crime designed to disgrace my own son and I suspect he has committed, or has arranged to have committed, the foul crime of patricide. It cries out for vengeance, Mr Devereux, and, should my opportunity arise, I will have it.'